KYDD

A KYDD SEA ADVENTURE

The Kydd Sea Adventures, by Julian Stockwin

JULIAN STOCKWIN

KYDD
A KYDD SEA ADVENTURE

MCBOOKS PRESS, INC.
www.mcbooks.com
Ithaca, New York

Published by McBooks Press 2008
Copyright © 2001 by Julian Stockwin
First published in the U.S.A. by Scribner, New York

Cover painting by Geoff Hunt.
Cover and interior designed by Panda Musgrove.

Library of Congress Cataloging-in-Publication Data

Stockwin, Julian.
  Kydd : a Kydd sea adventure / by Julian Stockwin.
    p. cm.
  ISBN 978-1-59013-153-4 (trade pbk. : alk. paper)
  1. Kydd, Thomas (Fictitious character)—Fiction. 2. Great Britain—History, Naval—18th century—Fiction. 3. France—History—Revolution, 1789-1799—Fiction. 4. Impressment—Fiction. 5. Wigmakers—Fiction. I. Title.
PR6119.T66K94 2008
823'.92—dc22

                    2008002056

Additional copies of this book may be ordered from any bookstore or directly from McBooks Press, Inc., ID Booth Building, 520 North Meadow St., Ithaca, NY 14850. Please include $5.00 postage and handling with mail orders. Shipping within the U.S. is free for multiple book orders over $75.00. New York State residents must add sales tax to total remittance (books & shipping). All McBooks Press publications can also be ordered by calling toll-free 1-888-BOOKS11 (1-888-266-5711). Please call to request a free catalog.

Printed in the United States of America

9 8 7 6 5 4 3 2 1

"AFT THE MORE HONOUR
FORWARD THE BETTER MAN."

—*Horatio Nelson*

CHAPTER I

"THE HONORABLE THE MEMBER FOR MOLTON." The Speaker of the Commons, in his full-bottomed wig, gave the floor to Edmund Burke in the crowded chamber.

Rubbing his long nose, the orator stood and glanced across to the opposite benches at the slumped figure of the Prime Minister, Pitt the Younger, who seemed resigned to events. It would not do, however, to underestimate Pitt, even if, as a man of peace, he seemed unsure of his direction in this new war with the French.

Burke drew himself up and spoke effortlessly above the disorderly hum. "Is this House aware that at this very moment, in a time of crisis without parallel in the history of these islands, His Majesty's government sees fit to let its chief means of defense, the Navy, its sure shield"—he paused and looked impressively about him—"rot at anchor in its ports, while the enemy is at liberty to issue forth on his awful missions of destruction?" He was aware that behind him, ready for any excuse to interject, was the fat, mustard-waistcoated figure of Charles Fox. Discredited for his earlier support of the French Revolution, he was nevertheless leader of His Majesty's loyal opposition—and a liability.

"No doubt the Honorable Gentleman is sensible of the fact that our most valuable possessions in the Caribbean lie trembling in daily

expectation of a descent by the enemy? That the City clamors for protection for its commerce? That we, the loyal Whigs"—he ignored the raucous splutter behind him that could only have issued from the embittered Fox—*"demand as conditional to our continued support to this Ministry that measures be taken to protect our commercial interests. And strong measures, which are swift, effective and decisive!"*

Pitt slouched farther down in his seat. What did they know of the real situation? Admiral Howe with the Channel Fleet was in port, true, but he commanded the only strategic fleet Britain possessed at this time, and would answer to the nation for its preservation until it was fit enough to grapple with the enemy. Howe would not jeopardize its safety. Still watching Burke, he leaned over to the man on his left and whispered, "Desire the Admiralty to make a showing off the French coast—just two or three ships of force will suffice." That would be enough to mollify Burke, who had only spoken to point up his own grand gesture of conciliation. Howe could spare two or three of the more elderly vessels. "Allow that it is a matter of some urgency," Pitt added wearily.

From the quarterdeck of the ship-of-the-line *Duke William*, nothing could be seen of the passengers in the ugly little hoy thrashing its way through the gray-green seas toward them. It was making heavy weather of it, bluff bows slamming into the short, steep waves kicked up by the stiff northerly. Drenching sheets of spray were flung skywards before whipping aft over the small craft.

Duke William's officer of the watch lowered his telescope with a grunt of exasperation. It was important to know quickly the results of their swift press-gang raid inland. *Duke William* had to be in a position to catch the evening tide to enable them to reach Admiral Howe's fleet at Spithead before it sailed.

With a new captain and a hard horse first lieutenant, the old ship had a poor reputation and would never attract volunteers. Furthermore, this was a full five days after the declaration of war against revolutionary France, and the Impress Service and individual press-gangs had between them cleared the Thames of seamen.

From his own pocket, Captain Caldwell had paid the hire of a pair of coaches to take a press-gang in a lightning swoop down the Portsmouth road, hoping to pounce on seamen who had taken refuge in the country or, failing that, seize some sturdy rural lads. An illegal act, but they could be spirited away well before magistrate or sheriff could intervene, and once at sea they were beyond reach.

The hoy drove on, its single-reefed mainsail board taut, its angle to the tide-driven waves resulting in an awkward screwing motion. Sprawled miserably on the bottom boards under a tarpaulin were some thirty wretched, seasick men and boys, the press-gang harvest.

Taking an appreciative pull from a bottle, the petty officer in charge returned it to his shipmate and wiped his mouth on the back of his sleeve. "Get it inside yer, Davey, while yer've still got the chance, mate."

The two men crouched in the lee of the weather gunwale, knowing they were out of sight from the ship. It would be their last chance before arriving aboard out in the great Fleet anchorage of the Nore.

Spray rattled again on the sail, and a thin, cold rain drifted across them. As the petty officer hunkered down farther, his black hat wet and gleaming, his shoe caught a lump in the tarpaulin, bringing a muffled cry. He lifted the edge, and a dark-haired young man of about twenty stared up at him with dull brown eyes. The petty officer grinned and dropped the tarpaulin.

The young man tried to ease his position, but it was hopeless: confined as he was by other wet bodies, seasickness and the continual

violent motion of the hoy, he lacked strength to move. Nearby, a
pale flaccid face lifted. The empty eyes looked into his and as he
watched, a weak spasm produced from slack lips a green ooze that
tracked across the sunken cheeks. The sight brought on the inevitable, but there was no more of his meager breakfast to bring up.
Subsiding weakly after a series of dry heaves, Thomas Paine Kydd
laid his head once more on the wet, hard boards.

Only a few nights earlier, he had been enjoying warmth and com-
panionship in the Horse and Groom in Merrow village, a public
house that dated back to the first King Charles; its age and solidity
spoke of the bucolic calm of that part of England. Three miles up the
road was Guildford, a popular staging halt on the way from London
to the trading ports of the south and west. There, in the last days of
the peace, he had seen from his wig shop in High Street grim faces
of naval officers staring from coach windows as they clattered over
the cobblestones on their way to the Angel posting house.

He had heard in the shop that this war was going to be quite
different from the stately clashes of empires earlier in the century.
It was not going to be a traditional war against France. Instead,
it would be a fight to the death against the howling mob that had
overwhelmed all the forces of the state and had now put to death
their own king. In the Horse and Groom there had been bold talk
that night, and this time not only from Stallard and his crew, as
usual ensconced in secret conclave in the snug. It was widely held
that the midnight rides of "Captain Swing" and a rash of rick-
burnings were the work of Stallard and his men, and Kydd tried to
avoid their company.

The loss of the American colonies and the fall of Lord North,
spectacular victories in India and the rise of the younger Pitt had not
disturbed this quiet corner of England, so it had been all the more
shocking when a wider world had come smashing in on the night
the press-gang had made its move. Tipped off by a sheriff's man who

wanted to rid himself of undesirables, they had sprung their trap with practiced ease.

One minute it was noise and laughter, the next an appalled silence in the smoke-filled taproom at the sight of sailors appearing at every exit. They were in a costume like those to be seen in the theater, complete with pigtails, black tarred hat and short blue jacket. And each had a cudgel in one hand, which he tapped slowly in the opposite palm.

Patrons were allowed to leave, but at each door they were separated into those who would go home to relate their escape to wide-eyed loved ones, and those who would begin a long journey to their fate on the high seas. Kydd had struggled but, under the weight of superior numbers, was soon overpowered.

The trip east to the Isle of Sheppey had taken two days. They had avoided towns, and the men had been handcuffed to a tarpaulin-covered wagon like common criminals. Kydd had felt bitter and hopeless by turns, not able to find comfort in cursing as Stallard seemed to do, or in the fatalism of the two merchant seamen also caught up in the press.

They were kept for two more days in the dank holding cells in Sheerness's Blue Town, a bleak garrison town, at the tip of the desolate island at the mouth of the Thames. It seemed to Kydd that he had arrived at the end of the earth. He was almost relieved when it was time to board the hoy. Then he saw, for the first time, the forest of masts set in an iron-gray winter sea, and knew he would need all the courage and strength he could muster for whatever lay ahead.

Now he tried to ignore the steady trickle of icy rainwater, on its way to the bilge, that coursed down his neck and back.

Suddenly the tarpaulin was flung aside, and Kydd took in the brightness of the pearly winter sky above, the reluctant stirring of damp men and, dominating all, the colossal form of a great ship. It seemed all gunports and lines of yellow and black timber, unknown fitments and black ropes. It towered up to the deck-line, and then above to an impossibly complex structure of masts and yards, black and ominous against the sky.

His eyes sought meaning in the rush of detail. The massive sides of the ship were near enough to touch. At such proximity the pockmarks of age and battle were all too clear, and at the point where the fat side of the ship met the muddy gray waves of the Thames estuary, dark-green weed betrayed the urgency with which the ship had been summoned from her foreign station. In the dark beyond the open gunports Kydd could discern unknown movement. From a small opening near the waterline discolored water dribbled on and on into the sea.

"Let's be havin' yer, then, me lads!" the petty officer said, and released them with a brisk clinking of metal. Kydd rubbed his wrists.

High above, a figure in a gold-laced coat and black cocked hat appeared at the deck edge. "What the devil— My God, get those men inboard at once, or I'll have the hide off someone's back, I swear!"

The sailor moved quickly. "That prick Garrett," he muttered. "Watch, you bleedin' lubbers—like this!"

He moved easily along the gunwale of the hoy to where a series of small steps marched vertically up the tumble home of the ship's side. On each side were handropes, shiny with use. Stepping lightly across at the highest point of the hoy's wallow, in one movement he transferred his weight to step and handrope simultaneously and swarmed up the ship's side.

The remaining sailor blustered at them from behind, and the first moved forward. He grabbed the ropes but his feet slipped on the rain-slick wood and he fell into the sea, still dangling from the rope. He squealed in fright until the sailor hoisted him up by the scruff of his neck. The others held back in fear. "Fer Chrissake, get up there!" the sailor urged.

No one moved. The hoy rose and fell, the slap of waves between the two vessels loud and forbidding.

Something stirred in Kydd. He pushed the others aside, snatched a look upward and acted as he had seen the seaman do. He jumped across the chasm between the two vessels, his feet scrabbled on the narrow step and he paused to gather his strength. Then he began to climb, not daring to look down. A sudden shaking of the handrope showed that his example had been followed.

Kydd emerged over the thick bulwarks onto the upper deck. It was a scene of unutterable complexity, the deck sweeping far forward, massive cannon in rows along it, and above him a black web of lines connecting masts and spars higher and thicker than any tree imaginable. The rock-like stillness of the ship was in noticeable contrast to the lively movement of the hoy.

The high, irritable voice shrilled, "Over there, you fool!" The officer was standing near the ship's wheel, legs akimbo. "*There, you damn idiot!*" he snarled, and stabbed his telescope toward the mainmast.

Kydd shambled weakly toward it, tripping on a ringbolt in the deck.

"Good God!" the officer exclaimed. "So *this* is what we're going to meet the French with!" He turned to the plainly dressed older man standing with him. "Heaven help us!"

The man's expression did not change but he murmured, "Yes, Mr. Garrett, heaven indeed help us."

The young farmhand had finally stopped howling in terror at the black, malodorous confines of the lower hold and was now looking up through the hatch grating at the marine sentry and sobbing quietly. The rest lay draped over the bulk stores, mainly huge casks, that extended out into the noisome gloom.

The air was so thick it was difficult to breathe. Although *Duke*

William barely noticed the waves, creaks and cracks randomly punctuated the darkness, terrifying for those who could not know what they meant. The only relief from the all-conquering darkness was the dim wash of tawny light that patterned down through the gratings from the few lanthorns on the deck above.

Lying back on a cask top, Kydd strained his eyes at the shadows of the hold. Around him he could hear moans and coughs, weeping and obscenities. Men moved restlessly. At the very edge of his perception, he became aware of movement, out of sequence with the ponderous creaking from the working timbers. Then he heard the scrabble of tiny paws as pinprick flashes of red appeared and disappeared. He shuddered and fixed his gaze resolutely on the lanthorn.

A broken mumbling started on one side. A voice Kydd recognized as Stallard's snarled back and the mumbling stopped. The man next to Kydd stank, a musty uncared-for rankness. Kydd inched over the top of the big cask to get away—and slid off with a cry. He fell into what seemed to be a shingle beach. He stood up in confusion and moved forward. Each step into the shingle ballast brought a renewed roiling of an acrid stench.

A shape appeared over the edge of an adjacent cask. "Give us yer hand, mate," it said. Kydd hastily scrunched over and did so. The human contact was gratifying and he found himself hoisted surprisingly easily onto the top of the cask. "Don't want ter go wandering around too much, cully. Yer can find dead 'uns an' all down there!"

It was difficult to make out who was talking; Kydd kept silent.

The man eyed him. "Truscott. Didn't move meself fast enough when they came." He grunted. "Shoulda known better. A pox on the bastards, anyway."

Kydd felt a surge of anger at those who had torn him away from his rightful place in life to this world of squalor and misery. "What happens now?" he asked.

"Why, that's easy enough. We go before the First Luff, who'll rate you landman 'n' me able seaman—mebbe quartermaster's mate if I'm lucky. And then we gets to be part of the crew of this 'ere vessel."

"So how long'll this be—I mean, when can I go back home?"

The man chuckled harshly. "Forget home, lad. You're crew of the *Royal Billy* all the time she's in commission—you gets to leave her only if she goes to Davy Jones's locker by bein' wrecked ashore or sunk in an argyment with a Frenchie."

"But . . ." The idea was too overwhelming to take in.

"Look, chum, you're a pressed man," said Truscott, "same's me. We don't get to go ashore, we gets paid less 'n a private soldier and we've less say about what we do next than a common bloody trull—so do yerself a great favor and get used to it. You're now a foremast jack in a man-o'-war, 'n' that's that."

Kydd breathed deeply, reaching for calm, but frustration boiled within him. He smashed his fists on the cask and gave a long hopeless roar of impotent rage.

Truscott sighed. "Don't take on, lad. Nothin' you can do now. Listen—there's them who are goin' to suffer"—he glanced significantly at the broken farm-boy—"and they're goin' to be the muckers who'll be on every shite chore there is, fer ever more. 'N' there's them that'll work it out 'n' make right Jack Tars of 'emselves—and that's no bad life when you comes at it the right way." He cleared his throat. "Ye'll not expect to be one right off, but—"

"You're just talking piss 'n' wind, you are!" Stallard's acid voice cut in from the dark as he scrambled over to them. "He wants to know why he's a prisoner down here in this stinkin' hole, not what wunnerful prospects he has!" His voice rose as though he were addressing a crowd. "We're here because we ain't got no rights—none!" He paused. A groan sounded in the dark. "Only 'cos we're born in a cottage, not a mansion, we're no better'n a flock of cunny sheep—do this, go there, yes, sir, no, sir. Whatever they say, we do. You see any whoreson *gentleman* down here, then? Not a chance!"

"You'd better keep your trap shut once we're at sea, mate," Truscott said.

"Don't you worry, Mr. Sailor Man," Stallard retorted. "I may know a thing or two about that—you just be sure you know where you'll be standin' when it comes down to it."

Kydd bit his tongue. Stallard was mad if he thought he could get away with his petty seditions here—there was no chance of a mad gallop away into the night and anonymity in this closed community.

"Yer frien' had better learn quick," said Truscott, in a low voice. "If he gets talkin' wild like that he'll be decoratin' a yardarm before he knows where he's at."

Stallard glared at him, then slithered over to Kydd. The lanthorn gleam caught his eyes. "Kydd knows what it's all about," Stallard said. "Ain't that right, mate?"

Kydd said nothing.

"We're town-mates, from Guildford," Stallard told the figures draped on the casks about them, "and they've learned there to have a care when they deal with us—or they could get a midnight visit from Captain Swing." He cackled. Noticing Kydd's silence, he added, "We stand for our rights in the old town or we lose 'em. That's what we say, ain't it, me old cock—ain't it?" He thrust his face into Kydd's.

Kydd kept quiet.

"Well, then! I do declare! Can it be Kydd's a toady to the gentry—a stinkin' lickspittle? Mebbe a—"

Something gave way. Kydd threw himself forward and smashed his fist into Stallard's face, but as he did so he cracked his own head against the low deck beams. Stunned, he fell back, and Stallard dived on him, punching, clawing, gouging.

"Stow it, you mad buggers!" Truscott thrust himself between them, pulling Stallard off Kydd by his hair.

Stallard knelt back. Dark runnels of blood came from his nose and smeared over his face. "Don't think I'll forget this, Kydd!" he said.

Kydd looked at him contemptuously. "You're gallows-bait, Stallard—y'r cronies won't save y' now!"

He was interrupted by a clumping at the grating, and a petty officer appeared at the hatchway. "Up 'n' out—move yer scraggy selves!"

They emerged onto the orlop deck, the dull yellow glow of the lanthorns appearing almost cheerful after the Stygian darkness of the hold.

Awaiting them were a pair of marines, in scarlet with white cross-belts and muskets, standing rigidly. The boatswain's mate had two seamen with him.

"Topsides, gemmun!" the petty officer rasped. "First Lieutenant wants to make yer acquaintance."

They were herded together, making their way along several gun-decks and up endless ladderways to the main deck. Here they were assembled on one side, sheltered from the fitful drizzle by the extension of the quarterdeck above before it gave way to the open area of the boat stowage.

The Master-at-Arms arrived, flanked by his two corporals. He was a stout, florid man with dark piggy eyes that never seemed to settle. "Toe the line, then!" he rumbled at the petty officer.

Shoving the pressed men together, the petty officer showed them how to line up by pressing their toes up against one of the black tarry lines between the deck planking.

From the cabin spaces aft a small party of men emerged; a lectern and a small table were set up. Then an officer appeared in immaculate uniform and cockaded bicorne.

The Master-at-Arms stiffened. "Pressed men, sir!" he reported, touching his hat.

The officer said nothing but stopped, glaring, at the line of men. He took off his hat and thwacked it irritably at his side. He was short, but built like a prizefighter. His dark, bushy eyebrows and deep-set eyes gave him an edgy, dangerous look. The rich gold lace against the dark blue and white of his uniform cloaked him with authority.

In his sensible country fustian, which was now filthy and torn, Kydd felt clumsy and foolish. He tried to look defiantly at the officer while the wind flurried down the boat space, sending him into spasms of shudders.

"I'm Mr. Tyrell, and I'm the First Lieutenant of this ship," the officer began. "And you're a parcel of landmen and therefore scum. A worthless damn rabble—but you're now in the sea service of King George and you'll answer to me for it." He stomped across until he was within arm's length.

Kydd saw that the dark eyes were intelligent as they roved up and down the line. "Forget what you've heard about jolly Jack Tar and a life on the rolling waves. It's a nonsense. We're now at war, a hot bloody war, and there'll only be one winner at the end, and that's going to be us. And we win it by courage and *discipline,* by God!" He paced past them in a measured tread. "So listen to me! On board this ship you'd better soon understand that we have only one law and that's called the Articles of War. The quicker you learn that, the better for you." He paused. "Show 'em the cat, Quentin."

The Master-at-Arms looked at the boatswain's mate and nodded. The man stepped forward and, from a red baize bag, carefully extracted a thick, ornate rope handgrip ending in nine strands of much thinner line, each carefully knotted. He teased out the yard-long strands so that they fell in cascade in front of him.

"Every man jack of you is now subject to the Articles of War—and there it says that the penalty for disobedience is death . . ." Tyrell held his audience in a deadly fascination. ". . . or such laws and customs in such cases used at sea," he snarled. "And that means I may need to ask Mr. Quentin to scratch your back with his cat. Isn't that so, Quentin?"

"Aye aye, sir, Mr. Tyrell."

In the shocked silence Tyrell paced back to the table, then turned, his eyes cold. He let the silence hang, doing his work for him. No sound from the men broke the deathly hush, but the mournful keening of a pair of seagulls carried clearly across the water.

Tyrell handed his hat to the clerk and took his place at the lectern. The clerk opened a large book and prepared quill and ink. "You will answer my questions now and this will help me decide how best you will serve. I will rate you here and provide watch and station details later to the officer of your division."

He glanced at the clerk. "Volunteers?"

"None, sir," the clerk said, expressionless.

Tyrell's eyebrows rose. "Begin."

The clerk consulted his book. "Abraham Fletcher," he called.

A scrawny, apologetic-looking man shuffled forward.

Raising his eyes heavenward, Tyrell asked sarcastically, "Profession, Mr. Fletcher?"

"Tailor's cutter," the man mumbled.

"Sir!" screamed the Master-at-Arms, outraged.

"Sir!" agreed the man hastily, knuckling his forehead.

"Then you're just the man the sailmaker would like to see," Tyrell said. "See that Mr. Clough gets to know about him. Rated landman, Mr. Warren's division. Next."

It did not take long to deal with them all: Tyrell was clearly in a hurry. "Get them to the doctor. If he refuses any, he's to give his reasons to me personally." The book slammed shut. "Then they muster at the main capstan, lower deck. Tell the boatswain."

A single long squeal from somewhere aft cut through the bustle. All movement ceased. A seaman near Kydd stirred. "Something's on, lads," he muttered.

Minutes later, out of sight on the deck below, several boatswains' pipes shrieked out together—low, high, low. Their slow calls were a barbaric yet beautiful and frail sound carried on the buffeting wind.

"Ah, Captain's come aboard," the seaman said.

Tyrell hurried off up the ladder.

"He'll have to come up this way, mates," the seaman added.

The Captain appeared from below. He was wearing full dress uniform, sword and decorations with white gloves and gold-laced cocked hat, and was accompanied by a small retinue. He moved slowly, his lean figure ungainly, bowed. Before he began ascending the ladder to the deck above, he stopped and looked about him— suspiciously, Kydd thought.

Over the distance of the width of the deck his eyes rested for a moment on Kydd, who froze. The eyes moved on. The Captain resumed his stately climb up and out of sight.

Nobody spoke.

Chivied by the boatswain's mate, the pressed men moved on down to the dim orlop deck, to a cursory glance by the surgeon, then back to the lower gundeck. They found themselves trying to keep out of the way in the busy confusion of preparing the ship for sea.

Kydd had the chance to take in more of his surroundings. A few yards away from the capstan, the weak winter sunlight still penetrated through the main hatches on all the decks, on down even through the orlop below to the hold, casting an unearthly bright glow on the seamen taking the last of the stores aboard. On either side, great cannon stretched away into the distance, the implements of gunnery ready to hand beside them, lashed to the deckhead, while more homely articles were stowed at the ship's side in neat vertical racks between each gun.

The main jeer capstan was at the center of the deck, all gleaming polished wood, its massive shaft extending up to disappear through the low deckhead. Kydd could almost feel the vessel's strength— the sweep of mighty beams, the thick angular knees and the wrist-thick rope breechings of the guns. The gunports were still open, and through them he could see the wan glitter of the sea a few feet below. He went to the opening and looked out.

Several miles away over the sea, he could see the dull green and brown scarred cliffs of Sheppey. Halfway along the undulating coast was the square tower of a Saxon church on the skyline amid a tiny huddle of rain-washed gray dwellings. He wondered briefly who could be living in such a bleak place. With a pang he realized that for all the chance he had of setting foot there, they might as well have been on the moon.

He pulled back inboard, and despite himself his pulse quickened. Whatever else, he was now caught up in the age-old excitement of a ship ready for sea, outward bound; maybe to lands far away, per-haps to meet mermaids and monsters, and even adventures like the ones described by Mr. Swift.

The light from above dimmed to nothing as, one by one, the hatches were secured. Now only the light reflected through the gun-ports from the sea remained.

Shortly, from forward, Kydd heard irregular muffled thumps as a party of men began to close and seal the gunports. Now the cold sun-light and chill breeze were cut off, and an oppressive gloom advanced on them. There was no natural light or air now, only a suffocating closeness with uneasy overtones of dread.

Then lanthorns were lit, their dull yellow-gold light catching the flash of eyes, buckles and seamen's gear, and revealing a nervous young officer arriving down the hatchway ladder.

As Kydd's eyes grew accustomed to the dark, he saw that the gun-deck, which before had seemed a spacious sweep of bare decks, now appeared crammed with men. It was difficult to make sense of all that went on, but there was no mistaking the role of the big capstan. Deck pillars around it were removed and capstan bars more than ten feet long were socketed and pinned in a giant starfish pattern, a taut line connecting their ends to ensure an even strain on all.

"Nippers! Where's those bloody nippers?" bellowed a petty officer.

A ship's boy stumbled up with a clump of lengths of rope, each a few yards long.

"Bring to, the messenger!"

A rope as thick as an arm was eased around the barrel of the capstan, the ends heaved away forward to be seized together in an endless loop. Activity subsided.

"Man the capstan!"

Kydd found himself pushed into place at a capstan bar, among a colorful assortment of men. Some, like himself, were still in shore-side clothing of varying degrees of quality, others wore the scarlet of the marines.

"Silence, fore 'n' aft!"

Men stood easy, flexing arms and shoulders. Kydd gulped. It was only a few days since he had been standing behind the counter, talking ribbons with the Countess of Onslow. Now he was a victim of the press-gang, sent to sea to defend England. It crossed his mind that she would be outraged to see him transplanted to this context, but then decided that she would not—hers was an old naval family.

"Take the strain, heave 'round!" The distant cry was instantly taken up.

Following the motions of the others, Kydd leaned his chest against the capstan bar, his hands clasping up from underneath. For a moment nothing happened, then the bar began to revolve at a slow walk. A fiddler started up in the shadows on one side, a fife picking up with a perky trill opposite.

"Heave around—cheerly, lads!"

It was hard, bruising work. In the gloom and mustiness, sweating bodies labored; thunderous creaks and sharp wooden squeals answered with deep-throated shudders as the cable started taking up. The muscles on the back of Kydd's legs ached at the unaccustomed strain.

"Well enough—fleet the messenger!"

A precious respite. Kydd lay panting against the bar, body bowed. Looking up, he caught in the obscurity of the outer shadows the eyes of a boatswain's mate watching him. The man padded back and forth like a leopard, the rope's end held on his side flicking spasmodically. "Heave 'round!"

Again the monotonous trudge. The atmosphere was hot and fetid, the rhythmic clank of the pawls and the ever-changing, eversame scenery as the capstan rotated became hypnotic.

The pace slowed. "Heave and a pawl! Get your backs into it! Heave and a pawl!"

Suddenly a pungent sea smell permeated the close air, and Kydd noticed that the cable disappearing below was well slimed with light blue-gray mud. A few more reluctant clanks, then motion ceased.

"One more pawl! Give it all you can, men!" The officer's young voice cracked with urgency.

Kydd's muscles burned, but there would be no relief until the anchor was won, so he joined with the others in a heavy straining effort. All that resulted was a single, sullen clank. He felt his eyes bulge with effort, and his sweat dropped in dark splodges on the deck beneath him.

It was an impasse. Their best efforts had not tripped the anchor.

Along the bars men hung, panting heavily.

There was a clatter at the ladder and an officer appeared. Kydd thought he recognized him. The man next to him tensed.

Garrett strode to the center of the deck. "Why the hell have we stopped, Mr. Lockwood? Get your men to work immediately, the lazy scum!" The high voice was spiteful, malicious.

Lockwood's eyes flickered and he turned his back on Garrett. "Now, lads, it's the heavy heave and the anchor's a-trip. Fresh and dry nippers for the heavy heave!"

Kydd was exhausted. His muscles trembled and he felt light-headed. His bitterness at his fate had retreated into a tiny ball glowing deep inside.

"Now, come on, men—heave away for your lives!" Lockwood yelled.

The men threw themselves at the bar in a furious assault. The heavy cable lifted from the deck and thrummed in a line direct from the hawse. Nothing moved.

"Avast heaving!" Garrett screamed.

The men collapsed at the bars, panting uncontrollably.

Garrett sidled up behind Lockwood, whose pale face remained turned away. "You have here a parcel of lubbers who don't know the meaning of the word work," he said. "There's only one way to wake these rogues up to their duty, you'll find." He moved forward and glared at the men contemptuously. Only one side of his face was illuminated, adding to its demonic quality.

His chin lifted. "Boatswain's mates, start those men!"

Unbelieving murmurs arose as the petty officers hefted their rope's ends and closed in.

"Silence!" Garrett shrieked. "Any man questions my orders I swear will get a dozen at the gangway tomorrow!"

"Heave 'round!" Lockwood called loudly, but with a lack of conviction.

The men bent to their task, but their eyes were on the circling boatswain's mates. There was no movement at the capstan. A vicious smack and a gasp sounded. Then more. Still no displacement of the thick cable, which was now so tight that it rained muddy seawater on the deck. The blows continued mercilessly.

Kydd heard the *whup* a fraction before the blow landed, drawing a line of fire across his shoulders. The buried resentment exploded, but a tiny edge of reason kept him from a cry of rage or worse.

There could be no possible escape. While that anchor was so fiercely gripped by the mud they would remain at their Calvary.

"'Vast heaving!" The bull-like roar of the boatswain broke into the agonized gasping of the men. He was not contradicted by the two lieutenants.

"All the idlers to the bars—that means all you boatswain's mates, and you, the fiddler!" He tore off his own faded plain black coat and went to the capstan. "Shove along, matey!" he said, to an astonished marine.

"And it's one, two, six an' a *tigerrrr!*" he roared. *"Heeeeave!"*

Men fought the bars as though against a powerful opponent. Kydd threw himself at the capstan bar in a frenzy of effort. Spots of light swam before his eyes and he knew no more than the hard unyielding wood of the bar and the gasps and groans from beside him in the sweaty gloom.

Quite unexpectedly there came a single clank. Then another. Kydd found himself moving forward.

"Walk away with it, lads. Anchor's a-trip."

Almost sobbing with relief, Kydd kept up the pressure, desperate to avoid a loss of momentum. The clanks now came so regularly that they were almost musical.

A shout came down the ladder from the relay messenger, acknowledged by Lockwood, who turned quickly and ordered, "'Vast heaving! Pass the stoppers!"

Light-headed with relief, Kydd hung from the bar.

"Well done, lads!" the boatswain said, and retrieved his coat. Garrett was nowhere to be seen.

Kydd gazed muzzily down the length of the ship, then felt the gundeck fall to one side with a stately, deliberate motion, slowly, then faster. He clung dumbfounded to his bar.

An old seaman chuckled. "Don't worry, mate, she's casting under topsails, just taken the wind. Now let's see those shabs topside do a bit o' work."

The roll slowed and stopped, then returned, remaining at a small but definite angle. Incredibly, there was no other indication that this massive structure could now be moving through the water. Quickly the capstan and gear were secured, and Kydd fell back with profound relief.

A boatswain's mate appeared at the top of the ladder and piped, "*Haaaands* to supper!"

That made Kydd keenly aware that he was fiercely hungry, but in the hubbub nobody seemed to care about the bewildered pressed men who stayed where they were, not knowing what they should do.

Others rushed down the ladders, rudely shoving them out of the way as the mess was rigged for supper. Tables hinged to the ship's side were lowered into place between each pair of guns. Benches and sea chests became seats, lanthorns shed light over the tables.

Kydd hovered in the darkness at the centerline of the deck, watching friends greet each other, others hurrying past with mess-kettles and kids. Before long the savory smell of the evening meal washed past him. He was left alone. He watched the jolliness and familiarity with a pang, realizing that it reminded him of the fellowship and intimacy of his local tavern, and longed to be part of it.

His stomach contracted violently and he could stand it no longer. Hesitantly he approached the nearest mess, who were listening with appreciative attention to an engrossing yarn from a small, dark-haired sailor clutching a wooden tankard and gesturing grandly.

The story finished with a flourish and helpless laughter, and they returned to their food. Kydd stood awkwardly, wondering what to say. The conversation died away, and they looked up at him curiously. "I'm—I'm new on board, just been pressed," he began.

They roared with laughter. "Never have guessed it, mate!" a stout, red-faced sailor said, eyeing his country breeches.

"Just wondering, have you anything I can eat?" Kydd said.

"Why, which would be your mess, then?" the stout man replied.

"Only just got on the ship . . ." Kydd tried to explain.

"Well, Johnny Raw, you'd better go aft 'n' ask Mr. Tyrell ter give yer one, then, hadn't you?" A hard-faced man leered and looked around for approval.

"Shut your face and leave him be, Jeb. Shift outa there, younker," the stout man said, thumbing at a ship's boy sitting at the end of the table. "Bring your arse to anchor, mate, we'll see you right." He added, "Dan Phelps, fo'c'sleman."

Kydd introduced himself, sat down and looked around respectfully.

The hard-faced man leaned across to him. "So yer new pressed, are yer? Know about the sea, do yer? No?" He didn't wait for a reply. Jabbing his pot at Kydd, he snarled, "Yer'll suffer, yer clueless lubber. You're really gonna hurt."

The conversations tailed off, and around the table sea-hardened men stared at Kydd.

Phelps's eyebrows rose. "Give no mind to 'im. We has a sayin'—'Messmate before a shipmate, shipmate before a stranger, stranger before a dog.'" He glared around and the talk resumed.

Kydd remained quiet.

Phelps chuckled, then turned to the old man at the ship's side and called, "Crooky, lend our guest some traps—we can't have him keelin' over on his first day."

Kydd nodded gratefully as a wooden plate landed in front of him filled with a gray oatmeal mix and occasional lumps of meat. Ravenous, he spooned up some of the oatmeal but was instantly revolted. It was rancid, with flecks of black suggestive of darker secrets. The meat was a mass of gristle and definitely on the turn. There was nothing for it: he was famished, so he bolted it down without pause. The gristlebound hunks stayed in the bottom of the bowl.

The repulsive food restored his energy, and Kydd's spirits rose. He finished his meal and looked up, aware that he had been too hungry to pay attention to his duties as a guest at table. "Er, where are we going, d' y' reckon?" he asked. It was still a matter of amazement to him that their busy world was traveling along while they sat down to table.

"Give it no mind, lad, it's not our job to know the answer t' that." Phelps sniffed and leaned over to the grog tub. He waved his pot at the old man. "Light along a can for my frien' here, Crooky."

Kydd gingerly took a pull at his tankard. It was small beer, somewhat rank with an elusive herb-like bitterness, but he nearly drained it in one.

"I thought sailors only had rum," he said, without thinking.

Phelps grinned. "We does, but only when the swipes runs out." He pursed his lips. "You sayin' as you want to try some?" he said, in mock innocence.

Kydd looked around, but the others did not seem to notice; they were all comfortably in conversation. "Are you offering?" he said.

"Wait there," said Phelps, and lurched heavily to his feet. He went forward out of sight and returned with his jacket clutched tight around him as though against the cold. He resumed his seat. "Give us yer pot, mate," he instructed. Kydd did as he was told and caught the flash of a black bottle under the table. Then his tankard was returned.

He waited casually, then lifted it. It caught him by surprise. In the dull pewter of his tankard was a deep, almost opaque mahogany-brown liquor. Its pungent fumes wafted up with a lazy potency, which dared him to go further.

The buzz of conversation swirled around him. He took a swallow. This was not issue three-water grog, but neat spirit, and its burning progress to his stomach took his breath away. He surfaced with a grin. "A right true drop!"

Phelps's eyebrows lifted. "You'll not get that sorta stingo usually, cully, but if yer play your cards right with Dan Phelps"—he tapped the side of his nose—"yer mebbe could see more of it."

Kydd raised his pot again. This time he was prepared for the spreading fire, and gloried in the flood of satisfaction it released. His whirling anxieties subsided and his natural cheerfulness began to reassert itself. He finished the last of the rum with regret.

The piercing squeal of the boatswain's call abruptly cut through the din. "Be damned. Starbowlines—that's us. Fust dog-watch." Phelps lurched to his feet and disappeared into the throng.

The mess traps were cleared away rapidly and Kydd found himself the only one still seated. "Move yer arse, mate," he was told, and once more found himself alone in the midst of many.

Instinctively he turned to follow Phelps, who, he remembered, his head swimming, had left with the others up the main hatch ladder. It led to an almost identical gundeck from the one he had left, so he continued on up the next ladderway, muscles alive with discomfort, emerging into darkness. The night had already fallen.

Overhead, past the hulking shadows of the boats on their skids above him, he saw the paleness of huge sails in regular towers, each at the same angle and each taut and trim. Nearby, but invisible, he could hear the regular plash and sibilance of the sea, and as he stood he became aware of a background of sounds meshing together. It was a continuous and oddly comforting interplay of creaks, dings, slattings and all manner of unfamiliar mutterings.

Out into the starless night on either hand the darkness was broken only occasionally by the flash of a white wave. He felt rather than saw that they were traveling steadily through the water, a hypnotizing, unchanging sliding which gave no impression of headlong speed, and he marveled once again.

He was still comfortably warm from the rum, and ambled along, wondering at the vast mystery of the ship with all its unfathomable shapes, sounds and implied dangers. The sights above disappeared abruptly as he passed under a deck, the unmistakable outline of a bell in its belfry silhouetted briefly against the pallid fore course.

Loath to return between decks, he noticed a short ladder leading upward. He mounted, and found himself directly under the sails, the downdraft from them buffeting him with a deluge of cold air. He looked about quickly. Forward there was nothing but darkness, but aft he could make out men standing together, eerily illuminated by lights coming up from a low angle.

He moved toward them along the gangway next to the boats.

"Where you off to, matey?" A sailor had him by the arm. It was too dark even to make out his face.

"Lay aft, that man!" Garrett's high-pitched voice came from among the cluster around the lights.

There was no point in hiding, he had done nothing wrong.

"At the run!" Garrett screamed. Tortured muscles burned as Kydd staggered over to the group. They were around the ship's wheel and the light from the binnacle was shining up into their faces.

Garrett stalked up to Kydd and peered into his face. "When I say move, you fly! Stand at attention, you scurvy rogue. Who the devil do you think you are that you can just stroll about my quarterdeck under cover of night?" Garrett leaned forward, jutting his face at Kydd, who flinched. A stale smell of brandy hung about the officer.

Kydd stood rigid, all traces of the rum falling away. He had no idea what offense, if any, he had committed.

"Nothing to say?" Garrett asked dangerously. "Nothing to say?

You know you're caught out, and you know I'm going to punish you." Garrett swayed forward, looking closely at Kydd's shore clothing. His head jerked up. "Ah. So you must be one of that sorry-looking crew the press brought aboard today."

"Yes, sir."

"Then you'll have to learn that common seamen don't just wander about on the quarterdeck when it suits them. It is reserved for officers only—for your betters." He rocked on his heels and cocked his head skyward as if looking for inspiration.

"I've a mind to give you a spell in the bilboes to help you remember." His gaze snapped back to Kydd. A vicious look, and then a saintly smile spread. "But I'm too soft. I'll let it go—just this once. But if it happens again"—the voice rose to a biting crescendo—"by Harry, I'll make you rue the day you ever set foot in this vessel!"

Somewhere high above a sail started a fretful slapping. The man at the wheel eased a spoke or two and the noise stopped.

"Get below—now!"

Kydd turned wordlessly and made his escape. He hadn't asked to be part of this. He was a wig maker of Guildford and belonged there, not in this alien company.

He plunged down the ladders. He was friendless and unknown here, cut off from normal life as completely as it was possible to be. Not a soul aboard cared if he lived or died; even Phelps must regard him as a form of street beggar deserving of charity.

At the end of the last dog-watch, hammocks were piped down and Kydd was tersely advised to be elsewhere. Once hammocks were slung, every conceivable space was occupied. "Get the softest plank you can find and kip out on that," was the best advice he was offered. These men would be relieving the watch on deck at midnight and had little sympathy for a lost soul overlooked by the system.

Worn out by the trials and challenges of the day, he was driven by some instinct to seek surcease in the deepest part of the ship. He found himself in the lowest deck of all, stumbling along a narrow dark passage past the foul-smelling anchor cable, laid out in massive elongated coils.

Kydd felt desperately tired. A lump rose in his throat and raw emotion stung his eyes. Despair clamped in. He staggered around a corner, and just at that moment the lights of a cabin spilled out as a door opened. It was the boatswain, who looked at him in surprise. "Got yourself lost, then?" he said.

"Nowhere t' sleep," mumbled Kydd, fighting the waves of exhaustion. "Jus' came on the ship today," he said. He swayed, but did not care.

The boatswain looked at him narrowly. "That's right—saw you at the jeer capstan. Well, lad, don't worry, First Luff has a lot on his plate right now, sure he'll see you in the morning." He considered for a moment. "Come with me." He pulled at some keys on a lanyard and used them to open a door in the center of the ship.

"We keeps sails in here. Get your swede down there till morning, but don't tell anyone." He turned on his heel and thumped away up the ladder.

Kydd felt his way into the room. It stank richly of linseed oil, tar and sea-smelling canvas, but blessedly he could feel the big bolsters of sails that would serve as his bed, and he crumpled into them.

He lay on his back, staring up into the darkness at the one or two lanthorns in the distance outside that still glowed a fitful yellow. Then he jerked alert. He knew that he was not alone and he sat up, straining to hear.

Without warning, a shape launched itself straight at him. He opened his mouth to scream, but with a low "miaow" a large cat was on his lap, circling contentedly. Kydd stroked it gently and the animal purred in ecstasy, then stretched out comfortably and settled down. Kydd crushed the animal to him. First one tear, then another fell onto its fur.

CHAPTER 2

IT WAS THE CRUELEST JOURNEY, from the womb-like escape of sleep and a gentle dream of home—the musty little shop, his mother watching him as he stitched dutifully at a periwig, the sun splashing in through the thick windows—back to this waking nightmare.

Then came a vigorous shaking. "Rouse yourself—you're wanted on deck!" The boatswain's distinctive voice brought Kydd to his senses. "On deck. First Lieutenant means to muster all pressed men." The light from the lanthorn he carried deepened the lines in his face and sent a glow into the far corners of the sail room. "You'll get the number of your mess then. And your watch 'n' station."

Kydd struggled to his feet. "Thank 'ee, sir, I'm—"

"Get going—ask y'r way to the quarterdeck, abaft the mainmast."

In the cold gray of dawn, the pathetic line of pressed men shuffled miserably.

Kydd recognized the homespun and weatherworn old felt coat of a peddler, the patterned stockings, soft bonnet and greatcoat of a sedan-chair man, the leather knee breeches and smock of an agricultural laborer. They looked out of place here.

The wind off the sea was raw and blustery. Kydd's plain broadcloth coat gave little protection and he shivered.

The sea dominated in every direction, winter-hard, blue-gray, its vastness amazing to someone whose only experience of great waters had been the Thames at Weybridge. A slight breeze flurried the surface, but Kydd's eyes kept returning to the metallic line of the horizon. The ship slipped through the sea in a continuous, unvarying motion. Day and night they would be moving like this, much faster than he could run, eating up the countless miles without ever stopping. And over the line of horizon was the outer world—that plane of existence containing the dangers and fables that were part of the folklore of his society. Where previously it could be marveled at or ignored, now it was advancing to meet him, both threatening and beguiling.

The man at the wheel stood braced impassively, occasionally looking up at the weather leech of the main course, easing a spoke or two if it appeared to be on the point of shivering in the useful quartering breeze. Nearby, the officer of the watch paced slowly, his telescope of office under his arm.

High up the mighty mainmast nearly overhead, on the sturdy platform of the main fighting top, figures could be seen preparing for some maneuver. As Kydd watched, one man swung out and appeared to hang down from the main yard. He moved out, the men in the top paying out a rope as he made his way along the hundred-foot spread of the yard. Even at this distance Kydd could see that the sailor was disdaining to cling on, instead balancing between the tiny footrope he stood on while leaning familiarly against the big spar.

Kydd watched in awe. Then there was movement and the Master-at-Arms growled, "To yer front!"

The First Lieutenant strode briskly out from the cabin spaces aft, accompanied by a junior officer. His clerk hurried after him with books and paper, quill and ink. Two men set up a table at which Tyrell and the clerk then sat.

Tyrell looked up at them from under his bushy eyebrows and nodded to the lieutenant, who touched his hat and went over to the pressed men to address them. "Pay attention! You will now be assigned your watch and station. This is very important. It will tell you your duty for every motion of this vessel, be it by the actions of the sea or the malice of the enemy. You will present yourself at your place of duty immediately when you are called by the boatswain's mates or any other in lawful authority over you." The men stared at him with attitudes ranging from dumb resentment to outright fear. "And if not found at your post, you will answer for it at your peril!"

The proceedings were efficient and rapid. In a short while Kydd was left standing holding a piece of paper bearing terse details of his future existence aboard *Duke William*. It appeared that the officer of his division, a Lieutenant Tewsley, and his deputy, Mr. Lacey, master's mate, would also have these details to hand. Possession of these particulars seemed to Kydd a mark of finality. With them he could no longer claim, even to himself, that he was a temporary, unwilling visitor to their world. He was now unarguably an official part of it, and therefore subject to the most solemn penalties under the Articles of War.

A tendril of his dream brushed briefly over his mind and he felt lonely, vulnerable and frightened. Apart from the hotheaded Stallard, there was not a soul aboard whom he knew, someone he could trust, to whom he could reveal all his present fears and anxieties. One thing was sure: from now on he could rely only on himself, his own strength of mind and will. Blinking, he focused his attention on the First Lieutenant.

Tyrell finished scrawling in the margins of the book and rose. For a long moment he paused, his deep-set eyes fixed on the disconsolate group. Then he turned to the junior officer and snapped, "For God's sake, arrange an issue of slops immediately. I'll not have this ship looking like a dago doss-house!"

• • •

The bird-like purser's assistant held up a blue and white striped open-necked shirt. "Here's a fine rig for a sailor," he said. With it were some white duck trousers and a wide black leather belt.

Kydd took them. The material was strong but coarse; it would never do in Guildford, but he could see that here its robustness would serve its purpose. He couldn't help noticing how soft and pale his fingers were, and he wondered how long they would take to become brown and tough like a sailor's. There was no escaping it—soon he would be a very different person from the one he was now.

The assistant rummaged about and produced a short dark blue jacket adorned with plain anchor buttons and with it a glossy black tarpaulin hat and other seaman-like gear, and added them to the small pile. "Try them on."

It felt like dressing up, but it was plain that the short jacket and loose-bottomed trousers gave a great deal of freedom for movement. There was need, perhaps, for a bit of work with needle and thread to smarten them up, but they would do.

Trousers—these free-swinging garments were peculiar to the sea profession, and they felt loose and strange. Kydd had been in "kicks"—tight knee breeches—all his life, and so had everyone else of his acquaintance, high and low. He put on his glossy tarpaulin hat at a rakish angle and chuckled grimly at the sheer incongruity of it all.

"So you'll not be wanting these again," the assistant said, disdainfully holding up Kydd's sorry-looking country clothes. Without waiting for a reply he stuffed them into a sack.

A ship's boy led the way up the ladder for several of the group who had mess numbers on the lower gundeck. It was deserted, and at a point where the bows began their curve in, forward on the starboard side, Kydd took a long hard look at the place that would be his home in his new life.

It was the space between two monster long guns, now with their fat muzzles lashed upward against the ship's side. As he had seen the previous night, there was a table that could be lowered, revealing neat racks for the mess traps—wooden plates, pewter cutlery and bowls. Self-consciously Kydd added his new canvas ditty bag to the others hanging up along the ship's side. Each bag had an access hole halfway up the side, which was a practical means of keeping clothing and personal effects ready for use. Even in the dimness the impression he had was of extreme neatness and order, a Spartan blend of lived-in domesticity and uncompromising dedication to war. The whole purpose of the ship's existence was as an engine of destruction to be aimed at the mortal enemies of his country.

He emerged warily on deck to slate-colored skies and fretful seas. The sails were braced round at an angle to the northerly, and there away to starboard, from where the wind blew, was a mottled coastline, all in greens and nondescript browns. There was no way of telling where this was. To Kydd it might be England or a hostile foreign shore. It was entirely different from what he could remember of the rolling greensward of the North Downs.

"Damn you, sir! Do you think this is a cruise, that you are a passenger on my fo'c'sle?"

Kydd had not noticed the officer standing among the men at the foot of the foremast. In confusion he faced him and attempted to address him.

"Respects to the officer when you speaks to him, lad," a petty officer said testily.

Kydd hesitated.

Exasperated, the petty officer said more forcefully, "You salutes him, you lubber." Seeing Kydd's continued puzzlement, he knuckled his forehead in an exaggerated way. "Like this, see."

Kydd complied—it was no different from when he had to address the squire at home. "Kydd, sir, first part of starboard watch."

"Never mind your watch, what part of ship are you?" the officer asked tartly.

The question left Kydd at a loss. He saw the great bowsprit with its rearing headsails soaring out over the sea ahead. "Th' front part, sir?"

The men broke into open laughter and the officer's eyes glittered dangerously. Kydd's face burned.

A petty officer took his paper. "Ah, he's afterguard, sir, new joined."

"Then he'd better explain to Mr. Tewsley at the forebrace bitts why he is absent when parts-of-ship for exercise has been piped!" The officer turned his back and inspected the clouds of sail above.

"Get cracking, son!" the petty officer snapped. "You'll find 'em just abaft the mainmast—that's the big stick in the middle."

Kydd balled his fists as he set off in the direction indicated. He had not been treated like this since he was a child.

Around the mainmast there were scores of men, each in defined groups. They were all still, and tension hung in the air. A group of officers stood together in the center, so he approached the most ornate and saluted. "Kydd, first part of starboard watch, and afterguard," he reported.

The officer's eyebrows rose in haughty astonishment, and he looked sideways in interrogation at the young officer at his side.

"One of the new pressed men, I think, sir," the officer replied, and turned to Kydd. "Report to Mr. Tewsley at the forebrace bitts— over there," he added, pointing impatiently to the square frame at the base of the massive mainmast. Kydd did so, feeling every eye on him.

"Thank you, Kydd," a lined, middle-aged lieutenant replied, looking at Kydd's paper. "Bowyer, your mess," he told a seaman with iron-gray hair, standing near the maze of belayed ropes hanging from their pins at the square framing of the bitts.

"Aye, sir," the man replied. "Over here, mate. Jus' do what I tells you to, when I does," he muttered. The group of officers in the center of the deck conferred, the rest of the ship waiting.

Bowyer leaned forward. "That was the Cap'n you spoke to, cully. Don't you do that again, 'less you've got special reason."

The discussion among the officers grew heated in the inactivity, the Captain standing passive.

Bowyer looked curiously at Kydd and said in a low voice, "'Oo are you, then?"

"It's Tom—Thomas Kydd, who was o' Guildford."

"Joe Bowyer—an' keep it quiet, lad," Bowyer said, from the corner of his mouth. "It's always 'silence fore 'n' aft' when we're handling sail for exercise." He snatched a glance aft. "Jus' that we've done a dog's breakfast of the sail drill, and someone 'as to catch it in the neck," he muttered, his voice oddly soft for a long-service seaman.

Kydd noticed the petty officer closest to Tewsley: his face was set and hard as he watched the officers and in his fist was a coiled rope's end. Kydd stood with the others, unsure even where to put his hands, but the confidence in Bowyer's open face was reassuring.

Tewsley had the calmness of age, but he also kept his eyes fixed on the group on the quarterdeck.

The Captain turned on his heel and took position before the man at the wheel. He looked up once at the maze of sails and cordage, then down to the teams of waiting men. "Hands to make sail," he ordered. His voice came thinly, even with the speaking trumpet.

"Sod it!" Bowyer's curse made Kydd jump. "Captain's taking over."

Kydd puzzled at the paradox. "Th' Captain shouldn't take charge?" he asked.

Bowyer frowned. He gave a furtive look aft and replied gravely, "'Cos he's not what you might call a real man-o'-war's man—got his step through arse-lickin' in Parliament or some such." He sucked his teeth. "Don't trust him in sailorin', yer might say."

The Captain raised his speaking trumpet again. "Stations to set main topsail."

Lifting his voice, Tewsley called, "Captain of the quarterdeck!"

Kydd looked about in surprise, expecting another gold-laced officer. Instead the hard-faced petty officer came forward.

"Carry on, Elkins."

The petty officer rounded on his men. "Youse—double up on the weather buntlines, and you lot t' the clewlines." To Bowyer he ordered tersely, "Lee clewlines."

Elkins moved to the bitts at the base of the mast from which hung masses of ropes, and Kydd noticed that there were openings in the deck on each side down which ropes passed to the deck below. "Stand by topsail sheets, you waisters!" Elkins bellowed.

Bowyer crossed quickly to the row of belaying pins at the ship's side, just where the shrouds of the mainmast reached the bulwarks— the men already there moved to make room for him.

As much to them as to Kydd he said, "Now, Kydd, when I casts loose, you tails on to the line with the rest o' them land toggies."

The tension was almost palpable. Most of the ordinary sailors Kydd could see around him were clearly not of the first order, and he guessed that they were stationed here because they could be brought more under eye from the quarterdeck. All were uneasy and watchful.

The man at the wheel now had a second assisting him in the freshening wind, and the ship showed a more lively response to the hurrying seas.

The Captain brought out a large gold watch and consulted it ostentatiously. "I shall want to see topsails set and sheeted home at least a minute faster. If this is not achieved"—he glanced about him—"then hands will not be piped to dinner until it is."

At Bowyer's snort, Kydd turned. "He means no grog until he gets 'is times," he growled.

"Stand by!" A boatswain's mate placed his call to his lips, eyes on the Captain, who nodded sharply.

The peal of the call was instantly overlain with shouts from all parts of the deck.

"Lay aloft and loose topsail!"

Men shot past Kydd and into the main shrouds to begin a towering climb to the topmast. Bowyer jumped to the clewline fall and lifted clear the coil of rope, thumping it to the deck behind him. Kydd was shouldered roughly out of the way as the line was handed along until all had seized hold of it. He joined hesitantly at the end. Bowyer expertly undid the turns until one remained, the line of men taking the strain. He looked across in readiness.

Tewsley was staring hard upward and Kydd followed his gaze. Men had made the ascent up the shrouds to the maintop, and were even now continuing on past and up the topmast shrouds, moving up the ratlines in fast, jerky movements. They reached the topsail yard—an arm waved.

"Lay out and loose!"

Kydd was startled by Tewsley's roar, which seemed too great to have come from his slight frame. In response seamen poured out along the yard on each side and began casting off the gaskets retaining the sail. Watching them moving far above, he felt his palms go clammy at the thought of the height at which they were working, much higher than the top of any building he had ever seen. He stole a glance back at the Captain, who stood impassively, still holding his watch before him.

The sail began dropping from the yard.

"Sheets!" Tewsley snapped.

"Topsail sheets!" roared Elkins, to the deck below, and was answered by an instant rattling of ropes against the mainmast.

"Clewlines!"

Bowyer cast off the last turn and the lee topsail clewline swung clear.

The rough hairiness of the rope felt alien to Kydd, but being at the end of the line, he manfully put all his weight on it—and was immediately pulled off his feet.

He scrambled up, roundly cursed by those in front.

From nowhere came the hiss and fiery crack of a rope's end over his back. The pain caught him by surprise, clamping his chest in a stab of breathlessness. He swung round to see Elkins coiling his rope for a second lash. Instinctively he threw up his arms to shield himself.

Surprise, then cruel satisfaction passed over Elkins's face. "Well, damn me eyes! Raise yer 'and to a superior officer, then, you mangy dog!"

Bowyer threw in his position as first on the line. Racing up behind Kydd, he felled him with a glancing blow to the ear. "No, he wasn't, Mr. Elkins—he's a iggerant lubber who doesn't know 'is ropes yet." Panting and staring at Kydd rather than Elkins, he continued, "Give 'im a chance to learn—only bin aboard a dog-watch."

Ears ringing, Kydd staggered to his feet.

"Silence!" Tewsley strode over, his face red with anger. "Take charge properly, Elkins, or I'll have you turned before the mast this instant."

Elkins wiped his mouth with the back of his hand, his eyes following Tewsley. "Ease away clewlines."

Taking up position in front of Kydd, Bowyer threw over his shoulder, "Sorry fer that. See, yer heaves on the sheets, but when settin' sail you overhauls the clewlines 'n' buntlines—let it out, mate," he said, tugging at the line to let it go forward.

Kydd did as he was told, too stunned by events to question anything.

"Handsomely!" Tewsley growled, as the rope surged.

On the main yard, at the weather tip, a man sat astride the yard-arm, his feet in the "Flemish horse" footrope at the end, his task to keep the loose line of the sheet fed into the sheave at the best angle as the sail was sheeted home.

Querulous, the Captain called across, "Get your men to work, Mr. Tewsley—they seem to have gone to sleep!"

"Er—sir, we—" began Tewsley, in astonishment.

The men at the clewlines and buntlines didn't hesitate: unskilled as they were, and under the Captain's eye, they lost no time in paying out the line faster and faster.

"Avast there," roared Tewsley, but it was too late. At the topsail, the clewline dropping the corner of the sail had been slackened faster than the sheet pulling from beneath could keep up. Instead of a controlled glide to the yardarm, the topsail was now free to flog itself about in sweeping lashes. The topsail sheetman at the end of the yard ducked and parried, but there was nowhere to hide. The cluster of three massive blocks at the lower corner of the topsail, now a plaything of the hundred-foot expanse of sail, bounced the man off the yard. He fell in a wide arc outward and into the sea, his piercing shriek of despair paralyzing Kydd until it was cut off by the sea.

Kydd rushed to the side and saw the man, buffeted by the side wake of the ship, quickly sliding astern and away into the gray seas. The man's arm raised briefly to show he had survived the fall and Kydd turned to see what would be done. The Captain, however, did not move, frozen in a stare forward.

"Sir!" the young officer of the watch entreated. It was not clear whether the Captain had indeed taken over the deck. "Sir, do we go about?"

The Captain stood as though in a trance.

Tewsley threw himself toward the wheel and roared, "Down

helm—hard! Get that hatch grating overside. Let go lee main braces, main tack and sheet!" Spinning on his heels, he bawled forward, "Flow head sheets—clear away the lee cutter!" Ponderously the ship's head fell away from the wind. Tewsley paused and looked toward the Captain, who showed no apparent recognition. "Main clew garnets and buntlines—up mainsail!"

The great mainsail spilled its wind and began to be gathered up to the yard.

Glancing aft to the far-off tiny dot in the sea, Tewsley snapped, "Brace aback—heave to!" The effect of the backed sails balancing those normally set allowed the vessel to come to a stop, drifting slowly downwind. Touching his hat, Tewsley reported to the Captain, "Ship heaving to, sir. Larboard cutter on yard and stay tackles for launching."

The Captain's eyes seemed to focus slowly. "That is well, Mr. Tewsley, but I was looking to Mr. Lockwood to act in this matter." He stepped over to the poop deck ladder, touching it as though curious, and nodded to the young officer of the watch. "Carry on, Mr. Lockwood," he said, almost without interest.

From his place Kydd saw the boat hoisted from its chocks and lowered overside. It was a complex process and took far more men to achieve than the size of the boat seemed to suggest would be needed. He joined the crowd at the ship's side to watch.

It was too distant to see what was happening, and many opinions were expressed, but eventually when the boat drew near again, the chatter died away at the sight of a canvas-covered form lying along the thwarts between the rowers.

The bowman stood in the foresheets and neatly hooked the mizzen chains. The boat lay bobbing alongside, oars tossed vertically. The coxswain stood and cupped his hands. "'E's dead!" he shouted.

Kydd tailed on to the yardarm whip that hoisted the dead man inboard, secured to the grating. The surgeon, a lugubrious man in rumpled black, pushed through the throng and bent over the still form. "Broken bones and morbid cold—there was never any question." He did not look up.

The two bells remaining of the exercise time went slowly for Kydd. The sailor's sudden transition from hero of a lofty world to dead clay was much to take in. His experiences of death previously had been like Old Uncle Peel in a huddle on the high street, and the solemnity of the succeeding funeral. He pulled himself together. There was nothing he could do for the man.

At eight bells—midday—the peal of the boatswain's calls ended their drill. The Captain evidently did not wish to press the point about times. "Hands to dinner!"

Bowyer turned to him and said sourly, "Let's get below. I've a need to get outside a grog or two after this."

Grateful for his invitation, Kydd followed him down the fore hatchway, arriving in the now familiar gloom of the lower gundeck. It was alive with talk, and the tone of the voices and glaring eyes left him with no doubt about the subject.

They thrust past to reach their mess, which Kydd noticed was conveniently not far from the hatchway, just at the point where the round of the bows straightened into the long sweep aft. He thought to count the number of guns from forward. His mess lay between the third and fourth guns. It was already nearly full and now he would be meeting his messmates. What would they make of an unwilling outsider like himself, who knew not the first thing about their strange, dangerous world?

Bowyer grabbed the lanthorn that hung above the table and held it up next to Kydd's face. "Listen, you bilge rats," he said against the din, "this here's Tom Kydd, pressed man o' Guildford, an' he's our new messmate."

There was a hush, and Kydd watched the faces turn toward

him, varying in expression from frank curiosity to blank disinterest. "Pleased to meet you," he said, in as neutral a tone as he could manage.

A scornful "Pleased ter meecher!" came from a sharp-faced man on one side. "We don't have that sorta talk here, cully."

"Stow it, Howell," Bowyer said shortly. "Don't you pay no mind to 'im, the old snarley-yow. He is—or was, I should say—a merchant jack and pressed same as you, 'cept he's makin' more noise about it."

Next to Howell a pleasant-faced lad stood up and leaned over to offer his hand. "Dick Whaley, pressed outa the *Maid o' Whitby*, same as Jonas here." Kydd took the hand gratefully.

Howell snorted. "What he's not sayin' is that I was bo'sun aboard while he was afore the mast—and don't he forget it!"

Whaley laughed. "And here we're a pair of foremast jacks both. At least we've a chance fer some prize money. In the old *Maid* we was just floggin' up and down the coast with a belly full of sea coal, and never the sight of a frolic."

"Let him sit, Joe." At the ship's side was a considerably older seaman, nearly covered with faded tattoos. His mild, seamed face gazed steadily at Kydd.

Bowyer thumbed at the old sailor. "That's Samuel Claggett, fo'c'sleman to the quality. Been aboard since the last age, so we 'as to keep 'im in humor."

While Kydd found his place at the end of the bench the conversations took up again. Diffident, he said nothing and tried to listen to the others. His eyes slid to the men opposite and were caught, to his astonishment, by the glittering black orbs of a Chinaman, the first he had ever seen. The man sat without speaking, his shaven head reflecting the lanthorn glow. Bowyer noticed Kydd's start of surprise and said, "Say 'how' to Wong, then."

"Er, how!"

"*Ni hau!*" the man replied.

"Wong Hey Chee, able seaman and right heathen but a good hand aloft when it comes on to blow." Bowyer's introduction did nothing to affect Wong's steady stare. "Was a strong man in a circus, was Wong," Bowyer continued admiringly.

Kydd shifted his gaze to the last man, opposite Claggett.

The man gave him a civil nod, but remained wordless. He had a sensitive face, which bore the unmistakable mark of intelligence. His eyes were dark and unsettling.

"Yes—an' that's Renzi," Bowyer said. He leaned forward and lowered his voice. "Says nothing, keeps to himself. A rum cove, if you asks me. I'd leave him be, mate, bit quick on the trigger 'e can be."

Kydd looked back at Renzi and realized what was bothering him. Although clearly at home in a comfortable but plain seaman's rig, the man did not have the open, trusting manner of a sailor. Neither did he have the close-gathered tarry queue of the older seaman, or the long side-whiskers and wild hair of the younger. His almost blue-black hair was as short as a monk's. He was further taken aback when he realized that the man's gaze could best be termed a glare. He wondered if he had offended in some way.

His thoughts were interrupted by shouts of appreciation greeting the arrival of the grog monkey, a well-used, two-eared wooden kid. It was thumped on the table in front of Claggett, who lost no time in sending an odd assortment of pots and tankards, well filled, back to their expectant owners.

"That's yourn, then, Kydd." He slid over a brassbound wooden drinking vessel. Kydd lifted it. It was old-fashioned, the size and shape favored by thirsty countryfolk, but where they would fill it with cider or beer, the sweetness of rum eddied up to him. He was amazed—there was well over a pint of the liquid.

"Here's to you, Tom lad," Bowyer said, and upended his own pot.

Kydd felt an unexpected flush of pleasure at the use of his forename. "And Mr. Garrett—damn his whistle," he replied, lifting his tankard in salute. The taste had an unexpected coolness.

Bowyer's eyes creased. "Three-water grog, this is only. You'll be lucky ter get grog twice a week in *Royal Billy*—you're catching on, mate!"

They both drank deeply. The liquor spread warmth through Kydd's vitals and he could feel the anxiety draining from him. A smile broke through.

"That's the ticket! Can be a hard life, a sailor's, but there are, who shall say, the compensations!"

Kydd drank again and, amid the animated ebb and flow of talk, studied his shipmates once more. Wong was listening impassively to Whaley describing the hardships of a voyage to Esbjerg, while Claggett was speaking softly to a man sitting next to him.

Kydd lifted his pot to drink, but as it tilted he saw over the rim that Renzi's glowering, intense eyes were on him. Disconcerted, he gave a weak smile and took a long pull at his grog. The eyes were still on him, and he noticed the unusual depth of the lines incised at each side of Renzi's mouth.

"Where's that useless Doud? We'll die of hunger else," Howell demanded. The others ignored him.

"Hey-ho, mates, and it's pease pudding and Irish horse!" A wiry, perky young man arrived and swung a pair of wooden kids under the end of the table.

"About time, damn you for a shab!" Howell's sneer in no way discommoded Doud, whose broad grin seemed to light up the entire mess.

"Come on, Ned, we're near gutfoundered," said Whaley, rubbing his hands in anticipation. The lids came off the food, and the bread barge was filled and placed on the table. Mess traps were brought down from their racks and the meal could begin.

After his previous experience Kydd had no expectations. On his plate the pease pudding was gray-green, flecked with darker spots, and clearly thickened with some other substance. The beef was unrecognizable, gray and gristly. Kydd couldn't hide his disgust at the taste.

Bowyer saw his expression and gave a mirthless chuckle. "That there's fresh beef, Tom. Wait till we're at sea awhile—the salt horse'll make you yearn after this'n!"

He slid the bread barge across to Kydd. Lying disconsolate on a mess of ship's biscuit were the stale remnants of the "soft tommy" taken aboard in Sheerness.

Kydd passed on the bread and gingerly took some hard tack. He fastened his teeth on the crude biscuit, but could make no impression.

"Not like that, mate," Bowyer said. "Like this!" Cupping the biscuit in his palm, he brought his opposite elbow sharply down on it and revealed the fragments resulting. "This is yer hard tack, lad. We calls it bread at sea—best you learns a taste for it."

As they ate, Kydd was struck by the small concessions necessary because of the confined space: the wooden plates were square rather than round and therefore gave optimum area for holding food. Eating movements were curiously neat and careful: no cutlery waved in the air, and elbows seemed fixed to the side of the body. It was in quite a degree of contrast to the spreading coarseness of the town ordinary where tradesmen would take their cheap victuals together.

The last of his grog made the food more palatable, and when he had finished, Kydd let his eyes wander out of the pool of lanthorn light to the other mess tables, each a similar haven of sociability.

He remembered his piece of paper. "Joe, what does all this mean?" he said, passing over his watch and station details.

"Let's see." Bowyer studied the paper in the dim light. "It says here you're in the first part of the starboard watch—with me, mate. And your part of ship is afterguard, so you report there to Mr. Tewsley for your place o' duty." He paused and looked affectionately at the others. "And the other is the number of yer mess. You're messmates with us here now, and on the purser's books for vittlin' and grog under that number. Not that you'll get fair do's from Mansel, that bloody Nipcheese." Bowyer smiled viciously. "Yeah— those duds you've just got, you'll be working them off a guinea t' the poun' for six months yet. And with a purser's pound at fourteen ounces you'll not be overfed, mate."

He looked again at the paper. "You're in Mr. Tewsley's division, o' course, so yer accountable to him to be smart 'n' togged out in proper rig, and once yer've got yer hammock, it says here you'll be getting your head down right aft on this deck. Show yer where at pipe-down tonight." He returned the paper. "That's all ye need to know fer now. All this other lot are yer stations—where yer have to be when we go 'hands ter unmoor ship,' 'send down topmast' an' that. You'll get a chance to take it all aboard when we exercises."

Kydd needed more. "What's this about a gun, then?"

"That's your post at quarters. We get ourselves into an action, you go to number-three gun lower deck"—he pointed to it—"but I doubts we'll get much o' that unless the Frogs want ter be beat again." Taking another pull at his grog, Bowyer grinned.

But Kydd wasn't about to let go. "When do I have t' climb the mast, Joe?"

Bowyer's laugh stilled the table's conversation for a moment. He leaned forward. "Tom, me old shipmate, you're a landman. That means nobody expects you to do anything more'n pull on a rope and swab the uppers all day. Me, I'm an able seaman, I c'n hand, reef and steer, so we gets to go aloft, you don't." Finishing his grog, he looked across at Kydd, his guileless gray eyes, clubbed pigtail and sun-bleached seaman's gear making him the picture of a deep-sea mariner. He smiled good-humoredly. "That's not ter say you'll be a landman for ever. What say we take a stroll around the barky? Starbowlines are off watch this afternoon 'n' yer could be learnin' something."

They came out by the big fore hatch onto the upper deck. Up a short ladder and they were on a deck space at the foot of the fore-mast, beneath its sails and rigging. The wind was raw and cutting, and the odd fleck of spray driven up by the bows bit at the skin.

"Now, Tom, this 'ere raised part is the fo'c'sle deck, an' at the other end of the hooker is another, and it's the quarterdeck, and we move between the two parts by means of them there gangways each side. Gives a pleasin' sweep o' deck, fore 'n' aft."

Kydd nodded. "So is this then the upper deck?" he asked.

"It's not, mate. The upper deck is the top one of all that can run continuous the whole length, so it's the one next under us. We often calls it the main deck, and this one the spar deck, 'cos we useta keep the spare spars handy here."

Looking about, Kydd tried not to be awkward. "But I see one more deck above this, right at the end."

"Aye, that's the poop deck—important on a smaller ship keepin' waves from comin' aboard when we've got a following sea, but all it really is are the Captain's cabins all raised up off the quarterdeck—the coach, we calls it." Bowyer looked meaningfully at Kydd. "You should know, Tom, that the fo'c'sle is the place fer common sailors." He turned and looked aft. "And the quarterdeck is fer officers. If you're not on dooty you don't go there or—"

"I know," said Kydd.

"It's a kind of holy ground—same even fer the officers," Bowyer said seriously, "and they 'n' you should pay respec' when crossin' on to it."

Kydd's quizzical look did not bring an explanation.

Bowyer tilted his head to gaze up at the complex array of masts, yards, sails and rigging with something that closely resembled affection. "Now, lookee there, Tom. Any ship-rigged packet has three masts, fore, main and mizzen, and the names of the yards and sails are nearly the same on all of 'em, so you need learn only one. And the ropes an' all—they take their names from the masts and sails they work, so they're the same."

Kydd tried to adopt a nonchalant pose, holding on to a substantial-looking rope. Bowyer winced. "Be careful now, Tom—we scratches a backstay to get a wind, and we don't want ter tempt fate, now, do we?" He moved on quickly. "And we rate our ships depending on 'ow many guns we 'ave. This one 'as three decks of guns, the most of any, near enough, so we're the biggest, a line-of-battle ship." The guns on the fo'c'sle glistened blackly with damp. "We've got near one hunnerd o' the great guns, the biggest down low, where we lives. We can take on anything afloat, me lad. You pity the poor bastard that finds 'imself lookin' down the eyes o' these beauties."

The chill wind fluttered Kydd's jacket and made him shudder. By mutual consent they passed down the ladder to the deck below. It was mainly enclosed, but open to the sky for a distance between foremast and mainmast, here crossed by thick skid beams on which the ship's boats were stowed.

They passed the open area to go aft. The big main hatches were here below it, a passage deep into the bowels of the vessel, and garlanded with cannonballs like lethal strands of black pearls. Past the imposing bulk of the mainmast was a final ladderway down, but across the whole width of the deck aft, their way was now barred by a darkly polished bulkhead with doors each side.

"There's where the Admiral lives, Tom—an' like a prince!" Bowyer moved closer and spoke reverently. "And that's where they plan out the battles 'n' such." His mouth twitched. "'Twas also the place where Jemmy Boyes and his mates went afore a court-martial. Mutiny, they called it, although it were really them only talkin' wry—the year 'eighty-seven that was." He looked forward, his mouth compressed to a hard line. "It were our own fore yard-arm where they was turned off, God save 'em."

For a moment he stood, then went over to the ladder and looked down. "We have two more decks of guns below us, 'n' then it's the waterline."

"And where were we at the purser's?"

"Well, I didn't say we had no more decks under the waterline," Bowyer said. "In fact, me old gullion, we have the orlop under the lower gundeck, and that was where you was before."

He cracked his knuckles. "Interestin' place, the orlop. Right forrard you get the boatswain and Chips. They both have their cabin and their stores. But turn round and right aft you get the saw-bones, the purser and *their* stores—and not forgettin' the midshipmen's berth."

He looked down, as though the deck were transparent. "And all the middle bit is where the anchor cables are laid out in tiers, and where yer go down inside the gun magazines. Lots o' dark, rummy places about, down in the orlop. Wouldn't advise rovin' about down there without yer've got a friend." He swung round with a grin. "And then all that's left below is the hold. But I guess yer know all about that—it's where the pressed men go afore we sails. It's where all the water and vittles are stowed, and when we clears for action all the gear gets sent down there." Bowyer punched him on the shoulder. "So now you knows all the decks, we'll go visit 'em!"

There was no hanging back, and for the remainder of the watch Kydd found himself plunging after Bowyer—down ladders, along rows of huge guns, on gratings out above the sea and, in fact, to places it was impossible to believe might belong on a ship of war. A cookhouse with monstrous cauldrons simmering over an iron-hearted fire. A manger, complete with goats and chickens. A cockpit—but no cocks that Kydd could detect. And many—multitudes—of objects and places that Bowyer clearly thought important, but had no meaning to Kydd.

They happened to be under the boats when four double strikes sounded from the belfry just above. "Know what that means, Tom? It's 'up spirits' and then supper, me old griff!"

In a whirlpool of impressions Kydd followed Bowyer down to the lower gundeck and the welcome fug of the mess. Howell looked up sourly. "You tryin' to make Kydd a jolly Jack Tar, then, Joe?"

"You sayin' he shouldn't be?" Bowyer snapped.

"I'm sayin' as how he don't know what he's a-comin' to. He's not bred to the sea, he's a landlubber, don't belong." He became heated. "Can you see him out on the yard in a gale of wind, doin' real sailorin'? Nah. All his days he's gonna be on his knees and arse up with a holystone—that is, when he's not huckin' out the heads or swiggin' off on the braces!" He leaned forward and told Bowyer earnestly, "'S not right fer you to fill his head with grand ideas—he's never going to be a sailorman. Sooner he knows it, better for him."

Pointedly ignoring him, Bowyer took down their mess traps. "We've got first dog-watch straight after, so we takes a bit o' ballast aboard now, Tom, mate!"

It was still light on deck, showing up the swarm of small vessels around them, which were seizing the opportunity to slip down Channel with an unofficial escort of such unchallengeable might.

Kydd followed Bowyer closely, apprehensive because this was to be his first sea watch, and gingerly joined the waiting group near the mainmast.

"You! Yeah—the cow-handed sod with Bowyer!" Elkins's grating shout broke into his thoughts. There was an animal ferocity in the hard face and Kydd froze. "Come here, you useless grass-combin' bastard." Elkins thrust his face forward. "If ever you makes a sawney o' me afore the quarterdeck again, you're fishmeat, cully!"

Kydd felt defiance rising, but he kept silent, trying to withstand the assault of the man's glare.

Abruptly, Elkins seized his jacket savagely in both hands at the throat and pulled him to his toes. Speaking softly and slowly, but with infinite menace, he said, "A lumpin' great lobcock like you would do well to know where he stands afore he thinks to get uppity—you scavey?"

The hard, colorless eyes seemed to impale Kydd's soul. The thin lips curled. "O' course yer do, cully," he said. "You're a Johnny Raw, new caught, who's goin' to learn his place right quick—ain't that the case?"

He released Kydd slowly, keeping him transfixed.

Bowyer's troubled voice came in from behind Kydd. "No call fer that, Mr. Elkins," he said.

Elkins turned on him.

"I'll be lookin' out for Kydd, don't you worry, Mr. Elkins." He grabbed Kydd's arm and steered him back to the mainmast. A young officer watched, frowning.

"Don't do to cross Elkins's bows, shipmate," Bowyer muttered, pretending to test the tension of a line at the bitts.

Kydd had never backed down from anyone in his life—even the raw-boned squire's son treated him with care. But this was another situation, filled with unknowns.

"See there, Tom"—Bowyer was trying to engage his attention—"we're bending on the new mizzen t'gallant." Kydd allowed his interest to be directed to the second farthest yard upward at the mizzen. Men were spreading out along the yard, that side that he could see past the large triangular staysails soaring up between the two masts. "You'll remember we saw Mr. Clough and his mates sewing in the tabling for the t'gallant bolt-rope?"

Kydd recalled his curiosity as they stepped around the cross-legged men busily plying their needles. Those were no delicate darning needles: instead they were long and heavy, three-sided implements, which they drove through the stout canvas using a leather device strapped to their palms.

"Clap on here, mate," said Bowyer. "We're sending up yer sail now to fix on to its yard." A long sausage of canvas had made its way on deck, and an astonishing amount of rope lay in long coils next to it. "We uses the buntlines to haul it up for bending, but it being a t'gallant and all, the line is too short to come from aloft, so we bends on some extra."

Kydd let it all wash over him. It was beyond his powers to retain, but he was sure that Bowyer would be on hand later to explain. At the present moment he urgently needed to find his bearings and, indeed, himself.

The watch passed quickly in a flurry of hauling, belaying and repeating this on other ropes in sequence with events, the canvas sausage making its way up the mast to its final glory as a trim, smartly set sail. Dusk was well and truly drawing in when the pealing of boatswains' calls erupted forward. "There yer go, Tom, the Spithead nightingales are singin'. Larbowlines are on deck now, 'n' we can go below—but first we've somethin' to do, brother."

Kydd followed him down to the lanthorn-lit forward end of the main deck. It was crowded with men, gathered closely around a quartermaster's mate standing just abaft the foremast, and next to a small pile of clothing and other gear. Lieutenant Tewsley was there, hat held informally in his hand and his seamed face somber.

Bowyer coughed self-consciously. "This is what we do for them what goes over the standin' part of the foresheet."

At Kydd's look of incomprehension he said, "That is to say, them which tops their boom dies at sea—like Ollie Higgins did this forenoon off the main yard."

Kydd felt a stab of guilt at the stark memory of the man cartwheeling into the sea, knowing that it had been buried in the avalanche of images and experiences to which he had been subjected since.

Bowyer continued, in a low voice, "We gets into Spithead tomorrow, so we holds an auction on his clobber now. If we c'n find a little silver for 'is widow, well, it's somethin'."

The auction proceeded, low shouts as bids were cast and clothing fingered in quiet remembrance. Noticing Bowyer involved in the bidding, Kydd wondered what to do. There were only pennies left of what he had had in his pocket when pressed, and only volunteers received the bounty.

"'Ere you are, Tom," Bowyer said, and passed over a well-worn seaman's knife and sheath. "Ollie was a topman, and you can trust 'is steel to be the best." Kydd hesitated. "Go on, mate, take it—he won't be needin' it now, and he'd be happy it's still goin' to do its dooty."

Kydd's helpless fumbling at his pocket made Bowyer touch his arm. "Don't worry about that, mate. You'll find nobody cares about us—we 'as to look to ourselves. Yer'll not see a penny o' yer pay for half a year or more, so we'll square yardarms some other time."

Self-consciously, Kydd undid his broad belt and strapped on the knife, settling the sheath into place on the flat of his right buttock as Bowyer had his.

Bowyer paid over several more silver coins and was handed a crackling bundle of olive-gray skins. "This is what yer'll reckon best, Tom, out on the yard in a winter nor'easter—an honest seal-skin warmer under your jacket. Keeps out the cold like a hero."

Outside the purser's store on the orlop Kydd tried again. "Look, Joe, you don't have to—"

"Leave it be, Tom!" Bowyer said, gruffly.

Kydd drew his issue hammocks and meager bedding. Bowyer fingered it doubtfully. "Listen, mate, only way yer goin' to get a good kip in a hammacoe is if I tells yer how. So let's be at it—we're on watch right after hammocks are piped down. I'll give yer a hand." Bowyer clicked his tongue at the haphazard bundle of stiff new canvas and bedclothing and deftly rolled them tightly together, securing them with half hitches. He threw the result over his shoulder. Thrusting his way aft, he found Kydd's numbered position.

"You'll be slingin' yer 'mick here, being as you're afterguard. Part of ship stays together so's yer can be found in the dark for a shake— yer oppo's alongside yer, o' course."

Seeing Kydd's look, he explained, "The man who does the same job as you but in t'other watch."

Kydd nodded, but he was overwhelmed. An unbelievable number of men were moving about in the dim lower gundeck, all busily slinging hammocks, and it seemed inconceivable that they could fit into so limited a space.

With the ease of long practice, Bowyer secured one rope to a batten fastened on the deck beams overhead. "Watch this, Tom—can't show yer twice, have me own 'mick to sling." He teased out the parallel knittle lines at the ends of the hammock, then extended the canvas, taking the opposite end to another batten. "Guess you'll want to try it low, first up," Bowyer murmured, and Kydd could see that there was a method in the madness about him. To maximize space, adjacent hammocks were slung clear, either high or low. Bowyer had eased the lines so that Kydd would be in the lowest of them.

The hammocks also overlapped to the canvas in a fore and aft direction. It became clear that this had an additional benefit when Bowyer invited Kydd to climb into his hammock for the first time.

The seasoned sailor chuckled at the inevitable result—like a skittish horse, the hammock skipped out of reach every time Kydd lifted a leg to lever himself in, quickly finding himself dumped smartly on deck the other side.

"Yer gets aboard only like this," Bowyer said, and with one lithe movement, he grasped in both hands an overlapping hammock clew overhead, and this taking his weight, his first leg positioned the hammock for the other leg to thump in alongside.

Reversing the movement, Bowyer dropped to the deck. "Now you, mate."

CHAPTER 3

IN THE LIGHT NIGHT WINDS, sailing easily full and bye on the starboard tack, there was little for the watch on deck to do. Keyed up to expect hours of toil, Kydd was surprised to find how relaxed the watch before midnight could be. After an initial fuss at the braces, tacks and sheets, the sails were finally trimmed to the satisfaction of Warren, the officer of the watch, who then reluctantly stood the men down, save those about the binnacle.

One thing, however, Kydd found disconcerting. Where the mess decks were gloomy, lanthorn-lit caverns, on deck it was positively tomb-like. A low overcast obscured the night sky and his eyes strained in the winter night to distinguish main features, let alone the dozens of ropes, ringbolts and sharp edges that lay invisibly in wait. It was quite impossible to make out the faces of the others. They were phantoms in the darkness: their voices had the curious quality of being overloud when close, and too distant when farther away. Only moving shadows against the dim whiteness of the deck disclosed their presence.

Kydd stayed close to Bowyer as they went down the ladder to the main deck. There, in the waist of the ship, they would be on instant call, but could shelter from the spray and keen wind. It didn't escape Kydd that they would also be out of sight of Warren and the others on the quarterdeck. They hunkered down, backs to the bulwark, the old hands among them coming together in companionable groups to converse in low tones and while away the watch. Kydd sat on the periphery of Bowyer's group, content to listen.

The hiss of the ship's wash out in the darkness was hypnotic. Sitting on the deck, leaning against a gun carriage in the anonymity of the night, Kydd felt a creeping unreality, that stage of tiredness when a floating light-headedness bears the spirit on in a timeless, wondering void.

Disembodied voices rose and fell. His mind drifted, but returned to hear what they were saying.

"No, mate—I saw 'im! Didn't do a bloody thing, just watched while Ollie went over the side. Did nothing 'cept stare, the useless ninny."

"Yeah, you saw him, but he was givin' a chance fer Lockwood to do somethin' for himself. He had the deck, didn't he?" Kydd recognized Bowyer's troubled tones.

"It won't fadge, Joe," someone replied. "The Captain 'as the ship. There's no buts in it. It's his dooty to look after the people, same's it's our dooty to look after the ship."

"Now, what I don't like is this. When it comes to a situation, it's 'sharp's the word and quick's the motion' but he just stood there! Yes, sir, just froze right up!"

"So we gets a dirty great Frenchie, yardarm to yardarm, offerin' to ventilate our sides—ain't no time to be stoppin' and starin'."

"I seen a scrovy like that!" a voice chirruped from out of the dark.

"Oh, yeah?"

"Did so too. He was touched, that's what he was, used t' stare like that—into his vittles, out the window, nobody could speak to him. Right scareful, it was."

"What happened to him, then?"

"Well, one evenin' he fell down in the pothouse, kickin' 'n' twisting 'n' scarin' the daylights out of us all until they took him off ter the bedlam."

Kydd snorted into the gloom. "Bloody rot! You're talkin' of the falling sickness. Poor juggins to have you as his friend. It's a kind of fit. An' what I saw this afternoon wasn't the fallin' sickness."

Another voice challenged, nearer. "So what was it, Mr. Sawbones?"

Conscious that he had attracted attention to himself, Kydd could only answer lamely, "Well, it wasn't, that's all."

The exchange drifted into an inconclusive silence.

The edge of an unseen sail fluttered sharply and quietened, and an occasional muffled crunch of waves came from forward, in time with a slight pitch of the bows. Kydd shifted his position.

He heard Bowyer from farther away: "Can't blame the skipper, Lofty. He's new, 'n' he's had to take over the barky from Halifax without the smell of a dockin', poor lady."

"That's all gammon, 'n' you know it, Joe."

"No—what I'm a-saying is that, as bloody usual, in this war we've been caught all aback 'n' all in a pelt—skipper's got to get the ship out to meet the Frogs 'n' 'e's cuttin' corners."

The man grunted loudly. "Pig-shite! You always were simple, Joe. What we 'ave is a Jonah! Seen 'em before. They doesn't know it even but they 'as the mark! An' it's evil luck that comes aboard any hooker what ships a Jonah, as well you know, mate."

The murmurs died away, and Kydd shivered at the turn in the conversation. He took refuge in the continual run of shipboard noises—the ceaseless background of anonymous sounds that assured him his new world was continuing as usual.

There were a few coughs before a deep voice announced, "When we makes Spithead tomorrer, I'm goin' no farther than yon Keppel's Head—get me a good sea coal fire ahead, a muzzler of stingo under m' lee and I'll not see daylight until we fronts back aboard."

"Stow that!" someone whooped. "I've got a year's pay says there's no fubsy wench in Portsmouth Point's goin' unsatisfied while I've got the legs to get me ashore."

The babble of voices was broken by one of the older men. "Presumin' we get to step off."

"Course we will! On the North Ameriky station for near two years—stands to reason we dock first to set the old girl to rights afore we join the Fleet. Gonna take at least half a year—we're forty years old, mate, and you know she spits oakum in any sort of sea!"

"Yeah, that's right! We had thirteen months ashore off of *Billy Ruffian* in 'eighty-eight, an' she was in better shape than we by a long haul."

"Jus' let me get alongside my Polly—she's been a-waitin' for me 'n' my tackle since St. Geoffrey's Day."

The excited chatter ebbed and flowed around Kydd, until it crossed his mind that if the others went ashore, then there might be a chance for him to slip away. A few days' tramp along the London Road and he'd be back, God be praised, in the rural tranquillity of Guildford.

Distant bells sounded from forward. A hand on his arm broke into these happy thoughts. "Stir yerself, Tom. Now we can get our heads down until mornin'," said Bowyer.

Their way lit by a lanthorn carried by a ship's corporal, they passed down to the lower deck. Shadowy figures, the last of the larbowlines, hurried past.

After the cold dankness of the open air, the heat and fug of the broad space, full of slowly swaying hammocks, was prodigious. The air was thick with the musty odor of many men in a confined space and the creeping fetor of bilge smells. With fatigue closing in on him in waves, Kydd stumbled over to his hammock. Stripping off his outer clothes, he followed the example of the others and rolled them into a pillow. He then addressed himself to the task of getting in. It took only two tries before he was aboard, agreeably enfolded by the canvas sides. Some cautious wriggles and he found that the hammock was remarkably stable and, in fact, astonishingly comfortable. The meager "mattress" conformed to his shape and the single coarse blanket was hardly needed, with the heat of so much humanity.

Lying there, too exhausted to sleep, he let his eyes wander restlessly over the scene—the loom of hammocks all around, the dark closeness of the deckhead above and the last few moving figures. Then the lanthorns were removed, and he was left alone with his thoughts in utter blackness.

There was an air of excitement and anticipation as the far-off soft green and gray-black of the land resolved into the Isle of Wight, and Portsmouth, with its sheltered naval anchorage of Spithead. The weather had held, and there was nothing to disturb the winter-bright pearlescence in sea and sky. *Duke William* glided in under all plain sail toward the long dark smudge ahead that was the Fleet at anchor.

A wearisome forenoon had been spent on the ship's appearance, for it was well known that Admiral Howe was no friend to the indolent. Besides a thorough holystone fore and aft, salt-stained sides were sluiced with fresh water, brightwork brought to a thorough gleam and the sea-dulled colors around the beakhead and figurehead touched up to their usual striking splendor.

Around the catted bower anchors and aloft, men had been working since daybreak. It was clear from the short tempers on the quarterdeck that more than appearances would shortly be judged.

Along the line of the deck the gunner's party were busy at the twelve-pounders with wadhook and shot ladle, removing the live charge and shot from each new-blacked gun. At sea a ship had to be ready to meet any enemy appearing unexpectedly with immediate fire. Now the guns would carry nothing more lethal than a blank saluting cartridge.

The hawse bucklers were removed from the eyes in the bows, the massive twenty-five-inch cable roused out from the tiers below and passed through them before being secured to the bower anchor. Finally the sea lashings were removed, leaving the anchor suspended only by a single stopper. Amidships, the barge and cutter were readied for lowering, the barge crew going below to shift into their smart gear. Kydd noticed activity on the poop deck around the flag locker. Bright bunting, vivid on the gray day, was carefully checked, with the ensign and jack laid out ready for the staff.

Duke William neared the land, which now took on more detail. Kydd marveled at the number of ships about—tiny tan and white specks of sails up and down the coast as far as he could see: merchantmen, passenger craft and cumbersome naval auxiliaries. But dominating all, stretching over a mile of sea, there were at least a score of great ships-of-the-line at anchor, all arrogance and lofty grace. Closer still, it was possible to note the details of the small craft ceaselessly moving against the low-lying shoreline and the medieval white stone ramparts. At the narrow entrance of the harbor, he saw an untidy clutter of small, rickety buildings perching close by.

It soon became apparent that they were making for the outer end of the cluster of moored ships.

"All hands, bring ship to anchor!"

Hardly a soul stirred, long since standing to at their posts. A rope thrust into his hands, Kydd snatched a glance aft at the small group on the quarterdeck.

The Captain, easily recognized with his large gold-laced cocked hat and imperious bearing, stood in the center of the deck. Next to him was Tyrell's restless stumpy form, with Garrett close behind.

Within earshot, but at a respectful distance, were the Master in his plain black coat and a group of midshipmen.

Lieutenant Tewsley watched the quarterdeck while Elkins kept his eyes on Tewsley and Bowyer watched Elkins.

Kydd held the lee main topgallant clewline as though his life depended on it and waited for whatever would come.

"Stand by to take in topgallants—man topgallant clewlines, fore and main clew garnets and buntlines!"

Bowyer made no move; neither therefore did Kydd.

"Haul taut! In topgallants—up foresail, up mainsail!"

Bowyer threw off his turns and went to it furiously, frantically imitated by Kydd, bringing in the rope hand over hand, the wind spilling thunderously from the big sail above them.

Duke William slowed perceptibly, progressing parallel to the shoreline under topsails and staysails. Kydd could not keep his eyes from the scene—so many huge vessels, so much power and threat.

Bowyer moved over to the clewline and Kydd followed. "Which is the Admiral's ship?" he asked.

Bowyer's hands on the rope, he cocked his head toward the largest. "*Queen Charlotte,* a hundred guns—Chatham built, same's *Victory,* but much newer." His eyes rested dispassionately on the big ship. "But not ever as sweet a sailer on a bowline as that old lady."

Silently they neared the anchorage, but even to Kydd's eye, they appeared to be passing well to seaward of the dense gathering of ships. His not to reason why, he waited, grateful for the warmth generated by his recent exertions.

Caldwell raised his speaking trumpet. "Helm a-lee! Topsail clew-jiggers, buntlines! Man jib downhaul!"

The ship exploded into action, almost the entire company energetically at some task. Kydd tensed, noticing that the vessel was ponderously beginning a turn toward the anchored Fleet and incidentally the shore.

"Haul taut! Let go topsail sheets, topbowlines! Clew up!"

The turn grew faster, and Kydd's quick glance aft took in the men at the wheel energetically spinning it to counteract the swing. It appeared that they were heading straight for the last three vessels in line.

"Down jib! Settle away the topsail halliards—square away there!"

The previously taut, finely trimmed sails were now baggy masses pressing against the forward sides of the mast, for as Kydd could see, they had turned directly into the wind, meaning to slow the ship in her onward course toward the anchored vessels.

Then the wind dropped, fluky and unreliable, and with reduced retarding effect on the fore part of her sails, *Duke William* glided on unimpeded.

Kydd looked at Bowyer beside him, who was watching the approach with rapt attention, his face hardening. Kydd felt a sudden stab of fear. "Joe—Joe, what is it?"

"Christ save us!" Bowyer blurted, staring forward. "We're falling aboard *Barfleur*!" He reached for the familiar solidity of the forebrace bitts.

Kydd looked back at the quarterdeck—the wheel was hard over, but their slow way through the water did not give sufficient bite to the rudder and the bow's reluctant swing was agonizingly too ponderous. Looking down the length of the ship, he saw that beyond their long bowsprit loomed the after end of a vessel quite as big as they, toward which they seemed to be sliding inexorably. There was frantic activity on her quarterdeck and poop, booms beginning to stick out in despairing efforts to fend off the inevitable, white faces, angry shouts carrying across the water.

The maneuver had failed in its purpose; the falling light winds blowing against the wrong side of the sails were insufficient to stop the forward momentum of the heavy battleship—a sad misjudgment. And under the eyes of the Admiral.

Kydd watched the drama deepen on the quarterdeck. Captain Caldwell had the speaking trumpet up, but no words came. He looked sideways briefly at Tyrell, who refused to catch his eye, standing square, oak-like, and with eyes in a fierce stare forward. No one moved.

It did not take much imagination to picture the result of the impact of a couple of thousand tons of out-of-control warship on another; Kydd, to his surprise, felt only a strange detached control as he awaited the outcome.

A flurry of shouts took Kydd's attention forward again. On the fo'c'sle, someone with quick wits had taken advantage of the presence of the fo'c'slemen, the most skilled and reliable seamen in the ship, to stop the downward descent of the jib and to boom it out sideways from its usual fore and aft position. It took the wind at a slant, and as the sail jerked higher, exposing more area, it tautened and added a lateral force to that of the rudder, and the ship's head began to move a little faster. They were now very near, close enough to make out on the decks of the other ship running figures, faces at the gunports, a lazy spiral of smoke from the galley chimney.

Beside him, Bowyer remained still, with a grave but calm expression as he watched. Kydd held his breath and braced himself.

Their bowsprit speared across the last few feet of *Barfleur*'s poop, snapping the ensign staff like a twig, instantly dowsing the huge flag. Her spanker boom shuddered and jerked in response to the twanging of rigging as it parted, and a loud *scr-e-e-eak* ended as quickly as it started.

Still swinging, the bulge of their bows narrowed the distance to her ornamented stern galleries, but Kydd saw that they had a chance—the gap was sufficient—and they were on their way past.

The elaborately carved and gilded windows of the First Rate shot by, it seemed at a bare arm's length, Kydd catching sight through one window as they swept past of a shocked white face, without a wig.

Their momentum carried them on for several hundred yards before they brought to, and they sagged away downwind in ignominy. Now flat aback, the vessel began to gather sternway, and under the last helm order this led to the remaining sails filling once more on the original tack. In silence they went around again, wearing ship, to repeat the whole maneuver. This time they crept in, turning and coming up into the wind well separated from the nearest vessel. The anchor was let go when forward motion ceased, the gun salute banging out from forward to send clouds of acrid smoke smothering aft around Kydd.

The ship now fell to leeward until checked by the paid-out cable, leaving the vessel at anchor in her final position.

At supper liquor flowed around the mess tables and tongues loosened. "What a bloody shambles! Seen better handlin' on the village pond."

"Lost it again. We've got ourselves a right Jonah, mates."

"Yair—he's bin called away by Black Dick to account fer hisself 'n' I doubts he'll be a-pacin' his own quarterdeck for much longer."

"Meantimes, he's goin' to be killin' orf sailors, lads, don't forget that."

Bowyer said nothing, looking thoughtfully over his pot. He leaned forward. "Did you ever stop to think, mates, that he's only had the *Royal Billy* a few weeks—and not forgettin' a fourth part of his crew are new pressed?"

It didn't have any takers.

"I seen like dat in Lisbon. They take the *capitão* ashore—they shoot him!"

Kydd turned in surprise to the man at the end of the table. He was a sorrowful-looking, wall-eyed Iberian with a flaming red kerchief in place of the usual black.

"Savin' your presence, Pinto, the dagos sometimes got the right slant on things." Claggett's pronouncement did not invite comment.

Bowyer gave a twisted smile. "That's Pinto, Tom. A Portugee with some sorta quarrel with shoreside. 'N' cox'n's mate—that's why you ain't seen him before," he added, as though it were an obvious explanation for his absence for meals at sea.

With a quaint flourish, Pinto flashed his teeth and bobbed his head. "Fernando da Mesouta Pinto, your service," he said melodiously. "We ha' not met?"

Unsure, Kydd nodded in return. "Thomas Kydd o' Guildford," he said, and seeing the polite inclination of the head added more loudly, "in England."

"O' course, Thomas. And you are pressed? What did you before?"

The conversations died away, eyes turning curiously to Kydd. He was aware that Renzi, in his accustomed position at the ship's side opposite Claggett, had his dark eyes on him as well, but he refused to give the satisfaction of noticing.

"Perruquier!" he said defiantly, and took a strong pull at the grog. The hubbub at the other tables flurried and ebbed, but when he set down his tankard there was no comment.

"Fine thing fer a man in Guildford," Claggett said mildly.

Howell gave a harsh laugh. Then he leaned across the table and mock-toasted the bow-backed man next to Kydd. "About as fine a thing as bein' a gennelman's flunkey aboard a king's ship, eh, you—Buddles?"

The man made no reply. His eyes dropped as he shied away from the confrontation, his face turning toward Kydd.

Kydd was shocked at the extremity of misery he saw.

"What's this—nothin' to say? Yer tongue lyin' to under a storm jib, then?" Howell leaned back and half turned to his neighbor.

"Nah—he's missin' his woman! He's quean-struck on the old

biddy—I saw them together in the tavern."

"Leave him, *companheiro*." The voice sliced through the talk quietly.

"What's he to you, Pinto?" Howell said loudly, and glared at him. "That looby a friend of yourn?"

In a movement of snake-like quickness Pinto thrust over and seized Howell's kerchief. He yanked the man toward him—and toward a glint of steel that had simultaneously appeared at Howell's throat. "You a pig," Pinto said, in a low and perfectly even voice.

Howell's hands fell away slowly, far too late to intervene. He was careful not to move. "You—you're mad, you dago bastard!"

Pinto held him with his brown, liquid eyes, then slowly released him, withdrawing the knife at the last moment. From first to last there had been no expression of emotion. Pinto resumed his place opposite Kydd and, unexpectedly, smiled at him. At a loss, Kydd smiled back, finding his gaze sliding along to Renzi, who sat perfectly still and as watchful as a cat.

Claggett cleared his throat and addressed the now silent table. "You're caught fightin', Pinto, yer'll get your back flayed at the gratings. And you, Howell, you know damn well that Buddles ain't no sailor, and he's got a family 'n' bantlin's an' all. They could be on the parish now, fer all he knows."

A smothered sob escaped Buddles.

"Come on, Jonas, leave him be," Whaley begged. "We've got Portsmouth Point under our lee, 'n' I'm hot for a cruise there tonight—let's see if your Betty still remembers yer."

Howell glowered.

"Where'll you be headin' for, Ned?" Whaley asked Doud, whose countenance had brightened considerably at the direction the talk was taking.

Kydd bit his lip. The thought of returning to land and walking in a street, any street, seeing men in breeches, women in dresses and laughing children, stabbed with poignant appeal. He downed the last of his grog. "What about you, Joe?" he asked Bowyer.

A slow, shy smile spread across his face. "Well, Tom, you see, I've an understandin' with a lady, name of Poll. We goes back awhile." His face softened. "We gets leave to step off, she'll be a-waitin' for me at Sally Port, 'n' if not, then we'll get 'wives aboard' all the while we're at moorin's. 'S only human." The kindly gray eyes rested on Kydd. "She'll know some young lass as would welcome an arrangement with ye, Tom, don't you worry. It's the right way fer a sailor."

"All hands! The hands ahoy! All hands on deck—lay aft!" The boatswain's mates echoed each other along the gundeck.

"Well, mates, we says our farewells to Johnny Hawbuck, I believe." Bowyer seemed relieved at the swift return of the Captain and therefore early resolution of the situation.

Howell stirred. "Aye, but that means it's going to be Mantrap instead—it'll be a hell ship."

Claggett broke through the murmuring: "Maybe, but don't count on it. Black Dick'll have his cronies he'll want to satisfy, 'n' who knows? We could get a real tartar like Bligh!"

"Could be—but at least Bligh was a reg'lar built sailorman. Damn near four thousan' miles in that longboat 'n' never lost a man."

Whaley punched Doud playfully. "Yeah—and at least now we'll know if it'll be the larbowlines first ashore."

It was the first time that Kydd had seen both watches of the ship's company mustered together on deck, nearly eight hundred men. Bowyer had been right—the figure of the Captain stood clear above them at the forward nettings of the poop deck, waiting as the men congregated below. His officers stood behind, rigid and ill at ease. From all parts of the ship seamen came, covering the quarterdeck from the binnacle to the gangways. Quickly the rigging filled with men eager to improve their view.

Kydd, with his messmates, took position near the center, by the rail of the main companionway.

"Can't say Mantrap looks well pleased—wonder why?" Bowyer muttered.

Claggett looked bemused. "No sign of the new owner. Surely they're not giving Shaney Jack his step over Tyrell?"

Pinto's vicious curse drew a sharp look from the petty officers.

Wong grunted. "If him, I *Hung Fu Chi!*" The contempt in his bland face was the first expression Kydd had ever seen on it.

The wondering murmurs continued until Caldwell nodded at Tyrell, who snapped, "Still!" at the boatswain.

From a dozen silver calls a single steady note pealed. A slight shuffling of feet and silence spread. Captain Caldwell strode forward to the break of the poop to take position, legs astride, hands behind his back. In front of him, the ship's company of *Duke William:* petty officers, hard men, the freely acknowledged backbone of the Navy; the tarry-pigtailed long-service able seamen, relaxed but wary; the idlers—the armorer, cooper, sailmaker, carpenter and their mates in their outlandish working clothes; the yeomen—coxswain, quartermasters, gunner's mates; and the landmen, anxious, not understanding.

The Captain cleared his throat and began. "I've called you all aft to tell you the news." His voice, not strained in shouting orders, was a pleasant patrician baritone. "But first I want to congratulate the fo'c'slemen on their quick thinking this morning. It may have prevented an unfortunate accident from occurring. Well done."

There was a ripple of indistinct comment.

He paused, looking grave. "We shall need that sort of initiative and attention to duty where we will be going."

Significant looks were exchanged. If Caldwell was talking about sea duty in the near future, then not only would estimates of leave time ashore need to be revised but they would be putting out into the Atlantic winter in an old, leaky vessel in certain peril of their lives. Faces hardened and attitudes took on a sullen cast as they waited for what came next.

"As most ready for sea, we sail in a little while on a very important task. A vital task, and one on which England's very existence may depend."

Disbelieving stares and mutters came from all sides: the men had been quick to notice Caldwell's use of "we"—clearly he had got away with it, there would be no new captain.

"You don't need me to remind you that we are now at war with France. And this time we're dealing with a set of murderous bandits who will stop at nothing." His voice whipped and rose in dramatic flourishes. "We proceed with *Tiberius* and *Royal Albion* with frigates for the coast of France to clamp our hold on their deep-sea ports in time to prevent their fleet coming out to fall upon these islands. And our folk at home are right to put their trust in us to defend them. Ours is the just cause and ours will be the victory. Let me hear your spirit, men—an huzzah for old England! Let me hear it!"

There were sparse cheers and stony looks.

"And another for our brave ship!"

The cheers held a little more conviction.

"A three times three for His Majesty!"

This time the shouts were more good-humored, for it was not the amiable "Farmer George" who was the cause of their immediate discontent. Volleys of cheers echoed over the water, Caldwell and all the officers marking time with their hats.

The final cheer died away. Satisfied, Caldwell carefully replaced his cocked hat and stepped forward again. "This ship is now under sailing orders. The hoys are already on their way out to us in order that we may complete stores ready for sea as soon as possible, and I know you are ready to do your duty. Unfortunately it is not possible to grant leave ashore," he continued smoothly. "You will, of course, appreciate the need for all hands at this time."

A surge of muttering spread outward in the sea of faces. Growls from the petty officers did little to stop it. Caldwell looked pained and waited. The murmuring grew in volume. Now and then individual shouts could be heard.

Tyrell stood rigid, his chin thrust out, his eyes dangerous slits.

More shouts erupted. Tyrell snapped at the Captain of Marines and a line of marines descended each side of the poop and forced their way forward down each side of the deck. On command, they halted and turned inboard, their muskets held tightly across their chests.

The men drew back, the growls replaced by looks of savage discontent.

Caldwell resumed in the same smooth tones: "I shall not be able to be with you during this period, unfortunately. I have urgent business in London. However, I'm sure you will give your support to Mr. Tyrell, who will act in my place until I return." He nodded at Tyrell. "Carry on, please." Accompanied by his clerk, he made his way down the ladder and disappeared into the cabin spaces, leaving a somber group of officers on the poop.

Tyrell moved forward. "Hands to stations for store ship," he ordered brusquely.

"No liberty—what about wives and sweethearts?" The vigorous shout came from the anonymous center of the mass of seamen and was immediately taken up by all around. Boats now putting out from shore, crowded with enterprising womenfolk, gave point to their grievance.

"Silence!" Tyrell roared. His hands, clamped on the rail, writhed under the intensity of his anger. "You're under discipline, you mutinous rascals. Any one of you wants to forget this, then I'll see his backbone at the gratings and be damned to him. And it's no use baying after skirt like a set of mangy dogs. It'll do you no good. We're under sailing orders. You're a vile set of lubbers, no control, and I will not have the discipline in this ship undone by letting a crowd of drabtail trulls come swarming aboard."

"Why—the poxy, cuntbitten bastard! The—the—" Words failed Whaley.

Murmurs spread and grew in passion. As the shouts and catcalls peaked a shrill voice sounded clear above the disorder: "Death to tyrants—and an end to slavery!"

Kydd recognized Stallard's high, intemperate voice.

Tyrell went rigid; the shouting died away. The Captain of Marines barked an order, and the marines on each side slapped their muskets to the present, a storm of clicking in the sudden silence as they cocked their weapons.

The seamen shied at the sudden movement, unsure and fearful at developments. The officers on the poop in their blue, white and gold stood, legs apart, looking down, grave and silent.

Tyrell's murderous expression did not falter. Slowly and deliberately he went down the side ladder alone to the quarterdeck and into the mass of seamen. Directly challenging with his eyes individuals on one side and the other, but never uttering a word, he passed through them, past the mainmast, then with a measured tread back along the other side. Kydd caught his darting glance—a fierce, dangerous glint that held the same intelligence he had seen before. Unchecked by any movement, Tyrell made his way to the opposite ladder and back up to the poop. Taking position dead center, he stopped, holding the still mass of men with his gaze for a long minute. "I don't know who that fool was," he roared, "but he'll swing when I find him—and if he has any friends of like mind, they'll dangle next to him." His eyes flicked up the naked masts with the ease of long habit, and down again. "I'll have no more of this nonsense," he said, his fury in icy control. "We're paid to fight the King's enemies on the high seas, not pansy about in port! We sail to meet the French in a short while, and I mean to have this ship in fighting trim by then—and damn the blood of any knave who stands in my way! Hands to store ship!" The moment hung. Then, with sullen reluctance, by ones and twos, the men dispersed.

Kydd looked at Bowyer. The man still stood, his face a mask of sorrow. It was not hard to understand why: he was staring out over the mile or so of sea to the long stone landing place, and the colorful crowd gathering there. "It'll be a long time afore we gets to see Spithead again, mate," he said, in a low voice, and turning abruptly stepped firmly to the seaward side of the deck to join the brooding group of men at the forebrace bitts.

By the thump of the Admiral's evening gun *Duke William* had completed taking in stores. Kydd's back was seizing up with fatigue after the unaccustomed hours of drudgery manning the tackle falls used to sway in the innumerable forms of stores. Supper was a cheerless meal, with Whaley away in the gunner's party and Doud nursing a wrenched shoulder. The inevitable acid barbs from Howell went unheeded in the depressing quiet and even Wong slumped over his meal.

Kydd noticed Bowyer's set expression and, not liking to intrude, turned to Claggett. "We's got good reason to feel aggrieved, lad. What yer don't know is that *Duke William*'s been on the North Ameriky station for two years, 'n' before that the Caribbee. She's well due t'get a proper docking. When you's at sea for years you gets druxy timber. See here . . ." He reached down and fumbled around in the gloomy recesses beneath the lashed muzzle of the gun. His hand came up with a dark substance. "This here is spirketting, believe it or not." As far as Kydd could see it might have been so much forest mulch—a perfectly black piece of wood flecked with tiny white dots. Claggett squeezed it in his palm and a pool of brown-stained seawater formed on the table. "It runs fore 'n' aft the whole ship. If you knows how a ship works at the seams in any kind of sea, you'd be powerful concerned 's how even a First Rate's goin' to swim in the kinda blow you gets in Biscay in winter!" The seamed old face turned to Kydd. "You'll've heard of what happened to the *Royal George* in the year 'eighty-two. A ship-o'-the-line same's us, they didn't see their way clear t' givin' her a good refit 'n' the bottom fell clean outa her as she lay at her moorings, right here in Spithead."

Long-faced, Bowyer fidgeted but listened as well.

"Admiralty says as how a land breeze overset her while heeled over fer a repair, but my cousin was cox'n's mate aboard 'n' he said as how there was a great loud cracking first, afore she went under." His old eyes rested unseeingly on the ship's side. "Took more'n a thousand souls with her, the women, the Admiral—they're all down there together still, mate."

The somber mood cast a pall, and Kydd made his excuses. He rose and made his way to the companionway. There was an ugly edge to the messdeck talk and he was troubled by it. He went up to the next gundeck. An argument had developed into a fight. Inside a tight ring of onlookers two men smashed into each other in brutal silence—meaty thuds, gasps and panting. It was not a match of skills: the transient flaring hatreds of the blood-smeared antagonists demanded immediate release. What chilled Kydd was that instead of the cheery crowds to be seen around any fights ashore, here the watchers growled and muttered against a glowering, dangerous quiet, taking long pulls from their grog and no joy in the action. He moved quickly to the ladder.

On the upper deck he saw that it was getting toward dusk, an overcast building overhead that brought with it a lowering, claustrophobic atmosphere. Lights were beginning to flicker ashore. The fitful offshore breeze carried out to him the scent of horses, mud and sea coal smoke, the comfortable smells of land.

He stared hungrily at the shoreline, as he gripped one of the myriad ropes coming down to the ship's side; his foot rested on the low fife-rail of the fo'c'sle.

His mind wandered across the small stretch of water to the odd few figures still waiting forlornly at the Sally Port. Farther along, washing fluttered among the tightly packed houses of Southsea and he could discern the ant-like movements of carts and people. Folk would be wending their way home now to a welcome by the hearth, and victuals worthy of a man. He remembered that at this time his mother would be at work on the Tuesday beef pie in the old kitchen at the back of the workshop. He and his father could always be sure of a fine hot meal, no matter how hard the day. In fact, he realized, if he were over there on the foreshore he could board the London stage. For a few silver coins he could be at the Angel post house in Guildford the same day, safe and sound, and telling his story.

He tore his gaze away from the tantalizing sight of land. All around the ship boarding nettings had been rigged and the rowguard in the pinnace pulled slowly around the vessel. On deck close by was the bowed figure of Buddles. Kydd felt a sudden burst of fellow feeling for the man, who was taking his plight so desperately hard. He moved over to greet him, but Buddles jerked around, staring at him from swimming eyes. He turned away to shuffle below, without a backward glance.

Kydd stared over the water. Who could say how long he would have to wait before he saw his family again? It was quite possible that his ignorance of the sea might cost him his life in some accident, or perhaps there would be a great battle . . . Emotion welled up. He clutched at the rope.

"Why, Tom, you're giving no mind to that cat-blash now, are ye?" Bowyer's voice was gentle, and his hand came to rest on Kydd's shoulder.

Unable to speak, Kydd brushed aside the gesture and continued to stare obstinately out to shore.

Bowyer held his ground. "Damn me eyes, I must be a sad dog not to see when a man's suffering the blue devils. Do ye—"

"I don't give a tuppenny damn!" Kydd said thickly. "Go t' hell for all I care!" He could not look at Bowyer. Shouts and harsh laughter floated up from the deck below, and Kydd burst out with a curse. As he tried to control himself, he felt an arm around his shoulders, just as his father had done not so very long ago. Then it had been in the matter of a worthless doxy, now it was an older seaman touched by his unhappiness.

Kydd pulled himself together with a great effort. "There wasn't need for that, Joe—I'm sorry."

"That's all right, me old shipmate," Bowyer said.

"But if I can get on land over there, I can post to Guildford in just one day!" he babbled, and saw a shadow pass over the sailor's face. "That's not to say . . ." He realized that whatever he said would be either empty or a lie.

Bowyer laughed softly. "Yer folks still in Guildford, then?"

Kydd nodded. "Where's yourn, Joe?"

Bowyer walked over to the gratings in the center of the deck. "Come on over the galley here, mate—it's a mort warmer." They sat companionably, well placed on the gratings above the warmth of the ovens from the decks below.

"Your kin, Joe?"

"Well, I'm one o' Jonas Hanway's boys," Bowyer said simply. "Don't rightly know m' dad, 'n' when I was a nipper m' mum gave me up to Hanway's Marine Society fer to go to sea."

"When was that?"

"When I was eight—bin at sea since."

"And you've never lived on the land all that time?"

"Never felt the need to."

Kydd felt a surge of bitterness. "Well, you c'n be infernal sure *I* feel the need. I didn't ask to be part o' this stinkin' world. Being taken by the press like a common damn prigger, and thrown on board like—"

"Hold hard, young 'un!" Bowyer's forehead was uncharacteristically creased. "Way I sees it, you has just two things you c'n do about it—get yourself into a fret all the time over what can't be undone, or do somethin' about it. What I means is, there's no chance you'll get yourself back to Guildford any time soon, so you'll be spendin' all your time on board. You then has the choice—stay a landman and take all the shite going, or learn to be a *sailorman* and live a life!"

Kydd did not answer.

"There's worse things to be—them poor bastards in red coats carryin' a musket, why, no warm hammock to go to end of day, no reg'lar vittles of any kind, and marchin' with a humpin' great pack thing when they want ter go anywheres." He watched Kydd looking moodily over the fast darkening stretch of water, the rowguard pinnace creeping unseen past his line of sight. "An' we get the chance for prize money! Know the Flag and Anchor in Southsea? No? I'll interdooce yer to the landlord. Taut hand o' the watch, as was. When he was a younker he shipped as able seaman in *Active* when they took the *Hermione*, Spanish frigate—earned 'emselves more'n three hundred years' pay in one hour, that arternoon! Only a score of years old 'n' he buys himself his own taphouse!" He knew he had Kydd's attention now. "We don't say as how it happens to all, but we get a good fight and it's gun money an' head money . . ." Bowyer allowed his eyes to gaze out dreamily. "'Cos it depends on yer rate, how much you get." He made himself more comfortable, leaning on his elbow over the gratings to catch more warmth. "But then money ain't all. For a man o' character, why, he c'n learn more about the way of things from what he sees in foreign parts than ever he could in stayin' by the fireside 'n' readin' books. Me, I'm just an old tarry-breeks, but me first voyage as able seaman was in *Resolution* in 'seventy-nine—Cap'n Cook that was. Voyage of discovery, Tom—the Great South Sea, ice islands in the Ar'tic, the women on O'Whyee. Their menfolk did for 'im, you know, on the strand, when he couldn't git back to the longboat where we was at."

It was almost completely dark now, but somehow it fitted the mood. Light from the decks below came through the gratings, gently patterning Bowyer's face in alternating squares of light and dark, a slight breeze whiffling his thinning hair.

"You're bred t' the sea, Joe. I just know . . . how to make wigs."

"Don't you pay no mind to that!" Bowyer said warmly. "A sailor has it inside, just a-waitin' to have it woken up in him—I could tell, first time I clapped peepers on yer, Tom, you has the makin's." He gave a slow smile. "Like it's said, 'Begotten in the galley and born under a gun. Every hair a rope yarn, every finger a fishhook and 'is blood right good Stockholm tar!'"

Kydd laughed.

"Yeah—you're quick on your feet, got a good headpiece on yer, 'n' you keep your eyes open. And you've the build for it," Bowyer said. "*An'* you have an eddication—means a lot these modern days. I'd be gunner's mate be now if I could figure them books."

Kydd sat back. There was some truth in Bowyer's words. Clearly, if he was to be imprisoned aboard for some indefinite time it made sense to avoid staying at the bottom of the heap. But he was rated on board as the lowest form of life, a landman. Without an academy for sailoring how could he qualify upward?

Bowyer seemed to sense his thoughts. "You make your own chances, cuffin. You show willin', you'll get yer start." He smiled broadly. "Like this. Tomorrow forenoon, when it's part of ship for priddying down, we goes together to the maintop—up there, Tom! First step is leavin' the deck to the land toggies, and go where a sailor goes—aloft!"

Kydd glanced up at the arrogant thrust of the great black masts and spars against the cold dusk clouds and his heart quailed.

"*Haaands* turn to, part of ship! All the hands!"

The afterguard part of ship in the form of Elkins was waiting for them the next morning, and under the eye of the boatswain and Lieutenant Tewsley he lost no time in dispatching the men in parties to their respective tasks.

"Bowyer, brace pendants with Pinto," he ordered.

Glancing at Kydd, Bowyer said to Elkins mildly, "Be a chance to get Kydd aloft, learn some ropes—can I have him up there?"

"No," said Elkins shortly, "you've got Pinto. Kydd stays on the holystones."

Bowyer paused. "Then, Mr. Elkins, I'd be obliged if you'd allow me to join him."

Elkins looked at him, astonished. His jaw hardened. "You're a clinking fool, Joe, always were, so get down on yer hunkers and get scrubbin' with 'im, then."

Kydd looked up from rolling up his duck trousers to see Bowyer do the same next to him. "I thought . . ."

"This life, you can't always get what yer want—but you can learn to take it. Move over, mate."

Captain Caldwell had made it quite plain that he regarded efficiency and smartness to be equivalents. As First Lieutenant, Tyrell would be judged on appearances, and this would mean at the very least continual hard labor for all. The gunner's party toiled at their pieces; each cannon would receive close attention from canvas and brickdust, then be blackened with a shining mixture of lampblack, beeswax and turpentine. This left little time for vital work on vent and bore, or even chipping roundshot.

And, of course, there was the appearance of the decks. While the seamen were aloft, the unskilled laborers of the sea rolled up their trousers, and with decks well a-swim from the wash-deck hose, and with sand liberally scattered over the planking, they began the soul-grinding misery of holystoning the decks. In a line the men moved from forward, on hands and knees and pushing a book-shaped piece of sandstone. Thomas Kydd was one of them. Twenty yards of the quarterdeck on, his knees were red and sore with the gritty sand and little splinters, but his chief suffering was the bitter pain from the icy water that pulsed relentlessly from the hoses carrying detritus to the scuppers. It was monotonous, painful and humiliating. It was only the uncomplaining presence of Bowyer that kept him going through the long morning.

At four bells the job was at last complete to the satisfaction of Tyrell, but there was no relief. One by one the articles of running rigging—the operating machinery of the ship—needed to be checked for chafing and in many cases re-reeved, end for end. Nothing prepared Kydd for the effort this would take. Even the lightweight lines of the topgallants and royals were nevertheless hundreds of feet long and in themselves were an appreciable deadweight. The same with the blocks—the big pulleys through which ropes were hauled: these were unexpectedly immense when seen close to, on deck. One top block was so massive it took four men to lift it to its fall for hoisting. With agile topmen at the summit of the towering mast tending the sheaves of the blocks, it needed the humble laborers to manhaul ropes, seized to a girt-line, up the entire height of the mainmast.

Unexpectedly, Elkins bellowed across the deck. "Bowyer—in the maintop, clew garnets." He paused just long enough to be noticed. "Kydd—get up there with him."

"Come with me, Tom lad," Bowyer said quietly, "and be sure and look where you want ter go, never back where you've been."

In one move, Kydd's view of his place in the scheme of things was changed. After a lifetime of living and moving in two dimensions, he was now to join the select band of those who would know the third.

He gulped and followed, aware of the eyes of his previous fellow laborers on him.

Bowyer crossed to the side of the ship, seized the aftermost shroud and in a little half jump hoisted himself up on to the broad top of the bulwark. He swung down to the main channel on the outside of the hull, the true beginning of the tracery of rope ladder leading up aloft. "Let's be havin' yer!" he called.

Kydd grabbed the same shroud and kicked his legs up. To his mortification he found that with feet correctly on the bulwark, he hung backwards over the deck from the inward-sloping shroud, unable to move around to the outer side.

Bowyer's hand reached for his collar and with surprising strength pulled Kydd upright and around. They stood together on the bulwark. Even these few feet of altitude were sufficient to alter forever his notion of the ship. Every man on deck now was lower than he; the deck itself was observably in plan, and he felt a curious pleasure at the satisfying curve of the deck-line as it swept far forward.

"Right, now, Tom, you goes first, 'n' I'll be right behind you."

Bowyer stepped aside, and there was nothing now before Kydd but the main shrouds leading up to a final focus—the big platform of the main fighting top.

He addressed himself to the venture. The thick shrouds soaring up had thin lines across them to form a ladder. He began to climb, feet feeling shakily for the thin rope, looking obediently upward.

"Don't put yer hands on the ratlines," Bowyer called from below him, "use the shrouds—they'll never give way on yer."

Kydd had a brief but intense picture of the thinner line snapping in his clutching hands, letting him hurtle backwards to his doom. Nervously he moved to grip tightly the thick black vertical shrouds, shiny with use.

Despite himself, he became aware of his increasing height, the shrouds on the other side getting closer, the deck dropping away below. He continued upward, foot finding the next ratline above while he hung on grimly; a push upward and a pause at the new level while his other foot relocated; then moving his hands gingerly one by one.

He knew he was not moving efficiently, but at least he was safe like that. His leg muscles burned with fatigue and he stopped for a moment to rest.

The shrouds shivered and Bowyer appeared on the broad span of shrouds next to him.

"I'm fine, Joe," Kydd said.

"Yeah—but watch that feller over there." Bowyer was pointing to the opposite ratlines. A seaman was mounting the shrouds in a fast, economic swing. "See how he uses his hands to pull himself up, only rests his feet. Doesn't go at it like he was climbin' stairs."

Kydd watched the graceful continuity of the sailor's movements; a fluid motion he could now sense was achieved by hauling forcefully on alternate hands, the feet just following. He tried it; the transfer of effort to the hands felt awkward at first, but he could feel the potential for a more connected movement. He persevered, his concentration on the required actions diverting his mind from his situation.

The main top approached with a reality it never had from the deck, foursquare and solid, with a big lanthorn rearing up oddly from the after edge. His arms ached. He knew now where the best seamen got their deep chests. Stopping for a breather, he idly looked down.

It was a mistake. What he saw was an ugly distortion—an impossibly narrow deck on which the people moving about it had become flattened, elongated disks, their feet blipping out in front of them like penguins'.

But what was so hard to take was the sheer vertigo of being at a killing height while clinging halfway up a vertical surface. Animal instinct made him freeze, pinned helplessly somewhere between heaven and earth. He clung fiercely, his eyes closed.

A shaking in the shrouds told him that Bowyer had arrived next to him. Whatever Bowyer said, Kydd vowed to himself that he would not release his hold. Perhaps Bowyer could work some rescue plan to lower him to the deck on a rope.

"Bit of a hard beat to wind'd, first time aloft," Bowyer mused. "Um, ever you gets in the situation you needs yer bearings fast. What I does, I looks at where I'm at first." He waited. "These here shrouds, Tom, very curious ropes. See here, they've got four strands, not yer usual three. And they're laid up *with* the sun, not like your anchor cable, which you may've noticed is laid up agin the sun."

Kydd allowed his eyes to slit open. Inches before his eyes was one of the shrouds, ordinary enough in itself, a stout rope several inches thick. It was tarred but this close he could see every microscopic detail of where it had been whitened by the weather. On impulse, he pressed his face to it, feeling its sturdy roughness against his skin and smelling the rich odor of tar and sea salt.

"'N' up there, you gets a good view of the catharpins. You c'n see there, Tom, how we use 'em to bowse in the shrouds—keeps the lee rigging well in when yer ship rolls."

Taking no chances, Kydd moved his gaze slowly upward, following the line of shrouds to where they disappeared into a large hole in the black underneath of the top.

"Get a move on, you heavy-arsed dogs!" Elkins's impatient bawl carried up clearly. It only served to make Kydd hold on tighter.

"Shall we go a bit farther, matey?" Bowyer said, inching a little higher.

Kydd willed the movement, but it stalled in a backwash of fear.

At that moment into his consciousness seeped an awareness of angels. It was a pure sound that enveloped his soul. He listened, enraptured. It was a light tenor, and it soared so sweetly that he could swear it belonged to the upper celestial regions.

> *Life is chequr'd—toil and pleasure*
> *Fill one up the various measure;*
> *Hark! the crew with sunburnt faces*
> *Chanting Black-eyed Susan's graces . . .*

Bowyer chuckled. "That'll be Ned Doud. Quite th' songbird is our Ned. Let's go visit, Tom."

The spell had been broken. With his heart in his mouth, Kydd followed Bowyer up.

They passed under the shadow of the great fighting top, then up through the large aperture next to the mast and its complexity of massive jeer blocks and heavy rope seizings, to emerge onto the platform of the top itself.

"Well, Joe," said Doud happily, "never thought to see you come up by the lubber's hole." He was sitting cross-legged, making a plaited bunt gasket using his own fox yarns.

"Came up to see what the noise was, did we not, shipmate?" Bowyer said, but Kydd had taken a deep breath and was looking about him in giddy exhilaration.

The maintop was impressive—it could take twenty men comfortably on its decked surface, and was bounded at the after end by a rail and nettings, and on both sides by the next stage of shrouds stretching up to the topmast.

Cautiously Kydd got to his feet and went to the edge. Although it was only some seventy feet above the deck, it felt like a separate world, one of peace and solitude. Farther out there were more ships at anchor, and beyond a noticeable increase in the depth of the countryside.

"Bear a fist, will you, Ned, reevin' the clewgarnet," Bowyer asked.

He slipped out of sight over the side. Kydd went over to see him pass from a downward hanging position on the futtock shrouds to drop to the main yard, with the dull white canvas of the course carefully furled in a fine harbor stow above it. Bowyer lay over the yard before swinging down, his feet finding the footrope, and moved outward to where the clewgarnet blocks hung below the yard.

"Watch yer back, sailor!" Doud said, pushing past Kydd. He was watching the clewgarnet rise from below, suspended on a fly block next to the mainmast as it was hauled up by the laborers on deck. Feeling like a yokel on his first trip to town, Kydd admired the skill and cool assurance of the two as they worked, thoroughly at home in this unfathomable complication of spars and cordage.

At one point when Doud and Bowyer were both out on the yard they asked him to pass the clewgarnet down to its second stoppering on the hauling line, out to the blocks. This involved the team sharing the task of passing it along, right out to the end of the yard where the clew of the furled course now was, and bringing it back again to where it was clinched to the main yard.

Kydd's part was not onerous, but he had to move about the top and give his full attention to the whole picture. He sensed that this was no special task, but when they finally stepped down from the shrouds to the deck at last, he was elated. Nothing could have stopped his foolish laugh and the casual swagger.

Elkins was waiting. "So you knows a bit o' sailorin', then, Kydd—get below, my respects t' the boatswain, and we needs a sky hook to sway up the kelson."

Concentrating on the message, Kydd turned to go. "Where—?"

"Forrard on the orlop, you grass-combin' bugger. Get goin', sharpish like, we got work to do."

The boatswain pursed his lips. "The sky hook, eh? Well, lad, that's going to be difficult." His hand rasped on his dark-shadowed chin.

"I gave it out, as I recollects, to Mr. Walker for to raise a mousing. If you finds Matthew Walker, you'll find your sky hook, lad."

Nobody seemed to know how to find Matthew Walker and even appeared to find his search entertaining. Remembering Elkins's sharp orders, Kydd hurried on. It was Dan Phelps who finally came to the rescue.

"They're gullin' yer, matey—the cook, he's yer Matthew Walker!" Gratefully Kydd accepted directions to the galley.

The cook scowled. He was a big man, seeming not to notice the absence of a lower leg, which, with the grievous black ingrained wound on the side of his face, was legacy of a bursting gun, terrible pain and a saw on the cockpit table.

"What the hell are you two a-grinnin' at?" he snarled at his mates, who were deep inside the colossal copper vats, sanding and sniggering. He turned back to Kydd. "See 'ere, me old Jack Tar, you tell yer Mr. Elkins as how I've a sea pie to raise for damn near eight hunnerd men, and how does he expect me to do that without yon sky hook?"

Kydd toiled up the fore companionway, aware that the seven bells striking meant that it was a half-hour to noon, and therefore soon dinnertime. From nowhere a boatswain's mate appeared at the head of the ladder above, blocking Kydd's progress. He grinned evilly at Kydd before raising his silver call and emitting an appalling blast of sound. "*All the haaands!* Hands lay aft to witness punishment!" he bellowed at Kydd, then mock doffed his hat with its *Duke William* picked out in gold and red, and clattered past to the next deck.

Joining the streaming throng, Kydd found himself in the familiar area of the quarterdeck between the ship's wheel and the mainmast. He had been jostled to the front of the assembled company so his view of the proceedings would be immediate.

The marines were formed up across the poop, but the officers were in a group before the break of the poop facing the men. A clear area existed between them.

The Master-at-Arms and his corporals flanked two seamen, one of whom Kydd recognized as one of the fighters of the previous evening. He had bloodshot eyes but carried himself watchful and erect. The other he did not recognize, a slight gray vole of a man whose darting eyes were his only concession to fear.

Kydd searched about, looking for Bowyer, but could not see him. With the oppressive tension draining his newly won reserves of confidence, he needed some other to share his disquiet. The only one he knew was next to the ship's side, arms folded and with an impregnable air of detachment. Renzi.

Transferring his attention back to the little group near the wheel, he was in time to see Tyrell appear from the cabin spaces. The officer stumped to the center of the clear area, looking sharply about him. "Rig the gratings," he growled.

A brace of carpenter's mates pushed through the crowd of seamen behind Kydd, dragging two of the main hatch gratings aft. One was placed upright against the poop railings and lashed tightly. The other served as a scaffold for the victim to stand upon.

A boatswain's mate touched his forehead to Tyrell. "Gratings rigged, sir."

Tyrell glared around at the men and without referring to his paper snapped, "Caleb Larkin, cooper's mate."

The gray man shuffled forward. He blinked and looked sideways at Tyrell, but said nothing.

Tyrell nodded at the Master-at-Arms.

"Was found drunk and incapable, sir; did piss in the waist under cover of dark, sir." The piggy eyes looked at the man without particular expression.

There was a ripple of movements, a few murmurs. The tall boatswain's mate at the side of the gratings stroked his long red bag.

Larkin seemed resigned, and continued his odd sideways stare at Tyrell.

"An unspeakable act, you ill-looking dog! Have you anything to say?"

The man thought for a moment, then mutely shook his head.

Tyrell let the moment hang. "One week's stoppage of grog, Master-at-Arms' black list one month."

Larkin's head rose in astonishment. His shoulders twitched as if throwing off the evil threat of the lash, and dared a triumphant look forward at his friends. Astonished looks showed that his incredible escape was not lost on anyone.

The murmuring died away as Tyrell consulted his paper. "Patrick Donnelly, quarter gunner." He looked up and waited for absolute silence before nodding crisply at the Master-at-Arms.

"Fighting when off watch, sir."

There were louder mutters this time. The going tariff for fighting would be a spell in the bilboes or a lengthy mastheading in this cold weather. The tall boatswain's mate would be disappointed of his prey.

"How long have you been quarter gunner, Donnelly?" Tyrell began mildly.

Unsure how to play it, Donnelly muttered something.

"Speak up, man!" Tyrell snapped.

"Two year, near enough," Donnelly repeated. He had the unfortunate quirk of appearing surly when being questioned in public.

"Two years—a petty officer for two years, so you know well enough that a petty officer does not engage in brawling. Disrated. You're turned before the mast and will shift your hammock tonight."

Donnelly's dogged look created a wave of barely concealed muttering. This was hard. The reason for the aimless flaring and fisticuffs was well known: Donnelly had a sweetheart in Portsmouth.

Tyrell watched the men. His hard face gave no quarter. "Collaby!"

His clerk hurried over with a thin black leatherbound book. Tyrell took it.

"Articles of War!" he thundered.

"Off hats!" the Master-at-Arms bellowed. In a flurry of movement the entire assembly removed their headgear—the officers' cocked hats, the round hats of the petty officers and the amazing variety of the seamen's head coverings, ranging from shapeless raw woolen articles to the stout traditional tarpaulin hats.

In grim stillness all stood to hear the strict law of the Service. The sea breeze plucked the hair on hundreds of bare heads.

The words were flung out savagely. "'Article twenty-three. If any person in the Fleet shall quarrel or fight with any other person in the Fleet, or use reproachful or provoking speech or gestures' and so on and so forth, as well you know, 'shall suffer such punishment as the offense shall deserve, and a court-martial shall impose.'"

He slammed the book shut.

"On hats!"

"You shall have a court-martial, should you wish it. Have you anything to say?"

Donnelly looked stupefied. This was no choice at all—a court-martial could lead anywhere, from admonishment to a noose at the yardarm.

"No? Then it's half a dozen for fighting."

A fleeting smile appeared on the boatswain's mate's face, and he lifted his bag.

A wave of unrest went through the mass of men like wind through a cornfield. This was ferocious justice.

Tyrell waited, with a terrible patience. "And another dozen for the utter disgrace you have brought on your position, you damned rogue!"

Donnelly's head whipped round—apart from the fact that

eighteen lashes was far above the usual, his "offense" had no standing in law, however useless it would be to argue.

"Strip!" There was a chilling finality in the order.

Donnelly stared at Tyrell, his eyes wild. He stripped to the waist in deliberate, fierce movements, throwing the garments to the deck, stalked over to the gratings and spreadeagled himself against the upright one, his face pressed to the wooden checkerboard.

"Seize him up!"

The quartermasters tied his hands to the grating with lengths of spun yarn and retired. The boatswain's mate advanced, taking the cat-o'-nine-tails from the bag. He took position a full eight feet away to one side and drew the long deadly lashes through his fingers, experimentally sweeping it back to ensure that there was enough clear space to swing it.

Kydd stared across the few yards of empty deck to the man's pale, helpless body. His eyes strayed over to Renzi, who still stood impassive and with his arms folded. His anger rose at the man's lack of simple compassion and when he looked back at Donnelly he tried despairingly to communicate the sympathy he felt.

"Do your duty!"

Kydd was startled by the sudden furious beating of a marine drum on the poop. It volleyed and rattled frantically as the boatswain's mate drew back the cat in a full arm sweep. At the instant it flew downward the drum beat stopped, so the sickening smack of the blow came loud and clear.

Donnelly did not cry out, but his gasp was high and choked. The nine tails had not only left long bruised weals where they landed, but at every point where the tail ended, blood began to seep.

"One!" called the Master-at-Arms.

The drum began its fierce noise again; Donnelly turned his head to the side and fixed Tyrell with a look of such hatred that several of the officers started.

Again the whipping blow swept down. It brought a grunt that

seemed to Kydd to have been dragged from the very depths of the man's being.

"Two!"

Even two blows was sufficient to make the man's back a raw striping of bloody welts, the animal force of the blows visibly as violent as a kick from a horse, slamming the body against the grating.

"Three!"

Donnelly did not shift his gaze or his expression from Tyrell's face. Blood appeared at his mouth where he had bitten his lip in agony, trickling slowly down in two thin streams.

"Four!"

The horror of Donnelly's torment tore at Kydd. It went on and on in endless sequence; the lower grating was now spattered with blood, and when the boatswain's mate drew back the cat for the next stroke, combing his fingers through the tails, bloody gobbets dropped from them.

Donnelly's eyes flickered now at each blow and started rolling upward, his grunts turning to smothered animal cries. His back was in places a roiling mess like a butcher's cut of raw liver.

"Twelve!"

The Master-at-Arms looked questioningly over to Tyrell.

"Quentin!" Tyrell snapped, utterly unmoved.

The tall boatswain's mate surrendered his position and cat to Quentin, who was left-handed—this would enable the stripes to be crossed.

Before he could begin his grisly work, Donnelly's eyes rolled entirely out of sight with a soft despairing groan, and he hung down.

The surgeon thrust over and examined him. Donnelly was semiconscious, occasionally rolling his head about and issuing tiny childlike whimpers.

"Sir, this man's—"

"Souse him!"

"Sir, I must insist! There is—"

"Then get below if you must. I will not have my discipline ques-tioned. Carry on, Quentin."

A fire bucket of seawater bearing the cipher of King George was produced. Measuring his distance, Quentin dashed the full contents against the man's back.

Donnelly shrieked just once and hung senseless.

A midshipman crumpled to the deck.

Tyrell scowled. "Cut him down," he grunted.

Chapter 4

At a somber dinner Kydd pushed away his wooden platter. It was not possible to eat after the scenes he had witnessed. "Some says as how you're not a real sailorman till you've got your red-checked shirt at the gangway," said Bowyer.

Nobody laughed.

"Pat should never've got more'n half a dozen," Doud said, playing with his hard tack. Various growled comments supported him, although Renzi sat in his usual, watchful silence.

"How the bloody hell can y' take it like this?" Kydd flared. "Are we animals t' be whipped? Even a pig farmer takes better care o' his stock. What lunatic way is this?"

"Yer right enough, lad," Claggett replied. "But yer have ter understand our sea ways too. See, we're different to youse ashore where you hang a man for stealin' a handkerchief or clap him in a bridewell fer bein' half slewed in the street."

"Me brother was transported ter Botany Bay fer twitchin' just two squiddy cock pheasants," Whaley agreed.

Claggett nodded. "Well, what I means to say is that if we chokes off everyone on board what does somethin' wrong, why, soon we'd have no one left to man the barky. Besides which, makes no sense to bang anyone up in irons doing nothin' fer too long, or we'd soon be gettin' shorthanded. An' that makes no sense if we meets a blow, or comes up with an enemy." He finished his grog. "So everythin' we does is short and sharp, and back on course again, yardarms square, 'n' all a-taunto!"

In a low voice Bowyer added, "But there was no call for Tyrell to come the hard horse like that. Pat's a right good hand. Has a short fuse only."

Kydd brought up the subject again when the two returned to the maintop. Bowyer was working on one of the many blocks. His keen-edged knife split the frayed strapping, which pulled away from the deep score around the wooden shell of the block. He began a short splice on a new length of rope to create a circular shape.

"Joe, you *really* think floggin' a man is right?"

"It's one way o' discipline, we do hold with that, but there's them what makes too free with it, and that's demeanin' to our honor," Bowyer said seriously, twisting the splice to make it lie more easily. His marline spike had an eye, a length of twine secured it to his belt and Kydd guessed that this was to prevent it from falling on the heads of those below.

"Here, clap on to this," Bowyer said.

Kydd did as he was told, extending the circle so Bowyer could ply his wooden serving mallet to apply a tight spun yarn covering continuously around.

"It's important to us—that is to say, we." Bowyer smiled at Kydd. "A sailor has pride, 'n' so he should. There's none can hold a candle to us in the article o' skill. I'd like to see one of them there circus akrybats step out on a topsail yard, take in a stuns'l when it comes on to blow. Or one of yer book-learned lawyers know the half of how to cat and fish a bower anchor."

The covering finished, Bowyer put the serving mallet aside and flexed the stiff circle. He settled it over the scored part and offered

the block to Kydd. "Hold it in place here, mate," he said, and prepared to apply a stout round seizing at the base of the block to
bowse the strap close in. "You see, Tom, when we gets a thunderin'
squall comes up and we has to get aloft and get in sail, we don't
want no misgivin's about the jack next to yer on the yardarm. In
the short of it, I'm saying we has our loyalty, and it's to our mates,
our ship and the Navy." He seemed uncomfortable with expressing
sentiment, but finished firmly, "But we expects it back, shipmate."
The seizing was finished with riding turns and crossed. "There you
are, Tom—take pride in yer work 'n' you can be sure it'll return
the compliment 'n' look after you, just when yer come t' need it."
Bowyer carefully gathered up the odd bits of twine and stranded
rope, and put them in his leather belt pouch. "Ned, keep a weather
eye for that toggled lift coming up, mate," he told Doud. "Kydd is
goin' to be a-learnin' some bends 'n' hitches."

He reached for a light jigger tackle belayed to a cleat and helped
himself to its end. "Now, Tom, this could save yer life one day. It's
called the bowline, an' it's the only one you c'n tie one-handed."

Bowyer was a good teacher, patient and with a vast fund of salty
asides to give meaning to what was being done. He made Kydd
practice each action until it was instinctive. "Middle of a gale o'
wind ain't no time to be puzzlin' over which way to bend on a line—
your mates relying on yer an' all."

Kydd descended from the tops to the lower world with a twinge of
regret. Something of Bowyer's simple contentment at the exercise of
his sea skills was attractive to him, especially when contrasted with
the harsh imperatives of life on the lower deck. He imagined wist-
fully what it would be like to be a true son of the sea.

Toward evening one or two boats were still circling the ship,
forlornly hoping for a change of heart, but whenever they closed
on the *Duke William* they were menaced with the threat of a cold

shot hove through their bottom. Eyes aboard the old ship watched hungrily, but it was common knowledge that Tyrell had told the Master-at-Arms that if any came aboard, then he himself would be turned before the mast as a common seaman. Even so, shoreside grog somehow found its way on board and before the end of the dog-watches there were eight men in irons—long bars along which iron shackles slid, seizing them by their legs as securely as the stocks ashore.

At supper there was little avoiding the topic.

"It's fair burstin' me balls just watching them trugs in the boats!" Whaley tried to laugh, but a cloud of depression hung about him.

Howell leered at him. "Like as not, boy, we're goin' to ground on our own beef bones waiting for somethin' to happen, and no steppin' ashore in the meantime, not with our hellfire jack of a first luff! So best you get used to the idea, cully!"

Kydd tried not to notice Bowyer's downcast silence. He looked over at Wong. The man's forehead glistened, but otherwise his bearing gave nothing away, and therefore Kydd almost missed the slight movement of his hands. His pale stubby fingers held a tankard, and as if of its own tiredness, the pewter slowly crumpled into a shapeless ball, the rest of Wong's body remaining quite motionless.

"And so say us all, that so, mate?" Doud's attempt to draw in Buddles failed, the man's misery was so deep.

Doud got to his feet. "Gotta see a man about a dog," he said, and hurried off, but not before receiving an approving wink from Claggett.

"Hear tell as how you're skylarkin' in the tops now, Tom." Whaley looked at Kydd with interest: for a landman only days aboard to have made it aloft so soon must indicate something of his mettle.

Kydd flushed with pleasure. He was being included in the general conversation for the first time in this mess, and felt pleased that it was Whaley, the born seaman, who had done so. "Couldn't help it—Joe would've given me a quiltin' with a rope's end, else," he said, a wide smile firmly in place.

Howell stirred with irritation. "Said before, younker, you're a landman 'n' not bred to the sea. Ye'll take a tumble off a yard first blow we gets and—"

"Clap a stopper on it, Jonas. Man wants t' be a sailor, is all."

Doud arrived back, and Kydd recognized what was going on in the play with the jacket and Buddles's pot.

Doud pushed across the pot with its dark mahogany contents. "Get this in yer, cuffin," he said quietly. "Things'll look different after, you'll see."

Buddles stared at him, then took a good swallow, sputtering his thanks. No one seemed to know quite what to say to him, and stared at the table or looked pensively at each other.

The conversation turned to other subjects over the greasy boiled salt pork, which followed.

When all was eaten, Bowyer spoke. "Tip us your 'Dick Lovelace,' Ned, I have a hankerin' after somethin' sad, mate."

Doud gave a pleased smile. "Upon the usual terms, Joe, me old shellback."

"You shall have it, Ned."

There was a general movement up from the table, and Kydd followed them up to the fo'c'sle just as the evening began to draw in. Warmed by his grog and pleasure at their company, he joined the others at the fore bitts. He found himself grinning benignly at total strangers.

Lanthorns were hung in the rigging, their golden pools of light more tawny than bright. Over the darkling sea he could see points of light appearing in the other ships also, and gradually he felt his open, cheerful attitude to life begin to return.

Another group of men were in a circle on the other side of the deck. A fiddler perched on the carronade began executing a neat but intricate air. A regular thumping resolved itself into a sailor in a white double-breasted waistcoat with brass buttons and blue and white striped trousers, dancing alone inside a rope circle. Kydd went across to watch. The sailor remained in the same spot, dancing a complex measure that involved the lower part of his body alone. With no expression whatsoever, arms folded immovably across his chest and rigid above the waist, he danced, feet pointing as they kicked, slapped and rose in time with the fiddler.

"Dancin' heel 'n' toe? Why, 'tis the hornpipe, matey!"

Kydd glanced back. Doud was making play of downing his due libation, and prepared to sing. This attracted the others, who very soon made themselves his adoring audience, finding places on the deck and fife-rail. Kydd settled down among them.

"Well, I'm blessed, lads, see who's come to join us!"

From up the ladder appeared Buddles, looking confused. Kydd tried to include him in the cheerful group, but the man did not seem to hear his words.

"Leave him be, Tom," Claggett said.

The hornpipe crew finished, and the fiddler came over to sit cross-legged on the fore gratings. He tuned his fiddle carefully, experimentally plucking at the catgut.

More sailors arrived, some hanging back in the outer shadows. Even with his face obscured, Kydd could recognize Renzi. He was an enigma, a mysterious figure who made Kydd feel uneasy.

Theatrically Doud gargled a few trills, which brought the gathering to a quiet. They waited expectantly. "The tale of Dick Lovelace, shipmates, who in the character of foretopman in the *Mermaid* is carried off to the Spanish Main, away from his true love and on to his fatal destiny."

The fiddler drew a long, low chord that split in two, leaving a single high note hanging. Doud stood on the grating next to him, legs akimbo, and sang. His voice was every bit as pure and clear as Kydd remembered from his experience at the maintop, and the clean, sparing accompaniment on the violin complemented it well. They all sat enraptured as the melancholy song continued, the chorus always the same:

> *Turn to thy love and take a kiss*
> *This gold about thy wrist I'll tie*
> *And always when thou look'st on this*
> *Think on thy love and cry.*

The song finished and there was a stillness, each man allowing his thoughts to steal away to secret places and treasured times, faces softening at intimate memories.

Buddles, it seemed, was bent on destroying the mood. He faltered unsteadily forward, pushing through the men toward the forward end of the fo'c'sle. Cradled in front of him was a twelve-pounder cannonball.

"What're yer doing, you stupid great oaf? Holy Christ! Can't you steer straight, you useless farmer?"

One seaman leaped to his feet and scruffed Buddles's shirt. "Look, whoever you are, mate, get outa here before I douse yer glims!"

Buddles looked at him in bewilderment. "It's Mary!" he said thickly.

The seaman dropped his hands in astonishment. "Wha—"

"No—please let me pass!" Buddles resumed his shamble forward. No one stopped him. He reached the larboard carronade and stopped, breathing heavily, for he had reached the farthest he could go forward. He stood bewildered.

"What's he doing? Shies that over the side 'n' Mantrap'll be down on us like thunder!"

"He's brainsick, poor lubber!"

"Let him go, he's harmless. How about 'Black Eyed Susan,' Ned?"

Buddles didn't move, standing irresolute.

Attention quickly returned to Doud, who took another pull at his grog in preparation. The fiddler produced a gay introductory elaboration in the right key and prepared for Doud's entry note.

"Stop him, you fools! Stop him—blast you!" Tewsley, carrying a glass of wine, stepped out into the lanthorn light in his ruffled evening shirt. He gestured sharply forward with his glass.

Buddles had mounted the low fife-rail and from there was shuffling out along the projecting cathead, still cradling the cannonball.

Some of the quicker-witted reached out, trying to seize his jacket. Buddles looked back, a look of utter contentment on his cadaverous face. "I have to go to Mary now," he said quietly, as though comforting a child, and embracing the heavy iron shot closer, stepped out into the void.

There was a rush to the side. A lanthorn was brought, but all that could be seen on the glitter of oily black water was a continuing stream of bubbles.

"Rowguard!" roared Tewsley, but the boat was half a ship's length away, and all Kydd could do was stare at the diminishing popple of bubbles and think in cold horror of the man's life ending in so many fathoms of dark water below them.

He stumbled away from the excited crowd, needing to be alone. He brushed against someone. It was Renzi, standing back from the others.

"You—you," Kydd gasped, "get out o' my way." He made instinctively for the ladder to the deck below. There he turned and lurched to an open gunport, retched into the darkness and hung there, weak and trembling, despising himself for his weakness.

It took a while for him to register what he was hearing from the tight group of men sitting farther forward. They spoke very quietly, but there was no mistaking Stallard's urgent, hectoring tones. "For fuck's sake, you *can* do somethin'! Why do yer stand for it? Never heard of any being made to eat shite like on board this boat!"

Kydd heard a growled reply too soft to distinguish, then, "O' course! That's what they think yer worth. Meanest lobsterback gets a whole shillin' a day."

There was more rumbling. "Ah, now that's where you're dead wrong. If you ain't been paid, then law's on your side—and my bloody oath, yer don't have to work until you have, see. And I oughta know—tell yer about it one day, I will.

"So we finds somewhere we can talk. Just don't want to hear any more low cackle about lyin' down and takin' anything they wants to dish out."

The voices died away, and Kydd could hear no more. When he pulled himself back inboard they had gone. He drifted listlessly back down to the lower deck, listening without interest to the desultory chatter, and was glad when the end of the dog-watch brought the hammocks down.

He lay back trying vainly to keep the misery-etched face of Buddles out of his mind. The violent contrasts of the day had left him empty and sick. It was no good: sleep was beyond him and he determined on activity as the only alternative.

He eased himself to the deck in the blackness, grateful that his hammock was so close to the main hatch. Careful not to disturb the sleepers whom he could hear breathing, snoring and grunting, he shuffled along on hands and knees. It was only when he got to the hatchway that he stopped to consider where he would go. The next deck above would be the same as this, full of sleeping bodies, and indeed the one above it, for all the time in port there would be no need to maintain a full watch on deck of half the men. Then he remembered the orlop deck below where he had spent his first night aboard, courtesy of the boatswain. The long walkway around the periphery—that would do.

The orlop had a pair of lanthorns at the after end. The men in irons lay sprawled asleep on the deck, a marine sentry suspiciously glassy-eyed against a door. The rest of the orlop forward was in blackness, and Kydd began pacing around the walkway.

He was totally unprepared for the sudden attack. An iron-hard pair of hands gripped him by the throat and dragged him choking and helpless across the deck to the gratings of the main hatch. "Shall I croak 'im?" his attacker whispered hoarsely. Kydd was forced to his knees.

"Wait—we'll find out what he knows first," returned an urgent whisper.

A tiny light, a purser's glim—a reed in an iron saucer burning rancid fat—was uncovered, and in its sputtering light Stallard's face appeared, devilish and delighted. "Well, if it ain't me old royster, Tom Kydd." There was just enough luminosity to reveal about half a dozen other figures among the shadows.

The pressure on his throat eased and he dropped to the deck, heaving burning breaths in spasms. A hand grabbed his hair and forced his head back. "Just we needs to know why you're creepin' around down here, Kydd. Stands to reason you're not here for the sake of yer health," Stallard said.

Kydd gulped air and tried to order his thoughts against the roaring in his ears and the savage adrenaline rush. "Couldn't sleep— needed to—"

His hair was jerked savagely back, and a meaty hand gripped his throat. "You gull us 'n' you're shark bait, matey."

"No—he's square, I know him from a-ways back." Stallard's look became speculative. "See, me 'n' me friends here don't think it right we should have to go out to sea in this leaky old boat and drown like rats, so we're goin' to take action." He looked around for confirmation, which he got. "The committee has to meet here, 'cos you know why, and we voted we stand for our rights as human beings, not poxy slaves.

"We're now goin' to organize the whole crew, and when those fuckin' whistles blow to force us to sea, we're just goin' to refuse to sail."

Kydd's reply was left unsaid at the sight of Stallard's wolfish grin.

"And that means we ain't a-goin' anywhere! Like to see their faces when we stands up for the first time and demands our rights. Fair stonkered, they'll be! They can't do a bloody thing if we're all together in this." He nudged Kydd. "And that's why we wants to know where you stand in all this, me old mate."

Kydd said nothing.

"Don't forget, Kydd, you make a noise, someone finds us, you'll be seen right here with us all, so you may as well come in now and do somethin' useful." Stallard rubbed his chin thoughtfully. "Yeah—for some reason, people like you, they'll listen to what yer say, and we're gonna need leaders when we makes our stand." He stood up. "We starts work tomorrow, Tom, 'n' first meeting at the tables at noon. See you then, mate." Stallard held out his hand, and Kydd knew that if he didn't take it he would never leave the orlop alive.

In the blackness he couldn't find his way back to his hammock. Not that sleep was possible—his mind was racing. He crawled over to the side of the ship and sat with his back to the hull and his head in his hands. There would only be one end to such madness: mutiny in the Navy could never be allowed to succeed, whatever the provocation—even he could see that. According to a local penny broadsheet, even after four years they were still ranging the Great South Sea for the remaining mutineers of the *Bounty*. Tyrell would have no compunction against sending armed men against them instantly, leaving no time for discussion or negotiation. There would be bloodshed, and if he did not show on the right side Stallard would be too desperate to allow him the luxury of time to decide.

His thoughts rushed on. Supposing he were to warn the quarterdeck right now? He would not be believed without evidence, and in any event his very being rebelled against betrayal. Should he wake Bowyer and ask him what to do? Easier said than done—all he knew was that Bowyer slung his hammock with the mizzen topmen, and they were lost somewhere in this vast city afloat.

Restlessly Kydd eased his aching limbs. The deep groans and creaks seemed to take on disturbing meaning in the claustrophobic dark. Perhaps Stallard was right: if the ship was a deathtrap, then indeed they had a case. The newspapers always seemed to carry reports of ships lost at sea for unknown reasons; it was easy to think of one now. But Stallard was a hothead, fomenting trouble to satisfy his craving for cheap adulation; he had no real idea of the consequences of his actions. This situation was different: there was nowhere to hide afterward and it was most certainly a hanging matter.

Time dragged on and Kydd began to feel drowsy. He would leave decisions to the morning, after he had spoken to Bowyer.

He was drifting off, hardly noticing the bumps and thuds on the hull, when he was jerked awake by the urgent squeal of boatswains' calls and pandemonium everywhere. "*Haaaands ahoy!* All the *haands!* All hands on deck!"

There was groaning, curses and lanthorns waving about in the gloom. Kydd was jostled violently in the confusion. He tried to make sense of what was going on, and grabbed the arm of a boatswain's mate.

"Haven't you heard, mate? Captain's returned aboard suddenlike, and it's the French—they're out! The Frogs are at sea!"

"What the stinkin' hell are yer doin' still here?" Elkins pulled Kydd round to face him. "Yer station for unmoorin' ship is the main sheets—geddup there!" He knocked Kydd away from him and stormed about in the chaos, looking for the men of his division.

It was bedlam on the night-black lower deck, its hellish gloom lit fitfully by lanthorns—a struggling mass of men, white eyes rolling in the shadows, the occasional gleam of equipment. Kydd's heart thudded. In a matter of hours he might be fighting for his life out there, somewhere. His mind flooded with images in which he could see himself cut down by maddened Frenchmen as they swarmed aboard after a fierce battle. He gulped and mounted the ladders for the upper deck.

On deck, the darkness was lifting, slowly, reluctantly. A dank, cold dawn began the day.

The decks themselves were unrecognizable—braces, sheets and halliards were off their belaying pins and led out along the decks for easy running. The upper yards were alive with men. Urgent shouts shattered the dawn.

Along the somber line of warships there was a similar bustle and lights began to appear all along the shore.

Bowyer was already there, but did not answer Kydd's greeting, shoving a rope into his hand. "Clap on ter that and don't move from there."

The landmen were pushed into place, their slow incomprehension maddening the petty officers, who used their starters liberally on backs and shoulders, while the seamen moved far above them—on the tops, out along the yards and to the end of the jibboom.

The pace slowed, and Kydd saw a coalescing of groups about the officers. Tewsley paced deliberately, accompanied by Elkins, whose face wore a look of dedicated ferocity.

"*Haaands* to the braces!"

One by one, the massive lower yards were altered from their perfect cross-ship position to a starboard-farthest-forward angle, the better to catch the cold, steady breeze from the northwest.

On the fo'c'sle Kydd could see the men crowded around the anchor tackle, although he could not see what they were about. He knew that deep below him at that moment the capstan would be manned by every hand left over from duties on deck, and he was grateful to have his work out in the open.

The bustle subsided, and Kydd ventured a glance at Bowyer. He was looking up to the men waiting on the yards, and sniffing about for the precise direction of the wind.

He noticed Kydd and said quietly, "Easy enough—she'll cast under topsails to larb'd, 'n' then out going large. He shouldn't have anythin' to worry of."

Bowyer was subdued; Kydd realized that he was probably thinking of the woman he was leaving. "Joe, d'you think there'll be a battle?"

"Mebbe, and then again mebbe not. Who knows?" Bowyer looked away, and down to the rope he held. He let it drop and walked to the side of the ship facing Portsmouth and did something with a coiled line. There seemed no point in following.

"Grapple that buoy, damn it!" came faintly from forward, followed by a triumphant, "Man the cat! Walk away with it, you lead bellies!"

From the quarterdeck echoed a booming shout. "Make sail there! Lead along topsail sheets and halliards. Lay out and loose!"

Kydd saw sail suddenly blossom from the topsail yards. The men on deck worked furiously at the tacks and sheets.

"Lay aft the braces, you lubbers—larboard head, starboard main, and larboard your cro'jick!"

From having her head so steadfastly into the wind, tethered by her anchor, *Duke William* began to move ever so slightly astern. With counter-bracing on the fore, her bow paid off to leeward, faster and faster.

"Haul taut! Brace abox!"

Kydd was working too hard to watch, not really understanding what he was doing but determined to give it his best. The wind, more brisk than he remembered, had a salt tang to it.

"Starboard head braces! Brace around those headyards!"

There was a distinct lurch as the headsails took up at precisely the time *Duke William* ceased her sternward motion. Having curved around to take the northwester on her starboard cheeks, she now paused; the big courses were sheeted in and she straightened for the run south to St. Helens.

Portsmouth now lay astern, the little cluster of dwellings, tap-houses and Tudor forts dwindling into an anonymous blur. Kydd found that he had been too busy to think of the forlorn tiny scatter of women who were all that remained of those still hoping against hope at the Sally Port. They would know now that the only way they would see their menfolk would be in their dreaming.

Astern also was the fat bulk of the ninety-eight-gun *Tiberius* smoothly following in their wake, the whiteness of her new sails evidence of her recent docking. Ahead was *Royal Albion,* her stern galleries glittering before the salt stains of the open sea could dull them. A pair of frigates was even farther ahead, under a full press of sail, drawing away visibly on a course that would take them ranging far ahead out to sea.

The low dark green and black of the Isle of Wight slid by in the early morning, the busy little waves hustling inshore toward the far-off port, which Kydd knew would be waking to another dawn, another working day. He hoped that his duties would keep him on deck. He felt both exhilaration and fear; the altered perceptions that come from leaving land and committing body and spirit to the sea. In one sense he yearned for the certainties of life on land, the regularities that made up the day, the steady work and sleep, the warmth of being part of a wider community. But he was aware as well that, alone of his family, he was going to see great times, be part of a world event. Deep within he felt his spirit respond to the challenge—the young wig-maker of Guildford was fading into the past.

They passed St. Helens and shaped course more westerly for the

Channel. Portsmouth finally slipped out of sight behind the Foreland and they steadily forged ahead down the coast for Ventnor and the last of the land. The breeze freshened and at nine knots *Duke William* was sailing about as fast as she ever would. The sea hissed along her sides at an astonishing rate. Kydd doubted that even a horse at a fast trot would find it possible to keep up.

They reached St. Catherine's Point, and beyond the prominence ahead in grand fashion *Royal Albion* reared up, then fell in a broad swash of white. Then it was their turn, the first sea sent in earnest by the broad Atlantic, sending their bow with its great jibboom spearing up to the sky, then to crash down in a stomach-stopping smother of foam.

"Aye, see how she curtsies to Neptune when she reaches his kingdom," Bowyer said, smiling.

Sails bellied out and hardened as the regular winds of the open sea predominated. In place of the fluky, changeable airs of inshore there was a steadiness, an assertion of the primacy of sea over land.

Kydd's exhilaration began to ebb. The familiar outline of hills, fields and towns was now an anonymous green and black line becoming more insignificant each time he looked. To a countryman like him it was deeply disturbing to relate only to a wilderness of water, with nothing that could remotely be termed a fixed object.

The ship was now very much alive. She rose and fell with vigor to the waves, forcing Kydd to move from one handhold to another, too afraid to trust his feet. Bowyer didn't even notice, securing the lines into seamanlike hanks at the belaying pins, his movements sure and precise. "Fair wind at the moment—should make soundings in a day or so if there's no more westing in it," he said, after a considered look at the ragged sky.

"And then we'll face up with the French—the enemy?" Kydd tried not to sound fearful.

"The Mongseers? No, mate, with this wind they're away off out of it," Bowyer said. "Won't come up against them till we weather Ushant, 'n' then only if they wants to come our way." He smiled briefly. "They may be out, but it won't be this way they're coming. Off to the Caribbee or somewhere, my guess. Anyhow, our job's to put a stopper on any Frog that wants to get to sea from now on."

Kydd hung on as he took this in. So there would be no battle soon—he didn't question Bowyer's judgment. He looked up at the masts. Now clothed with sails, they gave an impression of a certain clean beauty and grim purpose. He tried a few paces and hung on. There was definitely a rhythm: as he watched, the line of the deck forward lifted, hung and settled, and lifted again. He tried a few more steps and looked back at Bowyer, who grinned at him. Boldly he crossed the deck to the windward side and grabbed a shroud, the wind in his teeth. Playfully, the wind plucked his hat and sent it spinning over the deck and out to leeward.

"Don't worry, cuffin, I'll find you another—but promise me next time you rigs yer chin-stay when you're on deck," Bowyer said.

There was never a definite time. Never an exact defining instant at which England finally vanished. One moment the far line of the land was there, only just, and the next time Kydd remembered to look, there was nothing but a horizon innocent of anything but the rimming seascape. It should have been a special moment, leaving his native country astern, but he only felt a curious separation, one in which England carried on with its own cares, duties and pleasures down one line of existence, while Kydd and his watery world went another.

At breakfast on the lower deck Kydd kept quiet. There was just too much to take in. Between decks there were new sounds: creaks, groans and random cracks that gradually resolved into a regular sequence—a long-drawn-out deep-throated shudder, followed by a volley of creaks, before a descending sigh of minor sounds. It was also a strange feeling 'tween-decks when there was no horizon visible to act as cue; body perceptions said that the entire structure was rearing up and plunging down, but the eyes just as firmly insisted that everything was solidly unmoving.

No sooner had they completed breakfast than Kydd was startled by the sound of a drum, loud in the confined space of the lower deck. Cutting through the hubbub in rhythmic rolls, its martial sound volleyed irresistibly, an urgent beating, on and on. Instantly there was turmoil. It was clear that this was nothing ordinary—the concentrated look on men's faces told him that. With thumping heart it dawned on him that this must be the call to arms, a clarion call to duty. If this was battle he could not be more unready. His anxiety turned to fear that he would let his shipmates down, that by his act others would suffer. He stumbled through the welter of activity.

"Bear a fist, then, you useless lubber!" yelled an unknown figure, passing over a detached mess table.

He joined the stream of men striking the tables, mess traps and all their homely articles into the hold below.

The guns were being readied. Where before they had been mere background features of the living spaces, much the same as the old oak sideboard in the living room in Guildford, now they seemed to come alive, to crouch like beasts in Kydd's sharpened imagination.

"Kydd—is that you?" A young lieutenant with a frown looked at him.

"Yes, sir!"

"Number-three gun, then," the lieutenant said irritably, more interested in his piece of paper. He moved on.

Kydd moved smartly to the gun indicated. It seemed enormous. Around it was a crowd of men casting it loose and taking up positions. The gun captain acknowledged his presence with a surly nod, busy checking his equipment.

The lower deck was crowded with men, even though only one side of guns was in operation, on the weather, and therefore higher, side. With shrill squeals gunport lids were raised on pulleys, allowing natural light to flood in and giving a close view of the sea outside. It suddenly dawned on Kydd why the inside of the ports and timbers around the guns were painted in so bright a scarlet. The wind streamed straight in through the gunports, making him shiver but bringing a welcome clean sea tang. He wondered what else might be out there, and ducked down to look out.

The sea, bright after the gloom, slid past only a few feet down, individual flecks and flurries in perfect clarity. But of the enemy there was nothing, just endless marching waves, looking much closer and more alive than on deck. It was surprising to feel the calming effect of the horizon. He had made his first vital discovery of the sea: that in a world where every single thing seemed to be in motion, here was something that was fixed and solid, could be relied on—the line of the horizon. Straightening, he dared a look at the man next to him. He was thin and ugly, and wore a beaver hat as shapeless as it was characterful.

The man glanced around and caught Kydd staring at him. He was very ugly, his face foreshortened like a monkey, the forehead disappearing too quickly into a stubble of hair. "You lookin' for a souse in the chops, cock?" he croaked, in a grog-ravaged voice.

Kydd mumbled something and tried to give his attention to his opposite number, an Iberian by appearance. The man saw him, but looked away in contempt, probably because he was a landman.

The gun captain straightened, and held up his arm. The man was all muscle, and with his striped shirt and red bandanna closely tied over his hair, resembled a pirate. His eyes were hard and took in everything.

"Silence! Silence, fore and aft!" It was the young lieutenant, shrill with anxiety, pacing down the midline of the ship. "The Captain desires me to inform you all that it is his intention to exercise the great guns every morning without fail."

So much for the enemy and mortal combat, thought Kydd, not sure whether to be relieved or disappointed.

It seemed the officer did not know whether to keep his black-japanned speaking trumpet behind his back or ready in front of him. "We have the heaviest guns in the ship, and therefore the most decisive weapons in battle. If we can hit harder, faster, then we will win. Otherwise we will lose. So we are going to practice and practice until we are good enough—and then we practice some more until we are the best. Mark my words, any man who hangs back will be dealt with instantly."

The seamen waiting by their guns watched him tight-faced or warily as their experience told them.

"Gun captains, prove crews in your own time! Carry on."

The man in the red bandanna spat on his hands. "Me name's Stirk." He fixed them with his fierce eyes. "Now, there's them what don't know me methods yet"—he took in several of them with his glance—"and there's them what do. Ain't that right, Doggo?"

He was addressing the ugly man next to Kydd, who grinned a gap-toothed acknowledgment. "Yer has yer ways, is the right of it, Toby."

"Then let's get to it. Slow time it is. Cast loose, Jewkes."

The gun was lashed by its muzzle into docile obedience like an ox by its nose. Jewkes, a nervous, slightly built man, pulled himself astride it and cast off the lashing, which he coiled neatly on the eyebolt.

"Watch yer arse," another said, and paid out the side tackles in long fakes, while others passed over the implements of gunnery—crow, handspike, sponge.

"Level guns!"

Once the quoins were slammed in place, the cocked-up appearance of the massive piece took on a more straight-eyed and businesslike appearance.

"Tompion!"

The muzzle gaped open.

Stirk stood back and looked appraisingly at them all. "Right, let's 'ave a few changes. Bull, I want you on the crow—yeah, take it, then. Pedro, we'll 'ave you on the rammer this time."

A barrel-chested man with a near bald head pushed out and grabbed the crow from unresisting hands. The Iberian sauntered across to claim a long stave tipped with a cup-shaped piece of wood. Tension was reflected in his glittering dark eyes.

"Doggo, I want you to lead on the left tackle, 'n' you, whasser-name, join 'im."

Kydd moved across and found himself in a line of men at the tackle fall. He placed himself unobtrusively at the end.

Stirk considered. "Well, that'll do fer now. Remember, you doesn't pull yer weight, I comes down on yer hard, as yez know." He took his position at the breech of the gun. "Now, ye know me method—we gets it straight afore we gets it fast. So we go through the drill, b' order. Stand by!" He glared at his gun crew one by one. "Run out th' gun!"

While those with implements watched, Kydd and the others tugged at the tackle. The monster gun sullenly ground a foot or two toward the port. On this point of sailing the deck was canted, so the work was all uphill.

"Stap me," marveled Stirk, "but you're a useless pawky lot! Let's 'ave some real 'eavy in it, then."

The gun moved out faster, but Kydd was dismayed at the effort required to shift the three tons of cold iron.

"That's better! Now, come on, gemmun, remember yer drill! Youse—clear the breechin' from the truck. You 'n' you fakes out the tackle falls nice 'n' neat. Yer don't want me remindin' yer all the time, now, do yer? So—prime! We doesn't take action here. Point yer gun!"

He looked at Jewkes, standing by nervously. "Look, mate," he said, "keep yer trainin' tackle close up—bight yer fall after she fires, 'cos side tackles'll be runnin' out quick 'n' they don't want it foulin'. Handspike. I want youse right here 'n' watchin' me all the time— t'ain't no good admirin' the view. Now the piece is ready to fire. Hey! Put that gun tackle down, you, Kydd! Gun goes orf, it'll fly out 'n' take you with it!"

Kydd's face burned.

"Gun has fired. Denison 'n' Cullen with Jewkes on the trainin' tackle fer now."

With the cannon's recoil they would need no training tackle for the real thing.

The long black gun rumbled inboard, helped by the inclined deck and the training tackle fixed to the rear. Fully run in, its massive size, chest high to Kydd, was overawing.

A brief image of the parson and his gun—there had been a spiteful crack from a barrel not much bigger than his little finger: what kind of earth-splitting sound would come from a gaping maw nearly the size of his head, Kydd wondered. His palms began to sweat.

"Yours now, Lofty. Let me see some speed." The man was good at the task. Taking advantage of the gunport, he sinuously arced out of the port to face inboard, plying his sheepskin-tipped stave into the muzzle at the same time. Three twists to the left going in, three to the right coming out.

"Let's be 'avin you, then, Cullen. Where's yer powder?"

A doleful-looking sailor went through the motions of going to the midline of the vessel, where a grinning ship's boy pretended elaborately to give him a cartridge from a long covered container.

"Load with cartridge!" Stirk ordered.

The invisible cartridge was stuffed down the muzzle to Cullen's armpit. He whipped out his arm, by which time the Iberian had advanced with his rammer. Thrusting forcefully several times, he leaped back, the action like a dance movement.

"Wait for it, Pedro—me priming wire 'as to feel the cartridge, 'n' then I signals an' that's when you carry on." He gave a wintry smile. "But that was smartly done, cully. Shot yer gun."

An imaginary wad was slapped into the muzzle as two men bent to the shot rack, pretending to heave a shot on to the cradle. It would need two to carry the great thirty-two-pound shot to the muzzle, where the cradle would tilt the ball in.

"Pedro?"

But the dark-eyed man was already there, plunging the rammer down. "Wad!" he shouted before Stirk could speak.

A "wad" was passed into the muzzle, more plunges with the rammer and they stood back.

"Good. Now we does it in one. Run out the gun!"

The exercise warmed Kydd, and he tore off his jacket and waistcoat. It was not hard to learn the motions; the difficult part was to learn to pull together with the others and to stop his muscles trembling at the unaccustomed effort.

Ahead of him on the tackle, others were finding it hard as well, with panting and feverish mopping of foreheads. Doggo had doffed his shirt altogether, the feral hair over his neck and shoulders glistening with sweat. "Now, lads, yer needs to get low into it, like this," he said, leaning into the line of the rope.

The young lieutenant appeared distracted. "Cease exercise. Stand down."

Stirk sat on the rear of the gun carriage, looking at them with a sardonic smile. A desultory chatter drifted around.

"What're we waitin' for, then?" Jewkes said, peevish.

Bull Lynch snorted. "Why—yer goin' anywhere?"

"Let's jus' get the exercise over. Need to get me head down fer a caulk."

The lieutenant reappeared, looking apprehensive. He raised his speaking trumpet. "Pay attention, the gundeck. The Captain means to exercise the great guns today with the discharge of one round from each gun."

He hesitated, then ordered, "All guns, load with cartridge!"

Kydd's heart quickened: he would hear the guns speak now.

Stirk rose. "C'mere, nipper," he said, to their ship's boy. "Now run along an' get me pouch from the gunner's mate."

Kydd had noticed the ship's boys stationed at each gun, some no more than ten years old, and had been touched by their youthful high spirits. He could not help but wonder how they could possibly endure in a great sea battle.

"You, Denison, match tub—and, Cullen, yer knows yer sponge'll need water." Stirk checked carefully around, then went to the gun-lock atop the breech of the gun. Carefully removing the lead apron, he attached a lanyard to the mechanism. Cocking it, he watched closely as it clicked a fat spark. Satisfied, he straightened. "Thanks, younker," he said to the panting boy waiting behind with the pouch. He smiled at the lad. "So where's yer ear tackle, then?"

The boy brought out a grubby white rag, which Stirk fastened with mock roughness around his head. It was in the form of two circlets that went around the head, intersecting at the ears where there were large pads.

The others began tying their kerchiefs and bandannas over their ears as well. Kydd felt awkward and apprehensive as he followed suit.

Slinging the powder horn over his shoulder, Stirk waited for the loading process to complete. This time, there was a real cartridge—a light-gray cylinder with coarse stitching, which held Kydd with a horrifying fascination. It went in, bottom end first, seam downward.

"Slow time, lads. We get it right first."

More carefully than before, the dark Spaniard plied his rammer.

This time Stirk had his thumb on the touchhole to tell by the escaping air when the charge was seated.

A wad and then the iron ball itself. To Kydd, it looked huge. Stirk noticed his interest. "Right ship-smasher, that. Go through two feet o' solid oak at a mile, that 'un will."

The cradle tilted and the cannonball disappeared into the gun. Another wad would be needed to keep it hard up against the cartridge against the roll of the ship.

"Run out!"

In a sudden bout of nervous energy, Kydd hauled mightily on the tackle.

Stirk took his priming wire, more an iron spike, and by piercing the cartridge through the vent hole ensured that naked powder was waiting for the jet of flame from the quill tube. The gunlock pan was filled with bruised gunpowder from the powder horn, and Stirk raised his hand. "Stand by to fire!"

A flurry of clicks echoed along the gundeck as the gunlocks were cocked. Gun captains stood behind their weapons, lanyard in hand, and kept their eyes on the lieutenant, who plainly was waiting for word from the quarterdeck far above.

The ship heaved slightly, muffled creaks startling in the silence. The morning wind was strengthening and buffeting those closest to the gunport. Kydd caught a glimpse of a lone seabird wheeling low over the sea.

Still the waiting. The tension became unbearable.

Kydd stole a look at Stirk, who was calm but poised. He wiped moist hands on his trousers.

A distant shouting and a face appeared at the forehatch. "Stand by. Number-one gun—fire!"

In a split second, Kydd saw it all. At the first gun, only two guns forward, the gun captain tugged hard at the lanyard. After the briefest delay came the stupefying din, the visceral push of the blast. It left him stunned. Then a vast, enveloping mass of smoke roiled out for a hundred yards or more before it was blown back in again. It swirled around them, briefly hiding the waiting gun crews.

"Number-two gun—fire!"

Kydd knew what to expect and closed his eyes. The cannon was nearer and there was a vicious iron ring to the blast. He flinched; a trembling started in his knees.

Now it was their turn. Stirk stepped back to the full length of the lanyard and waited for the order, a peculiar grin playing on his lips.

"Number-three gun—fire!"

A series of images was split by violence—the stabbing tongue of fire at the muzzle instantly replaced by acrid gunsmoke, the maddened plunge of the great cannon past Kydd to the rear, the frantic whipping of the side tackle until the gun came up to its breeching with a bass twang, the artistic arching of Stirk's body to allow the cannon to charge past as if he were in a bullring.

And then it was over.

CHAPTER 5

As KYDD CAME ON WATCH in the afternoon, it was clear that the weather was on the change. The wind had backed from a previously favorable light northerly, and was now more in the west—and strengthening. It moved forward of the beam and the old battleship had to thrash along close to the wind instead of a comfortable full and bye. Her bluff bow met the increasingly steep but still relatively short waves of the Channel head on in a series of smashes that sent cold spray sheeting into the air, then stinging straight aft. Overhead, the lowering cloudbase had turned into a dull, racing overcast. Combers started to appear, vivid white in the unrelieved green-gray.

By three bells the wind had increased and it became necessary to shorten sail. In came the topgallants and the main and mizzen topgallant staysails; to balance this the small jib was set. Kydd found it increasingly unpleasant. In weather that on land would have people reaching for thick coats and scurrying thankfully for shelter he found himself standing waiting on the upper deck as each sail maneuver called for more hauling, then more inactivity. His suffering increased when drifts of light rain bore down in curtains of misty drizzle. The rain suddenly got harder, then stopped, leaving him shivering in the keen wind.

The others on watch did not offer sympathy—to them it was

an inevitable part of being a sailor, to be endured quietly and with resignation. Some pulled on foul weather gear—shapeless woolen monmouth caps and lengths of tarred canvas that hung down like aprons, mainly used by those going aloft. Luckier ones had a grego, a rough, thick coat, and over it a layered tarpaulin surcoat.

Kydd had none of these. His short jacket over the waistcoat had soon become sodden and his trousers kept up a steady stream of water into his purser's-issue light black shoes. Cold crept remorselessly inwards to his vitals.

It seemed an age before the watch was over and Kydd was able to make his way down to the mess. The warm fetor of the gundeck, its buzz of talk, was welcoming. Supper was beginning, and the grog monkey swam dark with rum.

Kydd sat in his wet gear, letting the rum and the surrounding fug do their work.

Bowyer stripped off his old tarpaulin overcoat, but underneath he seemed just as damp as Kydd. "Grievous wet, Joe," Kydd said.

"Well, if you takes it ter heart every wet shirt yer gets, why, yer'll fret yourself into a stew. O' course, if you has yer sealskin warmers—wear 'em under the waistcoat yer does—but I guess you'll want tarpauling gear o' sorts. Have to see ol' Nipcheese about that."

He seemed to find the grog as acceptable as Kydd. Draining his tankard regretfully, he said, "I'll see yer right on that, mate, don't you worry. Can't be havin' you die o' cold before we makes a topman of ye, now, can we?"

Kydd looked at Bowyer, in his faded seaman's rig, and felt a surge of warmth toward the man. He gulped at his grog, sighed and smiled, looking around at his new friends, then rested his eyes on the stout side of the ship. As usual condensation was running over age-blackened timber, but strangely, it slowly transformed, from a harsh confining prison wall into a sturdy barrier protecting him against the unknown vastness of the ocean outside.

Suddenly the ship gave a bump out of sequence, followed by a pitch of considerable vertical distance. The sudden movement caught Kydd unawares, and his grog spilled down his front.

"Gets a mort worse afore it gets better," Howell said, watching Kydd over his pot.

Doud ignored him. "What's the chance of a real blow, Sam?" he asked Claggett.

"Depends on what you calls a real blow." Claggett stared moodily into the distance. "We'll have Portland comin' abeam b' six bells. If it doesn't back even more to th' west we can do it on this board, if that's what yer mean." Doud waited patiently. "But if we don't make our westin' soon, why, then we'll be hook down ridin' it out in Torbay or somewheres. You know how it'll be, Ned."

Kydd broke in. "What about the Frogs?"

They looked at him with surprise. "Why, the buggers can't move with this westerly," said Whaley. "Bailed up in harbor, they be, can't sail against a foul wind, see."

A deeper lurch came. Kydd could swear he felt the unseen wave pass all the way down the ship, the bows first rising to it, then as the wave reached midpoint, falling off down the other side.

Bowyer grinned. "Let's get yer foulies, then, Tom. Yer on fer the last dog-watch."

Dusk drew in, but there was no easing in the weather. The wind by the hour swung west, strengthening as it did so, a hard, continuous blow in place of gusts and buffets. Scud raced overhead, ragged and low, and the ship labored heavily.

"There goes our run!" said Corrie, one of the watch. He pulled viciously at a line. "Couldn't have stayed in the north for just another day, oh, no! Now we'll be floggin' about all over the oggin, lookin' for a slant."

It was clear that *Duke William* was unable to keep as close to the wind as the other two vessels. She sailed as near as possible but she sagged sadly away to leeward of the newer ships, the line of three becoming a gaggle.

From the main top of the *Royal Albion* ahead a solitary flicker of light appeared. Kydd glanced up: their own maintop lanthorn produced its fitful beam for *Tiberius* astern.

He gazed at the three-decker ahead, working her way through the seas in a welter of foam, rising and falling in a foreshortened bobbing, clawing at the wind. As he watched, the vessel altered her perspective, changing tack to conform to *Duke William*'s labored course, the line now whole again.

"That'll please the buggers. Now nobody's goin' to fetch Start Point on this tack," Corrie said. A cluster of signal flags made its way in jerks up *Royal Albion*'s rigging, the bunting stiff to the wind. "That'll be night orders, 'n' welcome to it," he added, with a sniff. "Like as not, it'll come on a real muzzler tonight, an' then what's the use o' orders?"

The rain had stopped, but the wind steadily increased. Inside his new tarpaulins Kydd shivered, the slapping of the cape-like folds feeling awkward and uncomfortable. The odor of tarred canvas was strong and penetrating.

A bulky figure in old, rain-slick foul weather gear stumped along the deck in the gathering darkness. It was the boatswain, accompanied by his mates, going about on a last checking of gear before it was too dark to do so. He passed Kydd without recognition, then stopped and came back. "Gettin' your sea legs, then?" he rumbled. "One thing about foul weather, soon sorts out th' sailors from the lubbers."

Then there was the familiar round of trimming—the tightening, easing, bracing and other motions deemed necessary by the officer on watch on assuming the deck, after which the men huddled beneath the weather bulwarks. The binnacle lamp was lit, and extra men sent to the wheel. The small group on the quarterdeck paced abjectly in the dirty weather, wet streaming from their foul weather gear. The night drew in.

Kydd pulled his tarpaulins close, imitating the others who, sitting with their backs to the bulwark, had wrapped a weird assortment of gear around them.

"O' course, it could all end for us in an hour, yer know," said Corrie.

"How so?"

"Jus' think, here we is, thrashin' along with the wind shiftin' all the time, who's to say where we'll be at the end of the watch in the dark?"

There was no answer, so he went on, "Frenchy coast only thirty mile or so off hereabouts, 'n' it's sure enough iron-bound—worst part o' the whole coast, is that. What if we gets to tack south when the wind heads us? We'll be piled up afore we know it."

Bowyer grunted, "Leave him be, Scrufty. You knows they keeps a proper reckonin' on the quarterdeck. An' we must have passed this way no more'n half a hundred times."

"Ah, yes, but we're talkin' about a bit of a blow, at night, tide set 'n' all, and a cap'n who doesn't know his arse from his elbow about shiphandlin'.

"Don't forget, we gotta weather the Shambles first—ever seen 'em under a tide-fall? Nasty, black, 'n' ready to tear the heart outa a good ship afore yer knows it," he said.

"But—" began Kydd.

"An' by me calc'lation they're just about here. Could be right in our course, mates, only a half a mile ahead 'n' jus' waitin'."

Kydd couldn't help it. He stuck his head above the bulwark and peered into the dark sea fret ahead, the *Royal Albion*'s lanthorn light long since disappeared into the thick murk. In his imagination he could see only too vividly the black rocks rearing up to smash and splinter their way into their vessel, the victorious sea close behind.

At the end of the watch they wearily slung their hammocks.

"I'd keep me gear handy if I was you, mate! Somethin' 'appens, an' it's 'Turn up the hands,'" came a voice from the darkness. Kydd peeled off his clothes, still damp from before, and wearily swung himself in. The ship was moving more—less of a roll, more of an uncomfortable jerky pitching which the hammock, slung fore and aft, could not easily absorb.

He drifted off to sleep, and a disjointed dream arose, troubling and frightening, of himself borne away unwilling on the back of a huge wild bull, thundering unstoppably toward a great precipice that somehow he knew lay ahead.

Waking with a start, he was confused, disoriented. Lanthorns swayed and flickered in the musty gloom, voices murmured and turned querulous; he struggled to make meaning of it all. Thumping his feet on deck, he felt the motion of the ship markedly more irregular and violent.

"Starbowlines! All the starbowlines! Out or down! Out or down, you farmer's sons, rouse out!"

The boatswain's mates moved about quickly, urgently. There was no time to lose. Warm and pink, Kydd stumbled into his damp clothes, then the awkward tarpaulins. He found himself losing his balance and crashing into cursing men half glimpsed in the dimness.

Still befuddled with sleep, he emerged up the main companionway to the open deck. As soon as his head topped the coaming he was into the full force of the gale, a turbulent streaming wind hammering and lashing at him, wild and fearful. In the darkness he could see by the light of the binnacle that now there were four men on the wheel, leaning into it hard, grappling, straining. Spray whipped past in spiteful blasts as he staggered in the hammering wind to the binnacle, where an unknown figure shouted in his ear, jabbing with a finger.

He was expected on the main deck, down in the waist. He turned to go back down the ladder, but something made him pause. The length of deck forward was barely visible, but there was a furious grandeur in the rise and fall of the entire length of deck, an eager and responsive coupling of the ship with the wildness of the sea. A mounting exhilaration replaced Kydd's fear, and instead of returning down the companionway he staggered forward along the side of the deck, holding on tightly as he went. It was impossible to see out to the sea itself, but waves smashed on the ship's bluff sides and he tasted the salt spray on his lips.

Looking up he saw that only some of the sails were still in place, each pale and taut as a board. A strident chorus of thrums and musical harping in the rigging gave a dramatic urgency to the scene. He hung on at the mainchains, reluctant to leave.

Something in him reached out—and was answered. A fierce joy touched his soul. It didn't matter that the situation was perilous or the ship doomed. From that moment on Kydd knew in his heart that he would be a seaman. He clung to this revelation, taking the bursts of spray in his teeth and grinning madly. The bows would rise, then smash down, flinging the seas apart, shuddering and racking, then gloriously rise again.

"Tom!" Bowyer's concerned shout and hand gripping his arm startled him. "No need—don' wait here. Geddown to th' waist!"

His honest concern was evident and Kydd laughed, eyes shining.

More men emerged from below, whipped and buffeted by the hard winds.

"Double reef—topsails—" shouted Bowyer.

A man grunted and swung himself up into the weather rigging.

"Go down—reefing tackle, forebrace bitts!"

Others pushed past and mounted the ratlines.

"Go—" Bowyer shoved at Kydd impatiently.

Kydd stood and watched as Bowyer pulled himself into the rigging. Hanging there for a moment, Bowyer shouted something, then looked up and began the dangerous climb, the wind streaming his gear out horizontally.

It was madness—but without hesitating Kydd grasped the shrouds, swung himself up and followed.

In a way the darkness isolated him from the fearsome dangers. The wind tore at him, pummeled and shook him, but in his exalted state he was invulnerable. He looked up and saw Bowyer reach the futtock shrouds, then disappear into the main top.

Downward the deck was vanishing into murk. There was just Elkins, who gestured and shouted up at him.

Upward Kydd climbed, gripping the slick black rope firmly. At the futtock shrouds he hesitated—through the despised lubber's hole close to the mast, or hang upside down to get round and onto the main top?

There was no choice for a seaman. For the first time, he worked his way upside down to the edge of the main top. His head and shoulders rose above it, but then he discovered that he didn't know how to get the rest of the way.

The men were gathered in the darkness of the top, waiting for the yard to be laid so they would not be reefing a full drawing sail. Suddenly one caught sight of Kydd, whose face loomed pale against the outer darkness.

"Christ in heaven—it's a ghost!" he screamed.

The others jerked round.

"Tom! What are you doing, mate?" Bowyer leaned over and hoisted him over bodily. He clung to Kydd as though he would tumble away.

A large shadow against the pallid sail resolved itself into the captain of the top pushing across. He stood for a moment clutching at a downhaul, looking into Kydd's face. Bewilderment was succeeded by distrust as he tried to make sense of the intruder. The wind slammed at him and his open seaman's face was puzzled; then his expression changed to acceptance and finally he bawled, "You'll do!"

Kydd turned to Bowyer, who pushed the lee tricing line into his hands, himself taking the weather. Their eyes met—and Bowyer nodded slowly, a deep smile spreading over his whole face.

In the relative shelter on the main deck below the boats, the watch resumed.

"See yer mate is a regular foul weather jack, then, Joe," said one.

Bowyer grunted casually. "Yair—expect to see him out on the yardarm soon, mate."

A vicious squall bullied and blustered at the ship for long minutes; *Duke William* heeled and staggered, then recovered.

"Needs to learn a bit more about th' sea afore he c'n call hisself a sailorman," an older voice continued.

"Ah, leave him be, Nunky."

"No, what I means is, that which you doesn't hear about unless someone gives yer the griff. Ye know what I mean."

"No, I don't, Nunky, what *do* you mean?"

"Ye'll not hear this from any else." The fierce hiss of seas along the hull nearly drowned the words. "'Twas a long time ago, lads, 'n' we needed water bad. Shipped in *Seaflower* we was, on a v'yage to the Spice Islands, and we landed a party ashore to look fer water. Now, I wuz a green hand, thought I knew it all, so when I climbs over this 'ere sand hill, all I thinks about is water. That's when I sees 'em! Seven of 'em! Each one enough to set a sailor's heart afire. Right saucy ladies they wuz. So I sets meself down in the rushes to watch. Then I notices they's passing around this ointment, see, putting it on 'emselves. So I creeps nearer an' nearer, and when they wasn't looking dips me finger into the jar."

A violent clatter from aloft drew attention until the helmsmen let the bows fall away, and the sail filled again.

"Then I rubs it in me eye and, dang me, I gets so surprised I nearly cries out! What I saw then was they were mermaids. Damn me fer a chucklehead—the ointment clears me eyes and I c'n see 'em plain as day. So I creeps away again, goes back aboard 'n' tries to forget. Then we makes Port Anjer an' we steps ashore like. An' what do you think I sees there?"

"What did you see, Nunky?"

"With me eye treated with th' ointment, I sees that the doxies walkin' up and down the street, bold as brass, are really mermaids in their steppin'-ashore disguise. Yessir! Means that any trug you takes on a cruise could be a mermaid—and they'll suck yer soul out, as any sailor knows!" He eased his position.

The younger voice spoke again. "Can yer see 'em now, Nunky? I mean, has yer got the power still?"

"Well, now, this is where I makes me mistake, being young an' all. See, I ends up half cut on this arrack, see, and I thinks as 'ow I'd like to make me respects to the girls. We gets down on the job 'n' while she unrigs, with me eye I sees as 'ow she's a mermaid! 'Be damned,' I says. 'Ye're a mermaid, we'll not swive!' She gets taken right aback, I'm tellin' yer. But then she gets all cunning like, 'n' asks me how I knows. 'With this eye I has, so none o' yer tricks!' I says. But mates, she flew at me like a harpy 'n' with her long nails she douses me glim in one!" He sniffed disconsolately. "When I comes to, there I see this doxy—an' she's jus' yer usual fusty luggs a-grinnin' at me! And that's as 'ow you'll notice I've got no starb'd peeper to this day!"

The morning came with no relief to the foul weather; the sea was an expanse of seething waves, each with a feather of spume on the crest whipped away by the onrushing blast of the gale. It saw *Duke William* diving, shuddering, her bowsprit burying in the white seas ahead before emerging in a broad smash of spray.

Kydd thrilled to the spectacle. He instinctively knew that snugged down under treble-reefed topsails the old battleship was in no real danger, and he set his teeth to the gale. Movement along the deck was hard work. He staggered forward, the deck diving down and down while he tottered on his toes as light as a child, before the irresistible heave up that made him as weighty as a hippo with legs that felt like lead. The spray rattled aboard constantly, striking his tarpaulins like hail and reddening his cheeks, the wind never ceasing its forceful bluster. Encrusted salt made his eyes sting. It was with guilty relief that he went below at midday for the rum issue.

Even in the close coziness of the lower gundeck there was a swash of water, most coming through the hawse bucklers, which were taking the underwater pressure of the bows when they plunged heavily beneath the waves. Lanthorns swung together, sending shadows swaying over the packed messdeck, the strained, tired men and double-breeched guns. Kydd slid into his place at the table and, bracing himself against the surging movements, let the rum spread its cheeriness through his vitals.

"Nor'-westerly like this can go on fer days," Howell muttered, staring at the ship's side.

Claggett glanced up. "An' what else can you expect in Biscay of an Eastertide, Jonas?" he said.

Kydd put down his tankard and turned to Claggett. "So this is y'r storm?" He grabbed for the table edge as a roll turned into an unexpected lurch.

"Not as who would say a storm, mate," Claggett replied. "More of what we'd call a fresh gale, is all." He took another pull at his grog and glanced at Bowyer. "A storm is somethin' that makes yer very 'umble, like—it's when the hooker has ter give up goin' ter where it wants ter go and she lies to, or scuds, only where the storm wants ter send 'er."

Bowyer grimaced softly. "He's right, cuffin. A real blow can be very awesome, makes yer right fearful when yer comes down to it, like." He stared through Kydd. "Comes a time when yer knows that there's a chance that yer might not live—sea jus' tears at the barky like it was an animal, no mercy a-tall. That's when yer remembers yer mother an' yer sins."

Claggett nodded slowly. "It's when yer finds out if yer ship is well found 'n' you can trust yer life to 'er. Or not."

Kydd took another swallow of his rum and listened.

Bowyer stirred uncomfortably. "Fer me, I feels pertic'lar for the merchant jacks in foul weather—ship's gen'rally small 'n' always the crew is less'n it should be, owners being so horse-cockle mean 'n' all. Poor bastards, they might fight fer their lives, but it's for nothing—that size in wild weather they got no chance a-tall."

With a crash from forward and a rumble of gear along the side, *Duke William* rolled before an unseen rogue wave, seawater spurting from the caulking around the lee gunports to add to the swill on deck.

Kydd was no longer a prey to seasickness. He had quickly developed a feel for the ocean's rhythms, and he could sense the shape and timing of the seas that rolled under *Duke William*'s keel, learning how to move with rather than fight against the motion. And after his experiences in the hoy at the Nore he knew enough to be grateful for this. He refused to join in the cruel taunting of those seasick unfortunates in the waist, helpless in their misery.

Pinto arrived with the noon meal. In the absence of a galley fire it was poor stuff—chunks of cheese so hard it needed real effort to carve at it, even with sharp seamen's blades. Kydd's gorge rose when he noticed long red worms squirming at the cut, but raw hunger griped at him.

"Saw bosun at the fore shrouds lookin' wry," Doud said. "Chucks'll have us rackin' at them lee lanyards this afternoon, I guess." He chewed hungrily at his hard tack.

Whaley gave a short laugh. "Seen the weather brace o' the fore topsail? Bin so many times end for end it's naught but shakin's waitin' to be damned!"

"An' the bowsprit gammonin'," Doud added. "Bobstay's loose, 'n' in this blow the spar's workin' somethin' cruel."

Howell's lips curled in a sneer. "Goes ter show, barky is rotten in the riggin' and the deadwork as well. Ship only keeps afloat by the maggots holdin' hands. Be a bloody miracle if we ever makes port agen, I says."

Pumping began at three bells, and Kydd was sent to the chain pump in the second half-hour spell. The massive crank, worked by twenty men, could send the endless chain clattering around vigorously— two tons of water an hour could clear the pump well in a watch.

It was hard work; in the confined space of the lower deck the ro-tating crank handle needed a wide range of movement, the weight of the column of bilge water and the resistance of dozens of leather disks a deadweight to be heaved against in a tedious round of move-ment. The clanking, rattling boredom went on and on, Kydd's back taking the worst of the strain, and it was an intense relief to hear the "Spell-oh!" at the end of his trick. He stretched and stumped up the ladders to rejoin his watch, sure that the blast of wind that met him as he emerged on deck was wilder than before.

"*Haaaands* to shorten sail!"

Bowyer came up, his hair plastered to his skull and water streaming from his tarpaulin cape. He bent forward to shout to Kydd: "We're going ter play safe 'n' close reef topsails, then bend on the fore storm staysail—but none o' yer tricks now, mate, it's too chancy."

The sea was now smoking at its crests, a continuous horizontal sleeting of fine spume covering the surface like a ground mist. The wind held real force, its sound a continuous low roar as it passed through the taut rigging, and Kydd held grimly to the fore and aft rigged lifelines.

The watch gathered forward—the fo'c'sle was a frightening place to be. Ahead, the bowsprit out to the flying jibboom rose skywards as though to spear the racing dark clouds before swooping down to smash into the waves ahead in a violent paroxysm of white. It stayed under for long seconds before rising, streaming water. At times a rampaging comber would thump violently against the weather bow, sending solid water sheeting over the little group, making Kydd gasp afterward at the cruel cold of the wind blasting against his sodden clothing.

Kydd felt a hand on his arm. It was Corrie. "Now yer can see why they calls it the widder-maker," he yelled, pointing at the bowsprit. "Some cove's gotta get out there jus' because they left it late."

"Stir yerself, Corrie!" Bowyer growled. "Yer got work to do."

With lifelines around their waists paid out slowly, the two, with three others, timed their move out onto the gangboard gratings of the bowsprit to the horse, a single footrope dangling in space under the big spar. The bows plunged—the men dropped to the bowsprit and clung. Kydd watched dismayed as white seas closed viciously over them. The onrushing wave then exploded against the beakhead in sheets of spray, which fell heavily on him. By the time he had cleared his eyes the bowsprit was emerging with dark dripping figures still clinging.

In short, hasty jerks the fore topmast staysail came down and was gathered in. Bowyer climbed to the top of the broad spar, his arm around the forestay, fisting the wildly flogging staysail. His eyes, however, did not miss the next wave, which seethed in, leaving his head and shoulders clear. When the wave receded Kydd saw that Bowyer's tarpaulins had been stripped off, hanging loose.

He kicked them away and continued in his shirt. The storm stay-sail was an easier matter. The long cylinder of canvas was passed out and bent on the forestay with beckets, Bowyer's nimble fingers quickly passing the toggles as the canvas mounted the stay.

It was the sharpest sea lesson that Kydd had received yet: only skill, bravery and the ignoring of personal discomfort would give a man any kind of chance in these conditions. Any less and he would be eliminated.

"See that? Lightnin'! We're in for it now, mates!" Corrie was staring out at the Stygian cloud mass to the southwest. Another soundless flash low down on the horizon to leeward, but no thunder, any distant sound impossible to hear against the storm noise.

"No, it ain't, that's gunflash, that is," Doud said.

"Don't talk such flam. Who'd be fightin' a war in this?" Corrie countered.

Bowyer frowned. "Them's distress guns!"

As if in confirmation, *Duke William* eased around and bore away toward. The alteration, of course, had the waves coming in at an awkward angle astern and her movement changed into a nasty cross motion, which soon had some of the hands looking thoughtful.

Low in the water, the merchant ship was in a sorry way. She was a small brig with an old-fashioned look about her. Her foremast had snapped off some eight feet clear of the deck and the entire rigging structure forward was snarled into hopeless ruin on her foredeck. All she could do was scud before the wind under bare poles. A few figures could be made out on her low poop, waving vigorously.

"Guess we must seem as some sort o' miracle," Kydd said to Bowyer. They were sheltering in the half deck, behind the men at the wheel. He pictured *Duke William*, bluff and grand, appearing out of the wildness and making straight for them.

Bowyer stared pensively over and did not reply.

The officer of the watch had his telescope trained on the unfortunate vessel and clicked his tongue. "She's not going to last for much longer unless they can get the water out of her," he said.

"Poor beggars at the pumps are prob'ly beat—or somethin' else," Bowyer said cryptically.

"Mr. Warren!" The Captain's voice came suddenly from behind them. "What's the situation?" The watch politely made room for him under the half deck overhang.

"Merchant brig, sir. Lost her foremast, seems to be taking in water. Can't see more than a few men on deck, could be shorthanded." He raised his telescope again. "Can't see any colors, but she's probably ours."

"Very well. Heave to, if you please, Mr. Warren. Least we can do is make a lee for them." Caldwell's face was set and pitying.

"Then?"

"No, Mr. Warren, no boat can swim in this." He cleared his throat. "I'm sorry. We can do nothing more—they must take their chances."

Kydd could hardly believe his ears. There were human beings, sailors, just a short distance away and they could do nothing?

"Was there when *Montrose* was lost off the Canaries," said the Master, to no one in particular. "Near two hunnerd soldiers there was, with we standing by. Went down in the night, they did. Heard their screams when it was they drowned. Cruel hard it were, we could do nothing for 'em."

Warren turned to the Captain and said urgently, "Sir, if we could come alongside to wind'd of them, and get a line across we—"

"No," Caldwell said flatly. "We drift at different rates, there is danger we would fall foul of each other. I cannot risk this valuable ship in such a venture. We'll stand by them until nightfall but then we must resume our station. That is our duty."

To that there could be no reply.

It was clear that the small ship's end would not be long delayed. She did not rise readily with the waves, which swept her decks like a half-tide rock, each one adding to the deadweight of water in her.

Crippled as she was, there was no way she could achieve any kind of steerage way and she rolled and wallowed at the mercy of the sea, surging and snubbing at some sort of sea-anchor out over her plain stern.

"Beggin' yer pardon, sir," said Bowyer, knuckling his forehead awkwardly.

Caldwell looked around in surprise. "Yes, er, Bowyer, isn't it?"

"Aye, sir. Well, when I was foretopman in *Diana* frigate we had to lie off a sloop in this sorta blow, 'n' we had to get men aboard. An' what we did, sir, was t' stream off a raft to loo'ard, with the men lashed on it." He shuffled his feet. "What I'm a-sayin', sir, is that if you sees your way clear to sendin' a raft, why, I'll be on it, sir."

Caldwell looked at him doubtfully. "That vessel will surely founder soon," he said.

"If we can fish a spar to the stump o' the foremast, we show some steadyin' canvas, fresh men at the pumps, she has a chance, sir."

"It will need more than one man."

Warren stepped forward. "I'll go, sir—give me another three men, and we'll do the job," he said.

Caldwell paused. "You do understand that, if you go, I must leave you to your own resources and return to station. You will have to make rendezvous with me when the weather moderates."

"Understood, sir."

"Then I must ask you now to consider carefully the risks. This is a very dangerous enterprise and may result in the loss of you and your party. You will do well to reconsider."

Warren looked at Bowyer and then at the doomed brig. "We'll go, sir."

CHAPTER 6

THE RAFT WAS COMPLETE: two spare stuns'l booms connected a pair of main hatch gratings, supported by an empty cask at each end. Each man lashed himself on twice, once under the arms and again around the waist. Bowyer himself checked Kydd's lashings, with Doud and Wong attending to themselves.

The boatswain looked dubious as he personally secured the streaming line and attended to the hoisting out of raft and men. It was a vertiginous experience, buffeted by the wind blast while suspended from the main yard tackle, then swaying perilously above the violent seas before dropping toward the maelstrom. Kydd wondered wildly why he had volunteered, but he knew that he would always stand by Bowyer.

They neared the hissing seas and suddenly a large wave shot upward toward them and they were sent spluttering and choking into the sea. Bowyer threw the hooked block clear and they spun crazily until the line paid out by the team on the fo'c'sle took up.

There was little difference at the sea surface between solid water and flying spume, and Kydd choked and swallowed seawater helplessly until he thought to hold his head downwind. The sea felt almost warm in contrast to the wind-chilled air, but it was impossible to see anything of the larger picture. Spreadeagled on the grating, he felt the raft following the shape of the waves exactly; angling steeply up the fore side of the wave coming from behind, becoming briefly buried in its foaming crest before sliding at less of an angle down the other side. It went on insanely, riding the seas like a piece of debris, hurtling up and down on the waves but always on top like a cork and never overcome.

With a jerk the line tautened and Kydd rubbed his eyes to see the bulking mass of the merchant vessel very close. A rope slapped across his back. He grabbed it and found a bowline-on-a-bight already formed at the end, through which he put his head and arms before fumbling at his lashings.

He was pulled up, bumping on the weatherworn old sides as he reached the top, before being hauled in bodily, falling on Doud, who was crawling out of the way.

There were only two men on deck, both in old oilskins. They had gray, exhausted faces and moved slowly. "Lieutenant James Warren, His Majesty's Ship *Duke William*." Warren's words were carried away by the wind.

One of the men gestured to the single companionway in the center of the flush deck, and they descended to a tiny cabin flat. "In here," he said, in a hoarse croak.

They entered the small stern cabin, which was in disorder. "Lost our foremast a day ago, takin' in water fast, and—"

"Yes. Then you are?" Warren broke in.

"Charles Kelsey, master o' the *Lady of Penarth*, five days out o' Barry bound for Lisbon with jute," he said.

"What can we do for you, Captain?" Warren asked.

Exhausted, Kelsey gestured to the other man to speak. "Took your damn time coming, didn't you?" the man said bitterly.

"Sir?" Warren's jaw took a hard line.

"All the same, you King's men, always—"

"That's enough, Mr. Scully!" the older man said sharply. He

turned to Warren. "We've had a hard time of it since we lost the foremast. Please forgive the mate his manners." He glared at Scully and resumed, his voice strengthening. "We're shorthanded, you understand. Main need right now is help at the pumps."

Warren nodded at Bowyer, who touched his forehead. Scully grudgingly led the way. The pump was abaft the main hatch on the upper deck, slightly protected from the storm blast by a weather cloth spread in the shrouds, but open to the green seas, which regularly poured over the bow. Scully stumped off.

A single seaman was at the pump, which was much like a village pump with a handle to work up and down. The man swung listlessly at his task. No water emerged from the standpipe.

Bowyer took it in with a glance. "Rose box in the bilges is choked," he said. "Show me, would you, mate?" he said to the man.

There was no answer. The man went on pumping mechanically, up and down.

"Chum, we need to find the pump well," Bowyer said more loudly. He pulled the man clear, but the sailor stared about him in bewilderment. His hands remained extended, claw-like.

"The pump box, mate!"

They reeled off forward into the sleeting spray and down a companionway.

When Bowyer returned his face was grim. "Cleared it usin' the limber chain, so you can get started. Tom goes first, Ned spells 'im in an hour."

He glanced aft. "No use expectin' help—they're all below, betwaddled to the gills an' right out've it. They left their mate to do all the pumpin'."

Doud shrugged. "If you have ter go, not a bad way, is it? Yer wouldn't know anythin' about it."

Bowyer's look was scathing. "That's as may be. Better ter go down fightin' is my way." He looked at the tangle of splintered wreckage forward and flexed his arms. "Let's be started—we gotta get sail on 'er afore dark."

Kydd saw *Duke William* sail off into the smoking seas, disappearing into the white murk and leaving them on their own.

It was not until after night had closed in on the struggling vessel that the fore topsail yard had been seized upright to the stump of the foremast, and stayed to the empty fore-chains. By the wildly jerking light of three lanthorns the storm jib was hoisted as a trysail. It held, and with the mainsail a goosewing there was balance at last. Not only that, but a semblance of control was possible, for with the course braced up sharp and the jury trysail taut and drawing, it was possible for the ship to lie to, taking the seas regularly on the shoulder of her bow. The waves ceased to flood the decks and there was a noticeable increase of liveliness in response, helped by the steady pumping that was clearing the deadweight of water from within her.

In a huddle under the bulwarks, Warren gave his orders. They would be divided into larboard and starboard deck watches in the usual way, Bowyer and Kydd in the larbowlines and on for the first watch. Warren himself would stand both watches while the master and mate recovered from their exhaustion. "And listen to what I say now," Warren said, looking at them grimly. "The hold is not to be entered. I will take it as a serious breach of discipline if it is." They stared at him. "I have given my word to the master that this will be so, and any man that makes me break my word will rue it. No doubt you'll discover in any event, this vessel carries a cargo of bonded whisky under the jute."

Doud caught Kydd's eye. Warren noticed and continued, "Therefore any man who is found in the hold will instantly earn himself at the least a striped back. Do I make myself clear?"

Bowyer nodded, and the others conformed.

He broke into a smile. "Well done, men, I'll see that your efforts are properly brought to attention when we rejoin *Duke William*. Larb'd watch, turn to, the rest, try to get your head down in the forrard cuddy."

"Aye, sir. Any chance of some clacker?" Bowyer asked.

During the night the gale was fading and the *Lady of Penarth* was swooping energetically, glad to be spared. Even before the weak sun tentatively appeared above the horizon the master emerged from the companionway. He shuffled forward to check the jury rig, then went below without a word.

"Haven't seen Hellfire Jack on deck this morning a-tall," Doud said.

"As long as he sends up breakfast I'm sharp set!" said Kydd, patting his stomach. He was sitting on deck next to Bowyer.

Wong didn't say anything, but continued to whittle at a piece of white bone with a small but sharp blade.

"Often wonder what goes through that heathen's headpiece a-times, I really do," Doud said. "Never a sound—you'd think 'e pays for talkin' by the word! That right, Wong?"

The dark eyes lifted; the careful knifework suspended momentarily. "What to say?" Wong said, in his curious voice, then resumed carving.

"Where do yer come from?" Doud asked.

Wong laid down his work with a sigh. "China, Kwangchow south part," he said.

"What's yer dad do?"

"Dead."

"Sorry to hear that, Wongy, didn't know."

"Not sorry—he no good." He picked up his scrimshaw and carried on with it.

The freshness of the dawn seemed unwelcome to the men below, who stumbled bleary-eyed on deck, scruffy and seedy. The Navy men stared. They were a sorry-looking crew—dirty, scrofulous and scrawny. They resembled wharf rats more than sailors.

"If they're seamen then I'm a Dutchman," said Doud.

"'Oo in 'ell are you?" one said, looking a-squint at Doud.

"They got strange rats aboard this hooker," said Doud to Kydd. "They're speakin'."

"Yes—t' look at 'em they must've just come topsides for a breather straight fr'm the bilges," Kydd replied.

Doud regarded them dispassionately. "Strange, that. Always thought rats left a sinkin' ship. This lot seems to have left it a bit late fer that."

The first man advanced, ingratiating, shifting his battered tricorne hat from hand to hand. "Now look'ee here, me name's Yates—deck 'ands, we is. Where d'ye come from, I asks yer?"

Kydd replied, "We're from *Duke William*—King's ship. Saw y' distress guns and—"

"And we saved yer skins, is what 'e's a-sayin' of," Doud continued, his contempt plain.

The contrast could hardly be more obvious: Doud, a prime man-o'-war's man, strong and confident in his blue shirt and white trousers, and these three, in ragged shore clothes and repulsively unclean.

"We're thankful, t'be sure," Yates said, wheedling, looking from one to the other and furtively licking his lips.

"No bloody wonder the barky clewed up in trouble if they only 'ad these fer crew," Doud said contemptuously. He remembered Warren's threat. "Hey, you, what's this that yer carries a fat cargo o' whisky?" he said.

There was a defensive hesitation. "Ah—that's right, we 'as a load."

Doud winked at Kydd. "That's all I want ter know," he said.

• • •

The deckhands were as useless in practice as their appearance suggested when a yard was crossed on the jury mast.

"Prime!" said Bowyer, easing his back gratefully. "Now we'll stretch a bit o' square canvas an' we'll be able to set a course." It was a great satisfaction to ease carefully around and start riding the rollers eastward, heading for the noon rendezvous position that *Duke William*'s master had written out for Warren.

A change was evident also in Kelsey, who now paced the deck with a confidence that put a spring in his step. He stopped at where the Navy men were working at the foremast. "You men, I have to thank you for your work," he told them. "But for that we surely would not have survived." Nothing was said, but each found some task needing extra concentration. "I'd just have to say . . ." he went on, but hesitated. "God bless you."

"Well, Ned mate, should be back aboard soon," Kydd said to Doud that afternoon.

Doud was trying to put a whipping on a ragged brace end. "An' none too soon, mate. Never seen such a rat's nest—all twice-laid stuff, canvas yer can see through. This hooker's fer the knacker's yard it seems to me." He pursed his lips in disgust. "Missin' me tot, and that's the truth. You'd think that with a clinking great cargo o' liquor they'd could stove one in b' accident, after what we done fer them."

He glanced about, then leaned forward. "So, Tom, me old mate, when you has the watch tonight, you may see a little rabbit pop down the fore hatch, which in course yer won't notice." He allowed Kydd to glimpse a sizable gimlet in his pocket.

"I got a thirst on'll stun an ox—but I'll not ferget me friends." He grinned and continued at his work.

At dusk, Bowyer was at the wheel and Kydd on deck with him. Warren had gone below for supper with Kelsey, those off watch were in the cuddy for their supper and all was peaceful.

A figure appeared at the break of the fo'c'sle. Bowyer grunted, but Kydd smiled and whispered, "Ned going after a wet."

"Yer mean—"

"He's goin' to tap off some whisky," Kydd said.

"That's broachin' cargo—a hangin' matter," Bowyer growled.

Kydd's smile faded. "Says they're an ungrateful crew, not seein' us right after riskin' our lives, and so he's goin' t' even things up!"

"Still no reason ter break into cargo—Warren finds out, 'e's a gone goose. An' we're 'avin' no part of it—are we?" He looked straight at Kydd.

"You're in the right of it, Joe," Kydd admitted. "Ned's a bit too forward for his own good a-times."

Doud silently dropped out of sight down the hooded companionway to the hold.

Darkness clamped in, but an unexpected moon broke through the scurrying clouds for the first time, accentuating the whiteness of the foam crests and glittering in the inky troughs. It was strange to have the seas so close, a few feet away after *Duke William*'s thirty or more.

Doud cautiously emerged on deck, but instead of returning to the cuddy he hurried aft toward them.

"Ned?"

"Yes, mate."

"Well?"

"Well, I stand well flammed. In truth, I didn't catch so much as a whiff o' whisky, so help me."

Lieutenant Warren's appearance on deck put an end to the conversation. He peered at the binnacle and up at the vigorously drawing single sail, then concluded with a cautious pace around the decks. "Quiet watch?" he asked.

"Aye, sir," Bowyer answered stolidly.

"Should be up with *Duke William* at noon tomorrow," Warren said.

"Sir." Bowyer was not given to idle chat with officers.

"Notice anything unusual, Bowyer? Master seems uneasy about something."

"No, sir."

"Very well. You'll be relieved at midnight. Any worries, I'll be below. Goodnight."

With a last sniff at the weather he left.

"Good hand, is he," Doud said. "Others would have us squarin' off all the time, 'n' on our knees on deck and such. Hope he gets his step—deserves better'n the *Royal Billy.*"

"Why didn't you get y'r taste o' whisky?" Kydd asked.

"Well, that's the damnedest thing. I tapped three kegs, 'n' they were all full right enough—wi' sand!"

"You went to the right ones?"

"O' course! If I can't tell a cask o' spirits by the feel, I been wastin' me time ashore."

"Maybe some was carried as a ballast?"

"Nah—I was careful to choose three separate ones. The whole lot'll have to be the same."

They lapsed into silence. Forward the jury rig creaked constantly as it worked with the ship's roll.

"Makes no sense. If the Cap'n wanted ter bam the merchant by landin' the spirits fer his own 'n' switchin' sand in place of it, you'd think that 'e'd be smoked at t'other end."

Bowyer frowned as he braced at the wheel. Kydd perceived his disquiet at the way things were developing.

"Whoever does get his 'ands on two 'undred barrels o' whisky is goin' to end up with a pile o' guineas yer couldn't jump over." Doud unconsciously licked his lips.

"Doesn't explain th' sand," Kydd said.

There was a murmur from Bowyer.

"What was that, Joe?"

"Well, mean ter say—"

"Come on, spit it out, mate!" Doud urged.

"Er, don't like ter say it, but there is *one* reason I c'n think of."

"Yeah?"

Bowyer looked intently at the weather leech of the mainsail. "Could be this is a coffin ship, mates."

"It—what?" Kydd said.

"Not sayin' as it is, but there's them a'longshore who would send sailors to sea in a barky that ain't meant to make port. Then they collects on the ing-surance when she don't arrive."

"The sand?" Doud challenged.

"Yer can't see it? Whoever sets it up gets valuable whisky on the ship's papers so 'e can claim fer it as well, but 'e lands it for 'imself and loads aboard—"

Doud nodded. "Yeah, got a feelin' yer could be right. Stands ter reason."

Kydd shivered. The moonlit sea had somehow lost its exuberance.

"Poor buggers. But fer us they'd be shakin' hands with Davy Jones himself b' now."

Bowyer looked sorrowfully at Doud. "You are a simpleton, Ned, me old shipmate. Now think on this—they can't risk the barky makin' port, not with them kegs o' sand, they got ter make sure."

Nobody spoke. "They have ter be sure she goes to the bottom, 'n' that means that the skipper must be in on it. It's him what knows what's in the papers, nobody else."

Kydd couldn't believe that the tired old man would commit such cold-blooded murder. "But he'd go down as well—you saw how rough it was!"

"No, Tom, that there blow was not in the plan, no one could get away in a boat in that. What he needs ter do later is one night stove in the bottom, or somethin', and make off with the only boat. No witnesses, see?"

Doud whistled. "Then we need to tell Warren quick-smart—he'll know what to do."

"So who went down into the hold to find this sand? Agin his strict orders? You?"

The odd-looking sail forward shivered and flapped until Bowyer realized and paid off a spoke or two at the helm.

"Damn it, we have t' do something," Kydd shouted.

"What did ye say?" It was Scully, emerging from the after hatchway. He moved up and stood before them, legs apart and thumbs in his belt. "So all the King's men are on deck, are they? What's yer trouble, then—vittles not to yer liking? Or should I tickle yer with a rope's end ter make yer feel at home?" The moonlight threw his face into strong contrast.

Doud started up, but seemed to remember something and subsided.

"Take the hellum, Ned," Bowyer said, and handed over the wheel to a puzzled Doud before confronting Scully. "Now, Mr. Scully—sir. We found out somethin' about yer vessel, and we're vexed to know how ter handle it."

Scully tensed. "Yeah?"

"Well, it's like this. We know yer shipped a cargo o' whisky, 'n'—well, let me put it this a-way." He scratched his head to find the words. "Seems it ain't all it seems. See, we checked up on it, bored a little hole, like, 'n' all there was was sand. No spirits, jus' sand."

Scully stepped back. "Yer found just sand?" he said, in a dangerous voice.

Bowyer shrugged. "So I hates to inform yer—but it seems a good chance that yer cap'n is goin' to scuttle the barky 'n' claim the ing-surance."

"Who have yer told?" said Scully, after a moment's pause.

"Well, this is our difficulty, see. Our officer told us he'd stripe our backs if we entered the hold, so yez understands, we can't really tell him, like."

Scully's eyes flickered. "Yer did right to tell me, boys. Comes as a bit of a shock, our own skipper 'n' all. Don't you worry, cully, I'll tell yer officer as it was me who found out." He hesitated. "Yer did well, lads. I'll go 'n' tell 'im now, don't you worry."

They waited until Scully passed below.

"We keeps the deck, watch 'n' watch," Bowyer said firmly. "Ned, you go 'n' rouse up Wong 'n' tell him to lay aft here with us. Nobody's goin' to touch that boat."

Doud added, "Fer once in me life I'm right pleased to 'ave an officer in th' offing."

It was Doud on the wheel when dawn broke; a clear, bracing dawn that saw the white-capped seas hurrying toward them under the strong breeze—exhilarating sailing weather.

"Well, I own I'm at a stand as to why Warren didn't come up ter see us—not like him at all." Doud's frown deepened.

Bowyer opened an eye and considered. "Maybe he's been gettin' his swede down—he did put in double tides yesterday. I'll go below 'n' give him a shake, it bein' dawn an' all."

Kydd stretched his aching limbs. He was not yet able to snatch sleep wherever he was like the other seamen and his muzzy mind needed prodding into life.

Bowyer returned looking grave. "He's not in his cabin."

Doud looked at him. "Got to be—'ave you seen in the master's cabin?"

"Yeah. Nobody seen 'im since last night. I'm gettin' Mr. Scully."

The mate came on deck promptly. "What's the trouble?"

"Can't seem to find Mr. Warren," Bowyer said.

Scully frowned. "Seemed fine last night—told him o' yer worries and he said he'd wait till first light an' investigate. Didn't seem fazed at all, he didn't, just went back ter sleep."

"Hadn't we better go look fer him?" said Doud.

There was no very great number of places that would need searching in the small merchant ship, and it was not long before Scully came back with his men.

"Can't find him," he said, watching for reaction.

"Yer can't find 'im?" Bowyer was incredulous. "A barky this big 'n' yer can't find 'im? 'E 'as to be somewhere!"

"No. We looked all over—'e ain't aboard." He took on a set, dogged expression. The deckhands stood behind him, expressionless.

Bowyer glanced at the others. He spoke deliberately. "I think as how this c'n only be yer skipper. He knows Mr. Warren's been tipped off and is goin' to investigate this mornin', 'n' he thinks to get in first."

"Them's serious words," the mate answered. "You're saying as 'ow our cap'n is a murtherer!"

"Can't help it," Bowyer said gravely. "What do you think? 'E's the only one keeps the ship's papers, that right?"

"That's right," Scully said reluctantly.

"An' 'e's the one who sets the course 'n' that—knows just where we're bound."

"Yes."

"And last you saw of 'im last night was when he was a-restin', not to be disturbed, I hear?"

"Well, yes."

"We've been on deck all night, so it's got ter be 'im."

Scully considered this. "What you're sayin' is that I should take some sorta action."

This time it was Bowyer who waited silently.

"Right, then—I will. There's no sleep fer anyone until I do. I'm goin' to take him in charge, suspicion o' murther!"

"Don't like this, mates!" Doud said, after Scully had left the deck. "Don't like it a-tall. Not right, takin' a ship from the Cap'n like that."

"What else can he do?" Bowyer replied. "He's right—none of us is goin' to get much sleep until he's in bilboes or somethin'."

Kydd felt uneasy. "What I don't get is how Kelsey sent Mr.

Warren over th' side without our hearin' it."

Doud answered in a low voice. "What I reckon, Tom, is that 'e thwacked Mr. Warren on the noggin from behind, 'n' launched 'im out o' the stern windows, like."

"It's over now, lads," said Bowyer, "and 'ere's Mr. Scully."

Scully returned, with a satisfied look. "Right we are, mateys. 'E's lashed to a chair in 'is cabin and'll give us no more grief." He stood astride and folded his arms. "We owes you a lot, you boys. Least we can do for yer is to stand yer watches. You get yer heads down and leave 'er to us."

Bowyer cocked his head. "Shouldn't we be comin' up with *Duke William* soon?"

Scully seemed evasive. "Well—yeah, we're gettin' to the rendez-vous position, but don't forget, it's fer noon, so we has to stand off 'n' on until she comes up. Anyways, you're all free o' work—ye're passengers."

It seemed natural to go forward to the fo'c'sle, where they arranged themselves to avoid the occasional spray bursts over the bow and took advantage of the tentative warmth of the morning sun. The sea was sparkling now, cheerful and exuberant, a royal blue in place of the previous gray, and with the seas coming from astern it was a comfortable lift, a heartbeat's pause and then a gentle curtsy down.

Wong drew out his scrimshaw and began plying the blade. It was turning out to be a lissome naked Oriental girl, lying full length and seductively propped up on her elbow. Doud lay down and closed his eyes, while Bowyer took a length of line and began to instruct Kydd on the more arcane bends and hitches.

The morning wore on. It felt odd to have no duties but, then, it seemed neither did the crew, who appeared to be taking it easy aft with Scully.

"Wonder who they think is goin' to set this hooker to rights for 'em?" Bowyer mused. "Won't be *Duke William*—we done our bit. Strange."

Kydd finished a carrick bend with his eyes obediently closed. In the dark of night there would be no convenient lights nearby. "That right, Joe?" he asked.

"She's right, Tom. It'll do fer now, mate."

Stretching, Kydd turned to Bowyer. "Joe, we've got the Captain under key in his cabin, but even a poxy thief gets a chance to say his piece. What say we hear him out?"

Bowyer looked down. "Yes, mate, it sits a bit awkward with me as well. Why don't you nip below 'n' see what the bugger 'as to say for 'imself?"

Down the single companionway Kydd turned aft to enter the stern cabin.

"Yes, mate?"

It was Yates the deckhand, getting to his feet outside the door to the cabin. It was obvious he had been placed there.

Kydd was reluctant to tell Yates his reasons. "Mr. Scully here?" he asked.

"Er, yer might say yes. 'E's sleepin' in 'is cabin right now." Kydd hesitated. "But 'e won't thank ye for interruptin'—he's put away two bottles this forenoon."

"Thanks, mate, it can wait." Kydd clattered back up the ladder and hurried back to Bowyer.

"Seems to me they did the right thing to guard 'im, 'e bein' a murderer an' all," Bowyer said.

Kydd stood his ground. "I want t' hear Kelsey without there's anyone else about," he said.

Bowyer smiled. "An' how are you goin' to do that? Gettin' past Yates, I mean."

"You sway me down on a line over the transom an' I get in through th' stern windows," Kydd said promptly.

The smile disappeared. "That's a risky business, cuffin. Is 'e worth it?"

"Let's go," Kydd said impatiently. They strolled to the poop as if on a pleasant walk. Only the man at the helm was on deck and he was facing forward.

Bowyer found a topping lift fall and used the end with a bowline as a stirrup to lower Kydd over the low sternwork. It was easy. One window was already open, and as he swung over he hooked his feet inside and Bowyer lowered him in.

The master was sitting lashed in his chair, gagged and with his chin on his chest. He looked up in astonishment as Kydd approached and loosened the rag. "Rogues!" he shouted. "Damned scurvy rascals!"

Kydd clamped a hand over Kelsey's mouth but it was too late. A rattling of keys in the lock showed Yates was investigating.

"Er—into the side locker!" Kelsey said urgently, nodding toward the long built-in seat at the side of the cabin.

Kydd opened it and tumbled in, remembering to lower the lid quietly. It was stuffy and damp in the locker, odorous with the musty stink of age-old tarpaulins.

"Yes, I'm talking about you, Yates!" Kydd could hear Kelsey plainly. "Take my ship away from me like this—I know your lay, Yates, you and Scully both."

A meaty smack sounded. "Clap a stopper on it, old man. You don't give no orders any more."

"You'll regret this!"

"Save yer breath, cully, yer'll need it later. 'Ere, this'll stop yer yattering!"

There was no sound for a short while and then the door slammed. Kydd waited for a little while, then climbed out. Once more he loosened the cloth gag. Bending close, he said quietly, "Is it right the ship's goin' to be done away with for th' insurance?"

Kelsey started, and stared at Kydd. "Not by me!" he said bitterly. "Open that drawer—you'll see a letter from my wife in Lisbon expecting to meet me there."

Kydd found the letter, which confirmed Kelsey's story. "Is it true that you're the only one touchin' the ship's papers?" Kydd asked him.

"Yes, that's right enough. But you should know that in the merchant service it's the mate that's responsible for stowing the hold. He can stow what he likes there and nobody would be the wiser. And about Mr. Warren—I'm sorry to hear of it, and all I can say is it wasn't me did for him, but you'll admit I'd be damn foolish to risk you men on my neck if I'd already made up my mind to scuttle."

Kydd nodded. At the window he signaled to Bowyer to lower the line, and stepped in the bowline stirrup. It was only a short distance up the transom and he quickly clambered back on to the poop.

At that moment Scully emerged from the companionway. "What in hell?" he shouted. Striding over, he confronted them.

"You've been talkin' with Kelsey! You're in it with him!"

Bowyer looked at Kydd, who said, "Yes, cully, I've been talkin'— and got quite a different yarn to yours."

Bowyer stared and Doud stood up. "What do yer mean, mate?" he asked.

"I saw a letter proves he meant to make Lisbon—and it's always the mate who stows the hold."

Scully bit his lip. "Yates!" he bawled. "Get the others and get up here!" He pulled a small pistol from his pocket and cocked it with his left hand. "Don't any of yer move!"

Doud edged away to the shrouds as though in fear of the pistol while Bowyer still held Kydd's bowline and stared into Scully's eyes.

Kydd knew what he must do. "Bilge rat!" he yelled, and launched himself at Scully. The pistol swept round but Bowyer whipped his rope back, pulling Scully into its bight and off balance. Simultaneously Wong leaped forward and head-butted Scully, who went down with a gasp, the pistol discharging harmlessly over the sea.

It was no contest. Wong quickly pinioned Scully, who flopped helpless in his grasp.

"Joe!" warned Kydd. Up the companionway had come Yates and others, who took the situation in with a glance.

Yates produced a knife—not a seaman's blade but a short curved weapon. The other men closed about him and it was plain that no quarter would be shown or asked. Other knives appeared.

The Navy men fell back while Yates moved forward, stopping at the mainmast bitts with its maze of ropes coming down and belayed around the pins on the frame.

With their backs to the bitts, Doud and Bowyer silently reached behind and each eased up a belaying pin, then both brought them forward and smacked them suggestively across their palms.

"You comin', then?" said Doud to Yates, who now faltered, and looked at the others for support.

It was all Doud needed. Like lightning his hand flicked up his belaying pin, which spun crisply through the air and at Yates's head. Yates screamed and clutched at his bloody face while the others turned and fled.

The man at the wheel was terrified but took no part in the fight, keeping the ship steadily on course in the same dogged way he had faithfully pumped.

It was a matter of moments to round up the others and free the master, who hurried on deck to confront his mate.

"We're not going to get much outa Scully," said Doud. He looked around. "Wong, me old shipmate, I think this 'ere Yates could do with a bath, don't you?"

Wong nodded. He dragged Yates to the ship's side, where the sea foamed a few feet down. In one casual move he bent, and seized Yates's ankles and hurled him over the side, then left him suspended upside down inches above the waves.

Yates struggled and shouted, but Wong effortlessly held on to his skinny frame. Then he let the man descend. Yates saw the sea come closer and wriggled frantically, but his head dipped under.

Wong waited until he saw bubbles, then hoisted him back up. Yates panted and spluttered. Again Wong slowly let him descend. The struggles became frenzied. When the bubbles came again Wong set him roughly on deck and folded his arms.

It all spilled out: Scully had made an arrangement with the owners of the vessel unknown to the master whereby he and his four accomplices would sink the ship, then take to the only boat, ensuring there would be no witnesses. It was barratry, an insurance swindle, and would have succeeded but for the storm. The men lost no time in damning Scully as the man who had killed Warren, and also revealed that he had planned to complete the deed that night by eliminating those remaining.

The master breathed in deeply and took control. "I'll fix our position and have you aboard your ship as soon as I can."

CHAPTER 7

THREE DAYS LATER, back aboard *Duke William,* Kydd and Bowyer were with the starboard watch up on the topsail yard, shaking out a reef. In the maintop sailors swore heartily when the inexperienced officer of the watch let the ship come into the wind. Ponderously, the seventy-five-foot yard swung as the wind caught the sail momentarily aback, then more sharply swayed it back—to bring up hard against the braces.

One moment Kydd was standing watching for orders, the next he heard a brief cry and turned to see a gap where Bowyer had been shortly before. He stared down and saw men hurrying over to a still form, face down and at a distorted angle. For a moment he was stunned. Then, in a rising storm of feelings he shouted, shrieked—and flew down the shrouds.

A small crowd had gathered around Bowyer. Kydd thrust past, distraught at the spreading dark wet stain beneath. Gently he pulled Bowyer around to face upward. His eyes were closed and he was very pale, blood issuing from his nose and ears. His breathing was unnatural; harsh and stertorous.

"Where's the doctor?" Kydd's hoarse cry rose above the hushed voices. He cradled the barely breathing Bowyer, feeling the warmth seeping from his body.

"Stand clear—what happened?" the surgeon asked breathlessly.

"Fall from the yard," said an officer, arriving from the quarterdeck.

The surgeon dropped to his knees and felt for a pulse, his eyes passing briefly over the inert body. He rolled back an eyelid. Holding a small silver mirror to Bowyer's lips, he inspected the result. "He lives yet, but I'll not be sanguine about the outcome." He straightened and looked around.

In the shocked silence nobody moved.

"Broken bones bear on his brain—it must be relieved. Tie him to a grating and take him below to the cockpit."

The main hatch grating, which had so often seen the blood of floggings, was now smeared with the bright red of Bowyer's life-blood. There was no lack of men to help Kydd carry it below.

In the center of the noisome gloom of the cockpit Bowyer was placed on a table. Lanthorns could only provide their usual dim light, leaving much of the scene in shadow. The loblolly boys, broken-down men who were fit for no other work, stretched out Bowyer's limbs, tying them to stanchions. Then they stood back and waited for the surgeon to return with his chest.

Suddenly Bowyer's back arched and with a loud, tearing groan his body strained in a terrible convulsion. Kydd threw himself at his friend and tried to force him down. "F'r God's sake, help me!" he screamed at the loblollies, who were standing well back in the shadows.

They remained still, one rhythmically chewing tobacco.

"Help, for Chrissake!" Kydd sobbed. The body was rigid and contorted in a grotesque upward spasm. His efforts to press the spine down were hopelessly ineffective.

There was a movement in the lanthorn glow and the surgeon was at his side.

Kydd gasped with relief. "He—he's—" he tried to say.

"Opisthotonos," the man muttered.

Kydd stared at him.

"Not unusual in these cases—leave him, it'll pass." He casually up-ended a green bottle, wiped his mouth and replaced the bottle in the capacious side pocket of his black coat.

Kydd reluctantly let go of his friend and hovered next to the convulsed body, unsure and cold with horror.

The surgeon pulled at Kydd's jacket and said testily, "Be so good as to let me get on with it, will you?"

Kydd stepped back and watched as the surgeon rummaged in his chest, bringing out some steel instruments, which he laid on a small collapsible table next to Bowyer's head. The convulsion passed and Bowyer sank down.

The surgeon went to Bowyer's head and addressed himself to the task. A razor was flourished, and Bowyer's head was shaved around the seeping blood, leaving a monk-like tonsure.

"More light, you oaf!" he growled at the taller loblolly, who obediently held two lanthorns each side of Bowyer's head.

The surgeon felt the skull all over, then picked up a scalpel and, stretching the scalp with one hand, drew the blade smartly across in a three-inch incision. He made a similar cut at right angles at one end of the first incision, then peeled the scalp away in a triangle.

The sickly white of living, gleaming bone was clear in the close lanthorn light. The surgeon bent nearer and traced the long depressed fracture to where it continued under the scalp. Another incision and the whole was exposed. "Mmm, we have a chance, possibly," he muttered. He lifted a complex instrument. "Basson's patent trephine," he said, with pride. Carefully he felt around the floating skull plates until he found a sound area, then applied the instrument and set to work.

In the breathless silence the tiny bone-cutting sounds grated unbearably. Kydd looked away at the loblolly boys, who watched the operation stolidly. The men who had helped him carry Bowyer down retreated farther and Kydd caught the gleam of a tilted bottle. The lanthorns gave off a hot oily smell.

A young midshipman from their nearby berth lingered, fascinated, and glanced up at Kydd with a twisted grin.

The surgeon exchanged his trephine for another instrument and inserted it in the skull cavity. Kydd let his gaze drop to the wound and saw Bowyer's brain tissue, blood dripping slowly in small threads down the side of his face and to the deck. He could not control the sudden heaves—he staggered and held desperately to a deck stanchion. The surgeon straightened and glared at Kydd. "If ye're going to cast your accounts now, kindly do it somewhere else."

Kydd stumbled blindly toward the other men.

"Well, I hold myself in some amazement; he still breathes," the surgeon said later, waving away the lanthorns and stretching. He wiped his hands on his bloody apron, which he tossed to the loblolly boy, and took a long pull at his bottle. "You may have him," he said shortly. "The loblollies will attend in course." He disappeared into his cabin.

Kydd let out his breath. It was a waking nightmare, the blood-bespattered head all bandaged, the eyes receding into dark sockets.

They took Bowyer to the bay, the extreme fore part of the middle gundeck where the bows came to a point, and laid him down in a swinging cot, next to where the root of the mighty bowsprit reared outward.

One of the loblollies stayed, his tobacco chewing never ceasing.

His eyes dull with grief, Kydd sat with his friend. The hours passed; he willed with all his heart for some indication that the world had been set to rights again—for the eyes to flicker open, that slow smile—but there was only stillness and the hypnotic cycle of the rise and fall of the chest, a long moment of waiting, then another.

Kydd got up and stretched. There was no change; he would take a short break.

He returned to see the loblolly boy bent over Bowyer, working feverishly at the body. Kydd ran forward, guilt-ridden at having been absent. He realized that the loblolly boy had been at work on Bowyer's finger, trying to pull off the worn ring. Kydd wrenched him around and pinioned him against the fore bulkhead.

A crowd quickly gathered at the commotion.

The loblolly's eyes shifted. "But 'e'll not need that where 'e's goin'!" he whined.

Kydd smashed his fist into the man's face and drew back his arm for another blow, but felt his arms seized from behind. "Don't do 'im, mate—'e's not worth a floggin'!" someone cried.

Kydd fell back and the loblolly fled.

At three bells Bowyer gave a muffled groan and writhed in a weak spasm. Kydd lurched to his feet and held him down until it passed.

The vigil continued and Kydd's hold on reality drifted. Shadows appeared, offering him grog, food. His messmates came in ones and twos; an awkward word, a hand clapped on the shoulder, understanding. Bowyer's breathing was now almost imperceptible.

Exhaustion made Kydd's eyes heavy and his head jerked as he fought to keep awake. In this half-world of existence there was a merciful sense of detachment, a disconnection from events. Toward the end of the last dog-watch his mind registered a change . . . that there was now no movement at all. Bowyer's appearance was quite unaltered, except that he no longer breathed.

His best friend was dead.

"Rum do, Joe gettin' 'is like that," said Doud.

"Not 's if he were a raw hand—never seen such a right old shellback as 'e," Whaley mused.

Pinto leaned across the table, his liquid brown eyes serious. "You joke—but we say, when the Holy Mother want someone, she call, you come."

From the end of the table Claggett coughed in a noncommittal way and called them to attention. "Joe had no folks." The statement was bald, but downcast looks showed that the implications were clear. "He was one o' the Hanway boys, he were never one fer the 'longshore life." He glanced around. The shoddy purser's glim guttered. This time there were no sardonic words about the smell. "I'd say that Tom Kydd is as close as any to Joe," Claggett said.

"Where's he now, poor mucker?" someone asked.

"Saw him a whiles ago up forrard on the fo'c'sle," said Howell. "At the weather cathead," he added significantly.

"Doesn't someone go 'n' see if we can help?" said Doud.

Whaley hesitated. "Did go meself, Ned, but he wants to be on his own."

"Best to leave him so, I guess," said Claggett. "He'll get over it betimes."

Kydd was not alone, there on the fo'c'sle in the wind and thin rain. In his befuddled brain he felt a fierce and uncaring joy in the hard bulk of the bottle that lay hidden, nestling next to his heart. Phelps could always be relied on where rum was concerned.

In the gloom of the night the fore lookouts kept out of the way and no one else was foolish enough to wallow in the chill misery of wind and rain. Kydd took another drink from his secret store. It helped, but only if he didn't think. The trouble was there was no answer. Only blind fate. He took another swig. It burned as it spread into his vitals.

For some reason he found himself sitting on deck with his back to the carronade, looking up with owlish eyes at the huge pale span of the foresail. Strange that. There should only be one foreyard;

another seemed to be floating nearby. He leaned back to get a better view and toppled over. He struggled to sit upright again and fixed his eyes on the rain-black bitts to steady himself.

"Poor sod!" the larboard fo'c'sle lookout muttered to the other, jerking his head at the sodden, lonely figure. Neither could desert their posts—and that meant the result was inevitable. In a short while the Master-at-Arms with his corporals would be doing his rounds and would discover the poor wight. Then it would be irons overnight and the cat in the morning—at sea they were merciless when it came to a member of the fighting crew becoming useless from drink when at any time the enemy could loom up out of the night with all guns blazing. He'd be lucky to get away with just a dozen.

The lookout turned back to resume his stare out into the night.

The bottle tilted again. Bowyer had no right to leave him like this—he'd taken his advice and was well on the way to becoming a sailor. And now he had to sort it out for himself. It wasn't fair. Unlike many of the pressed men, Kydd had found a friend. In Bowyer, he'd had someone who could take this hellish world and make sense of it, put it in perspective for him. Give him purpose, a future, and be there when needed. Kydd's face contorted.

A figure emerged from the fore hatch, indistinct in the gloom. It hesitated, then came across and stood over him. Renzi looked down, with pity and revulsion in his expression. Blind sentiment played no part in Renzi's character—Kydd must take his chances along the road he himself had chosen. In his own past he had seen too many like him, worse in fact, for those with the wealth to do it could go to hell in their own way. Renzi moved away—but something made him return. He looked down again. Kydd returned the look with drunken resentment and Renzi swore harshly, for he knew he could not abandon him. Not when the man bore the uncanny resemblance that had haunted Renzi since Kydd first came aboard.

He jerked Kydd to his feet, tore the bottle from his grasp and hurled it into the night.

"Wha—how dar' you, s-sir!" Kydd spluttered, trying to dislodge the grip clamped on his collar. Somehow his feet found the deck and he wriggled free.

Renzi regarded him grimly.

Kydd bristled. "You never l-liked Joe," he said. "You don' like anybody, you slivey bast'd!"

Renzi had deep reasons for his detached position. But something had to be done: if he did nothing, disengaged himself—the result would be inevitable. A pang of memory stabbed at him.

"Wha's matter? Can't speak? Don't wanna speak wi' a common jack—you too high 'n' mighty, then?"

Kydd had changed, Renzi acknowledged to himself. Far from being a naïve young man from a country town pressed into an un-caring, alien environment, he was gaining confidence in his consid-erable natural abilities and had a very real prospect of being a fine seaman—if he survived.

"Ah, yes!" He looked at Renzi sideways with a leer. "I know—I know why you're at sea wi' the rest of us!"

He made exaggerated glances around to check for listeners. "You've done something, haven't you? Somethin' bad, I'll wager, 'n' they're after you. You go ashore, they're gonna nobble you. You're runnin', Renzi, running from somethin'."

Renzi drew a sharp breath. "You ignorant jackass. You don't know what you're talking about. Put a rein on your tongue before you say anything you might regret."

"It speaks! The gran' prince deigns to address th' mobility." Kydd made a bow, but staggered forward, colliding with Renzi. "Ge' your hands off me, sir!" Kydd said, wrenching himself free. He took a swing at Renzi, clumsy and wild. Renzi easily ducked under it, but knew that if he left now all would be over for Kydd. Tempted, he drew back—but Kydd's guileless face and dark features pricked him mercilessly. Stepping around him, Renzi seized his arms in a lock and frog-marched him toward the hatch.

"Ger' away—wha' you doing? Le' me go, you—"

He threw Kydd down the ladder and resumed his hold when Kydd picked himself up at the bottom. It continued until they were in the orlop. Renzi dragged Kydd over to the gratings between the pump room and sail stowage, and flung him down. "There, you fool! You want to give your life to the bottle, do it in company." He jerked up the grating to reveal, in the stinking blackness below, a huddled figure clutching a bottle. The face looked up anxiously, rheumy eyes and trembling grasp pitiful in its degradation. Renzi spoke scornfully. "Eakin, cooper's mate. Why don't you introduce yourself, Mr. Kydd? I'm sure you'll find you have much in common!" He let Kydd drop to the deck and left.

"Don't worry, mate, we squared it with Jack Weatherface. Good hand, is Tewsley." Doud spoke softly, as to a child.

Kydd said nothing, holding his head and staring at his breakfast.

"Yeah—look, we understand, cuffin. He was our shipmate too." Whaley reached over and squeezed his arm.

Kydd looked up wordlessly. His vague memories of the previous night were shot through with horror—waking from a drunken sleep to find the sickening Eakin pulling him down into the hold to evade the Master-at-Arms before clumsily going through his clothes for drink or valuables. He remembered also Renzi's pitiless grip and implacable face, and the cold ferocity of his movements. Kydd shot a glance over at Renzi in his usual place opposite Claggett. Silent and guarded as ever, he gave no sign of recognition.

Why had he done it? What had made Renzi break with character so much as to involve himself in a shipmate's fate?

Kydd needed answers—but not here.

At dinner, he watched Renzi quietly. No one knew, or particularly cared, where Renzi spent his time and, true to form, he slipped away afterward.

Kydd rose and followed. Renzi emerged onto the upper deck, then swung out to the fore shrouds and up to the foretop, where he disappeared from view.

He did not return. Kydd made his way up the ratlines to the foretop.

Renzi sat with his back to the after rail, a book balanced on his knee. Looking up as Kydd climbed into the top, he assumed an expression of cold distaste, but said nothing.

"I'm to thank you for y'r concern, sir," Kydd began.

Still no words, just the repelling look.

"I was much affected. My friend . . ." Kydd tailed off.

It was hard. Renzi felt himself weakening.

"Why did you interfere?" said Kydd abruptly.

Renzi put down the book and sighed. It was no good, he just could not bring himself to repel Kydd with his usual malignity. "Do I have to be in possession of a reason?" he asked.

"Your pardon, but you've never shown an interest in others before."

"Perhaps I choose to in your case."

"Why?"

Renzi looked out over the moving gray seas under the wan sunlight. How could he speak of the depth of feeling, the cold remorseless logic that had driven him to self-sentence himself—that same discipline of rationality that had kept him from following the others to self-destruction. It had its own imperatives. "Because you remind me of one who—I once met," he said finally.

Kydd looked at him, unsure of how to respond.

"And because I have seen others go to hell the same way."

"Then please don't concern yourself. I don't make a practice of it."

"I'm gratified to hear it." Renzi's educated voice seemed out of keeping.

"Who *are* you?" Kydd asked boldly. "I mean, what are y' doin' on a man-o'-war?"

"That can be of no possible concern to you."

"I see you do not care f'r conversation, sir. I will take my leave," said Kydd, aware that, despite himself, when speaking to Renzi he was aping his manners.

"No—wait!" Renzi closed his book. "I spoke hastily perhaps. Please sit down." It was rash, perhaps, but right now he felt a surging need for human interaction.

"Have you—are they after you?" Kydd said, looking at him directly.

Renzi toyed with the nice philosophical distinction between legal criminality and moral, but decided to answer in the negative.

"Then . . ."

"I was not pressed, if that is your impression."

Kydd eased his position. "So I must find that you are runnin'— hidin'—and from what, I do not know. Am I right?"

Renzi could not avoid Kydd's forthright gaze. "Yes, you are right," he admitted. How much could he speak of his situation and hope to be understood? Kydd was strong-minded—he had to be to endure—but he had no acquaintance with Descartes or Leibniz and their cold logic, no appreciation of the higher moral forces that might motivate a man of the Enlightenment.

Kydd smiled thinly. "You do not look a one who'd be craven."

Renzi half smiled and looked away. The months of self-imposed isolation, the deliberate lack of human contact, had been hard, but he had borne this as part of the punishment. But what if this could rightly be construed as *ultra poenas dare*—beyond the penalty given? The condition of exile might be sustained, yet he would have the precious mercy of human company.

He looked directly at Kydd, considering, and found himself deciding: if he was going to confide in anyone it would be Kydd. "You wish an explanation."

"If it does not pain you."

"No, the pain is past." He glanced at Kydd, feeling drawn to the intensity in the strong, open face.

"However, be so good as to bear with me for a space . . ." He paused for a long moment, then continued, "For philosophical reasons, which appear sufficiently cogent to me, I am denied the felicity of the company of my peers. This is not the result of a criminal act, I hasten to assure you."

Kydd could see that Renzi was having difficulty speaking of his burden and wondered if it had anything to do with his peculiar beliefs. "Then, sir, I will not speak of it again."

Renzi said nothing but Kydd saw the pain in his eyes. The deeply lined face spoke of complexities of experience at which he could only guess.

A silence fell between them. Sounds from the watch on deck faintly carried up to their eyrie.

"I beg you will tell me more of this philosophy, er, Mr. Renzi," Kydd said.

"Upon a more suitable occasion, perhaps, Mr. Kydd."

"Tom."

"Nicholas."

The cutter went about around their stern and came smartly up into the wind bare yards away, the brailed-up mainsail flogging violently. A heaving line shot up and was seized; canvas-covered despatches followed quickly. Mission performed, sail was shaken out again and the despatch cutter bore away.

"*All the haaands!* Hands lay aft!" The pipe came within the hour—it did not need much imagination to guess that something was afoot.

Salter was quite sure. "The Frogs have signed a peace, and we're on our way home."

"Nah—pocky knaves like that, they want ter bring us down first. It'll be the rest o' the Fleet comin' to help."

Stirk was more skeptical, but ready to listen. "Let the dog see the rabbit, Doggo," he said, elbowing him to one side.

The Captain stepped forward to the poop rail. "We have been entrusted with a mission." He paused, looking around him, delicately touching his mouth with a fine handkerchief before replacing it in the sleeve of his heavy gold-laced coat. "A mission that could see the beginning of the end for that vile gang of regicides."

There was quiet. A mission did not sound like something that could end the war—that would take a great battle involving the rest of the Fleet—but anything that offered a break from the monotony of sailing up and down on blockade duty would be welcome.

"We, together with *Royal Albion* and *Tiberius,* have won the opportunity to dart a lance into the very belly of the enemy. We are going to join with true Frenchmen who will rejoice to see their nation restored to its former glory—and make our landing together on the shores of France.

"You will all have heard how the wretches murdered their officers and govern their affairs by citizens' council. The rabble will retire in confusion under our disciplined advance. We will thrust deep into the heart of France, sweeping all before us, and bring to an end this squalid regime."

A restless muttering rippled through the men crowded on deck and in the lower rigging. An armed descent on the mainland of Europe?

"Mr. Tyrell leads our contribution, which will be two hundred men. He will be assisted by Mr. Lockwood and Mr. Garrett. They will be protected by the marines, for we shall be landing four guns, complete with equipment. As I speak, a strong force of Royalists is marching from across the Cherbourg peninsula to join with us. Our objective will be to free the great old town of Rennes and, having established our position there, we will be reinforced for the big advance to Paris—and victory! But by then we will long be returned on board. You need have no fear that you will be turned into redcoats.

"Now I am asking for volunteers—and might I add that they will certainly share in whatever spoils of war Providence brings."

Significant looks were exchanged. This was far more to the point than grand strategy.

"Volunteers may approach the First Lieutenant after dinner. God save the King!"

"Damn right I'm going. Not set foot ashore in eight months." Whaley's eyes gleamed.

"Want to clap eyes on them French women—wouldn't repel boarders should a saucy piece lay alongside!" declared Doud, his lewd gestures leaving no doubt as to his meaning.

Claggett did not join in. "Might be things are different to what you thinks," he said.

Howell sniffed. "What d'ye mean?"

Claggett leaned over. "I went in with the boats at Los Cayos and we suffered somethin' cruel. Moskeeters, stinkin' heat, an' never a morsel o' meat one day's end to the next. Cruel, I tells yer—you'll see."

Howell sneered. "Anyways, no chance o' that where youse are going! Just goin' to get yerselves separated from yer head by this here gillo-tin!"

"What about you, Tom?" Whaley said, tapping a piece of hard tack.

"Could do with a stretch o' the legs," Kydd said casually.

"Ye're all bloody mad," said Howell. "Mantrap and Shaney Jack both—it'll be seven bells of hell for all hands wi' them two. I'm stayin' aboard, where they won't be at."

At supper, Kydd eased into place opposite Renzi. "We join up with the Fleet in the morning, I've heard," Kydd said to him.

Renzi responded slowly, "Yes, I believe we shall."

"You volunteered." Kydd had been just as surprised as the others.

"As did you."

Renzi looked away, then back. "In the dog-watch it is my pleasure to take a pipe of tobacco on the fo'c'sle, should the weather prove tolerable."

Kydd's father smoked a long churchwarden pipe, but he had never taken up the habit. "I don't take tobacco m'self, but were you to need company . . ."

"Then I should be honored."

The fo'c'sle deck in the dog-watches was a place of sanctuary for the seamen. Out of sight of the quarterdeck, sailors chatted in ones or twos, spinning yarns and making merry. Some sat on the deck reading or sewing. Right at the forward end of the squared-off deck, before the massive carved work of the beakhead dropped away below, was a splendid place to be. On either side the busy wash of the bow-wave spread as the great bluff bow shouldered the waves arrogantly aside. Sliding aft, it rejoined the other side past the ornate stern to disappear into the distance in a ruler-straight line over the gray Atlantic. The jibboom thrust out ahead, the headsails soaring up to the tops and beyond, taut and eager. They dipped and rose with great dignity, it seemed to Kydd.

The vista seemed to please Renzi too. "There is a certain harmony in some works of man which I cannot but find sublime," he said, as they stood together above the beakhead. From inside his jacket he

KYDD

found his clay pipe, which he filled from an oilskin pouch.

Kydd waited until Renzi had his pipe drawing well, using the flame of a lanthorn swinging in the shrouds. He settled on the deck next to him.

"Have you thought, dear fellow, that tomorrow we could well be fighting for our lives?"

Renzi spoke so quietly that Kydd thought at first he was talking to himself. "Er, not really, no. But I'm sure that His Majesty will triumph over his enemies," Kydd added stiffly.

"Of course. Have you ever seen a battle?" The pipe was giving Renzi much satisfaction—he held it delicately by the stem near the bowl, luxuriating in the acrid fragrance.

"Not as one might say a battle," Kydd answered. The excitement of the militia being turned out to quell an apprentices' riot would probably not count.

Renzi inspected his pipe. "Then pray do not wish it—a battle. It must be the most odious and disagreeable occupation of man known." He caught something of Kydd's suspicions, for he hastened to add, "Yet some must be accounted inevitable—desirable, even."

"Does this mean that you—do not—"

"It does not. I will not seek glory in battle, but the rational course for personal survival is not to be found in turning one's back. You will not find me shy, I think."

"I'm sorry, I didn't mean—"

"We are to haul guns, I find. There will be precious little chance for laurels in that." He looked sideways at Kydd, with an amused expression.

"You wished to confide some matter t' me," Kydd said abruptly.

Renzi's face set. "Perhaps," he said.

Kydd waited.

After several more draws at the long clay pipe Renzi spoke. "I come from a family of landowners in Buckinghamshire. We were—

are not wanting in the article of wealth, you may believe." He paused, collecting his thoughts. "My education has been thorough and complete, and includes experiences which—of which I am no longer proud. I knew only the life of the indolent, the uncaring and unseeing—I confess, I knew no better. We have many tenant farmers, but my father was not content. His interest allowed him to see a Bill of Enclosure through Parliament that enabled him to increase his holdings. I conceive you know of enclosures?"

"Yes," said Kydd quietly, "I do. I share the name of Thomas Paine."

Renzi's lips thinned. "Then you know with what misery they are enforced, what hardship and want they can cause. It did not stop my father from sequestrating lands that had been under careful cultivation for centuries. In particular one small cottager did break his heart at the prospect—it did not move my father one whit. But it was when the bailiffs marched in to seize the land that they found the man's eldest and the hope of the family, whom I knew well, hanging by his neck in the barn." Renzi went on slowly. "My beliefs—I will not bore you—include a devotion to the Rationalist cause. A young man died. Legally there is no blame, but in the moral sensibility, it is as if we had tied the noose with our own hand."

Kydd's eyes narrowed.

"My family disowned the consequences of their actions. Were I to do likewise, then I would share in the crime. But if I acknowledge it, then logic—and I am a friend to logic—owns that a penalty must be served. And in my case, as judge and jury, I did pronounce sentence—which is to be five years' exile from home and hearth." Renzi looked away and added, a little too lightly, "A small price for an eased conscience, I believe."

Kydd had no idea what subtleties could drive a man to such a conclusion, but he found himself respecting and admiring the action. "Do y' not find the life—hard?" he said.

"There are worse things to be borne, my friend."

"How long—I mean—"

"It is but ten months of the first year."

Kydd had the insight to feel something of the bleakness of spirit that would have to be overcome, what it must have cost a cultivated man brutally to repress his finer feelings. He guessed that the reclusiveness would be part of Renzi's defenses and was ashamed of his previous animosity. "Then, sir, you have my sincere admiration." Kydd clapped him on the shoulder.

Renzi's hand briefly touched his, and Kydd was startled to see his eyes glisten. "Don't concern yourself on my account, I beg," Renzi said, drawing away. "It has just been an unconscionable long time."

In the morning, with the squadron wearing in succession and standing in for the French coast to the eastward, the enterprise had begun. They were under easy sail, for the transports from Plymouth would not reach them for another two days—but the time would not be wasted.

"Let's be seein' you now. All move over to larb'd, clap your eyes on this 'ere fugleman." The Master-at-Arms indicated a marine, rigid at attention with his musket.

The men jostled over to leeward and faced the red-coated and pipe-clayed marine with a mixture of distrust and interest. His sergeant glaring at him from one side and the Master-at-Arms on the other, he moved not a muscle.

"This man is a-going to pro-ceed through the motions of loadin' an' dischargin' a musket. You will pay stric' attention 'cos afterward you will do it." He paused and surveyed the restless seamen. "Anyone can't do it perfick by six bells joins me awkward squad in the first dog. Issue weapons!"

The gunner's party opened an arms chest and passed out muskets.

Curiously Kydd inspected the plain but heavy firelock. It seemed brutish compared to the handsome length and damascened elegance of the parson's fowling piece; this one had dull, pockmarked wood, a black finished barrel and worn steel lockwork, more reminiscent of some industrial machine.

"For them who haven't seen one before, I'll name th' main parts."

Within a bare minute Kydd had the essentials: the frizzen covering the pan had to be struck by a piece of flint, which would send a spark to set off the priming in the pan and thence to the cartridge. He looked doubtfully at the muzzle—the thumb-sized bore meant a heavy ball, and this implied a hefty kick.

"Right. We go through the motions first without a cartridge. First motion, half cock yer piece."

The fugleman briskly brought his musket across his breast and like clockwork brought it to half cock.

The seamen of the gunner's party went along the line, correcting and cursing by turns. The action of the recurved cock felt stiff and hostile to Kydd—but then it was necessary for a sea-service weapon to avoid delicate niceties.

"Second motion, prime your piece."

Priming was not difficult to imagine. Brush the frizzen forward, shake in the priming, shut it again.

"Third motion, charge your piece."

Take the remaining cartridge powder and ball, and insert it in the muzzle. Ram it down with the wooden rammer.

"Present your weapon."

Lock to full cock. It took a moment to realize that the words meant to aim the musket—present the muzzle end to the enemy.

"Fire!" The finger drawing at the trigger, never jerking—a satisfying metallic clack and momentary spark.

"Rest." The Master-at-Arms seemed content. "By numbers, one, half cock."

They went through the drill again and again until it was reflexive, the fugleman never varying in his brisk timing.

Finally the order came. "Issue five rounds ball cartridge!"

The cartridges felt ominously heavy, a dull lead ball with a wrapped parchment cartridge. Kydd put them in his pocket. Nervously he gripped his weapon and waited for the word to fire.

"First six! You, to you with the red kerchief—step over here to wind'd."

Kydd stepped over as number three.

"Face outboard—number one, load yer weapon."

The first man went through the drill. The man bit off the top of the cartridge and spat it out. The rammer did its work. A quarter gunner inspected his priming, making sure the powder grains covered the pan but no more, and the man looked at the Master-at-Arms.

"At the 'orizon—present!"

The musket rose and steadied.

"Fire!"

All within a fraction of a second—a click, fizz and *bang*. Gouts of whitish smoke propelled outward to be blown back over them all before clearing.

Roars of laughter eased the tension. As the smoke cleared the man was to be seen picking himself up from the deck. He had not been prepared for the mule-like kick. Kydd resolved to do better.

"Number two!" The man next to Kydd loaded his weapon. He was clearly nervous, and twice made blunders.

"Present!"

The barrel visibly trembled as it was trained, and the man unconsciously held the thick butt away from his shoulder, anticipating the recoil. Cruelly the Master-at-Arms affected not to notice.

"Fire!"

The musket slammed back and with undamped impetus caught the man's shoulder a savage blow.

With a cry of pain the man dropped his weapon, which clattered noisily to the deck.

"Now you all knows to hold the butt tight into yer shoulder. Number three!"

Kydd loaded his musket, carefully looking to the priming, ramming the ball vigorously down.

"Present!"

He raised the barrel and tucked the butt firmly into his shoulder. The tiny crude foresight settled on the horizon, but without a backsight or other cues Kydd decided to ignore it.

"Fire!"

Leaning into it, he pressed the trigger. The ear-ringing *blam* of the discharge sounded peculiarly less for his own piece than it had when he was standing sideways from the others, he noted. The recoil was heavy, but under control, and he lowered the musket with a swelling satisfaction.

The drill continued until every man had fired two rounds, after which half a dozen of them were called forward, the remainder relieved of their weapons.

"These men will fire at the mark."

This would be a round cask end dangling from the fore yardarm and steadied with a guy. The men took position on the poop.

"Number one, three rounds!"

At a range of a couple of hundred feet it was not surprising that there were no hits. Disappointed, the man stepped down.

"Number two!"

His first ball took the target near its edge, and it kicked spectacularly. A buzz of excited comment, and the next shot. It missed—the man reloaded quickly, blank-faced. Carefully he brought the musket up and squinted down the barrel. He left it too long—the muzzle wavered with fatigue, and after the musket banged off, the cask end still hung innocently.

There was a shout of derision and the man stepped down disconsolately.

Kydd moved forward. There was an undercurrent of muttering and he guessed that wagers were being taken. He loaded, took position, and the chattering died away. He took a long look at the cask end and brought the musket up, sighting along the barrel. The three-feet-wide target seemed to have shrunk in the meantime, for the merest quiver set the muzzle off the mark. Kydd tried to make sense of the single foresight, then remembered his recent experience and abandoned it. The sighting picture blurred, but in an act of pure instinct, he focused only on the target and let his body point through the gun at the mark.

He drew on the trigger—he heard the distant *thock* before the smoke cleared to reveal the target swaying from a solid hit. He was more surprised than elated.

A buzz of excitement went through the spectators, which died away to silence when he reloaded and took aim once more. He repeated the unconscious pointing and miraculously the target took another hit.

"Silence!" the Master-at-Arms roared, in the sudden commotion.

There must be more to it than this, thought Kydd, and at his last shot he tried to put more science into his aim. The little foresight settled on the target, Kydd finding it difficult to focus on both at the same time.

He knew immediately he pulled the trigger that he had missed, and a spreading sigh from the crowd confirmed it was so.

"Well done, lad—two of three is better'n most," the Master-at-Arms said.

At conclusion of the exercise Kydd was called over. "M'duty to Mr. Tewsley, and you are to 'ave an extra tot at seven bells."

• • •

"Nasty piece o' work, them muskets!" Claggett muttered.

"Why'd y' say that?" Kydd asked.

"If you was in a frigate, yer wouldn't ask!" Claggett replied with feeling. "You's servin' the upper deck midships guns with yer mates, all open t' the sky, an' it's a right smashin' match, yardarm ter yardarm. Then yer see that yer mates are gettin' picked orf, one after the other as they're busy workin' the guns. You wonder when it's goin' to be your turn next. An' it's all 'cos they have these buggers with muskets in the tops firin' down on yer 'n' you can do nothin' about it—a-tall." He drained his pot and glared at Kydd. "Ain't fer sailors!" he said forcefully.

"Bear away, shipmate," Doud said. "Kydd may get to settle a Frenchy or two fer you in a couple o' days!"

In the dog-watches the novelty of imminent action ashore lifted spirits and animated conversations. But it also generated nervous energy that found its release in yet more drill—close-quarters combat.

Kydd realized that this was a totally different affair. Instead of action at a distance, as with any gun, this would be a matter of man to man. The first to make a mistake would surely find himself choking his life out on his own blood. He wondered if he could stand up against some fierce bull of a Frenchman violently intent on his destruction. His imagination produced an image of a big *sans-culotte*, mustachioed, face distorted with hatred and closing in to batter down his guard and hack him to pieces. Kydd tried to focus instead on Lieutenant Lockwood.

"As you are new men, I will commence by mentioning the weapons you may be called upon to employ. First, we have the boarding pike." He moved over to the mainmast and selected one from the circle set around the base of the mast. "It is only used to repel boarders, but it is remarkably effective in that role." Lockwood passed it over. He had a cool, detached manner, which only added to the menace of what he said.

The pike passed from hand to hand, and Kydd gripped it nervously. Slender but strong, it had at its tip a concentrated forged and ground spike. It was seven feet long, and he could not help but wonder what he would do if called away as a boarder to be faced with these pointing at him from the enemy decks.

"And this is a tomahawk," Lockwood continued, holding up a vicious-looking small axe with a blade on one side and a spike on the other. "You will find that this is actually quite useful also in dealing with cordage, grappling irons and other impedimenta." He passed it over too. "When boarding an enemy ship you will have two pistols. These are useless"—he fixed the men with a meaningful look—"at more than a few feet range. If you decide to fire, discharge the pistol into the face of your opponent. The piece is then useless—you will certainly have no time to reload—but then you are possessed of a fine club." Nobody laughed. "Or throw it away." He reached behind him and produced a bundle of equipment.

The restless stirring died down, each man detecting a change in Lockwood's manner.

"But this is your main weapon. It is the boarder's best friend and you will practice its use constantly from now on until it can be relied upon in mortal combat to save your life, and therefore to take your enemy's."

Kydd watched, hypnotized, as Lockwood slipped on the equipment. There was a belt around the waist and a cross-belt over the shoulders. A scabbard hung on his left side from which, with a steely hiss, he drew a deadly-looking implement. "The sea-service cutlass!"

An arms chest lay on the gratings, and each man was told to take one. There were no scabbards, so Kydd stood with the weapon awkwardly in his hand. The cutlass was heavy, the wide working blade of dull speckled steel with a thin shine of oil, sharp on one side and coming to a robust point. The ropework hilt was almost enclosed with a black guard, which was plain and workmanlike. Kydd wondered whose blood the weapon had already tasted.

"If there is one lesson that I want to teach you, it is this one," and Lockwood called to an assisting seaman. The man came at him in slow motion. He raised his cutlass to deal a devastating slash down on the officer's unprotected head.

They both paused for a count of two.

"Watch!" commanded Lockwood.

They resumed their motions, but as the sailor's blow descended, Lockwood simply extended his arm and the tip of his cutlass rested on the breast of the seaman well before the man could connect with his own blade.

"This man deals the heavier blow—but now he is dead!" Lockwood said dramatically. "Thrust with the *point* always, never slash the blade. It only needs one inch of steel to decide the issue."

The advice seared itself into Kydd's mind.

"So, bearing that in mind, let us begin our drill. Robbard?"

Lockwood's seaman took position sideways on and flourished his blade.

"First position."

Robbard stood facing to his right, feet together, inviting attack.

"Right prove distance!"

He swung the cutlass warily out to his right.

"Front prove distance!"

The cutlass swept forward, the point weaving menacingly.

"Second position."

Bending his knees, Robbard slammed his foot a pace forward; from this he was able to demonstrate how he could both attack and retreat rapidly without moving his feet.

There were four body postures, and they practiced them all.

The cutlass positions were more difficult; some out to the side but covering the upper body, some hanging vertically down; in all, seven possible moves. Lockwood himself demonstrated them.

After an hour's work, he was able to bark a position and they could instantly assume it. "Guard—inside half hanger! Assault! St. George!"

Kydd could see how they fitted into a web of defensive and offensive moves—an outside guard, for instance, could well be the thing to ward off an assault, but in this he would wait and see. The main point seemed to be that for every act of offense there was a corresponding defensive move.

The cutlass felt less of a deadweight in his hands, but he knew that he would need much practice before he could feel confident—it would almost certainly save his life one day.

"Stand down—secure arms."

Reluctantly Kydd handed in his cutlass and prepared to go below.

"Hold!" Lockwood called. "Prince o' the poop!"

The seaman who had acted as his assistant grinned—then, snarling like a pirate, swarmed up the quarterdeck ladder to the poop deck. There he snatched up a wooden sword and flourishing it in the approved first position prepared to take on all comers. Lockwood smiled widely. "Robbard is defending, and is prince o' the poop for now—but any man may challenge him for the title, if they dare!"

There were cheers and catcalls.

"The man who is in possession of the poop at eight bells receives from me a fine bottle of claret," Lockwood declared.

The first man up was treated mercifully. Robbard circled him and tried a point. The man parried with an inside guard, which he tried to turn into an extended point of his own. Robbard saw it and swayed inside, tapping the man none too gently on the head. His opponent swore and started a furious assault, which Robbard

met like a rock, his sword flicking this way and that in a monotonous *clack, clok*. The man tired and drew back, at which Robbard
gave point and pierced the man's hurried St. George while he was
off balance.

Roars of appreciation greeted the defeated challenger ruefully
descending the ladder. Rudely pushing him aside was the next man,
an experienced able seaman with a tarry queue and thick-set body,
who bounded up the ladder.

"Have at yer, Sharkey mate!" he shouted.

Robbard chuckled and came to guard.

They were well matched, and Kydd watched fascinated. They
drove forward and back over the whole deck, their eyes holding
each other unblinking as they thrust and parried.

Once Kydd had delivered an elaborate wig to the small fencing
school in Chapel Street. He had stayed to watch, gripped by the
deadly swordplay, the glitter of rapier blade, the slither and clash of
steel on steel. The combatants had worn wire masks and the lethal
questing of the blades as they probed and parried was carried out
in chill silence, a ballet of death.

Here the pair grinned or stared ferociously by turns—Kydd
guessed they would look different when boarding a hostile deck.

Kydd felt an elbow in his ribs and turned to see Whaley offering
him a tankard. He accepted it gratefully and noticed that a crowd
of appreciative onlookers had gathered. He turned back to the combat in time to see the two grappling—Robbard's guard being slowly
overborne by his adversary's head stroke, pressing down. Their eyes
were inches apart as they forced against each other, when suddenly
Robbard let rip with a raucous raspberry. The other man jerked in
surprise, and Robbard's sweeping half-circle would have laid open
the man's ribs—according to the umpire.

"Damn me eyes, 'n' I'll challenge ye again!" shouted the man. It
took a pot of grog to persuade him to yield the deck.

Robbard strutted about on the poop, whirling his wooden sword in the air and crowing, the crowd cheering him on. The easy sail left little for the watch on deck to do and they joined the spectacle. Over to the westward the spreading red of a sunset tinged the scene and its players a ruddy color.

"That's your tie-mate, ain't it, Tom?" Stirk gestured with his pot. There was a swirl in the crowd and there was Renzi, mounting the steps in lithe, decisive movements.

Robbard stopped his capering and sized up the challenger.

Renzi threw off his jacket and stood in his plain waistcoat, his dark eyes fixed on Robbard's. He picked up his sword. A subdued murmur went up from the spectators.

Renzi said nothing, his mouth in a hard line, his expression ruthless. He stamped once or twice as if to test his footing, then whipped up his sword to the salute. Robbard mistook the move and came to a halfhearted guard, but did not return the salute.

Down came Renzi's blade, flicking in short, testing movements like a snake's tongue—darting, deadly. Robbard gave ground warily, circling to the left, all traces of comedy vanishing.

His forehead wrinkled in concentration, and when he finally made his attack it was in a burst of violence, his point thrust forward in a savage lunge. Renzi swayed coolly and in a beautiful inside half hanger deflected the thrust just enough to force Robbard to divert his energy into maintaining his balance. Almost casually Renzi took advantage of Robbard's brief recovery and changed his guard to a point, which flashed out—and came to a stop at Robbard's throat. The entire combat was over in just fifteen seconds.

Robbard stood motionless, the sword at his throat mute evidence of Renzi's skills. His sword fell to the deck.

Seeing Renzi's pitiless expression behind his motionless weapon, Kydd realized that there were depths to his friend's character that he had never seen.

The hush was interrupted by Lockwood. "May I?" He mounted the ladder and took up the sword. Robbard returned to the deck below in a daze.

"On guard, sir!"

The two faced each other and warily saluted. Then it began—a fight to the death, a no-quarter combat that was almost too fast to follow.

Swordplay continued over the whole poop deck, the clacking of wood never detracting from the deadly seriousness of the business.

The red sunset faded to a short violet dusk and as lanthorns were brought Lockwood stepped back and grinned. "Sir—I yield! The claret is yours."

Renzi nodded, and a small smile creased his face.

CHAPTER 8

Sir Philip Stephens glanced about *and coughed gently. The business would be conducted in the absence of the First Lord, the Earl of Chatham, who at the time was presumably answering questions in the House of Lords.*

The talk died away, quickly, respect for the Secretary of the Admiralty deep and sincere. This was a man who, beginning as secretary to Lord Anson, could bring to personal remembrance all the sea heroes of the second half of the century, and had more interest at his command than most of the Lords Commissioners themselves.

"Mr. Ibbetson, if you please," he murmured. His lean assistant opened a beribboned folder and passed it across without comment.

Sir Philip read for a moment, his spectacles balanced precariously at the end of his nose, and glanced up at the Board. "I have here a communication from the office of the Prime Minister, desiring an early response to his enquiry of the twelfth of March, which was"—he riffled the papers—"concerning our advice upon the matter of support for the Royalist cause in France, and in particular for any insurrection which from time to time may eventuate."

He laid down the papers and removed his spectacles. "You will, of course, know of Mr. Pitt's position in this. He believes that the country's interests are best served by circumspection in this matter, yet he is concerned to appear active and diligent."

Looks were exchanged around the table. Pitt's austere, reserved manner hid a keen intelligence, but lost him many friends. His preference in expending gold rather than lives would translate without doubt to tax increases later.

Sir Philip continued smoothly, "The Duke of York's, er, difficulties in the Austrian Netherlands would seem to make an action of some kind useful in drawing the attention of the regicides westwards."

Nodding heads around the table showed that the politics were well taken. Not for nothing was the Tory party known as "The King's Friends." And these were British troops in Flanders, the only real effectives on the Continent; anything that preserved their strategic presence was welcome.

Leaning back in his chair, Sir Philip said carefully, "It might fairly be said that we are out of luck in the matter of intelligence at this hour, yet we know of a rising in Brittany, attended by more than the usual success." His face wore a frown, however. "Maréchal du Pons is known to us from the last age, a stiff and unbending soldier, yet he has the trust of the people. I believe we must assist him."

He paused. Not all present would be keen in such circumstances to put British troops in a subordinate command. "I propose, therefore, a limited engagement of support—say, a battalion of foot and a few guns. If he presently triumphs, as I fervently hope, we will follow this with reinforcements of a more substantial nature. If he fails, we will be able to withdraw with naught but insignificant loss."

The following morning *Duke William* sailed into the rendezvous on the ten-fathom line, four miles to seaward of the small fishing port of St. Pontrieux, said to be in Royalist hands.

Kydd was fascinated. Over there was France, his first foreign shore—and it was the enemy! The very thought seemed to imbue the rugged Brittany coastline with menace. Somewhere over the dark hills was a country locked in war with his own. His island soul recoiled from the notion that there was nothing but dry land separating this point from the raving mob in Paris.

The rendezvous was crowded with shipping: nearly a hundred sail, dominated by the three big sail-of-the-line, several frigates and two lumbering transports. The rest were small fry: provisioning craft, water and powder hoys, a host of small sloops and armed cutters. They lay hove to, waiting impatiently for the word to move on the port.

Just before noon a deputation approached in a fishing boat, displaying an outsize white flag—the *fleur-de-lis* of the Bourbons.

"*Haaands* to cheer ship!"

As the little boat plunged past, seeking the broad pennant of the Commodore in *Royal Albion,* men crowded the rigging to cheer, the Captain graciously doffing his hat. The ensign of King Louis's Navy made its way grandly up to the mizzen peak.

In the boat a cockaded and sashed individual stood erect, waved and bowed, clearly delighted.

Within the hour the big men-o'-war had anchored, the frigates had taken stations to seaward, and the transports prepared to enter port. These would require pilots for the difficult rock-studded entrance, and even so they would then need to lie offshore among myriad islands, the tiny port's river entrance too difficult to navigate.

The transports got under way, passing close enough for Kydd to watch the redcoats thronging their decks. The thumping of martial music carried over the water.

"Don't stand there gawpin', tail on to that fall!" Elkins growled.

The launch eased alongside and the first of the four upper-deck twelve-pounders was readied to be swayed in. A delicate and precise operation, the long cannon, free of its carriage, had to be lowered into the boat that surged below in the slight sea. The slightest ill-timing, and the boat coming up with the waves would meet the mass of iron moving down and the result would be so much splintered wreckage. Lines ran from the yardarms in a complex pattern, balancing movements and loads with the use of tie blocks, guys and mast tackles in a complex exercise of seamanship.

What was surprising to Kydd in this difficult maneuver was that there was silence—no shouted orders. The boatswain controlled the men on the tackles through his mates and their silver whistles. Orders were passed by different patterns of twittering calls: a continuous fluttering warble sounded continuously while lowering, and at the right position a sharp upward squeal told the crew to avast.

It was hard work, and Kydd envied the seamen who waited in the boat.

After dinner the landing party assembled by divisions, two hundred men in their seaman's rig wearing their field sign—a white band on the left arm. The boats took them ashore, the men happy to be away from shipboard discipline. As the boats approached the landing place, Kydd looked around with interest. There was a wild beauty about it, rocky spurs among tiny beaches, the ragged land interspersed with dark-pink granite outcrops, and the port, a walled city, the ramparts connected to the mainland by an ancient causeway. Adding to the exotic effect was a subtle, exciting foreignness about the houses, the tiny farms and the patterns of cultivation. And the smell: after the purity of the sea, the odor of land—a mix of raw earth, vegetation and manure—had a poignant effect on Kydd. It reminded him of the countryside he had left, but it was overlaid with tantalizing alien scents.

On the quayside of the inner harbor the marines were formed up, their lieutenant languidly fanning himself. It seemed the elements were smiling on the enterprise, for the sun was breaking through with unusual brilliance.

"Hold water port, give way starboard—oars; rowed of all!"

The boat glided alongside the quay, oars tossed upright, and the men scrambled ashore, laughing, joking, the novelty of their surroundings refreshing but unsettling.

As soon as Kydd stepped off the boat onto dry land, the solid stone of the quay fell away under his feet. The boat had been perfectly steady, but despite the evidence of his eyes the land felt like the deck of a ship, heaving gently in a moderate swell. Mystified, he shrugged and walked away with a fine seaman-like roll.

From some windows drooped hastily found Bourbon flags, and banners with foreign words that seemed to offer welcome. Small groups of townsfolk gathered to stare at them, the ladies wearing quaint ornate lace headdresses, the men surly and defensive.

Petty officers called them to order: "Form up, then, you useless lubbers. Get in a line or somethin', fer Chrissake!"

Sailors could be trusted to lay aloft in a gale of wind, but the rigid mechanical movements of military drill were beyond them. A ragged group, they shuffled off. The line of marines on either flank marched crisply, and with more than a touch of swagger.

"Silence in the ranks! Corporal, take charge o' yer men!" The marine sergeant's face reddened at the shambles, but the seamen continued to chatter excitedly.

They moved through the narrow streets, the sound of their tramping feet echoing off the roughcast white houses. Windows were flung open and women looked down, throwing a blossom or screeching an incomprehensible invitation. The company emerged into the town square and halted. The previous shore party had prepared the cannon for transport, chocking them into stout farm wagons, which waited for them on one side.

"Stay where you is!" snarled the sergeant, as the sailors began to drift away, gaping at imposing stone buildings. The flanking marines chivvied them back until they stood together in a bored mass.

More ranks of seamen arrived from the other ships; they took position around the sides of the square, facing the central fountain, which was decked with bunting and draped flags.

"Who would believe it?" Kydd said. "I'm in France. It would make them stare in Guildford t'see me here like this." He shook his head, then laughed and turned to Renzi. "Where would we be, do you believe?"

Renzi pursed his lips. "St. Pontrieux. I was here before, in . . . different circumstances. It's in the northwest, in Brittany. Odd sort of place, mostly fishing, some orchards inland a bit. We know it as a nest of corsairs. It is supposed that they have moved elsewhere for the nonce. Don't remember too much else about it." But he remembered only too well Marie, whom he'd left in tears on the quay. But that had been a different man.

In the distance they could hear the military band. The stirring sound came closer, drums thudding, fifes shrilling, and into the square marched the Duke of Cornwall's 93rd Regiment of Foot, a burst of bright scarlet and glittering equipment, stepping out like heroes. At their head rode the officers on gleaming horses, with tall cockaded hats and glittering swords held proudly before them. Behind them stolid lines of soldiers marched, white spats rising and falling together, the tramp of boots loud in the confines of the square. The seamen fell silent, watching the spectacle. Screamed orders had the soldiers marking time, then turning inwards and forming fours. Finally the band entered, the sound almost deafening. The drum major held his stick high—double thumps on the drum and the band stopped. More orders screamed out and the stamp and clash of muskets sounded as they were brought to order. The soldiers now stood motionless in immaculate lines.

Kydd loosened his neckerchief and waistcoat. The noon sun seemed to have a particular quality in this foreign land, a somewhat metallic glare after the softness of more northerly climes.

The ceremonial party mounted the steps of the fountain, the

British officers deferring to a personage who had the most ornate plumed hat that Kydd had ever seen. It was worn fore and aft in the new Continental style.

"Silence! Silence on parade!" roared the sergeant major, his outrage directed at the sailors, who seemed to have no parade ground discipline whatsoever.

The square fell quiet, and the plumed individual climbed to the highest step. With the utmost dignity he began his speech. "*Un millier d'accueils à nos alliés courageux de l'autre côté de la Manche . . .*"

The sailors were mystified. "Wot's he yatterin' about?" whispered Jewkes to Kydd.

A ripple of applause came from the townsfolk.

"No idea," Kydd had to admit. He looked at Renzi.

"Welcomes the glorious arms of their friends across the Channel," he whispered. "Promises that God, with perhaps a little help from us, will send packing the thieving rascals in Paris."

The oration continued, illustrated by grand gestures and flourishes. The soldiers in their ranks stared woodenly ahead, but the sailors moved restlessly. At last it came to an end. The British army officer in charge stood alongside the orator and removed his own large hat.

"Three cheers for the *intendant* of Rennes!" He bowed to the man, who beamed.

Released from their enforced silence, the sailors roared out lustily.

"Three cheers for the Dauphin, and may he soon assume his rightful place on the throne of France!"

The townspeople looked surprised and delighted at the full-throated response from the sailors.

"And three times three for the sacred soil of France—may it be rid forever of the stain of dishonor!"

Hoarse with cheering, Kydd waved his hat with the rest.

A snapped order and the soldiers straightened, then presented arms. The band struck up a solemn tune, which had all the local folk removing their hats and coming to attention, followed by "God Save the King."

The soldiers turned about and marched off through streets lined with people, astride the road to Rennes.

Tyrell roared, "My division, close up on your gun!"

Kydd and Renzi hurried to the first gun, the marines falling back to take up position in their rear.

Fifty men took their place at the traces, a relieving watch of fifty following behind. Kydd wondered why no oxen were available to do the work.

"Mr. Garrett's division!"

At the head of his men, Garrett's horse caracoled as he fought to bring it under control. He managed it, and with an excessively bored expression started the horse walking ahead.

"What the devil are you about, Mr. Garrett?" thundered Tyrell.

Garrett looked down, astonished.

"Get off that horse! The men march, you march with them! Get off, I say!"

Sulky and brooding, Garrett dismounted. His fine hessian boots, which looked admirable on horseback, would be a sad hindrance on the march.

For the man-hauling, there was no time to make the usual canvas belts. A simple pair of ropes had to serve as traces. These were of new hemp, which, while strong, were rough and stiff to the touch.

Kydd adjusted his hat back and, passing the rope over his shoulder like the others, leaned into the task. The heavy cart was awkward to move and squealed like a pig as the massive old wheels protested at the weight of the gun. They ground off, taking the road out of town.

The band continued to play somewhere ahead, but the music

was too indistinct to inspire. Then someone in the relieving watch
started up:

> Come cheer up, my lads, 'tis to glory we steer
> To add something more to this wonderful year.
> Hearts of oak are our ships! Jolly tars are our men!
> Steadyyy, boys, steadyyyy!
> We'll fight and we'll conquer again and agaaain!

Kydd joined in with a will as they toiled along.

The houses fell away, and soon the cobbled road deteriorated,
holes making the cart jolt and sway dangerously. The road wound
into the hills and at every rise the relieving watch moved to double
bank the traces, getting in the way.

There was no more singing. The afternoon sun grew hot and the
still weather brought no consoling breeze.

"Halt. Chock the wagon."

Gratefully they resigned their places and sat on the grass verge,
waiting impatiently for the dipper of water.

They moved off again, this time with Kydd and Renzi in the relieving watch behind.

Kydd's hands were sore and, despite padding with his jacket, the
shoulder that had borne the rope across it was raw.

They trudged on. The sun descended, and word came to halt for
the night at an open place of upland heath. Kydd ached all over, but
especially in his legs, which were unused to marching. He selected
a tussock and collapsed against it while the marines foraged for
firewood. The rum ration would be coming round soon. "How far
have we come, do you think?" he asked Renzi.

Opening his eyes, Renzi considered. "Must be close to halfway,"
he said. "I recollect that there is another range of hills and Rennes
lies some way beyond, in the valley." He sighed. "Another one or
two days should see us in Rennes—I pray only that nothing delays

the Royalists marching to join us. We're far extended."

Kydd let his buzzing limbs relax. A single tent had been erected, probably for the officers—there was no time for a proper baggage train, and in any case it would all be over in a short time. The men had a single blanket each.

Cooking fires flared and crackled, the smoke pungent on the still evening air. Kydd felt a griping in his stomach—hard tack and tepid lumps of salt pork were all that was on offer.

"Jewkes, come with me, mate." Doggo eased his seaman's knife in its sheath and Jewkes grinned in understanding. The pair disappeared silently into the dusk.

Renzi removed his shoes and sat with his feet toward the fire. Kydd did the same. The early spring evening in the quiet stillness was pleasing. The fire spat and settled, the flames reflected ruddily on their faces.

"Mr. Tyrell must think I'm a fighting man enough, that I'm chosen," Kydd said.

Renzi grunted.

"Do you not think it?" Kydd said.

"My dear fellow, we had better face it that you and I are both chosen because we would not be missed, should the venture prove . . . unfortunate."

"Do you really think it will be so?"

Renzi sighed. "To me, though I am no military strategist, the whole affair seems precipitate, unplanned. We are but few—a battalion of foot and a hundred marines are all our fighting force. Our success depends on getting the guns to the Royalists to give them heart to win a small battle. If anything should prevent the joining . . ." He stretched and lay down full length, eyes closed.

With a start Kydd sensed the presence of shadows at the edge of the firelight. It was Doggo and Jewkes, bringing in a couple of chickens and some rabbit carcasses, which quickly found their way into the cooking pot along with a handful of wild thyme.

Replete at last, Kydd lay down, and drawing his coarse blanket over him, fell asleep.

He awoke in the predawn dark, bitterly cold and stiff. The fire had burned to ashes and the soaking dew had made his blanket limp and sodden. Struggling to his feet, Kydd eased his stiff limbs, then sat hunched and miserable. It was proving a far from glorious war.

After a lukewarm breakfast they set off in the bleak dawn. They had not made more than half a mile up the road when a horseman galloped toward them, coming to a halt in a shower of stones at the head of the column. It was a lieutenant of the 93rd Foot.

"Who is your officer, my man?" he said haughtily to the lead trace.

"I am," growled Tyrell, emerging from the other side.

"Er, I am desired by his lordship to make enquiries concerning the progress of our guns."

Tyrell glared up at him, the elegant officer seated nonchalantly on his immaculate chestnut. "We are proceeding at our best pace. Does his lordship require that I exhaust my men?"

"His lordship is conscious that an early juncture with our allies is desirable," the lieutenant said peevishly. "The regiment is at a stand, sir, and awaits its guns."

"Damn your blood, sir! These are our guns, and we go at our own pace. Be so good as to clear the road and let us proceed," Tyrell snarled.

The subaltern colored. Wheeling his horse around, he galloped off ahead.

Over the rise the road went downhill for a space and the traces had to be streamed astern to check the cart's motion. At the bottom the hauling resumed up a steeper incline, into the bare granite outcrops of the highest range of hills . . .

• • •

It sounded like a firework, just a flat pop and a lazy plume of smoke from halfway up the hill. There was a meaty slap and the first man of the starboard trace grunted and flopped to the ground, writhing feebly.

Stunned, the men let the gun grind to a stop.

"Take cover!" yelled someone. "It's a Frog!"

There was a general scramble for the shelter of rocks, someone fortunately thinking to chock the wheels of the cart. The marines doubled past and began fanning out, climbing slowly among the rocks of the hillside.

"You craven scum!" roared Tyrell. "Have you never been under fire before? Get back to your duty this instant!"

Crestfallen, and with wary glances at the hillside, the traces were resumed. Kydd felt his skin crawl. Next to him Renzi toiled away.

Again, the little pop. This time it was up the hill but on the other side of the road, leaving the marines helplessly combing the wrong side. Again it was the lead man on the starboard trace. This time the man was hit in the throat. He sank to his knees, hands scrabbling, his blood spouting between his fingers, drenching his front. Within minutes his life gurgled away.

"Keep it going! Don't stop!" Tyrell shouted, with a higher pitch to his voice.

"A pair of them working together—intelligent," murmured Renzi. "And not killing the officer—if they did we'd just carry on. As it is . . ."

Kydd didn't reply.

The guns squeaked on.

The new lead starboard trace man looked around fearfully, his arm half up as if to ward off any bullet.

Under the impact of the ball in his belly, he doubled up and fell screaming and kicking in intolerable pain. He was dragged to the side of the road, where he died noisily.

This time Tyrell did not try to stop the stampede. The unarmed sailors cowered behind rocks and tussocks, white-faced. Tyrell stood contemptuously alone. He signaled to the marine lieutenant, who came at the run.

Tyrell's terse orders were translated by the lieutenant, and the marines started to advance on both hillsides in a skirmish line. He waited until they were beyond musket range and called the men back to their task. The gun wagon had rolled backwards and into a watercourse by the side of the road, and it took considerable backbreaking work to heave it back on course and let the weary task resume.

Sore hands, raw shoulders—it seemed to Kydd as if the world was made of toil and pain. In front a man was leaning into it like him, a dark stain of sweat down his dusty back, and beyond him others. To his left was the other trace and Renzi, bent to the same angle but showing no sign of suffering. And always the cruel, biting rope.

The sound of horse's hooves at the gallop, and the lieutenant of Foot raced into view. In one movement he crashed the horse to a stop and slid from the saddle, saluting Tyrell smartly.

"The Royalists have got beat, 'n' you must fall back," he said breathlessly.

"Make your report, Lieutenant," Tyrell said coldly.

"Sir—sir, his lordship begs to inform you that the Royalists have met with a reverse at arms, and are in retreat," he said. "We are to fall back on St. Pontrieux, and he hopes to reach you with the regiment before dusk to escort the guns."

"Thank you, Lieutenant. Is that all?"

The lieutenant mopped his brow with a lilac silk handkerchief. "Well, they do say as how with the Royalists on the run Despard may now split his forces, and send his cavalry after us." He lowered his voice. "Tell the truth, it's amazin' how quick the Crapauds move! Outflanked du Pons completely, they did, 'n' if they take it into their heads to come after us, then we'll be hard put to stop them."

"That's enough, Lieutenant. Return to your unit," Tyrell snapped.

The talk of outflanking was disturbing. Even the most unlettered could conceive of the chilling danger of fanatic revolutionaries swarming past the redcoats, then falling on them from behind.

"Turn those guns around! Get a move on, you lazy scoundrels, or I'll see your backbone tomorrow."

"Change the watch—marines, rearguard!"

They ground off back where they had come, spurred by the thought of a hostile army possibly on their trail. The countryside now became brooding, malicious, the outcrops threatening to hide a host of snipers.

"Still, we've got the army at our backs. They'll hold 'em off—if they come!" Kydd said hopefully.

Renzi said nothing, but Kydd noted his half-smile.

The afternoon sun grew wan with a high overcast, but it did nothing to still Kydd's stomach. The long iron mass of the twelve-pounder was a brute to be served; Kydd hadn't thought he could hate something so much. The torture continued. There was always a small chance that the hurrying army in its turn could be out-flanked before it met up with them, but it seemed unlikely. The wheels squealed on, grinding grittily on the road.

There was a shout from the marines in the rear.

"Still!" Tyrell bellowed. The men ceased their labor. In the silence could be heard a faint, irregular tapping, popping.

"They're coming!" the marine lieutenant said. "Form line!" he ordered.

The marines spread across the road in three ranks, the front kneeling, and waited apprehensively.

Over the crest of the rise pounded a horse, pushed to the limit. It was the lieutenant of Foot, disheveled and wild-eyed. "We're cut to pieces! Got to us before we could form up!" He stopped for breath, his chest heaving. His horse was equally affected, snorting, wide eyes rolling and unable to stand still.

"What's the situation, man?" Tyrell snarled.

"They're through! You've a squadron of Crochu's cavalry in your rear, God help you!" Without waiting to see the effect of his words, he flogged the sweating beast around and galloped back.

In the stunned silence Tyrell spoke levelly. "Spike the guns. We leave them here."

"Mr. Dawkins!" Tyrell called the marine lieutenant over. "The best defense against cavalry?"

"A square, sir!" the young man said.

"Well, then, you will form square around the seamen on my order. When possible we move forward—"

He broke off as red figures on foot breasted the rise and staggered toward them. Some had their muskets and packs but many did not. They were ragged and torn, stumbling for the safety of their fellow kind.

"Duke Williams!" He addressed the sailors in a bull roar. "We fall back on St. Pontrieux. When I order 'square' you move for your life inside the lobsterback's square. If you're caught outside we can't help you. Understand?"

Kydd felt cold. His life had become the familiar sea world of masts and spars, where skills and intelligence could make a difference, not this bloody butchery.

"Keep together!"

They made off rapidly down the road, the marines warily in the rear, ignoring the pathetic stragglers still struggling hopelessly after them.

Kydd's legs burned, but he knew the penalty for fatigue.

A half-sensed rumbling became an ominous drumming, louder and louder, then over the rise burst Crochu's cavalry.

"Square!" roared Tyrell.

The marines trotted into place, fixing bayonets as they ran. Three ranks faced outward in a hollow square, enclosing the seamen and the pitifully few stragglers who had reached them, rows of bayonets in the front rank pointing seamlessly out in an impenetrable fence of steel, the muskets of the remaining ranks at the ready.

It was a frightful sight—the heavy crash of hooves and mad jingling of equipment seemed an unstoppable juggernaut. They were in blue and white with plumed silver helmets, holding at the ready pennoned lances and heavy sabers, which they swung loosely in anticipation. The sun picked out points of shining steel, which added to the men's dread.

In utmost terror, the exhausted stragglers saw their fate approach. Some screamed like children and tried to run, others made clumsy attempts to hold their ground.

The result was the same in all cases. A *chasseur* would detach from the squadron and canter toward the terrified man. The saber would rise, the horseman would lean gracefully into the task and at the right moment would slash down, slicing blood and bone like a butcher's cleaver—a brief death cry, and on the road would be another untidy huddle.

One brave soul tried to make a stand: he swung round to face the enemy, aiming his musket at the horseman. The *chasseur* rode at him, bending low over the horse's mane, his pennon held in pig-sticking fashion. The musket puffed smoke, but the bullet went wide. Instantly, Kydd saw the bloody spike of the lance emerge from the soldier's back. There was a tearing shriek as the impaled man was forcibly rotated on the ground to allow the weapon to be withdrawn by the *chasseur* as he cantered past.

One man at the extremity of exhaustion was only yards away. He staggered and swayed toward them, his eyes coal pits of terror, his mouth working. "God's mercy, let me in! For the love of Christ—" He could hear the thunder of hooves behind him and began blubbering and screaming.

The marines held firm, not a man moved to open the ranks. If the cavalry got inside the square it was the finish—very quickly.

"Open up, open up—let the poor fucker in!" sailors cried out.

"Still!" roared Tyrell, from the center of the men.

Casually, a lone rider turned and began his run, deliberate and measured. At its culmination the saber lifted and fell, slicing through hands pitifully trying to fend off the inevitable. The man's skull split like a melon and cascaded blood and brains.

A cry of rage broke from the seamen. "Fire at 'im, yer bastards! Get 'im!"

The marines, however, would not be drawn. The muskets would wait for the main charge, which must surely come.

Out of range, the squadron eddied and weaved, assembling for the charge. One of their number slashed at his horse's side and urged it ahead. The others followed at a brisk trot, heading straight for the unmoving square. Kydd could see the sun-darkened features of the horsemen, concentrating on their target, foreign, disturbing, frightening. The canter turned into a gallop, then a race, a full-blooded charge.

Kydd looked at the stolid faces of the marines, searching for some kind of reassurance.

"Steady, you men!" Dawkins called, voice cool and composed.

"Present . . ." The muskets rose and settled on aim.

The horses pounded nearer, nearer.

"Front rank—wait for it—front rank, fire!"

The muskets crashed out and the smoke rolled forward, hiding the horsemen, before it rose slowly, showing the riders considerably nearer, but also empty saddles. The muskets slammed on the ground and inclined forward, the bayonets a formidable barrier.

The horses pounded on.

"Center rank—fire!"

Again the crash of muskets, more smoke, but Kydd could see what the closer range told. One face dissolved into blood, the man swaying and falling, bringing down his horse. Another folded over and was left draped forward over the speeding horse's mane.

From this distance the expressions of the horsemen were clear—snarls, determination and, in more than one case, apprehension. And then they were upon the rigid square.

At the last possible moment reins were hauled over and the riders streamed past on each side. Unable to break up the square by sheer terror, they in turn made easy targets as the foam-flecked horses thundered past and more riders fell.

They turned and regrouped, some of the horses nervous, plunging and stamping. Again they came, but their high spirits had left them. It was a halfhearted performance, and afterward they turned and galloped back over the hill.

The seamen cheered to a man. Unused to doing nothing in action, they had found the experience daunting, and boisterously gave vent to their fears.

"Good thing there are no field pieces," the lieutenant of marines told Tyrell coolly. "A square cannot stand against a six-pound ball."

Nearby a cavalryman, wounded in the leg, crawled away on all fours.

An insane howl broke out, and a private of the 93rd burst out of the square and limped across to the wounded man. He shouted hoarsely, beast-like. The Frenchman stopped and looked back. He tried to stand, but fell again. As he sprawled he tugged at his saber, but it was trapped under his body. His movements grew agitated and at the last minute he fell on his back and his arms went up.

With what looked like a tenting tool the private fell upon the horseman, hacking and gouging frantically. Inhuman shrieks came from the writhing figure, helpless under the onslaught.

The bloodied instrument rose and fell in savage chops. There was no more movement. Still the butchery continued, but finally the man fell across the body, weeping.

"March!" Tyrell ordered.

The pace was punishing. Kydd trudged on, trying to keep up with the rapid rate of march, but he found himself beginning to slow. It was simply that his leg muscles would no longer obey—they felt like lead and refused to swing faster.

The others pulled ahead.

"I do conceive that they will be back," said Renzi.

Kydd had not noticed that he had fallen back as well. "Yes," he said, too beaten to say more, moving forward stubbornly, one foot in front of the other like an automaton. His eyes glazed, set on the road moving beneath him, his breath coming in ragged gasps.

They felt it first—through the ground came a vibration, a subliminal presentiment of doom. It became a sound, the hateful drumming of horses, and they knew then what to expect.

"Square!" bellowed Tyrell.

It was hopeless. Together with others who had fallen behind, Kydd saw the square form—and close. They were too late.

Around the corner came the hated cavalry: they would catch the square unformed and smash it, or they would have their way with the stragglers—there seemed enough about to offer them sport. Kydd knew he was going to die. Strangely, he felt no terror, only a great disappointment. He had badly wanted to be rated able seaman and fulfill his promise to Bowyer, but now . . . He could go no farther; he would turn and face his end. A rider on a black horse had already singled him out for his victim and was beginning his run.

Emotion flooded him, an inchoate rage. His back straightened and his fists bunched. He faced the *chasseur*—he would try to drag the rider off his horse or something. He shouted meaninglessly at his nemesis—but he found himself jerked off his feet.

"Here, you half-wit!" Renzi yelled. He had found a peculiarly shaped cleft rock back from the road and dragged Kydd over to it.

They made it with feet to spare, cramming into the space in a mad scramble. The horseman slid to a clattering stop, just yards away. He stayed for a moment, uncertain, then grinned, a flash of white teeth under a black mustache. He raised his sword hilt to his lips in mock salute and rode off after easier prey.

Sounds of battle drifted away down the road, getting fainter and fainter. The late afternoon insects could be heard and the peace of the countryside prevailed. But now they were alone—alone in the territory of their enemy.

"Up the hill—we've got to get away from here damn quick before they come back looking for us," said Renzi, extricating himself from the cleft.

The hillside folded into a small dry valley, thickly overgrown with mimosa and gorse. Plunging into it, they found the going tough, but fear drove them on. Twenty minutes later they had established a comfortable hundred-yard barrier of prickly growth. Hooves sounded on the road below—they dropped to a crouch and peered down.

Several cavalrymen reined their horses to a walk as they searched the sides of the road. An isolated scream sounded once but in the main they passed on up the road, prodding the scattered corpses as they went.

Kydd and Renzi crouched, motionless, the pungent scent of the undergrowth almost overpowering.

"We can't follow the road," Renzi whispered. "Despard will be marching on St. Pontrieux just as soon as he can. The road's going to be alive with soldiers."

It was impossible to tell what lay over the crest above but they had no choice. Fighting their way cautiously upward, they broke through the bushes into poor grass interspersed with weathered granite outcrops. Soon the road was out of sight.

"Nicholas, your pardon, but I am foundered, beat. Could we not . . ."

"Of course, dear fellow." It would mean the end of any chance to catch up with their shipmates, but Renzi looked about for somewhere to rest. The sun was already out of sight beyond the crest of the hill and the chill of evening was coming on. The resting-place would have to serve for the night as well.

The best that could be found was an overhanging rock under which they sat, Kydd groaning with exhaustion.

"It has a certain attraction, this country I find," Renzi said, musing through his own aching fatigue. "A definable quality of beauty that stems perhaps from its very wildness."

"Yes," said Kydd, in a muffled voice.

"A grandeur, a nobility that one supposes can only exist as a consequence of man's inability to impose his will on this rugged land."

There was no answering comment. Kydd's head drooped and he slid sideways against his friend.

Renzi could not bring himself to speak of his fears. Without doubt St. Pontrieux would be taken very soon and the British would give up the project, and sail away. He tried not to think of the consequence. Abandoned in a hostile land, he and Kydd would not last long.

While Renzi brooded and dozed, Kydd slept; a deep, profound and necessary sleep for a youthful body not yet fully hardened by sea life.

Renzi awoke shivering. It was dark and chill, the nearly full moon veiled in cloud. Kydd was awake and Renzi noted ironically that he was now leaning up against his friend.

"B-bloody c-cold!" Kydd said.

They both shuddered uncontrollably, hugging their knees.

"What o'clock is it?" Kydd croaked.

"Past midnight, is all I can say," Renzi replied.

Kydd stood up stiffly and cuffed himself. "This is no good—we shall die of the cold. We must go on."

"Yes, of course."

Their bodies aching and protesting, instinctively they headed for the top of the ridge. They trudged slowly, letting their muscles take up again, on and up the shadowed slopes. The moon-distorted countryside felt cruel and hard. Renzi foresaw them trying to hold to a steady course in the night, crashing into unseen obstacles, going in circles, awakening a hostile countryside. It was madness. Dark patches of tussocks lay everywhere and the hilltops in the distance were tinged with silver. It was deathly still, disturbed only by unseen scurries of wildlife. A soft flutter of wings signified either a bat or an owl, and a rabbit screamed as it was taken by a stoat.

They reached the top just as the moon retreated behind the clouds once more. They stumbled on in the dark, tripping over rocks and plowing through bushes, conscious all the while of gnawing hunger.

The moon emerged again, and Kydd jerked with surprise. On all sides they were surrounded by gigantic structures rearing up in black evil ranks, glowering down on them. His hair stood on end; there was something primeval and overpowering about them.

"Cromlechs!" Renzi breathed.

"What?"

"The Breton dolmen! I've never seen one before—a mighty building of stone, untold ages old. Built by an unknown people, for who knows what purpose?" Renzi wandered about the big stone circle, marveling. "Look, I do believe that we should wait until the morrow," he said, "until we can see where we should go."

"So we can gaze upon y'r stones?" Kydd snapped.

"Not at all," Renzi lied. "So that we are in no danger of having to retrace our steps."

"Then I wish you joy of y'r rest. I will continue." Kydd's face was indistinct in the shifting patterns of moonlight.

"You will find that St. Pontrieux has been taken," Renzi said softly.

A slight hesitation. "Do y' think I've not thought of that? Enough waste of time. I'm leaving."

Renzi noted the slumped shoulders, the dragging feet. Kydd was past caring. His heart went out to the lonely figure hobbling stubbornly through the gloomy megaliths and out of sight. For a minute or so he waited alone, then reluctantly went after him, only to see Kydd heading back toward him, head down.

"Be damned to both you and y'r stones, Renzi!" Kydd said thickly, swaying past and dropping to the ground in the lee of the central one.

"You will find that our mysterious ancestors always built at a prominence," Renzi said gently. "Tomorrow we shall have such a splendid view as will make you stare."

The long cold night eventually gave way to a gray misty dawn, the light of day turning the gaunt black megaliths to gray, lichen-covered crags. The mist stayed with the daylight, a quiet enshrouding white that dappled all things with a gentle dew. They cast about, and it was not long before they came across a well-worn animal track meandering along the ridge top. Hunger had become an insistent, hollow pain. They tramped on, not speaking.

A muffled sound carried through the mist. They stood absolutely still.

Hooves! It was impossible to say from where the sound came in the enfolding white and they remained rigid, ears straining. Then out of the mist trotted a small goat. It saw them and stopped in surprise.

"Breakfast," Kydd whispered.

"*Yes!*" gloated Renzi.

Kydd advanced slowly on the animal, which pawed the ground uncertainly.

"Pretty little one, come to me . . ."

A few feet away he lunged, and grappled the terrified animal by the horns, wrestling it to the ground. It kicked and struggled, bleating piteously, but eventually it lay still.

Kydd held it securely, its big frightened eyes rolling. "What do I do now?" he gasped.

"Kill it!"

"How?"

So focused on the animal were they that the little girl was able to come upon them unawares. "*Qu'est-ce que vous faites avec ma chèvre?*" she cried out, aggrieved.

"*Sois calme, mon enfant!*" Renzi said, in a soothing tone, removing his battered hat politely. "Your little goat, my friend thinks it has hurt its foot," he continued smoothly. He went to the goat and stroked its head. "You think it's hurt its foot!" he muttered at the mystified Kydd, who immediately began carefully to inspect a dainty hoof.

Kydd let the goat go and smiled winningly at the little girl.

"Who are you, *M'sieur?* A villain perhaps, or a lost Royalist?" she said, looking at them doubtfully.

"But, no!" said Renzi, frowning at the suggestion. "We are, unhappily, lost. We seek the farm of *Monsieur,* er, *M'sieur . . .*"

"Pleneuf?"

"Yes, child. May we know in which direction it lies?"

"I will tell you. It is back along the track. You go down the hill there."

Renzi smacked his forehead. "Of course! A thousand thanks for your kindness." He bowed.

"*Viens avec moi, mon fou!*" he told Kydd, beckoning to him unmistakably. They walked away, Renzi waving reassuringly at the little girl.

They followed the track down, the mist clearing as they went. Pastures and cultivated fields gave warning of the farm and they stopped at a safe distance.

"We must eat or we perish," Renzi said. "I have the liveliest recollection that in the barns they cure the most excellent bacon and keep stone jars of cold cider. Shall we proceed?" His eyes gleamed.

They stole toward the farm buildings, uncomfortably aware that in their seaman's rig they were utterly unlike the smocked and gaitered rural folk and would have no chance of passing themselves off as anything but what they were.

The ancient barn smelled powerfully of old hay as they slipped in through the vast doors hanging ajar. As their eyes adapted to the gloom, they went farther in, rummaging feverishly for stone jars or hanging flitches.

A sudden shadow made them look up, then wheel round—but it was too late. The man in the sunlight at the door held a fowling-piece, an old and ugly but perfectly serviceable weapon, its long barrel trained steadily on them.

"*Ah, Monsieur*—" began Renzi, stepping forward.

"*Non!*" The flintlock jabbed forward. "*Qui êtes vous?*" The dark-jowled farmer moved carefully into the barn to take a closer look. "*Diable! Les foutus anglais!*" The muzzle jerked up.

There was nothing they could say or do as they were marched out.

"*Par pitié, Monsieur!* We are famished, thirsty. For the love of Christ, something!"

The farmer said nothing, and outside the stables threw a key to the ground. He indicated to Kydd that he should open the massive old padlock. They entered a small stable. Still keeping the gun trained on them, he closed the lower door. Before the top half shut he leaned in with a triumphant look and spoke. He would immediately go to town and fetch soldiers, but out of pity he would first ask his wife to bring a little of the morning *mijoté* for them to eat, and possibly some cider.

The upper door slammed shut and they sank down on the straw.

"What're our chances?" Kydd said.

Renzi answered, with some hesitation, "Well, we can take it now that St. Pontrieux has fallen, probably without a fight. The soldiers therefore will be cheated of their victory, and will be in an ugly mood." He scratched his side—there were fleas in the stable. "What is worse for us, many of our men will have been saved because the ships will have taken them up, and this they will have seen. Perhaps it is not a good idea to be a sailor at such a time." The lines in his face deepened.

Kydd said nothing: if there was something to be faced, then he would face it without flinching.

There was a rattling of the padlock and the door was flung open. In the glare of sunlight they became aware of the mob cap and pinafore of a woman. Preceded by the farmer with his flintlock, she entered warily with a tray. She gave a little scream and the tray crashed to the ground. The farmer growled in bafflement. *"Les anglais!"* she faltered. "They—look so fierce!"

The farmer relaxed. *"Espèce de connard!"* he said dismissively.

He waited until fresh food had been brought, and swung in a stone jar. The door slammed shut and the two fell upon the food.

"Silly woman!" Kydd said, without malice, savaging a chicken leg that had found its way into the ragoût.

"I think not," Renzi said meaningfully. He tore ravenously at the country bread. It was infinitely the best meal he had ever had, the rough cider complementing the natural flavor of the Breton cooking.

Puzzled, Kydd looked at him. An urgent rattling at the door was his answer. It was flung open and the farmer's wife was standing there. "You must go now!" she said urgently, in accented English.

"Marie," Renzi said, in a low voice.

"No! Leave now! He will be back with soldiers soon."

"But—"

"Nicholas, I am married now. Married, *hein!* Please go!"

Renzi moved forward and held her. She sobbed just once, but pushed him firmly away. "Go to the house of Madame Dahouet," she said quickly. "It is the white house on the corner of the avenue du Quatorze Juillet off the square. She is a—*sympathisante.* Her son die in Paris."

Renzi stood reluctant.

"Take care, my love—*allez avec Dieu!*" She drew back against the door, her eyes fixed on his. "Go," she whispered.

CHAPTER 9

KYDD AND RENZI WAITED until the first light of dawn before entering the town. The river lay to their left, an easy signpost to the plaza they had left just days before. There were no more Bourbon lilies on display, no more white banners. Instead, the flag of revolution hung everywhere around them.

The town was silent, a curfew obviously in force. They removed their shoes and crept noiselessly toward the square, keeping well in to the side of the street. In the silence the measured tread of approaching sentries gave them adequate warning.

On one side of the square stood a tall structure in the dark. "Guillotine!" Renzi whispered.

Kydd shivered—the smell of blood hung in the air.

A sentry paced slowly by the guillotine. He was militia, dressed raggedly. His Phrygian cap had a tricolor cockade, just as the patriotic prints had it in the shops in England.

Timing their movements, Kydd and Renzi worked their way round toward a once grand house, which, as it was the only white building off the square, had to be their destination. The sky was lightening noticeably in the east when they reached it.

"Shy a pebble at th' window," Kydd whispered.

"You," Renzi hissed, sure that Kydd would do it better.

Kydd picked up a light stone, judged the distance carefully and caught the pane. It rattled and the stone fell.

Nothing. The first rays of morning were appearing; the gray dawn was fast disappearing in the promise of another fine day. Kydd tried again. Still nothing. The window remained shut. By now they would be easily visible to anyone chancing along the street. Kydd picked up another stone.

The door opened suddenly and noiselessly. They were yanked roughly inside. A sharp-faced woman glared at them. She had papers in her hair and wore a floor-length chemise and faded slippers. "You fools!" she said bitterly in English. "Do you beg to be caught?"

"Madame Dahouet?" Renzi enquired, with the utmost politeness, making an elegant leg.

Surprised, the woman bobbed in return. Then suspicion returned to pinch her face.

"Madame, might I be permitted to present my compliments and those of Madame Marie Pleneuf, who wishes to be remembered to you." He spoke in the flowery French of the old regime.

She fingered his dirty seaman's jacket doubtfully.

"I am, as you see, necessarily in disguise, Madame."

"Ah!" she said, satisfied. "Your French is very good, *Monsieur*." She went to the heavily curtained window and peeped outside, checking carefully. She spoke in English for Kydd's benefit. "It is not safe here, but I have a hiding place prepared . . ."

The hiding place was an ancient pigsty—still very much in use.

They looked at it in dismay. Fat pink and black pigs lay in a sea of mud and dung and on the far side of them was a rickety old wooden construction.

"No!" blurted Kydd.

"No *cochon* of a brave revolutionary would soil himself in that place. You are safe there."

"We can't—" Kydd felt sick at the thought.

The woman's eyes darted back across the yard fearfully, and she stamped her foot in exasperation.

Hastily, Renzi agreed. "Yes, Madame, you are right. This will prove an excellent hiding place—we thank you most heartily."

He lifted his leg over the low palings and plopped it down into the sty. The nearest pig rolled over to peer up at him. He brought the other leg over—the mud was ankle deep. As he began to wade over to the low entrance of the shed, the pigs scrambled to their feet, squealing and snuffling. Renzi, certainly no farmer, felt alarm at their huge presence.

"They won't bother you—go on, *Monsieur,*" Madame Dahouet said to Kydd, who followed Renzi into the mire.

Renzi reached the entrance, bent down—and recoiled. But there was no avoiding it: he went down on his hands and knees in the muck and shuffled in.

Kydd held his breath and followed. It was utterly black inside, despite the few tiny chinks of daylight that showed between age-distorted boards. The floor was a little more firm, but it was strewn with rancid straw, which made his eyes water.

"Well, now, look 'oo's come to visit." The deep-chested voice startled them.

"Who—?"

A bass laugh followed. "Sar'nt Piggott, Private Sawkins 'n' Corporal Daryton, at yer service, gemmun!" His fruity chuckle subsided.

The darkness lessened: it was possible to make out three forms leaning up against the back side of the shed. Inside it was steamy hot and close.

"Renzi and Kydd, seamen in *Duke William*. Delighted to make your acquaintance."

"Ooh—lah-de-dah! 'N' who's yer lady's maid, then?" the bass voice rejoined. "Yer'll find we're no frien's of the Navy—yer chums jus' sailed off leavin' us, 'n' there we was, fightin' rearguard while they offs to save their skins."

"Well, you soldiers didn't do so bloody well keepin' the Frogs off our backs when we was pullin' *your* guns!" Kydd retorted bitterly. A fly buzzed and settled. Kydd slapped at it, but it evaded him and circled to land on him somewhere else. More flies swarmed and settled.

He squelched over to the side wall and sat with his head down. He smacked viciously at the flies, which rose in clouds and returned immediately to the fresh muck now spread over most of his clothes.

A different voice piped up. "Yer gets to leave 'em be, else yer like ter go mad."

"Shut yer face, Weasel!" the deep voice said.

Renzi heaved himself up beside Kydd, saying nothing.

Kydd fidgeted, trying to scrape away some of the slime, and waved at the flies. "How long?" He groaned quietly.

There was no reply for a long time.

"I do think, my friend, that we may be here for some considerable time," Renzi answered. "We must wait for things to die down, and then . . . and then . . ." He tailed off.

"Nah! Yer 'aven't got a clue, 'ave yer? Well, we 'ave, see, 'n' if yez wants ter come in wiv us, yer learns a bit o' respeck first!"

"Give over, Toby, it ain't the fault o' they sailors we're 'ere, now, is it?" the third voice said. "Never mind 'im, 'e doesn't mean ter be pernickety. Wot we're goin' to do is—after it goes quiet like, o' course—is ter break out t' the south. We march b' night 'n' sleeps b' day, till we gets ter Spain. See?"

"Have you any idea at all how far it is to Spain?" Renzi said quietly.

"Well, I reckons we can do it in five days' march—I mean nights— 'n' in the 93rd th' quick march means a hunnerd and forty paces a minute, it is."

Renzi sighed. "If it were possible to go in a straight line, which I doubt, it's close to four hundred miles. That's near sixteen days—or nights," he added.

"How do yer know that, then, me old cock?" The bass voice came from Sergeant Piggott, Kydd noted, the grimy stripes now just visible under the dried muck on the big man's arm.

The day dragged on. The stench, the filth, the flies. Occasionally, the pigs would wallow and squabble and try to enter the shed, and were pushed away, squealing in protest.

"We have to steal a boat—there must be a fishin' boat or somethin'," Kydd burst out.

"Yeah! That's it!" the third man exclaimed.

"All the boats will be well guarded, and in any case in a small boat we wouldn't stand a chance in the open sea," Renzi said, in a level tone.

"We don't get to the open sea! We lie offshore an' wait for our ships on blockade to come t' us!"

"And the boat?"

"We get Madame to spy one out f'r us, and nobble the sentry—there's five o' us!"

The talk of escape died away as they waited hungrily for the evening food. This took the form of cheese between bread, wrapped in a napkin. Madame was not encouraging. "I will see. There are three sentries on the quay and the police barracks is nearby. But I will do my best."

Dusk fell. Then nightfall. The private whimpered in his fitful sleep and Kydd cursed listlessly at the cold filth covering everything.

They could not be allowed into the house, the stench hanging on the air would give the game away, and in any case it would be too much to bear, to clean up only to re-immerse themselves in this hellish stew. The corporal had turned over in his sleep and his face had become slimed; his attempts to scrape it off had spread it further. The sergeant snored like a rusty saw. Kydd leaned his head back and stared into the blackness.

It was not long before dawn when he heard the rapid tap of the woman's footsteps approaching across the yard. Kydd jerked upright. He and Renzi crawled to the entrance.

"Listen to me!" she called. "There is a beach not far from here. From it Monsieur Pirou goes to find the—how do you say it?—the *crémaillère* for the—curse this language! *Les langoustes.*"

"He goes to lift the lobster pots," said Renzi.

"Yes, it is only a small boat, but it may be sufficient for you sailors—I do not know these things."

Kydd's expression was eager.

"But, *attention*, Monsieur Pirou, if he is there, is not to be harmed! Do you understand? He does not sympathize but I will not have him harmed. He—he is an old man and a friend and—"

"We understand, Madame. Pray do not fear for Monsieur Pirou."

She studied Renzi's face. "Very well. Now, this is what you must do. The *voiture puisard*—the cart of the night, I think you say—passes by this house on its way to the country. Its odor, may I declare, will hide yours. I will stop it and you will get underneath and hang on. Get off at the first hill—you understand? The first hill. The beach is there."

"Excellent, Madame. A wonderful plan. It does credit to your intelligence."

Her face broke into a cold smile. "*Eh, bien!* In the last war my husband was a corsair, and much esteemed—you English have reason to remember his name, I believe."

Renzi laughed. "And our thanks are yours, Madame. No words can express our gratitude to you."

Her face hardened. "If you can do something to topple those . . . *crapules, les salauds,* I will be content! But *attend!* If you are taken up when you attempt your escape, I can do nothing! I must disown you. It will be understood that you hid in the sty without my knowledge. Understood?"

"Yes, Madame."

"Then here is a wineskin—of water," she added quickly. "You will perhaps need this on that sea." Her eyes rested on Kydd for a moment. "I wish you well, Englishmen."

It was easy. Crouching behind the front door, they heard the cart rumble closer. The sickly smell of the cesspit wreathed the air. The cart ground past.

Madame Dahouet flung open the door and ran out to the horse. "*Hélas! Mon pauvre chat! Monsieur*—have you seen my cat on your rounds? *Merde!* He has been gone all this night, I am so distracted!"

The fugitives looked hurriedly down the street, deserted in the cold dawn, then slunk quietly under the cart. Sure enough, under the giant tank there was a framework and sacks, which they pulled over themselves in the cramped, stinking space.

"Out of my way, Madame! No, I have not seen your cat. Now let me get on before your neighbors complain."

The cart trundled on. They felt it turn and straighten until all sense of direction was lost.

Kydd did not dare to peep out, and could only hope the others would be as careful. The cart swung once more, and the quickened pace of the horse meant that they would be on a road out of town.

There! A definite lift. The cart creaked and the horse's gait shortened—it was definitely a hill. He felt someone jab him in the ribs. He peered out cautiously: the country road passed beneath and in the bright early morning there was no one in sight.

He wriggled to the back of the framework and, like the others, dropped to the ground. The cart continued, its driver not looking back.

A track wound down to a tiny beach, overhung by trees. They slipped closer.

Drawn up above the high-water mark was a boat with a single mast. Sitting on the sand next to it in the early morning sun was a fisherman.

"Only one! This is gonna be easy meat!" Piggott crowed.

"He's not to be touched!" Renzi said quietly, turning to face Piggott.

The sergeant was thick-set and pugnacious, and leered aggressively. "It's 'im or us, simple as that. We has to go 'im—but you Jack Tars wouldn't unnerstand anythin' about that."

Kydd pulled Piggott round. "If y' lay a hand on 'im . . ."

Piggott hesitated. He noted Kydd's dangerous eyes and wiry strength. "Temper, temper! All right, 'e don't get touched. But tell me this, Mr. Fire Eater, 'ow do you think we're goin' to get the boat, then?"

"Like this," Kydd said, and advanced down the sand. The others followed. He had gambled that the fisherman would not be alarmed if they came normally, and he was right.

The man looked up as they approached, and his eyes widened at their appearance. He had an oaken, seamed old face and a neat beard. He dropped the net and scrambled to his feet. He spoke, but not in any French that Renzi knew. His voice was high and fluting, querulous.

"He's speaking Breton," Renzi muttered.

"*Monsieur,* unfortunately I have not the Breton tongue," he said in French.

"*Alors.* Who are you, that you stink so much?" Pirou replied.

"Tell 'im that we're takin' the boat now," Piggott spat.

His English gave the game away. "*L'anglais!*" Pirou gasped.

"Get him!" Kydd said, seizing an arm.

Pirou shouted desperately. They forced him to the ground, his frail old bones no match for the soldiers.

"*Mon brave,* I would be desolated were I to be obliged to silence you," Renzi said, hefting a rock significantly. The man subsided, but a fierce glint remained in his eyes. Renzi found a length of rope and they bound him.

"He comes with us," Kydd said shortly, knowing that it was too dangerous to leave him there. They carried him to the boat and lowered him inside.

"You three on that side," Kydd said sharply.

"Shut it, mate! See these?" Piggott tapped the stripes on his arm. "Sergeant. I'm takin' charge!" He walked around and stood menacingly over Kydd, who faced up to him, his eyes flaring.

The corporal thrust forward. "Now, Toby, we're goin' on the sea. Let them take over fer now. Come on, mate, they're sailors 'n' knows wot they're about."

Piggott glared, but eventually growled an acknowledgment.

With five men, the boat lifted easily. They carried it down the sand and into the water. The waves swept in boisterously and Kydd's heart lifted at the boat's eager bob. Exhilaration filled him.

Waves slapped the transom hard. "Bows to sea," he warned.

The soldiers clumsily obeyed and the boat rotated to seaward. They pushed it out knee deep, the waves surging in.

"Right—in th' boat," Kydd ordered, holding it by the squared-off transom. Renzi got aboard first and helped the soldiers over the side and, with a kick backwards, Kydd finally heaved himself in.

"Get down—only one man must be seen in the boat," Kydd hissed at the soldiers. Without a word Renzi took the oars, pulling strongly through the shallows out toward the blessed horizon, the wonderful salt sea smell penetrating through the stink of dried pig sludge.

After a while Kydd rolled on to his back and looked up at the blue sky and fluffy clouds. The boat bobbed and the water chuckled under the bow; the fishing gear smelled strongly but pleasantly and there was nothing more he could do but lie down and stare up dreamily.

A lazy half hour later, Renzi's long, comfortable strokes slowed and he stopped and boated the dripping oars. He stood up and, to Kydd's amazement, stripped stark naked.

"Come on in," said Renzi, and made a neat dive overside.

Kydd sat up. They were to seaward of a seaweed-strewn rocky islet. They would not be seen from the shore.

Renzi surfaced, spluttering, at the boat's side. "A mite cold for my taste," he said, through chattering teeth, "but needs must." He reached into the boat for his clothes and began to wash them in the sea.

"My oath! That's wot to do," said Piggott.

The mire dissolved into the clear green water, and five naked men shouted and laughed in the simple joy of being alive.

"Let's rig the sail." Renzi rummaged over the tightly rolled canvas, lashed with its own rigging, and tried to make sense of it. Pirou glared at them balefully, and when asked about it spat over the side, remaining mute.

The sail turned out to be a peculiar form of dipping lug, but it ran up the mast easily enough. The reason for the rig soon became clear: it could be maneuvered by one man at the tiller.

They continued their voyage, Kydd at the tiller now, the small boat scudding along in the pleasant breeze as it took them out farther and farther. The sun increased in strength, benign and warm.

The waves grew higher, the little boat swooping up hills of water, and down into valleys. Occasionally a boisterous roller would burst spray over them, and the soldiers started to look apprehensive.

They untied the old man, who rubbed his arms accusingly. The corporal suddenly heaved and vomited over the side, bringing on the same in the little private. They hung limply over the gunwale.

The sun rose higher. The distant land lost its distinctiveness, becoming an anonymous craggy coastline. A larger wave thumped the side and splashed them—the soldiers cried out in alarm.

The water felt cold and disconcerting, and swilled in the bottom of the boat. Kydd held the tiller tightly.

"We're sinking!" A squawk of terror came from the private.

Kydd hesitated. There was certainly a good deal of water in the bottom, and his face creased in anxiety. The boat felt sluggish somehow, not so willing.

The water was gaining, that much was clear—but why? The soldiers bailed frantically with anything they could find, and seemed near panic. He sensed their fear and felt it wash up against himself. The swell surged higher, now appearing menacing and sinister—it was amazing how different it was to be in a little cockleshell instead of striding the decks of a man-o'-war.

There was little that could be done to find the leak with the boat crowded as it was. The soldiers gabbled to each other in their terror, and cold dread crept over Kydd. To have got so far, and then to die by the very element he had yearned for! He gripped the tiller, his eyes searching for an answer.

Then he caught the triumphant stare of the old man—and realized what had happened. "He's pulled the bung! Get at it, Nicholas!"

Renzi thrust past the old man and, sure enough, the water was gouting in. He prized the bung from the fisherman's grasp and pushed it home.

The effect was noticeable. As the bailed water flew over the side, the boat returned to its previous jaunty bob.

"We must be out far enough," Renzi said.

The rocks and islands had fallen away astern and it looked a safe distance for a big ship to be traveling offshore. The vast seascape, however, seemed careless of their existence, exuberant rollers surging past, superimposed on a massive underlying swell that seemed to flex like mighty muscles moving under the surface of the ocean.

Renzi doused the little sail and took position at the oars again, keeping the bows facing the oncoming rollers with occasional tugs. They waited.

It had seemed a good idea, simply to wait for the blockading cruisers to happen by, but they had no idea of strategic naval movements and, as the day wore on, the idea lost its appeal and finally slipped toward fantasy. There must be over a thousand miles of coastline to blockade, and with how many ships? The chances that one would happen along just at this time were small, in fact vanishingly small.

The seas were now relatively slight, the weather kind and sunny, but that would not last—it could change with terrifying speed, faster possibly than they could make it back to land. The boat could not take even a small deterioration in conditions.

Kydd was aching with the fatigue that bracing against the constant jerking about was producing. It was a never-ending struggle to avoid being flung this way and that as the boat slammed to and fro. The corporal had lost his headgear and was touched by the sun. He was clearly suffering: weak from seasickness, he flopped about as the seas buffeted the tiny boat, his eyes rolling. The private was sunk in misery, facing outboard with both arms over the side. Piggott sat with his back to the mast, his eyes closed.

What if a ship finally came and it was French? The thought stabbed at Renzi, but it was the more likely outcome, given that they were only a few miles from France. He decided not to speak of it, but furtively checked the horizon. It was empty.

The sun lowered in the sky, and the breeze grew colder and strengthened. The sea took on a darker, more somber tint as the angle of the sun's rays dipped.

Renzi knew it would soon be decision time. It was inconceivable that they could survive the night. A tide set could carry them dangerously far down the coast, the weather might clamp in. The only option was to return.

They would have to kill the old man. It was the only way to be sure that he would not betray them. Then they could touch on one of the tiny beaches and hide for the night. He looked at the old fisherman, who sat near Kydd, looking back to the coast with a distant expression, his hands fidgeting—old, tough hands gnarled by the hard work of years.

"We have to return," Renzi said, and Kydd nodded. Renzi hoisted the sail, ignoring the old man's exultant look. He reached up to dip the lug for the return passage, but as he did so his eyes caught a subliminal fleck of white somewhere out to seaward. The boat swayed alarmingly as he stood up, but he was heedless. The horizon remained a stippled line, still with no sign. He scanned until his eyes watered and suddenly caught the distant flash of white again before it disappeared. "Sail!" he screamed.

Kydd leaped to his feet, the boat teetering over and just recovering. He dropped to the tiller and they altered course for the stranger.

"What if it's a Frenchie?" Kydd asked.

Renzi looked at him and shrugged.

The evening waves reared up higher, it seemed, dusky shadows in their wake, the beginnings of a sunset ahead. In a fever of excitement they saw the white fleck come in and out of existence, then remain steady.

"If it's a Frog, c'n we get away agin'?" the private wanted to know.

"I'm afraid not," Renzi replied. Almost anything afloat would outsail their little craft. There was no point in hiding the fact.

The white grew in size, resolving into three distinct blobs, and Renzi could see that it was a ship-rigged vessel on a broad reach, cutting their course ahead. Her hull was obscured most of the time by the heave of the swell, but it was sufficient to note that she had but one gundeck, and therefore was not *Duke William*. The disappointment was hard yet he had no reason to think that it would be *Duke William* and he was angry with himself for the loose thinking.

"*Une frégate française, je crois!*" the fisherman said, with great satisfaction.

The masts altered their aspect, and it was apparent that the ship was turning to intercept. "He thinks it's a French frigate," Renzi told Kydd quietly.

"*Ce vaisseau-là c'est* La Concorde *de L'Orient,*" the old man said definitively.

"What's he say?" Kydd said.

"Says that's *La Concorde.*"

"You sure?" Kydd said, his voice unnaturally intense.

"Yes."

"Ha!" Kydd shouted. He transfixed the old man with a look of triumph. "Tell the old bastard that it's a French frigate, all right—but she was taken by us in the first week of the war! By *Circe* 32, if my memory serves aright!" He laughed.

With a bone in her teeth the frigate came along in fine style—and, sure enough, above the yellow and black of her hull streamed out the white ensign of Admiral Howe's fleet.

The soldiers, roused from their stupor, capered insanely. The private tore off his red coat and waved it frantically over his head, screaming in delight.

"God rot me! An' what could yer do then, Tom?"

Stirk's interest encouraged Kydd to go on. He grinned at the circle of faces and said, "Well, what else could I do if I didn't fancy spendin' me days in a Frog chokey? It was over the fence and in with the pigs 'n' all their shite."

There was a hissing of indrawn breath. The dog-watch was well under way, the off-duty watchmen taking a pipe of baccy on the fo'c'sle in the gentle glow of the lanthorns, others with their grog cans.

"Hey now, Pedro! Yon Kydd—his pot has the mark of Moll Thompson upon it!"

The Iberian started, then grimaced. "For a story li' that, I give," he said, filling Kydd's empty tankard from a small beer tub.

"Where *is* Renzi?" Claggett asked.

Kydd looked at him levelly and said, "He's got his reasons right enough, Samuel. We just leave him alone, should he want it that way."

"Didn't mean ter be nosy, Tom, but yer must admit, he's a queer fish, is Renzi." Kydd said nothing, drinking his beer and still regarding Claggett steadily. "Yair, well, 'e's yer friend an' all," Claggett said.

"I were taken once, but it weren't the Johnny Crapauds!" Doggo's roughened voice cut into the silence, his features animated.

"Well, 'oo was it, then?" said Jewkes.

Doggo looked at him. "Why, it were in . . . let me see, year 'eighty-six, it were." He scratched at his side. "I were waister in the *Dainty* sloop, 'n' we took the ground one night on the Barbary coast. Not th' best place ter be, yer'll admit. Well, seas get up 'n' next thing she's a-poundin' something cruel. Starts ter break up, so's we gets thrown in the oggin all standin'. O' course, we nearly all drowns. In fac', it were just me left to tell yez the tale. Well, I gets dashed ashore 'n' just manages ter crawl up the strand, when all these A-rabs on 'orses comes ridin' up. I 'eard o' these Bedoos before, see, they're bad cess, but I can't do anythin' like I am. They ties me up 'n' rides off with me ter their camp."

His ugly face grew solemn. "There, mates, it were right roaratorious, what wi' me bein' a white man 'n' all. See, they wants me as their slave. 'N' that's what I was, sure enough—has to bow 'n' scrape, all togged up in saucy gear wi' turban 'n' all—you'd 'ave 'ad a good laff should you've seen me! Yeah, seemed I were there ferever."

"Did yer get away, Doggo?" Jewkes asked, bringing on a general laugh at his question.

There was a play at discovering his pot was empty. After it was filled again, Doggo continued. "Well, mates, seems an A-rab princess falls in love wi' me, takes me fer her own. Sees me un'appy like, it breaks 'er heart. So she decides to put love before dooty 'n' after a night o' passion sees me off afore dawn on a fast horse, 'n' here I is!"

The whole fo'c'sle fell about in laughter.

With the spreading warmth of the drink inside, the soft dusk and his shipmates about him, Kydd lay back happily, staring up at the stars just beginning to wink into existence in an ultramarine sky, and pondered at the extremes of experience that life could bring.

It was sheer luck that *Duke William* and her escorting frigates had been passing at that particular time. She had been on passage back to her station after landing her evacuees in Plymouth, and at no time would ever have contemplated a blockade of their part of the coast. In the sick bay men writhed in pain, wretches who would have reason to curse the experience if they survived, but Kydd had—and without a scratch. And the old fisherman had been set free with his boat, but had fiercely scorned the couple of guineas offered him by the frigate captain and sailed off making obscene gestures.

And, of course, the proud moment of being received in the great cabin by his captain to tell his story. "Remarkable!" Caldwell had said, making free with his scented handkerchief at certain points in the tale. Besides ordering a gratis issue of slops to replace their tattered and smelly clothes, he had courteously enquired if there was anything further he could do for Kydd.

"To be rated seaman!" Kydd had replied immediately.

Raising his eyebrows, the Captain had glanced at his clerk. "Should you satisfy the boatswain, by all means."

The tough old boatswain had been plain. It would not be easy. "Hand, reef and steer, that's only the start of it, lad. Good seaman knows a mort more. But I'll see as how you gets a proper chance to get it all under yer belt."

He was as good as his word. Paired off with Doud, Kydd found himself in every conceivable element of seamanship. From the tip of the jibboom to the royal yardarms, the cro'jack to the fore topsail stuns'l boom, sometimes frightened, always determined, he steadily made their personal acquaintance. Doud was a prime seaman, having been to sea since a boy; he was also an excellent choice as mentor. He challenged and cajoled Kydd unmercifully, but was always ready with a hand or an explanation.

"We'll take in a first reef in the topsails, I believe," said Lieutenant Lockwood. His serious young face studied the gray scud overhead.

"Way aloft, topmen—man topsail clewlines and buntlines! Weather topsail braces!"

The watch on deck was mustered: some began their skyward climb to the tops while others at the braces heaved laboriously around the yards to lay them square to their marks. The sails, no longer taut and working, flapped noisily.

It was Kydd's first experience at laying out on the yardarm. It was one thing moving out on a steadily pulling set and drawing sail, as he had already done with Doud, and another to achieve something on a loose cloud of flogging canvas.

The captain of the top was unsympathetic. "Weather yardarm, cully," he ordered.

"Where the sport is!" said Doud cheerfully—he would pass the weather earring, the most skilled job of all. Kydd just looked at him.

A heavy creaking of sheaves, and the topsail yard began to lower. The spacious maintop seemed crowded with men, and Kydd took a sharp blow in the side from the men working the reef tackles, which, pulling up on the appropriate reef cringle, had to take the deadweight of the sail.

Doud grinned at Kydd as they waited. "Be ready, mate," he warned.

"Trice up and lay out!"

"Go!" Doud yelled, and swung onto the yard. The inboard iron of the stuns'l boom was disengaged and the boom tricer hoisted it clear. Doud moved out quickly to the farthest extremity of the yard-arm and turned to straddle it facing inwards.

With his heart in his mouth Kydd followed. As he had learned, he leaned his weight over the thick yard until his feet were firmly in the footrope, pushing down and back, and arms clinging to the yard inched his way outward. It was worse than he had expected. The increasing beam seas were causing a roll, which was magnified by height—over to one side, a sudden stop, then an acceleration back to the other in a dizzying arc. In front and beneath him, the hundred-foot width of topsail boisterously flapped and tugged, and he knew he was being watched from below.

"Get movin', you maudling old women!" the captain of the top shouted.

Sailors were being held up by his slow movements, but he couldn't help it. It was heart-stopping to be up there, with nothing but a thin footrope and the yard—and empty space beneath his feet to the deck far below. He knew that soon he would not even have the yard to cling to—both his hands would be needed for work.

He looked down at the deck and the sea sliding past below, so foreshortened at the height of a church steeple.

This was how Bowyer had met his death.

"Haul out to windward!"

The men inclined to leeward and leaned over the yard, bracing against the footrope. Seizing one of the reef points, they heaved the sail bodily over toward Doud at the end. Kydd had no option but to follow suit. It needed all his courage to let go his hold on the yard and balance precariously forward, elbows clamping, and grab one of the points.

"Heave, yer buggers—let's see some tiger!"

It took three pulls and Doud had his turns over the cleat and through the earring on the sail in its new, reefed position. Inclining the opposite way, they hauled out again, achieving the same thing on the lee yardarm. Seized at its ends, the sail's central bulge was now slack and ready for reefing.

Kydd glanced at the men next to him. They worked calmly, industriously, thumping the sail into folds on top of the yard; first small, then larger, pinning them in place with their chests while they leaned down to get another, fisting and slapping the milling sea-worn canvas into place.

There was not much science in Kydd's efforts, but at least he did not let his reef escape. It was with real satisfaction that, holding it in place with the forward reef point, he brought the other up and secured it with an eponymous reef knot.

"Lay in, you lazy swabs!"

He joined the others on the maintop, and met Doud with a grin that could only be described as smug.

The carpenter pursed his lips. It wasn't a bad leak as far as it went, but it was in an awkward place. They were standing in the carpenter's walk, a cramped tunnel of sorts that went round the sides of the orlop, giving access to the area between wind and water in times of battle. It was an eerie sensation, to feel rather than hear the underwater gurgling rush on the outside of the hull. Kydd struggled along behind the carpenter's mate, with a bag of heavy shipwright's tools.

The carpenter bent to take a closer look. His mate obligingly held the lanthorn lower, into the black recesses behind a hanging knee. Water glistened against the blackened timbers of the ship's side.

"Maul," the carpenter said, after a moment. Kydd handed him the weighty tool. A couple of sharp blows at an ancient bolt started it from its seating. Kneeling down, the carpenter gave it a vigorous twist.

A furious half-inch-thick jet of water spurted in, catching Kydd squarely.

"Devil bolt!" the carpenter said. The bolt might have looked sound from the outside, but inside, there was nothing but false-work, crafty peculators at the dockyard having made off with the interior of the long copper bolt. "You'd better get down to the hold and take a squint, Nathan. This won't be the only beggar," he told his mate.

The deck grating was lifted clear, and the man dropped down into the blackness of the hold. The lanthorn was passed down to him.

They could hear him moving about, but then there was silence.

"See anything?" the carpenter called. He was driving an octagonal oak treenail into the gushing bolt hole with accurate smashing hits, the water cutting off to a trickle, then nothing.

There was no reply. "Nathan?" he called again, kneeling down to look into the hold. He was pushed out of the way abruptly by the carpenter's mate. His eyes were staring, his face was white, and he was trembling.

"What's to do, mate?" the carpenter asked softly.

The man gulped and turned to face him. "I s-seen a g-ghost! Somethin' down there—it's 'orrible. I gotta get out've it!"

The carpenter clicked his tongue. "Well, here's a to-do." He hesi-tated for a moment and said, weakly, "Now, Kydd lad, you go below and sort it out for us, my boy."

Kydd sensed the man's fear and felt an answering apprehension. There was nothing wrong with being afraid of ghosts, it stood to reason. He looked at the hole where the grating had been, then back at the carpenter.

"Go on, I'll come if you hails!" the carpenter mumbled.

With the hairs on the back of his neck standing on end, Kydd cautiously dropped down on top of the casks. He looked around fearfully.

There was nothing. He accepted the lanthorn, but its light was lost in the pervasive blackness and he could see little. The stench was unspeakable.

Nervously he moved away from the access hole and crept toward the edge of the casks. Before he reached them he became aware of a sudden discontinuity in the blackness on his left.

It took all his willpower to turn and confront it. It was a dim but definite ghostly blue-green glow, there at the edge of his vision, shapeless, direful. He froze. The light seemed to flicker in the dark of the farthest reaches of the hold but it didn't come closer. His eyes strained. The light strengthened, still wavering and indistinct. Something made him move forward. He reached the edge of the casks.

"Is all well, lad?" came an anxious call from the grating.

A muffled acknowledgment was all Kydd could manage.

The glow was still far off, down there in the shingle. There was no alternative. He slid over the edge and landed with a crash of stones. He looked up. The light was at a different angle now and seemed to be hovering, uncertain.

Heart hammering, Kydd crunched cautiously toward it. The source of the light lengthened and grew in definition, nearer, and the light of the lanthorn reached it, swamped it. The sickly sweet stench was overpowering, and he gasped with horror. The ghost was a dead body, what was left of Eakin, the cooper's mate, his putrefying remains luminescing in the blackness.

With *Tiberius* a speck on the horizon, a soldier's wind and Mr. Tewsley having the deck, it was time to take the wheel.

"Kydd on the wheel, sir?" said Doud, whose trick at the helm it was.

"Certainly," Tewsley said, and nodded at the quartermaster, the petty officer in direct charge of the wheel. The man looked dubious, but stood back.

The easy breeze meant that only one helmsman was needed at the man-high wheel, but Doud directed Kydd over to the lee position on the other side. "Jus' follow me. You're lee helmsman now, and while I watches the sails 'n' compass, you watches me. Ready?"

Kydd nodded, stepped up to the wheel and firmly grasped the spokes.

"Like this, mate," Doud said.

Kydd saw that the hand on Doud's inboard side was on an upper spoke while the outer hand was down on a lower spoke. He shifted his position and watched carefully. To his surprise the wheel felt alive—the little vibrations and jerks transmitted to him were a direct communication from the ship herself. He clasped the spokes tighter, watching Doud for his cues. He noticed that Doud's chief interest seemed to be not the compass, but somewhere up aloft.

"That's 'cos I'm watching the weather leech o' the main course— it'll start to shake if I goes too high into the wind. You gets a much quicker notice from the sails if you're off course, much better'n the compass."

It was very much a skilled job, much more so than Kydd had realized. It appeared that orders to the helm could take a bewildering number of forms—just to alter course away might be "hard a-starboard," "bear up," "helm a-weather" or "up helm," each with its shades of meaning. But what Kydd found hardest was the simple sea convention that to starboard the helm would make the ship turn to port. It wasn't until Doud mentioned that all helm orders had come unchanged down the years from the time when tillers were used to steer ships that he was able to make the mental adjustment.

"Right, mate, about time you took the barky yourself."

Nervous, but thrilled, Kydd took over, Doud right behind him.

"Steady, mate! She's carrying two spokes of weather helm—that means from the midships spoke, the one with the brass tip, you need two o' the spokes a-weather."

The wheel, as high as himself, felt huge at first, but to his great relief there was no sudden swing of the ship. The feel of the helm was a firm pressure to one direction, which he held steadily against, sensing the rush and vibration of the ship through the water coming straight to him. His confidence increased.

He peered down at the compass in the binnacle in front. The card hung lazily, the lubber's line at south-sou'-west by a point west—he had spent a whole dog-watch boxing the compass to prepare for this moment. Then he squinted up at the main course, uncertain what the quartermaster meant when he growled, "Keep your luff!"

Doud helped from behind, with an "Up helm a spoke!" or "Ease her!"

Kydd looked forward, at the sweet curve of the deck under the sails going right forward to where the bows came together at the distant bowsprit, the whole dipping and rising majestically as it obediently followed his course ahead. Under his hands was a living thing, responding to his touch, his coaxing. He sensed that the slight quartering swell needed meeting with the helm as approaching waves varied their pressure on the rudder. Odd flaws and inconsistencies in the wind, which he hadn't noticed before, now needed careful handling. A tiny flutter on the edge of the sail—up with the helm a couple of spokes and the flutter eased and disappeared. A lurch to leeward and over with the helm a-lee and back again—too much, the leech of the course started its restless flutter again; Kydd spun the wheel back—a bigger lurch, and bigger correction.

"Doud!" snapped the quartermaster.

Half gratefully, half reluctantly, Kydd surrendered the wheel to Doud, who killed the oscillation. "Nip over to the lee side, mate," Doud invited, and Kydd spent the remainder of the trick as lee helmsman, absorbing the art and reflecting on the wonder of it all.

CHAPTER 10

THE EARLY MORNING SUN was warming to the skin, and dappled the fo'c'sle with the bright crisscross shadows of the rigging. The bow crunched into the Atlantic rollers, sending spray outward in a rainbow, the long swell lazy and serene.

Kydd bent to his task: cross-legged he plied his needle skillfully, adding a fancy white edging to a seaman's short blue jacket. He was good at his stitching, and sailors brought him work, which he would perform for favors. It was a Thursday make-and-mend afternoon and many were taking the opportunity to relax in the sun. Etiquette was scrupulously observed. In such restricted quarters each had his personal space as he sat on deck, and unless he wanted otherwise he was treated as though he was invisible.

A shadow fell across Kydd and he looked up. "Nicholas! What cheer, mate?" he said, in surprise. It was not Renzi's way to seek out company, for he preferred a quiet conversation with Kydd alone.

Renzi smiled and struck a pose.

> *Is she not beautiful! her graceful bow*
> *Triumphant rising o'er enamored tides,*
> *That, glittering in the noonday sun, now*
> *Just leap and die along her polished sides!*

"Just so, shipmate!" Kydd replied happily. He was envious of Renzi's easy familiarity with words but enjoyed their display.

"Do you take a tuck in my waistcoat, I would be infinitely obliged," Renzi said, and squatted next to Kydd. He was struck by how much his friend had changed in just a few brief months. There was development and definition in his chest and arms, which sat well with his increasingly sea-darkened complexion, and his shining black hair was held back in a small queue. His experiences had toughened and shaped him, and his brown eyes now looked out with humor and self-assurance.

"Give you joy of your rating, sir," Renzi said formally.

"Why, it's to Ordinary Seaman, is all," Kydd said.

Renzi perceived the evident pleasure. "In Guildford they would not recognize you, Tom," he said, "what with the cut o' the jib of a seaman."

"Not that I've ever a chance of gettin' to the old town," Kydd replied, finishing the seam with a flourish of his capable brown fingers and biting off the thread.

Renzi hesitated, then pulled something from his pocket. Looking around, he pressed it on Kydd. "It's only a book, my friend, but in my time I've taken great comfort from its pages."

Kydd accepted it, flattered that Renzi thought he was a reading man. It was a slim volume printed with a tiny typeface—poetry by someone called Wordsworth.

"The man is a revolutionary—in the literary way, I mean," Renzi said. "You will sense the freedom and vitality. His verses are a paean to the sublime assertion of the individual; he brings . . . But, then, you'll see all this for yourself, Tom," he concluded lamely.

Kydd looked at his friend, touched by his thought. He fiddled in his waistcoat. "And I have something f'r you," he said, bringing out a screw of paper, which he handed over.

Carefully Renzi undid the paper. Inside was a good six ounces of small dark whorls, thin disks of the most fragrant tobacco he had ever encountered. "My friend, this is magnificent!"

Kydd was well pleased at the unfeigned delight. He had learned how to make a prick of tobacco from one of the gunner's mates with whom he had shared a watch in one of the hanging magazines. A wad of good strong tobacco leaves was spread on flannel. Sprinkled with rum, it was rolled up and tied to a deckhead cleat with spun yarn, rotated tightly along its length and left for a week or so. The resulting hard plug was then cut with a razor-sharp knife into thin disks of shag.

Appreciatively, Renzi drew out his clay pipe and rubbed himself a fill. Soon a powerful fragrance was on the wind and Renzi settled back against the carronade slide with a comfortable sigh.

Kydd picked up the waistcoat. Renzi's body had responded to seaboard life by becoming whipcord thin, and the garment would certainly need another tuck. He threaded the needle. "So much for the Mongseers!" Kydd grimaced. "Never a sign of 'em, and we trail our coats off their ports f'r weeks!"

Renzi's eyes were closed. "I wonder what's happening in Paris," he mused. "The mob will be baying for blood—but whose? The Jacobins ride the tiger—Robespierre needs victories if he is to prevail." It was not easy to live in this total isolation, without a newspaper, journal or even a rumor when to his certain knowledge the world was in flames.

Doud came up beaming with a tankard of small beer. "Well, Jack Tar, ahoy! I reckon we can't ask Tom Kydd now to desire the sextant for to pray fer us!" He gave the beer to Kydd, looking at Renzi sideways as he did so.

"You want a wet, Renzi?" he enquired.

"That is most kind in you, Ned," Renzi said, "and it's Nicholas, by the way."

"You are most welcome, Nick," Doud said, in mocking tones.

"It's Nicholas," Kydd said.

Doud grinned and left.

It was glassy smooth, only a long swell moving under the glittering surface of the sea. The sails drew, but only just, *Duke William* inevitably falling away in the line of three ships as they exercised together.

A distant thud was heard. Another—it sounded like a far-off door slamming. On the quarterdeck, telescopes whipped up and trained on the distant land. Another gun thudded—and a flurry started among the officers.

"What's that?" Kydd asked. He and Renzi were together now in the mizzen top as Kydd's station had changed since his advancement to seaman. With a grandstand view of the quarterdeck, they saw the marine drummer boy hastily take position at the main hatch.

"Quarters!" Renzi exclaimed.

They looked at each other and descended hastily to the deck, moving past the raucous volleying of the drum at the main hatch to their respective stations.

"What cheer, mates?" said Salter. "What's the alarum, then?" His eyes glittered in the lower-deck gloom as he cleared away the muzzle lashing of their gun.

"No idea, Will. Did see sail close inshore, but that'd be one of our frigates, I'll wager." Kydd had not been prepared to risk a rope's end by hanging about to find out.

This was a call for a full sweep fore and aft—anything that could not immediately be struck down into the hold was dumped overboard, and the sea astern was studded by floating debris. The men worked fast—this was no drill.

Renzi's action quarters was at one of the upper-deck twelve-pounders. There was perhaps a chance that Kydd would see him if he was called away to handle sails, which was his secondary battle station.

Down the fore hatch ladder clattered Midshipman Cantlow, still buckling on his dirk, his cocked hat askew. Kydd disliked him—the gangling man was older by far than the others, in his late twenties at least, not having the interest or ability to pass for lieutenant. He had once ordered a starting for Kydd over some trivial matter; it was not the colt whipping painfully across his shoulders that he remembered, it was the spite that had triggered it—Cantlow was embittered at his lot.

"What news—sir?" asked Stirk. He was ignored, Cantlow adjusting his cross-belt and scabbard over the threadbare uniform coat. He would take charge of the foremost six guns under a lieutenant of the gundeck. With a significant look, Stirk called over to Doggo loudly, "Looks like we got ourselves a right smashin' match, mate. Yer've made yer arrangements, then?"

Kydd looked at him sharply.

"Why, o' course—but it ain't no use, there won't be many of us left after the fightin' really gets started, we bein' down here in the slaughterhouse 'n' all," Doggo replied, his face blank.

"What are you yattering about, you useless swabs?" Cantlow said irritably, fiddling nervously with his dirk.

"Seen the doc sharpenin' his saws," Salter said gloomily. "Shoulda got the carpenter to do a better job—never could stand a blunt saw at me bones."

"An' where's the priest?" Velasquez added mournfully. "'Ow we can die wi'out we ha' a priest?"

"Silence! Do you think to bait me? You stinking, worthless scum!" Cantlow glared around.

"Why, sir," Stirk said, with a saintly expression, "we're cruel a-feared, 'n' we need some words, some strong words, from an officer to steady us in our time o' need—sir!"

Cantlow's venomous glare was interrupted by the arrival of Lieutenant Lockwood. "Report, Mr. Cantlow," he ordered.

"Well, sir, I—"

"You're useless, and stupid," Lockwood said, "so muster your men again and report." Lockwood took position on the centerline. Although he was young, his voice already had the crack of authority. "Still!" All activity on the gundeck ceased. "We have just been alerted by *Amphion* frigate that the French have taken advantage of this easterly to put to sea. But not from Brest. Four ships-of-the-line and frigates have sailed from Douarnenez to the south of here, and we think they mean to proceed to the Caribbean and our valuable sugar islands. They did not reckon on our vigilance, and now we will make sure that they never arrive!"

A savage growl arose from the gun crews.

"The weather in this light blow is not in our favor—but they have formed line and are offering battle. We will oblige them!"

A deeper-throated sound swelled into cheers.

"*Haaaands* to make sail!"

The boatswain's calls pierced into the excitement. Kydd ran topsides with the others of the gun crews assigned to sail trimming. The brilliant sun made him screw up his eyes, but he knew by instinct the position of the mizzen shrouds and his leap took him into the ratlines. He swarmed up to the mizzen top.

It was a chance to take in the scene of impending battle. Far ahead against the nondescript line of the coast were the enemy—four small clusters of ivory sails emerging from Douarnenez Bay and sailing large before the light easterly wind, four big vessels in line formation, taking advantage of the offshore winds of the morning. They were headed from right to left across *Duke William*'s bows, standing out for the Atlantic, but seemingly in no hurry to close and grapple.

On the starboard tack *Duke William* was heading toward a point of intersection ahead of them, clawing her way to windward in the frustrating light winds, doing her best to get within range. The ripple under her forefoot sounded like the contented chuckle of a country millstream at a sleepy knot or two.

"'Less we can get the old barky to lift up her skirts 'n' run, we're goin' to lose 'em," the captain of the top said bitterly. He looked over the flat seas to their fellow ships-of-the-line in staggered line abeam. *Tiberius* led *Royal Albion* by a short head, and both were significantly ahead of *Duke William*.

"Know what that is?" the man said sharply to Kydd, without turning his head. "That there's gun money 'n' head money 'n' mebbe even a mort o' prize money, that is. One chance we get in this bucket to lay 'ands on an honest guinea or two and we meets wi' a dead calm."

Others in the top rumbled their agreement.

A weather stuns'l was not a success, however, backwinding the main topsail, and it was struck. Swearing, they toiled at the sail, which had managed to wrap itself around the topmast stay when the halliards were let go.

As the day wore on, it became apparent that the enemy were equally affected by the lazy weather, straggling along in a slow, ragged line. At two, the wind failed altogether, and the ship hung lifeless in the water, sails barely stirring. She lost way and after ghosting along for a space she simply did not answer her helm and drifted, the slight swell causing an aimless clack of blocks aloft.

"*Awaaaay* all boats!"

Tumbling into the cutter, Kydd made room on the thwart for Renzi. The rowers would go double-banked in this attempt to tow *Duke William* into action, and together with the larger pinnace and launch they would do their utmost to close with the enemy. Even the Captain's barge took a line from the fo'c'sle.

It was cruel, backbreaking work: the hard thwart and unyielding oar, the burning pain in the back and arms, the hands turning into claws. With the inertia of two thousand tons their oars threshed the water uselessly while the boat remained dead in the water.

It took all of ten minutes of toil at the oars by hundreds of men to see the tiniest move through the water of the great battleship. They were now half a mile behind *Royal Albion,* who also had all her boats out.

"Pull, you scurvy lubbers!" The tiny midshipman's piping voice was almost comical as he tried to emulate the bull-roaring of Tewsley in the launch.

Although it was not strong, the sunlight glittered on the unbroken sea surface and reflected up into their faces. Kydd was grateful for his hat, but felt his face redden from the glare. They pulled on in silence, a steady long pull, leaning well back to get the straightest line from chest to feet against the stretchers athwartships.

A series of disjointed thuds sounded distantly, then cannonballs skipped and splashed audibly around them. Kydd glanced about him as he pulled, and was relieved to see that the shots were well scattered. One of the enemy ships was nearly hidden by clouds of slow-moving gunsmoke.

Nevertheless it was unnerving. The enemy had their broadside facing them while their own guns would not bear so far forward. They pulled on. More thuds, more balls. A long space, and then an avalanche of crumps. This time the sound was appreciably nearer and the balls skipped and smashed with venom among them. Some came between the boats and two struck the ship with a peculiar sound like a blunt axe smashing into rotten wood.

"Eyes in the boat!" piped the little midshipman, as some men missed their stroke looking over their shoulder.

There was a fierce muttering. It was one thing to be under fire with their own cannon roaring defiance from their wooden ramparts and another to be helpless in the open with no means of reply.

A catspaw of wind ruffled the water and subsided. Another came and went. Anxious faces looked toward the fo'c'sle but nothing changed.

A double rush of thumps and a storm of shot broke over them. One ball plowed into the bow of the pinnace and opened it like a banana, instantly cutting off the shrieks by plunging every occupant into the sea. Without waiting to be told, lines were slipped and the boats returned, the launch remaining to pick up survivors.

But the wind seemed to have returned. Sails were stirring, flapping desultorily, the huge battle ensign lifting momentarily and falling.

So weary were they that it was impossible to climb the Jacob's ladder over the stern and they were waved around to the entry port. Aching and sore, they mounted the side steps and made their way back to their battle stations.

On the lower gundeck the gun crews waited. Kydd sat against the gun carriage, head in his hands, exhausted.

"Denison, you 'n' Kydd change," Stirk said, giving Kydd a break from his arduous gun-tackle duty. Kydd nodded his gratitude. Cullen brought the round shot to the gun with Denison.

It was hot and fetid, even with the gunports open, but a whisper of a breeze now wafted cool sea air over them. Kydd was stripped to the waist, a red bandanna around his head. He closed his eyes and let the talk eddy around him.

"No, I tell a lie. An able seaman's share, that'd be over five poun' we gets to take one o' they Frenchies."

"O' course I'll do that—'n' if it's me, then I'd take it kindly if you could visit me sister, she's all I got. I'll ask Lofty ter write 'er name 'n' lodgin' out for you—she's a widder, yer knows."

"An' we'll hire a coach, Will, go to Winchester an' kick up a Bob's-a-dyin' they'll never ferget!"

Kydd forced himself to open his eyes. With both sides manned, the gundeck was crowded with men and equipment. The guns were already loaded, only awaiting the order to open fire. On the centerline were scuttled casks of water with vinegar, and long cases containing cutlasses and sea-service pistols lay open. It was the first time he had seen the vessel prepared in earnest for war. It was rare for a line-of-battle ship actually to fight: it did its work more by the threat of its existence, but now the greatest single weapon in history so far would have to justify its being.

He saw Cantlow in low conversation with Lockwood, and the gunner, Mr. Bethune, making his way slowly along in his plain black waistcoat, his bright eyes darting about in a last check before he went down into the magazine.

Painfully Kydd got to his feet and went to the gunport to lean out.

The enemy seemed to be holding their fire until the smoke cleared—it hung downwind of them in gigantic clouds above the sea, with little movement to disperse it. *Royal Albion* to larboard had some sort of signal hanging out and *Tiberius* was in the process of dowsing a staysail.

As he watched, the enemy man-o'-war last in line erupted in stabs of flame and was instantly enveloped in gunsmoke. Kydd flinched. In quick succession there were two loud crashes overhead some-where, followed by a terrifying splintering smash as a round shot pierced the side near the foremost gun.

Through a jagged entry-hole it smashed diagonally across the gundeck, taking with it the head of the rammer of the number-one gun, together with the leg and thigh of one of the gun-tackle crew and the hand of his mate. It slammed across the main hatch grat-ings, pulping the golden-haired powder monkey in its path, and hit an opposite gun squarely, dismounting it.

The screaming started—and the tearing sobs of a ship's boy un-able to comprehend the bloody carcass of his friend.

Kydd was paralyzed with horror. His eyes followed the procession of moaning, hideously bloody men carried down to the orlop and the hands of the surgeon.

"Get forrard 'n' give 'em a hand, lad," Stirk said, in neutral tones.

Kydd stared at him, then started for the scene of carnage.

Human tissue was everywhere. It did not seem possible that a body could contain so much blood.

"Get 'is legs, mate," a seaman said. Two others had a headless torso by the arms, quite untouched apart from its surreal shortening, ending in obscene white tendrils in a meaty matrix.

Kydd gingerly picked up the dead body's feet, noting the heavy wear in the shoes that the man had put on that morning. He started pulling the body backwards.

"What the fuck are you doing?" flared a man at the other end.

Kydd stood dumbfounded, his mind no longer working.

"He goes overside, mate," the other said kindly.

Numb, Kydd complied, and the body, slithering floppily, went out of the gunport to splash into the bright sea below. He resumed his place at the gun and tried to control his trembling. There would be another broadside soon. At the very next moment another cannonball might blast into the gundeck. This time it might be him.

Stirk stood with his arms folded across his hairy chest, slowly chewing a quid of tobacco, his face expressionless. His calm, his strength, reassured Kydd, whose trembling subsided.

"We'll settle those sons of whores! Serve 'em out the double what they did t' us!" Kydd said violently.

Stirk looked at him in amusement. "Yair—and when we get amongst 'em, we'll give 'em such a mauling as will have 'em beg for quarter inside an hour—on their knees!"

"Blast me eyes if we don't take all four!" Salter said, white teeth gleaming.

"A pity there ain't others—could do wi' the prize money," Doggo croaked.

The next flurry of thuds produced a fluster of confused bangs and breaking sounds from above, but no rending crashes into the gundeck.

Kydd tried to still his thudding heart. It was the uncertainty, the knowledge that out there was an enemy who was doing his best to kill him. His remaining time on earth might well be measured in seconds. To his shame his knees began to tremble again.

He snatched a glance at Stirk—the same neutral passivity, the unconcern.

Impulsively, Kydd moved closer to him and said in a low voice, "Toby, how c'n you—I mean, why doesn't it . . ." He tailed off, feeling his face burning.

Stirk frowned. "Yeah—I know what yer mean, mate." Idly stroking the top of the massive gun, Stirk went on, "Fair time ago, when I was a nipper, I shipped in *Terrier* sloop, out east. There was a yellow bugger, name o' Loola, in the fo'c'sle wi' us." He smiled briefly. "Weren't much chop as a seaman, 'n' he useta pray at this 'eathen god thing 'e 'ad, with a big belly and fool expression, but 'e 'ad his life squared away right pretty, answers fer everything. 'N' he said somethin' savvy that I never forget, ever. 'E said as 'ow it's dead certain yer'll get yours one day, but yer never gonna know what that day is when yer wakes up in the mornin'." He coughed self-consciously. "But yer 'as to know that if it *is* the day, then yer faces what comes like a hero—and if it *ain't* the day, then it's a waste o' yer life worryin' about it."

A few moments later the ragged strike of a broadside came, this time with no solid impacts sensed through the deck.

"Firin' at the rigging, they do," Stirk said derisively. "Thinks they'll cripple us so's they can skin out."

Taking a deep breath, Kydd felt his fear recede. He straightened, and ventured a smile. "Shy bastards—can't take a mill man to man!"

Stirk studied him and nodded.

Another spasm of cannon fire banged out. The noise was appreciably nearer now, and the sound of balls striking above had a vicious quality.

A boatswain's mate appeared at the fore hatch. "Sail trimmers aloft!"

Kydd realized that this included him. He ran up the hatchways, aware that he would now be facing a hail of shot unprotected in the rigging.

He was shocked by the disorder on deck. In place of the neatly squared and precisely trimmed appearance of the decks, there was a wasteland of debris—blocks fallen from aloft, some with lines still reeved through them, unidentifiable fragments of splintered wood and unraveled rope. Long gouges in the decking told of the brutal impact of iron on wood.

Looking up, Kydd saw that with the angle of strike of the balls several sails could be pierced at once, and there seemed to be holes everywhere in the sails aloft.

"Get going, lads, fore tops'l yard's taken a knock," the boatswain said. Directly above, Kydd saw that the outer third of the spar was hanging at an angle where a shot had mutilated the yard, and the topsail flapped in disorder under it.

He swung into the fore shrouds, cringing at the threat of another broadside in the rigging—but remembering Stirk's words, he thrust it brutally from his mind. As he climbed he looked to see where the French ships were. There they bore, strung out in a widely separated line passing across their bows. They were shockingly close, a bare mile away, while their own ships closed in roughly abreast of each other.

Royal Albion and *Tiberius* were ahead of *Duke William* and would soon fall upon the enemy, while the last French vessel, a large three-decker, would apparently be their opponent. The afternoon breeze had picked up and there was now no chance for the French to avoid action. Kydd reached the foretop and stood waiting for orders while others arrived next to him. A pair of capstan bars would be used in fishing the topsail yard, and he was one of the party assigned to perform the outboard lashing. A sullen bellow of guns rolled across the water. The third enemy battleship disappeared behind a wall of gunsmoke as she fired on the nearer *Tiberius,* but this time the smoke clouds dissipated, rolling slowly downwind.

On *Duke William*'s poop, fifes and drums began a jaunty, defiant tune—a *thumpity thump, thumpity thump* rhythm:

> *Hearts of oak are our ships! Jolly tars are our men!*
> *We al-always are ready!*
> *Steadyy, boys, steadyyy!*

The guns of the last French ship in line broke out in a thunderous roar and almost immediately the assault struck.

Unseen missiles slapped through sails and parted ropes—the whirring of chain shot was unmistakable, the two links sliding apart and whirling around through the air in an unstoppable scythe of death. They caught one man climbing around the futtock shrouds, effortlessly cutting him in half. The torso fell silently. A ball slammed past the side of the foretop, its passage so violent that it sent a man staggering over the edge, his scream instantly cut off when his body broke over a carronade below, scattering the gun crew. A twang and thrum of impacts on taut ropes and the onslaught was over. Kydd stirred from his frozen position, heady with the realization that he was spared. This was not to be his day for eternity.

"Pass the bloody lashing, then!" the boatswain's mate yelled from the top. His voice cracked falsetto with tension.

Kydd passed the seizing as fast as he could—the others tumbled into the shrouds and made the deck as he finished. He thought of Bowyer and made the lashing a good, tight, seaman-like one before he joined them. For no reason at all, a startlingly clear image of Guildford's High Street overlaid his vision—the sun out, the street streaming with gentlemen and their ladies, beggars, and children with their whipping tops and hobbyhorses playing outside the red brick Holy Trinity church.

The noise and smoke increased. The French were near, very near. Kydd heard a smart tap on the foremast as he completed and reached the foretop. Looking down, he saw a musketball rolling spent across the top. On impulse he picked up the flattened disk and put it in his pocket before sliding dizzyingly down the backstay to the deck.

A last look showed the enemy only a few hundred yards away, and their own bows beginning their swing finally to place their ship side by side with the looming three-decker. With a thrill of excitement Kydd knew that the time for real battle had arrived, and he clattered down the ladders at a rush.

Just as he arrived on the lower gundeck there was a roar of cheering as the great thirty-two-pounders opened up with a mind-numbing slam of sound. The deck instantly choked with smoke blown back in the gunports, thick acrid wreaths that caught him in the throat. He stumbled into Lockwood, disoriented. The smoke began to clear with the strengthening breeze and he caught sight of his gun, the figures of the crew emerging, Doggo's shapeless hat unmistakable.

Stirk's eyes gleamed—his concentrated expression had a ferocious intensity. The gun crew moved fast and economically on the reload. Kydd and Cullen hurried the shot cradle to the muzzle, lifting the deadly iron sphere into the hot maw.

Through the gunport the enemy ship was clearly visible across the narrowing gap of water, and for a split second Kydd took in the black and yellow hull darkening the frame of the port. There was debris falling in the water alongside it from their own cannon strike and he was aware of countless gun muzzles staring at him.

Velasquez's ramrod cut across his gaze as he plied it, his movements skilled and rapid, savage joy in his face.

Kydd went to the shot garland around the main hatch and rolled a ball on to the cradle. Standing on the grating was a ship's boy, his ears bound and his eyes enormously big and bright. He clutched his cartridge box to him like a teddy bear, his strong little legs bare to the toes. Kydd smiled encouragingly at him, but there was no response in the solemn, wide-eyed face.

They faced about just as the enemy replied. The noise was fantastic, for their own guns spoke at the same time, the crashing thunder seeming to go on forever as the guns played up and down the sides of the two great vessels. No more than a hundred yards away now, they couldn't miss, and Kydd knew that through the choking smoke their own ship-smashers would be doing deadly work.

Splintering crashes and screams somewhere in the gloom told of where the enemy shot had found its mark. As the smoke cleared he noticed a strange pattern of daylight two guns down, then saw that the ship's side between the gunports was missing.

Behind it a seaman sat on the deck, staring at his right arm, which was now no more than a stick, the blood coursing steadily down from it. He watched it with a puzzled frown, then slowly pitched forward.

A rhythmic tearing gasp nearby made Kydd wheel round. A man was lying on his side, hands clutching a long jagged wound in his inner thigh, trying painfully to drag himself toward the hatchway. He left a bloody trail.

Cantlow appeared from aft. His white face stared sightlessly. Pushing past Kydd, he made his way forward aimlessly.

Shouts and cheers penetrated the general noise, clear through the sharp ringing in Kydd's ears. Wildly thirsty, parched by the metallic-tasting powder smoke, he went to the scuttled butt of water amidships and ladled out a dipper of cool sweet nectar.

Again the gun crew rolled a shot into the muzzle and stepped back quickly. The French were now no more than a few dozen yards away, their harsh yells alien to the ear. They were answered with equal venom by the British seamen.

Velasquez spun like a dancer and sent the ramrod spinning in. But then he pirouetted and fell, the ugly tear of a musketball wound in his back.

Stirk bawled obscenely as he leaped forward and carried the writhing man tenderly to the rear.

"Double shotting!" Stirk roared. There would be two balls to one shot, the effect on accuracy greatly outweighed by the doubling of killing power. Their next ball was already on the cradle and they rushed it forward.

Stirk didn't wait for firing orders—this was a smashing match and only the faster crews would win. There was no need to sight. He jerked on the gunlock lanyard. The gun bellowed and slammed to the rear with increased recoil, the breeching rope twanging dangerously.

Through a freak break in the smoke Kydd could see the enemy side. It shuddered visibly under the impact of their double shot and a massive hole appeared magically in the center of his vision. Before the smoke closed in he saw that the enemy guns were still not run out and there seemed to be some sort of jerky activity behind the ports.

The other ship was less than fifteen feet away and when they came together the massive grinding impact sent Kydd staggering. The smoke drifted away and there was the enemy side within touching distance—pockmarked, splintered and with blood running down the side in thin streams from a rent in her sides.

Raging shouts burst out. The enemy seamen were feet away only and with bull roars the British seamen attacked them even through the ports, with ramrods and anything that came to hand: battering, smashing, killing. Cooler hands raced to the arms chest and the flash and bang of pistols stabbed the smoky gloom.

"*Awaaay,* boarders!" Lockwood's voice was hoarse. He stood with his sword out, his uniform grimed with powder smoke, eyes reddened.

Seamen nominated for the task ran for the hatchway, snatching pistols and cutlasses as they left.

Kydd turned back to the mêlée. Opposite, the enemy gunport framed a stout man with a mustache, who gestured violently with his ramrod.

Kydd remembered the cruelty of the French cavalry. Dropping the shot cradle, he ran over to the pistol chest and grabbed a weapon. It felt heavy and cold. Cocking it haphazardly, he aimed past the heads of the working gun crew at the man and banged off the pistol. It bucked viciously in his hand. Stirk and his men turned in surprise but, to his intense satisfaction, Kydd saw the man clutch at his face and drop out of sight.

Duke William had not quite come to a standstill, the enemy's side slipping past at a walking pace. Stirk's gun crashed out again, the crew working like madmen on the reload. Kydd's back and arms felt a burning ache, his efforts at the oars still taking their toll.

Another crunching impact brought long sounds of splintering. The enemy guns began firing again—but they were many fewer.

Kydd felt a peculiar exultation, a rising of blood lust, a call from his Briton forebears. He shrieked defiance as he worked.

A man staggered in a circle, a jagged spear protruding from the side of his chest. He turned and fell and Kydd saw that it was an oaken splinter torn from the deck and driven into him. The man writhed and flopped, and almost in a trance Kydd turned back to the job in hand.

The Royal Billys ran out the gun but suddenly the enemy beak-head was passing from view, a figurehead of a virago with a conical hat and clasping a spear, then empty sea. They had gone past their opponent without coming to a stop.

"Stupid crazy bastard—the fucking lamebrain!" Stirk raved, spittle on his lips underlining his fury. "'E 'asn't fuckin' backed tops'ls!"

It was elementary: to keep the ship in position while the guns made their play, it was necessary to heave to by putting the topsails aback. Kydd wondered at the scene on deck. It could be that the Captain had fallen and could not give the order.

The firing died away. "Clear away this shit," Stirk said dully.

Splinters and debris went out the port, the last wounded were taken below. Blood splashes were left—there were more important tasks at hand to ready the guns for the next bout.

Cautiously Jewkes leaned out of the gunport. "Wha—they're running, the shy bastards!"

Kydd and others joined him at the port and eagerly took in the scene.

The enemy ships had hauled their wind and now shaped course for Brest, their high stern galleries prominent as they sailed away. The battered rigging of the British ships resulted in their falling farther behind, the changed angle again making their guns impotent.

Maddened shouts and cheering stormed from *Duke William*'s gunports until the chase brought them into range of the batteries ashore. Wearing around, the squadron made a dignified retreat, deeply satisfied that the battlefield was now theirs.

CHAPTER 11

REALLY, OLD FELLOW, I was too busy to worry," Renzi said. They were sitting astride the cro'jack yard, busy splicing.

"And I," Kydd agreed, beginning the whipping around an eye splice. He made the turns as tight as he could—Bowyer had always said that you could tell a seaman by his ropework.

"Was it . . . hot work on deck?" he asked, in a noncommittal tone.

"Hot enough," Renzi replied.

Kydd wanted to share his newfound secret with his friend. "Heard a good enough piece of philosophy not so long ago," he began, and told Renzi of Stirk's secret.

"Oh, yes," Renzi said. "Same base truth in *Julius Caesar:* 'Cowards die many times before their death / The valiant never taste of death but once.'" He finished his splice with a workmanlike tuck, testing its strength. "Act two, scene two, I'd hazard." He saw Kydd's expression. "But that is not to detract from the essential verities in *both* sayings," he added hurriedly. "Perhaps one day we will sail to the Orient—I have a morbid desire to imbibe their metaphysics at the source."

France was a dim gray coastline on the horizon as the three ships proceeded under easy sail, the tasks of repair never-ending. As the adrenaline of the battle fell away, and fatigue set in, it was hard to keep going, but it was double tides—working watch and watch without a break—to get the ships seaworthy and battleworthy once more.

A double tot of rum went far to ease the pain. Kydd felt detached from his aches, and spoke out loudly: "A great maulin'—they outnumbered and outgunned us, but we saw 'em back to their stinking lair! A thunderin' good drubbin'!"

"Do you think so?" Renzi said, without looking up.

"Why? Do you not? We've sent 'em back to where they came from—they won't try it again."

"My dear fellow, in the larger scheme of things, this will be seen as a passing brush with a few of their ships-of-the-line—and you are forgetting one thing." Renzi stopped and looked at Kydd.

"What's that?"

"Those four came from Douarnenez and now they are in Brest."

"So?"

"So they have successfully concentrated their force. I don't believe they were headed for the Caribbean anyway. It was always a move to bring about this very thing."

Kydd remained silent.

"We did not bring the action to a conclusion, the enemy escaped us. Now there are nine of-the-line in Brest. They can sweep us aside and fall on our convoys and possessions at any time. I doubt if this afternoon will even be dignified as a battle." Renzi resumed his whipping on the rope.

Kydd glared at him. "I need a bigger fid," he said shortly, and disappeared over the edge of the mizzen top.

Renzi was right, of course—if he had stopped to think he would have come to the same conclusion. It was just that he was exhilarated by his first fight against the enemy. He had not found himself wanting: he had passed through horror and hardships and he was determined to revel in the feeling.

He stepped out of the mizzen shrouds onto the poop deck, and into the path of Midshipman Cantlow. "Well, now, the dam' keen Mr. Kydd." There was a drunken slur to the words and he slapped at his side with an old rattan.

Kydd said nothing, but stood impassive. The last thing he needed now was a run-in with the despised Cantlow.

"An' I've just caught him skulking in the tops!"

Kydd snorted. Although a midshipman was not an officer, they equated to a petty officer in terms of discipline. The charge of hiding to avoid work was nonsense, of course—the boatswain himself had set them to their tasks. His jaw clamped shut as he forced himself to say nothing. Cantlow, if ever he got his promotion, would be of the same dangerous mold as Garrett.

"Say somethin', then, damn your whistle!" Cantlow shouted.

Kydd knew better than to open his mouth while the midshipman was in this mood.

"You're in contempt, you vile lubber! Contempt! I'll teach you manners!" His rattan swept up and caught Kydd on his upraised arm.

Kydd threw up his other arm to protect his face, which seemed to enrage Cantlow. Slashing and whipping, he forced Kydd back to the bulwark, continuing the assault there mercilessly until he was forced to pause, panting.

Dangerously angry, Kydd glared at Cantlow. He remembered Cantlow's witless shambling on the gundeck during the worst of the fight and suspected the real reason for the drinking.

"Afright now, are you, Mr. Keen Kydd! Then take this, you shy rogue!"

His arm lifted again, but before the blow landed Kydd snatched the rattan out of his grip and with one hand snapped it in two.

Cantlow stood aghast. His eyes widened and he backed away. "Master-at-Arms—sentry!" he yelled, his voice high and constricted.

The officer of the watch on the quarterdeck below appeared irritably, moving out from the break of the poop to see what all the fuss was about. It was Garrett.

The bilboes were situated down in the orlop, in the cockpit. They consisted of a long bar of iron on which leg irons were threaded and Kydd was the only occupant, his ankles clamped in the irons, sitting uncomfortably on the hard deck. He was shaking with fury, as much from Cantlow's shameless toadying to Garrett as the lies the midshipman had told. He tried to turn over to take a new position but the irons would not budge. He swore helplessly.

Renzi could not visit him—the bilboes were outside the midshipmen's berth among other things, and Cantlow would surely make certain that Renzi stood accused of plotting with Kydd.

The weak yellow light guttered and the marine sentry coughed and hacked endlessly. It would be a long night before Kydd could account for himself to the Captain in the morning.

"Right, mate, get to yer feet—'tis yer time to explain yerself." The ship's corporal was not unkind, letting Kydd rub his ankles and stretch before moving off. They threaded their way to the main hatch, watched curiously as they passed.

Kydd felt the stares and lifted his chin. The Captain would see his part—Bowyer had taught him that the King's Service was hard, but in the end fair, which was more than could be said for justice ashore. He marched forward confidently.

They emerged from the main companionway onto the quarterdeck. Kydd, bleary-eyed and disheveled after a sleepless night, was taken by surprise at the scene. Every eye was on him: hands had been mustered aft in the usual fashion, marines lining the poop rail, the officers below. A space of deck lay between him and a sea of men facing him from the opposite direction.

Tyrell looked at him dispassionately as he was brought forward to where Caldwell stood behind his lectern.

"Orf hat!" the Master-at-Arms said. "Ordinary Seaman Kydd, sir, did use threatenin' language to a superior orficer, sir, did offer violence to the orficer and did use insultin' words, sir." He stepped back.

Kydd looked up into his captain's eyes. The same intelligent and gentle blue eyes—but there was weakness in the downswept lines at the side.

"These are serious charges, Kydd," Caldwell began mildly. He glanced at Cantlow and back. "I hope they will not be proven."

"No, sir," Kydd replied firmly.

"Silence!" the Master-at-Arms roared.

Kydd snatched a side-glance at Cantlow. He was in his best uniform and rested his hand on his dirk. His face was expressionless. Close behind stood Garrett.

"Are there any witnesses?" Caldwell asked.

"Sir!" snapped Garrett, and stepped over to the Captain's side, facing Kydd. "I saw it all, the rogue."

"What did you see?" Caldwell enquired gently.

"That rascal—that villain—"

"Have a care, Mr. Garrett."

"I saw him ranting at Mr. Cantlow after being remonstrated with for skulking in the tops."

"And?"

"And Kydd seized Mr. Cantlow's rattan and offered to 'fetch him a polter on his noggin,' begging your pardon, sir."

"Ah."

"That is not all, sir. I snatched the rattan from Kydd and broke it over my knee, at which he let fly with a stream of insults, which I will not trouble you to repeat."

A murmuring spread out over the crowded mass of seamen.

"I see." Caldwell looked at Kydd for a long moment, then turned back to Garrett. "It seems fairly clear to me . . ." he said.

Garrett could not help a quick look of triumph at Cantlow.

". . . that you yourself, sir, stand guilty of the gravest dereliction of duty!"

Garrett was stupefied.

"Were you not officer of the watch? Speak up, man!"

"Yes, sir!"

"Then why, pray, were you absent from your place of duty on the quarterdeck, and at the mizzen shrouds on the poop, when the safety of this ship depends on your vigilance and proximity to the helm? Hey, sir? Which is it, man? You saw it all and were absent from your place of duty, or you didn't see it at all? Well? You are stood down, and will wait upon me later to explain your actions." Caldwell drew a scented handkerchief from his sleeve and touched his mouth. "I will therefore ignore this testimony and call Mr. Cantlow." Cantlow stepped up and touched his hat. "It is customary to remove your headgear when addressing your captain, Mr. Cantlow. I find merely touching the hat an irritating modern affectation."

Cantlow flushed and took off his hat.

"Now, sir, what are the essentials of the charge?"

Cantlow's eyes slid over to Kydd and back. "I caught this man skulking in the mizzen top, sir, and—"

"One moment. Let us settle that matter first."

"Pass the word for the boatswain!"

The cry was taken up and, as if on cue, the burly figure of the boatswain appeared. He did not look at Kydd.

"What was this man doing in the mizzen top?" Caldwell enquired.

"Sir, Ordinary Seaman Kydd was, agreeable to my orders, engaged in puttin' an eye in the mizzen topsail slabline, afore it's meant to be re-reeved," he growled.

"Thank you. Mr. Cantlow?"

Cantlow hesitated, then blurted, "He wouldn't speak!"

Caldwell's eyebrows rose.

"Er, sir! He—he just stood there in dumb insolence. What was I to think, sir?"

"I would have thought that was obvious, but we'll let it go. The insults, if he didn't speak?" Caldwell began tapping his feet.

Cantlow's eyes fell. They rose again obstinately. "I have a witness, sir."

A ripple of disquiet spread through the men. Kydd sensed their presence behind him and was comforted—Bowyer had been right: if you were innocent you had nothing to fear.

"Oh?"

"Able Seaman Jeakes, sir."

"Pass the word for Jeakes."

A gangling black man pushed his way diffidently forward, his old canvas hat passing from hand to hand nervously.

"What can you say about this, Jeakes?"

The eyes in the dark features flashed white in anxiety.

"Take your time, Jeakes. We want to know the truth," Caldwell said kindly, glancing at Cantlow's stubborn face.

"Well, sir, it's like this 'ere, sir. I wuz shinnin' down from the maintop 'n' I sees Mr. Cantlow and Kydd, sir."

"You mean, you could see them from the main shrouds to the poop deck?"

"Well, see, we was sailin' full 'n' bye on the starb'd tack, sir. I could see down at 'em, like."

"What did you see?"

"Mr. Cantlow, sir, he was quiltin' the very 'ell outa Kydd, sir. Layin' into 'im wiv a will, he wuz, sir."

"I see," said Caldwell, looking sharply at Cantlow. "And then?"

"Well, sir, he stops, sir."

"Yes?"

Jeakes looked over his shoulder at the silent mass of men. If he told the whole story and it went ill for Kydd, they would take it out on him. But if he lied Cantlow might get another witness and he would find himself next to Kydd. "He stops, sir," he said unhappily.

"Speak up!" the Master-at-Arms said angrily.

"And then 'e 'as a go at Kydd again, sir," he added.

"Get on with it!" the Master-at-Arms spluttered.

"And Kydd grabs 'is rattan." The stirring among the men stopped.

"'N' then 'e breaks it, like!" The words fell into a heavy silence.

"Sir—in front of the men, sir! It's intolerable!" Cantlow said, incensed.

"Be silent!" the Captain said. There was the rub—Kydd might have been provoked, he might have been an innocent outraged, but he had been seen in front of others to have held his superior in contempt.

"Do you not feel that Kydd may have acted hastily? Remember, he has only been in the King's Service a short while."

"No, sir, it was a deliberate act of contempt," Cantlow said stubbornly.

"Then consider the consequences of your position, sir. You are perhaps bringing down punishment on one of the most promising seamen *I* have ever seen for what, I am sorry to say, seems like personal vengeance. I ask you again, can you not conceive—"

Cantlow missed the significance of the emphasized "I" and broke in sullenly, "It's a matter of discipline—sir!"

Tyrell leaned over. "No choice, sir, in front of witnesses. Kydd's guilty, and if—"

"I know my duty, Mr. Tyrell," Caldwell said testily.

He looked over Kydd's shoulder, avoiding his eye. "Articles of War," he ordered.

Kydd went cold.

The words of the relevant article rang out. It was a nightmare.

"Seize him up!"

It couldn't be happening—his world spun around him. The boatswain's mates stepped forward and waited. Kydd started and realized that they were waiting for him to strip. He slowly tore off his shirt, still smeared with the gray of powder smoke.

He let it fall and turned to look back at Caldwell, but the mild blue eyes were looking out to seaward.

"Twelve lashes," the Captain said, distantly.

The boatswain's mates seized hold of Kydd and dragged him to the grating. One held his arms spreadeagled while the other passed spun yarn around his thumbs.

His head twisted to the other side—Cantlow stood relaxed and, as Kydd looked at him, his head lifted and a slight smile appeared.

Out of sight the drum thundered away—and stopped. He knew what this meant and braced himself.

He heard the deadly hissing and the blow fell.

It was of shocking force and he felt as if his torso had been plunged into ice. Then came the pain. So murderous was it that it forced a desperate intake of breath before the scream, which Kydd forced to a hoarse grunt.

The sound of the drums floated into his consciousness, which began to retreat.

Again the drums ceased. He writhed at his bonds as the blows slammed him into the grating and the intolerable slash of pain cleaved deep inside. It was inhuman—he bit his lips and tasted the warm blood trickling down.

The agony continued. One part of him begged for release, anything that would halt the torture, but by far the larger part was of consuming fury, a blind rage—not so much at Cantlow and the injustice of it all, but in the betrayal by his adopted world.

The torment went on and on, the monotonous count, the fearful lashing.

Suddenly it was over. Kydd was dimly aware that he was hanging from the gratings and there was a sawing at the lashings. Unable to move, his vision whirling, he felt himself lowered to the deck, his back a roiling bed of unendurable pain. His arms were held, and Renzi's agonized face swam into view. "Whoresons!" Kydd said thickly. He didn't hear any reply, for at that moment his mind ceased to take any further interest in the world.

Renzi wrung out the rag, dipped it into clean water and dabbed at the frightful mess of purple and black that was Kydd's back. He was deeply worried—not about Kydd's physical condition, which after a few days was already showing signs of healthy healing, but at his brooding silence. Kydd went about his work sullenly, stiff with pain, and responded in monosyllables when talked to. Even Renzi was given short shrift. Now he sat on the chest, his back bowed.

"I am sanguine it will heal within the week," Renzi said.

Kydd grunted.

"You will forget all about it in—"

"No!"

Renzi stopped dabbing. "There's nothing you can do about it. You may as well—"

"I know exactly what I'm goin' to do about it."

"May I know what it is you propose?"

Kydd hesitated. "No."

"Very well. I'm sure you intend no fatal mischief for the sake only of immediate satisfaction."

"I know what I'm doing, if that's what you mean." The grim set of his face worried Renzi. He finished the job and reluctantly left Kydd alone.

• • •

"So all it takes is a few fuckin' stripes to get you thinking." Kydd looked up. It was Stallard.

"Bollocks!" Kydd said weakly.

"Just thought I'd give you the word, brother. There's a meeting tonight for all them that have had a gutful of this and fucking well want to do something about it." He waited.

"Where?" Kydd said, without thinking.

Stallard smiled. "Cable tiers, starb'd side, last dog-watch."

He looked around and leaned forward. "Password, 'freedom or death,'" he mouthed dramatically.

It was no part of Kydd's plans to plot mutiny, but the way he was feeling, there would be no harm in seeing what was in the wind.

Turning aft from the fore hatch, Kydd saw that the orlop was in its usual darkness amidships, the area between the surgeon, purser and others aft, and the carpenter and boatswain with their stores forward.

His senses on full alert, he padded down the walkway until he was abreast the starboard cable tier. The anchor cable had long since dried and the thick rope was ranged out in long coils, one on the other nearly to the low deckhead.

He wondered what to do next, when noiselessly a dark figure appeared in front of him. He sensed another behind. "What's the word?" the first whispered urgently.

"Freedom or death," Kydd said quickly.

The figures relaxed, signaling him to clamber up.

Inside there was ample room for the dozen or so men it contained. Kydd's nose wrinkled at the acrid seaweed and mud smell. A single shaded purser's dip was the only illumination.

"Meeting comes to order," Stallard whispered. He was the one with the light.

The others leaned forward over it to hear. With a start Kydd recognized one. It was Bull Lynch, from his own gun crew. Lynch stared back.

"First thing, meet Brother Kydd, who's joining us."

Heads nodded cautiously. Kydd's dull anger now turned to apprehension. It was untrue that he was joining, but now he would be considered part of anything that was decided.

"Now, brothers, to business." Stallard had the easy authority of the rabble-rouser. "We have to face it, friends, we ain't had a chance to do anything much lately, it being so busy, like." He glanced at each of them. "Until now! Brother Kydd is a townie, comes from my part o' the country, and I trust him. Got a headpiece, has Tom, and the two of us are going to work on a plan o' mine that's going to shake the buggers up somethin' cruel." He paused. "Been workin' on this plan for a long while, and even if I say it, it's a good 'un. We gets shot o' this life, and at the same time we gets set up with a purse full o' guineas—every man jack of us!"

The men stirred restlessly, darting uncomfortable glances at each other.

Lynch looked scornful. "Tell us yer great plan, then," he hissed.

Stallard looked resentfully at Lynch. "Brother Bull, I spent a lot o' time at me plan, please be s' good as to hear me out. What we needs is a plan what sees us safe from the law afterward, an' sets us up at the same time so's we don't need to go beggin'. I have that plan, an' it's guaranteed." He stared Lynch down and continued. "Now, listen to this. Hear the whole plan first afore yer makes comment, brothers.

"The night we makes our move—Johnny Hawbuck always comes up for a sniff o' air on deck before he turns in, has a gab with the officer who's got the deck. Gets very dark it does, that hour, so in one easy move we tips 'em both a thwack on the bonce with one o' them belayin' pins and it's overside for 'em both. Meanwhile, I gets to settle with Tyrell in his cabin; I got personal reasons to do this job. But then the beautiful bit—we beats t' quarters, everyone thinks we've seen the French up close but instead all we does is seize the boardin' weapons, as many as we want, all ready for us! This is how we, the h'oppressed slaves, can finally win our freedom. With eight hundred of us under arms we outnumber the bastards ten to one. No one can tell me we can't win—and that's why I needs you 'n' Brother Kydd to help organize 'em all."

There was dead silence.

"Now, you say, what next? Well, we has the ship. This here is a valuable property, is a ship-o'-the-line, and there's nations what'll pay bags o' gold for a line-of-battle ship. Not the enemy! No, we don't consider that, we're patriots, we are. No—we sell to a nation that ain't got one of its own, but is growin' big enough to want one. The United States of Ameriky!"

There were indrawn breaths.

"What about th' officers?" came a deep voice.

"Well, now, we gives 'em a fair trial, they has to answer for their conduct, that sorta thing. And then we tops 'em."

There was a long silence.

"Well—what d'ye think?" Stallard said impatiently.

Kydd was lost in horror, but he could find no immediate glaring flaw that would show it for the madness it was. It seemed he was caught up in a nightmare sweeping him to disaster.

Lynch was the first to move. "Never heard such a lot of cock shit in all me life."

His whisper shocked Stallard, who seemed to lose control. He grabbed Lynch by the shirt and choked out, "You fool! Here's a chance for you to do somethin', to make somethin' of yourself, and you won't fuckin' do anything. You're a sad dog, Bull, you'll never—"

Lynch stood up. "I'm gettin' outa here, I've a gutful o' your pratin', Stallard." He turned to go.

"No, you don't, Lynch. Brothers, stop him!"

The others hung back, worried and uncertain. The bull-like figure of Lynch waited, then his lips curled. "Seems yer've lost it, Stallard."

"You bastard! You yellow bastard!" Stallard breathed, and slid out his knife. Lynch's eyes opened wide, then he brought out his own.

The men fell back—the light was placed on deck, its guttering luminance now unchecked, playing fitfully on the scene.

Stallard circled warily. He held the knife like a dagger, point down, but Lynch held his across his palm low down and with the point slightly upward, following the line of his thumb. He tracked Stallard's movements without moving from where he stood.

It ended quickly. Stallard leaped forward, raising his knife for a sudden strike. Lynch picked up the signal and like a snake his arm extended. The blade gleamed and buried itself in Stallard's ribs.

With an astonished gasp, Stallard fell on his knees, staring at the wound from which scarlet was already pulsing.

Without expression, Lynch returned the knife to its sheath and began climbing out. There was a mad scramble as the others fought to distance themselves from the scene, for whoever was left would surely be blamed. Already someone might be coming, attracted by the noise of the scuffle.

Kydd needed no prompting and made to follow them up and over the cable, but felt his feet impeded.

It was Stallard. "Kydd, help! For fuck's sake, please help me. I've been stuck—bad."

Kydd hesitated.

"Tom—please! Don't leave me, for Chrissake!" Stallard coughed weakly, bringing up a copious amount of blood.

He collapsed on the deck, his strength visibly draining from him. "Don't leave me, Tom, please don' leave me to die—I can't die!" His voice became unsteady and the coughing turned into bloody spasms. He reached weakly for Kydd. "Please don' leave me alone, please, I beg of you. For the love o' God, stay!"

Kydd saw the anguished, terror-ridden eyes. If he left now he could not live with the guilt. "I won't leave."

Another coughing fit racked the dying man. Kydd held him while it passed, careful to avoid the blood. Stallard's eyes rolled and he started a maundering diatribe.

Outside a walkway deckboard creaked. Kydd clapped his hand over Stallard's mouth. Stallard struggled awhile, then subsided. Another sound came distinctly.

Kydd held his breath. There were footsteps coming from forward, the direction of the boatswain's cabin, and they came hesitantly. Stallard gave a spasm and moaned under Kydd's hand, which he clamped tighter.

The footsteps stopped outside. Scrabbling noises sounded on the outside of the cable. Kydd stared up at the rim of the coil. Stallard fell silent.

Renzi's face peered over the edge. "Tom?"

Kydd slumped, ashen with relief. He released Stallard, but the man's head flopped back, his eyes staring open. He had been suffocated—and Kydd had killed him.

Kydd had taken the manner of Stallard's death hard. "Nicholas?"

Renzi paused in bathing his friend's healing back. "Yes?"

Kydd looked away. "I'm goin' to run," he said.

Renzi couldn't believe it. Desertion could mean death—the majestic and brutal ceremony of being "flogged around the Fleet," three hundred lashes on the cruel triangle set up in the boat, which few survived.

It was madness—and where could he desert to, here at sea, a dozen leagues off the French coast? Kydd had been unhinged by his experience, that was clear.

"I plan to be quit o' the Navy within this sennight," Kydd said, in a low voice. He looked up—there was only desolation in his eyes. "I'll need help."

"Of course, dear fellow." Renzi felt a hundred questions crowding in—but before them all was the dawning devastation that he had lost his true friend, the only one he felt able to confide in. As a last service he would help Kydd the best way he could—help them to part, almost certainly forever. A lump began to form in his throat, for he knew that it was the end either way—Kydd would get away or he would be seized for punishment.

Kydd held out his hand. "I knew you would, my—dear friend." Renzi gripped and held it.

Renzi slipped away quietly from the group of men in the waist. Those on deck now in the graveyard hours of the middle watch had little to do. The darkness was relieved by the cool glitter of a quarter moon and as he climbed the ladder to the fo'c'sle it was easy to make out Kydd's lonely figure.

"Nicholas," Kydd mumbled. He was fo'c'sle lookout, a concession to his still painful wounds.

They were quite alone. For a while they stood together, watching the endless moon-silvered waves march toward them from ahead, a hypnotic sight, the continuous lifting and soft crunching of the bow spreading white foam on each side to mark their passage.

"A pleasing scene," Renzi ventured.

"Yes."

Kydd's wounds were healing, and he was able to wear his blue-striped shirt. An occasional cracking in the skin called for more goose grease, but soon he would be as fit as ever. The scar, however, he would carry for the rest of his life.

"You have your plans made now, I believe."

Kydd was silent for a space. "Yes, I have."

Renzi waited.

"I spoke t' Dick Whaley."

"And?"

"He said that every merchant ship has a hidey hole in the lower hold where they stow their best men from the press-gang, should they board. The powder brig will be with us very soon to replace our powder and shot. I will be aboard her when she returns to England."

Renzi's heart went cold. There would be no turning back.

"Nicholas—I have no right to ask it—" The moonlight cast deep shadows on Kydd's face.

"Ask, you looby."

"I will need to sweeten the brig crew, you know, to—"

"I understand. You shall have it." He thought of the guineas sewn in his second waistcoat. Kydd would need them all to sustain him for whatever lay ahead.

"Thank you. I—we might meet again somewhere, y' never know, in this poxy world."

Two days later the brig arrived. It was a boisterous day and, as she lay alongside, an irritable boatswain had to rig, in addition to the main yard tackle, a stay end quarter tackle on fore and main to steady the big barrels as they were swayed aboard. It was not difficult to arrange assignments to the working party in the brig— most sailors had a reluctance to be in such proximity to tons of gunpowder.

At the noon meal break Kydd feigned fatigue, curling up in a corner as though stealing a nap. The brig's crew looked at him curiously, then later invited him to share their victuals.

The *Judith and Mary* of Bristol was on charter to the Navy, a small, rotund but seaworthy vessel that had done the trip several times before. The crew quarters right in the eyes of the ship were tiny, but the men on each side of the table tucked into their meal with gusto. There was small beer to follow and Kydd drank it thirstily—it was no more than a few days old and was fresh and soft. He listened to the talk that followed. The *Judith* had reached her rendezvous late because she had sailed well out into the Atlantic to avoid any privateers at the entrance to the Channel. She was to supply *Duke William* and return to Devonport to de-store before going to Bristol for refit.

Kydd tried to hide his excitement—Bristol had no significant naval presence that he knew of. He took a deep breath. "Thanks for the scran. Might be I can return the favor."

The nuggety seaman opposite grinned. "No need fer that at all, boyo!" he said, in a pleasant Welsh borders lilt.

"No—what I mean is, there's maybe a bit o' gold in it f'r you."

The seamen looked at each other.

"How so, lad?"

For answer, Kydd stood up and, fixing them with blazing eyes, tore off his shirt to reveal the half-healed wounds, livid purple weals, some still weeping in places. "There's ten guineas in it for you if I'm aboard when you sail," he growled.

"An' a berth in a King's ship for us all if yer found," another seaman muttered.

"What do y' say?"

At first there was no response, and Kydd feared the worst.

Then the dark nuggety seaman stood up. "Name's Finchett—Billy to you. Welcome aboard the *Judith!*"

Giddy with relief, Kydd sat down.

"We has a little, who shall say, accommodation in the hold we useta make our own before, when the press-gang's out abroad. Ye'll be safe enough there, boyo." His palm came out, apologetically. "We needs to make other arrangements, you'll unnerstand."

The guineas chinked solemnly into the silence.

• • •

After the break, Kydd returned to the hold for work. *Duke William* required only half of *Judith*'s cargo of powder and soon they would cease their labor and return aboard.

Finchett clambered about over the top of the cargo as though checking their stowage.

There was much more light in the hold than there was on the old *Duke William,* but even so, there were dark recesses in the corners.

"Here you are, Tom," Renzi whispered. He had noiselessly appeared at Kydd's elbow with a shapeless piece of jute sacking. "Your gear—take it."

Kydd grasped it, touched by his friend's thoughtfulness.

"Last barrel, you men!" called down the boatswain.

Finchett gave Kydd a significant look and sauntered over to the after corner. Kydd followed, looking up through the hatch as though waiting for the can-hook to come plunging down again. His heart hammered. It was not too late to abandon the unknown, return to the warmth and safety of his mess—and his friends.

A bulky water barrel rested in the dark outer end of the lower hold. It had an old strop and toggle lying around it, and it looked just like the other sea stores. Finchett slipped the toggle and took the after chine in his fingers.

Checking around carefully, he lifted—the barrel split in two lengthways, hinging at the forward end. He let it fall again. "Get in when yer hears me shout 'n' don't come out till you hears a knock, two times two."

Kydd wiped his clammy hands on his trousers and looked back. Renzi had come over to see the arrangement and now stood quietly.

"It seems that this is goodbye, my good friend," Kydd whispered.

There was no answer. Renzi's face was away from the dull light and it was difficult to read his expression.

From the opposite corner of the hold came the loud splintering of wood. "What the hell are youse doing, yer useless lubbers?" came Finchett's shout. "Call yerselves seamen? I've seen better sailors in Mother Jones's barnyard!"

Kydd gulped. A quick glance back at Renzi and he had the barrel top lifting. There was no time to lose. His heart thudding, he climbed in and began lowering the top half over him.

"Tom—" Renzi's voice was hoarse, unnatural.

Kydd hesitated.

"I—I'm coming with you!"

Mind racing, Kydd crouched down—and immediately felt an opening in the end of the barrel. In the dimness he made out that the opening communicated with the rest of the ship aft in some way. On hands and knees he crawled through.

He looked back to see the figure of Renzi dropping in, and the barrel lid closing. It was now totally black.

Almost immediately there was a scrabble of sound outside as someone secured the strop, and then quiet. Whatever else, the minimum they could expect was a flogging for attempting to desert— Renzi was now as guilty as he.

Renzi must have found the opening too, for his elbows caught Kydd in the side.

"I really do beg your pardon," he murmured, and wriggled aside.

Kydd felt a rise of panic as claustrophobia threatened. He could feel deep frames as they crossed and curved away upward, a flat decking pressed down close above. They must be at the very lowest point of the vessel, where the rise of the keel led to the transom and rudder pintle. There would be rats and cockroaches crawling unseen among them in the dark.

The smell was bad, but less so than *Duke William*'s nauseous depths. It was very close and stuffy and Kydd panted in anticipation of the air expiring.

"I must be demented! Utterly bereft of my senses!" came Renzi's voice.

The motion was not helpful—the swash and hiss of waves above them was quite audible, and the little brig's liveliness was unsettling after the battleship's grand movements. Kydd lay full length, trying to relax. The jerk and wallow of the vessel was trying and he needed to brace himself against the hard beams. Time passed. He knew that they were still alongside from the irregular thumps as they bumped the bulbous sides of *Duke William*.

Muffled shouts penetrated. They were repeated, and knocks were heard, approaching from forward. Kydd guessed that a search was under way. The knocks came closer and he stopped breathing.

Kydd jumped at a vicious banging on their special cask. It stopped, but a shouted exchange then started. The words could not be made out but Kydd thought that he recognized Elkins's voice. He cringed—there would be no mercy from Elkins.

More shouts, answered distantly. Elkins was not moving on—he was a valued member of the boarding party for pressing in merchant ships because he knew all the tricks. They were trapped. The shouts became impatient. The distant voice answered shortly—but with a final banging it was over. Not daring to move, Kydd lay waiting. There were more isolated shouts, but they were moving away. Soon they died away and the two of them were left alone. The impossible seemed to have happened—and when finally the unruly bumping settled into a steady surge his heart leaped. They were under way, bound for freedom, and his life as a seaman in a man-o'-war was over.

It was almost an anticlimax. Without a doubt, for the rest of his life he was a marked man. The desertion was now actual, and even though he had been in the Navy only a few months, his name would be in a book somewhere, and all the dire penalties would fall due if he was discovered. It was a miserable situation.

He had given no thought to what he would do now. He could not return home, which implied survival elsewhere, but where? In wartime there was little call for a wig-maker, and his newfound skills as a sailor could find employment now only in the merchant marine, and there he would be in constant fear of the press-gang and someone recognizing him.

He would have to go somewhere like the colonies. His loyal heart would not allow him to go to the infant United States and he had heard that the new settlements in Botany Bay were in grave difficulties—no place for a fugitive.

The enormity of what he had done pressed in. He remembered Bowyer's face with its slow smile as he gently put Kydd right about some seafaring matter, and felt demeaned, dirty and criminal.

A double knock was followed by another, and the barrel top lifted. Thankfully they scrambled out. "Two of yez!" Finchett said, in mock astonishment. "Well, yer both come up on deck 'n' take your last sightin' o' *Duke William!*"

Cautiously they looked out from the hatchway, *Judith*'s low bulwarks making it inadvisable to show themselves on deck.

A mile or so off, *Duke William* was heading away from them, leaning into the stiffening breeze. With her yards braced up sharp, the big three-decker looked a picture of careless strength. And with her she carried Kydd's friends: Doggo, Dick Whaley—Ned Doud, of course, not forgetting Pinto and Wong. Kydd's eyes pricked, and glistened. Renzi touched his arm, but he still stared over the sea to the old ship-of-the-line. He gazed after her until first her hull sank beneath the curve of the horizon, then her topsails, lit redly by the setting sun, and finally, almost too distant to see, her royals. Then the sea was empty.

They sat together on the foredeck of *Judith*—the skipper had insisted they work their passage, and in the morning sunshine they were set to work seaming a threadbare foresail.

The brig met the seas in exuberant fashion, for she sailed up the long blue swells and down the other side instead of arrogantly shouldering them aside. The occasional breakers served to discommode, bullying her off course unmercifully.

The lighter spars and rigging seemed toy-like after those of a man-o'-war but the freeboard of only a few feet gave an exhilarating closeness to the rush and hiss of the sea.

"Tom, dear fellow," said Renzi.

Kydd had been quiet and introspective since their desertion, but had been respectful and considerate in their exchanges.

"Tom, we must give thought to our future." Renzi's impulsive act had changed his own circumstances fatally. Now there was no question of seeing through the high-minded redemption he had undertaken: neither could he return to his family with his tail between his legs. In truth he had no idea what to do.

"Th' colonies?" said Kydd, looking up with troubled eyes.

"A possibility." Renzi's half-brother was in Canada and after his infrequent return visits Renzi had no illusions about the raw, half-civilized frontier life of the new continent.

"A foreign land, then?"

Renzi hid a smile. He knew that Kydd, like others of his kind, had only the haziest notion of the outside world. "Again, a possibility," he answered. "We must consider carefully, of course." With half the world at war and revolutionary disaffection rampant in the other, it would be a deadly gamble to find which of them, old world or new, would prove a reliable hiding place.

He returned to his palm and needle. They had but a few more days to make a decision before landfall in England, and then it would have to be final. For the first time Renzi felt that events were slipping out of his control and his options were being extinguished, one by one.

CHAPTER 12

WELL, ME BOYOS, early tomorrer you sees old England agen—ain't it prime?" Finchett's announcement did not seem to cheer Kydd and Renzi and, perplexed, he left them to it. The pair moodily sat on the canvas-covered main hatch; there seemed no point in conversation.

Interrupting their introspection, from the masthead there was a sudden hail. "Sail hooo!"

A single vessel within hours of the English coast—there could be little doubt about its origins. The entire maritime trade of England passed up Channel this way, as did the ships of the Navy going about their business of war.

"Youse had better be ready to stow yerselves below agen."

This was eminent good sense. One of the darker acts of a King's ship was the stripping of seamen from homeward-bound merchant packets, a hard thing after a voyage to the Indies of a year or more.

"Deck hooo! She's a cutter under flyin' jib—'n' English colors!" Now there was no doubt: one of the many small warships on patrol. And her deep, narrow hull and that huge bowsprit meant speed. There was no way they could think of outrunning her.

The crew of the *Judith* had a protection from the press as a Fleet auxiliary, but these were personal to the bearer. There was no help for it: they would have to return to their black hole.

A last reluctant glimpse of the balmy day, and the cutter smartly tacking toward, and they returned below. It was uncomfortable and boring in their close black lair, waiting for the boarding to be over with, but it was infinitely better than the alternative.

The steady swooping movement was replaced by an uneasy bobbing—they had heaved to; a discordant bumping told them that the cutter was alongside. They resigned themselves to it: this might be the first of many such.

Faint shouts—probably Finchett expressing his views on the propriety of the Royal Navy interfering with the merchant service, and after an interminable time they felt the lurch and smooth take-up of sail once more. They waited for the signal, and before long they heard scrabbling at the toggle and the strop falling away. But there was no signal. Perhaps naval seamen were still aboard.

"Wait!" Renzi whispered. "We must be sure."

The air grew stale, then close. They started to pant and felt giddy.

"We have to get out," Renzi said. He tried to lift the barrel lid. It didn't budge. He heaved at it, with no result. Putting his back under the lid, he uncoiled his full weight against it. It gave a little, then slammed down again. "There's something on it," he whispered. "Give me a hand."

He guided Kydd in the blackness to put his back next to his own in the cramped space, and together they thrust upward.

Suddenly it gave and flew open. The hold was in darkness, of course, but on the next barrel a lanthorn stood, casting a dim yellow light.

They climbed out cautiously, but Kydd tripped on a dark shape on the deck next to the barrel. He bent to see what it was—and jerked up in horror.

It was a body. He bent again to roll it over—and his hand came away wet and sticky. "It's Finchett."

Renzi knelt and examined the corpse. "There's a wound in his back," he said. It didn't make any sense. Maybe Finchett had been wounded on deck and had tried to reach them, expiring after releasing the strop. Renzi realized their reconnaissance would have to be cautious—something was terribly awry.

Kydd remembered that there was a small hatch forward; it allowed entry into the hold without needing the big main hatch to be opened. They scrambled across the remaining powder barrels and reached the hatchway ladder at the fore part of the hold.

"Careful," whispered Renzi.

Kydd eased back the sliding hatch an inch. Sunlight flooded in, as did familiar sea sounds. The clean salt air was invigorating.

Renzi put his ear to the opening.

"What is it?" whispered Kydd urgently. He was beginning to feel ghosts.

"Quiet!" snapped Renzi.

Faint voices could be heard. They grew louder, and Renzi eased the hatch shut again.

"What?" Kydd asked.

Renzi looked at him gravely. "They were speaking French, dear fellow."

The cutter must have been a French corsair under false colors—a smart move, given the circumstances. They had boarded the unaccompanied powder brig, probably massacred the crew and even now would be carrying her into a French port.

They stared at each other. Their immediate future was now very much in question. If they surrendered they would probably be hove overboard; if they waited until they reached port and discharged cargo they would be discovered and would rot in a military prison; and if they hid in their hole they would die there.

Renzi struggled with alternatives, but logic led pitilessly to a series of dead ends. He climbed back down the ladder and put his head in his hands.

"Nicholas! Up here, man!" There was sharp authority in Kydd's voice. "We need t' know where we stand. Try to listen t' what they're saying."

Renzi slid the hatch open a crack and put his ear to it. There were two distinct voices, both young and strong, and another distant one, more mature. Their northern French dialect was difficult to follow, but he understood. The distant voice was giving the other two orders—probably the watch on deck, or what passed for it.

The orders themselves gave clues. What was *aller vent largue?* To go with the wind *largue?* That would be "large," of course— the opposite of close hauled. In that case they were going in the opposite direction to before. "We visit Madame Cécile's establishment when we reach Goulven"—where was that? This heathen dialect! But that meant it was somewhere in Brittany, almost certainly the north coast—they would not risk the longer voyage to Brest or points southward.

Renzi strained to hear, but there was only a tedious description of what they would find in Madame Cécile's brothel. "We're on our way to Goulven, which I believe to be on the north coast," he quietly reported. "We are running large to the south or sou'-west, and I suppose we will reach port tomorrow.

"I can hear two on deck and one aft. There may be more below."

Unarmed, they wouldn't have a hope, no matter how much surprise they commanded. He resumed listening. What he heard made him start, but the import was worse—it was desperate.

"They're saying that they hope they won't have their prize taken from them by the Navy bound for Brest," he whispered urgently.

Apparently an unknown force was sailing to make rendezvous with those in Brest. Together they could overwhelm *Duke William* and the two others, then be free to descend on any valuable British overseas possessions they chose.

Kydd was utterly resolute. "Nicholas, get yourself here!"

Tumbling down the ladder, he swung down to the capacious

water barrels along the centerline at the forward end of the hold. He tapped them until he found an empty one. Knocking out one end, he began the laborious task of manhandling it toward the ladder.

Renzi didn't question Kydd's judgment: he moved across to help him shift the water cask.

Through gasps of effort Kydd explained: "What would you do if y' saw your cargo of gunpowder afire?" The water barrel was upended at the base of the ladder. It was a simple matter to stuff it with packing straw. Kydd fetched bilge water, which he liberally sprinkled over the straw. "Need a lot of smoke, not much fire," he said, and brought the lanthorn.

His eyes shone—with exhilaration or fear Renzi could not be sure.

"Here goes—we get blown t' glory together or . . ." Kydd opened the lanthorn and ignited a wisp of straw. The tiny flame seemed to illuminate the entire hold, filling it with ruddy dancing shadows.

He dropped it into the barrel and wisps of gray-white smoke began to issue upward.

At the top of the hold the smoke gathered, swelling and building. Kydd fed in more wet straw while Renzi eased the hatch back a little and returned.

The smoke got thicker, stinging Kydd's eyes, but they did not have to wait long. Above them there was a yell of fear, the hatch slammed open and white smoke billowed up on deck. There was no attempt to get at the fire and Kydd could hardly blame them: tons of gunpowder ablaze was an awesome threat.

It wasn't possible to see what was happening but the sounds were graphic enough. Disordered slatting and banging of sails meant that the wheel had been abandoned, sending them up into the wind. Panic and shouting—the thumps and clunking amidships could only be the dory being launched.

"No—wait until they're well clear. They'll be rowing f'r their lives, I believe," said Kydd happily. He inspected the barrel—no need to let it blaze any more. He clapped its lid back on, choking the fire.

They emerged spluttering and red-eyed on deck. The dory was already a good half-mile away and making astonishing speed.

"So, what now?" said Renzi. The dory would surely return when they saw the fire die down.

"Get the boarding muskets," Kydd replied.

Renzi reserved his views about how long they could keep the dory at bay. Night would be coming soon, and they had to face the urgent problem of how the two of them alone could handle the brig.

They hurried to the master's cabin. There had been only a half-hearted attempt to clean away the bloodstains, but the small arms chest was in its place against the bulkhead. There were only old-fashioned pieces, but they had been carefully looked after. Kydd and Renzi loaded feverishly from the keg of powder and priming horn, the heavy balls rammed down over the charge.

There were six muskets, enough to deter all but the most determined onslaught. They returned on deck. Sure enough, the dory had stopped, rising and falling with the slight seas, oars held level. There were six of them by count, a prize crew not expecting trouble.

They continued to load until all six muskets were ready.

"I'll fire, you load," Kydd said briefly.

The dory bobbed about. They would have been spotted by now, and no doubt there would be an animated discussion going on, thought Renzi.

"So what is our plan, then?" he said lightly. He would not share his fears—he could only see them wallowing about out of control off the French coast and he put their survival time at hours at the most.

"We invite 'em aboard, o' course," Kydd said.

Renzi's eyebrows rose.

"To kindly work our vessel f'r us!" Kydd grinned.

The dory spun about and began the laborious return to the brig. Kydd trained a musket and waited.

It approached and stopped fifty yards away, outside reliable musket range.

"*Je monte à bord!*"

"What's he say?"

"He *says* he is coming aboard."

A fat man in a purple coat with gold lace was talking, offhand and confident. He had left his hat behind and his unwigged head was covered in corn-colored stubble. He signaled to the man at the oars, who resumed his pull.

Kydd squeezed off a shot. It sent up a waterspout close to the bow of the dory. A furious shout came from the fat man, followed by a more placating tone. The others in the boat watched sullenly.

Renzi took the piece and reloaded it.

"And?"

"He's offering to make it worth our while to let them continue on their way."

Kydd loosed another shot, resulting in another angry shout that ended in wheedling.

"He's saying that unless we yield he will not answer for the consequences," Renzi reported.

Kydd smiled grimly.

"He says he has a corsair crew who are difficult to control—would we care to put ourselves under his protection?"

It was deadlock. They could not hope to keep the dory away forever, but the dory was in a dangerous position so far to sea and a perilously long pull back to land.

"Tell them to swim for it, Nicholas, the fat one first."

"What?"

"If they want t' get aboard, they do it one on one—fat sod first," Kydd replied with relish.

A violent discussion began. The fat man shouted and gesticu-
lated, his main attention on the thick-set seaman in the bows.

"Another ball, dare I ask?" Renzi said.

The shot went over the heads of the French, and the ball must
have gone low, for the boat's occupants all ducked violently.

The fat man stood up and waved. Kydd sent another ball close to
his head and he collapsed back into the dory.

Tearing off his purple coat, he lowered himself, protesting volubly,
over the side of the dory. He splashed and spluttered his way toward
the brig, puffing and blowing like a grampus at the main chains.

Weapons reloaded, Kydd stood on deck, flintlock cradled as he
waited for the man to haul himself up. "Citoyen Hector Jouet," he
snarled, dripping seawater copiously on the deck, wariness struggling with defiance on his face.

Kydd looked at Renzi, who broke into mellifluous French, bow-
ing as he did so.

Jouet looked at him murderously and turned his back. Renzi cut
off a length of line and efficiently secured his wrists. He was to remain at rest on the main hatch.

Meanwhile, the dory had crept closer. The well-built man in the
bows was next. He plunged into the sea and with powerful strokes
came rapidly up with the brig. Kydd's musket idly lay in his direction as the man submitted to being bound, and sat next to the
glowering Jouet. The dory was now only thirty yards off. "Don't
worry, let's jus' get 'em aboard," Kydd said.

A mustached and wiry seaman next swam lazily toward them.
The dory was now only some fifteen yards off. The rower lay on
his oars. Kydd beckoned, his musket held loose. A man in plain
black stood up, his eyes even at this distance fierce and glittering.
His hand went inside his coat as though to scratch lice—but when
it came out, a long gleaming pistol came with it. He sighted down
the long barrel.

Behind Kydd came the sudden earsplitting crack of a musket. The man snapped rigid, then slowly fell forward to splash noisily into the water alongside the dory.

Renzi lowered the musket. "My bird, I think."

On the main hatch the five men sat, darting deadly glances at them. Renzi knew it would take only one ill-judged move and he and Kydd would die.

Kydd looked at them dispassionately. The brig had two masts, square-rigged on both, and a big spanker on the main. Three men could handle the vessel if they attended to each mast in turn. If it came on to blow—well, the whole thing was a gamble anyway.

"Get the fat bugger up here, Nicholas. Secure his feet an' sit him down forrard o' the wheel."

Renzi did so, and Kydd stood with the muzzle of his gun lazily covering the man. "Tell him he gets it in the belly first if there's trouble. Now the hard-looking bastard—he goes on the wheel."

The man padded forward and stood at the wheel, his black eyes unblinking in a mask of hatred.

"Better this ill-looking dog's under eye." Kydd shifted around so his flintlock covered both men.

"Now tell 'em all we're blood 'n' death desperate. If they try anything they're dead 'uns for sure, but if they behave they may get t' live."

Renzi felt as though he was in a cage of lions waiting to pounce if the trainer lost his nerve. He knew that Kydd's course of action was the only one possible, and he could only admire the cool thinking that had cut through hopelessness to a solution, and the toughness of the mind that had carried it through to make it work. "So, what course?" he asked. He was uncomfortably aware that neither of them had the faintest idea of ocean navigation, and they ran the risk of piling into the Scilly rocks or worse, if they were but points off course in the return to England.

"South-west!"

Renzi was dumbfounded—it would take them *away* from England. Then he understood. "You're going to warn *Duke William!*"

"Of course. If we return to England to tell 'em there, it'll be too late."

"But—"

"Do you want it upon your conscience that you betrayed y'r friends? And our desertion—they'll be so pleased to be tipped the wink, we'll be heroes."

They soon fell into a routine; always the whole five on deck and under eye at the one time, Jouet always under the muzzle of a gun. In everything they did, they moved slowly, carefully, their eyes everywhere, watchful.

The tension was fearful.

Fortunately their course did not require them to tack, and they bowled along south-westward with little attention to the tacks and sheets. When night fell the lanthorn Renzi hung in the rigging played on the three sprawled on the main hatch.

A three-quarters moon rose, bathing them in soft silver glitter, making it easier to check on their captives. Renzi stood guard, occasionally pacing slowly to keep awake, Kydd sleeping on deck beside him.

The moon rose higher, moving behind the swell of the sails. The ceaselessly moving lines of rigging projected stark black against the backlit sails, swaying hypnotically.

Renzi's eyes grew heavy, and when the moon was high in the night sky he woke Kydd for his watch. It didn't take him long to drift off into a deep, dreamless sleep.

The sudden concussion of a musket burst into his sleep. He sat up, eyes straining to make sense of where he was. Two of the French were standing, brought to a halt by Kydd's vigilant shot. "Tell them I've five other shots'll be waitin' for their next move!" he said thickly.

Renzi did so, reloaded the musket and settled down again.

• • •

Dawn found them both huddled together, muskets across their knees, bleary-eyed.

How much endurance had they left? It might be days before they encountered the squadron, if at all, for there was no knowing where they might be. All they had as a clue was a half-remembered mental image of the French coast, a picture of a low, nondescript coastline jutting out and going in again that they knew so well from their constant beating up and down.

And over there was the coast right enough, but Renzi did not recognize it in the slightest part. It was going to be a long, long vigil. He stood up and stretched. "Need to pump ship—going forrard."

Kydd nodded, and stood also, his musket loose and ready.

Renzi passed down the waist, warily eyeing the tense, glowering French. He eased himself and made his way back past them.

In a sudden lunge the wiry sailor made his move. He leaped from behind and a flash of steel flew at Renzi's throat before he could react.

"*Arrêtez-vous!*" the man snapped.

Renzi halted. It was a sailmaker's knife, small and curved and razor sharp. It rested against his windpipe. The man was hidden by his body, so there was no target for Kydd.

But Kydd had the gun instantly jabbing into the fat man. Eyes flashed murder over the space between—and there was absolute stillness. His hand on the trigger, Kydd hauled Jouet to his feet. Carefully, he edged sideways until he had the man at the wheel in sight and the stand of muskets behind his back.

It was stalemate.

Long minutes passed. Renzi held still, a thin half-smile his only concession to emotion. The fat man lay at Kydd's feet sweating, and the other Frenchmen bunched up behind Renzi.

There was no sound except the slap and crunch of the bow waves and the cheerful pattering of reef points on the sail.

The wiry seaman growled at Renzi.

"He says to throw down your musket."

"Tell him to—tell him what you like."

"He says—he desires you to know that my throat will shortly be cut."

"Remind him that the fat man gets it in the guts instantly."

The man with the knife made a scornful remark.

"His view is that Jouet's life is not worth preserving."

"Then I've still five shots ready for them." Kydd kept his musket on Jouet.

"He says that you will only get one or two shots away before they overcome you, and these are odds they are willing to take."

Kydd detected only the slightest tremor in Renzi's voice.

The tableau held—but there would soon be a sudden, desperate move on one side or the other and it would be over quickly in a flurry of death and mutilation.

In helpless fury Kydd glared at them. He jerked the muzzle up when the man with the knife inched Renzi forward. He was aware that the man at the wheel had abandoned it and was ready to spring on him, because the brig had fallen off the wind.

They closed in.

Then Kydd laughed. Harsh, maniacal laughter, barking away.

They stopped.

"They want to know if you've gone mad." There was anxiety in Renzi's voice.

Kydd stopped laughing. "Tell him if he drops his knife I might consider him my prisoner, or then again I might not."

Relaxing, Kydd looked at them contemptuously. Slowly he lifted his arm and pointed to the south. Hidden by the sails before but now revealed by their falling off the wind was the plain sight of a British sloop-of-war. She had seen them and was fussing over to investigate.

• • •

They lay at their ease on the little foredeck, no duties for them—the lieutenant of the sloop's prize crew had been most insistent. The sloop had hurried away to alert the Commodore, leaving the *Judith and Mary* to transport the two at their leisure to rendezvous with the *Duke William*.

A pigtailed old seaman coiled down the fore halliards. "You lucky buggers!" he said enviously. "Prize money on this little barky'll set yez up fer life or chirpin' merry forever."

"When we finally make it back," Kydd said dreamily. He would cut a figure in Guildford—gold watch, buy up one of the fashionable shops on High Street, his family wouldn't believe it. Only a few miles down the road was Hatchlands, a vast estate built for Admiral Boscawen after the last war—and now Thomas Kydd would be the one pointed out parading in town.

Renzi was wrestling with his conscience. He was less than a third of the way through his sentence—would striking it personally lucky make it ethically allowable to remit the remainder? He rather thought not.

Duke William backed her topsails and hove to. Curious faces looked down from her decks high above as Kydd and Renzi mounted the entry steps and came over the bulwarks onto the well-remembered quarterdeck.

Kydd grinned at the jaw-dropping surprise their appearance caused. Tyrell stumped his way rapidly from forward to confront them.

"Take them in charge! Put them in irons this instant!" he roared. Lockwood looked bemused.

"If you'll allow me to explain, sir," a voice behind them said smoothly. It was the lieutenant of the prize crew arriving from the entry port.

At that moment the Captain emerged from the cabin spaces. The lieutenant lifted his cocked hat politely and drew them both aside.

Kydd looked around happily. The sounds and smells he remembered surged over him—he nodded to Doggo on the wheel, and grinned cheekily at Elkins, who stood speechless by the mainmast.

The lieutenant doffed his hat again and left—he would have an anxious time on the voyage back to England.

Captain Caldwell came over. Kydd touched his forehead. "I think we might have misjudged you, Kydd," he said pleasantly.

"Couldn't abide t' see *Duke William* mauled so, sir," he said respectfully. "May I ask, sir, will we be in time?"

"Set your mind at rest, Kydd. The sloop has probably reached Admiral Howe by now and I daresay we'll be able to provide a warm enough welcome for the French when he comes out."

"Sir, will we get prize money f'r the brig?"

Caldwell coughed politely. His eyes slid to Tyrell and back again. "Well, as to that, you must understand that at the time you were technically deserters. I'm sorry."

Kydd's heart fell. So much for dreaming.

"But welcome back, Kydd. I can see a fine future for you in the King's Service, mark my words."

"Sir—I must point out—"

"Mr. Tyrell?"

"They *are* deserters!"

"Come now, Mr. Tyrell, let us not allow our zeal for the Service to overcome our common humanity."

Tyrell's black eyebrows contracted. "I must insist, sir. The regulations cannot be so lightly set aside—they knew what they were doing!"

The Captain hesitated.

"They should be taken in charge, sir."

Tyrell's obdurate manner unbalanced Caldwell. It would go hard with him if for any reason it could be shown later that he had failed in his duty to bring a deserter to justice.

"Very well. Take them below." He avoided Kydd's eyes and returned to the cabin spaces.

Kydd struggled to face it. The Articles of War and naval regulations gave little leeway once a crime was proven—desertion was a serious problem for the Navy and the penalties were savage, intended to deter. It was absolutely no use to appeal to natural justice: the law must take its course.

He sat appalled at the impossible-to-conceive prospect of three hundred lashes—and *Duke William* was at the end of her sea endurance and must soon sail back to England and the Fleet.

His feet were in bilboes once more—he would have to get used to it, for they would be in irons even after they arrived back in port. He tried to lie back, but could not, the bilboes twisting his leg irons.

What was so hard to bear was that he had involved Renzi, who sat in irons uncomplaining next to him. Kydd sank into a quiet misery.

Early the next morning the Master-at-Arms appeared. "Up!" he said.

Shackles were removed, manacles went on their wrists and they were led up to the upper deck—for exercise, Kydd assumed.

On the quarterdeck the Captain and Tyrell were waiting.

The Master-at-Arms saluted. "Prisoners mustered, sir!" His pig eyes swiveled curiously to Kydd.

Caldwell nodded and stepped forward. "You see there, Kydd," he said, gesturing over to leeward.

No more than a few cables off lay *Artemis,* the legendary crack frigate. She kept up lazily with the big battleship, effortlessly slicing through the water. She looked impossibly lovely—as new as *Duke William* was old, smart as paint and with fresh white sails, gold leaf gleaming on her scrollwork; she was an ocean racer, a lucky ship that had already made her daring captain a rich man.

Kydd turned his dull eyes back to the Captain. "Sir?"

"She has signaled us."

Kydd wondered what on earth this had to do with him.

"*Artemis* has prize crews away—she has signaled us to the effect that she would be grateful if we could spare a dozen seamen. I have answered that we can.

"Master-at-Arms, remove the gyves. These men are going to *Artemis*—thoroughly bad lot, glad to be rid of 'em!

"We'd better get rid of their associates as well. They'd be of like mind, I'll wager."

Dumbfounded, Kydd allowed his fetters to be struck off.

Captain Caldwell continued, "The boatswain has explained to me what happened. It seems that unfortunately we left you behind in the hold when the brig sailed. My apologies."

"Then th' prize money, sir?" Kydd said, greatly daring.

"Let's leave it at that, shall we?" Caldwell said smoothly. "Get your dunnage, and let me know who your accomplices are—they will be going with you."

Kydd and Renzi exchanged a quick expression of wild hope. Tyrell stormed forward, confronting the pair, but Caldwell gestured, placating. "Thank you, Mr. Tyrell. Kindly prepare to be under way in fifteen minutes, will you?

"Now, Kydd, you go as a volunteer and able seaman according to the books—but let me warn you"—the Captain's expression softened to a half-smile—"you'll find life in a frigate just a little bit different from that in a ship-of-the-line!"

Author's Note

Kydd is based on real life. I feel that I would devalue what the eighteenth-century seaman really achieved were I to exaggerate or distort facts for the sake of drama—for me, a particularly odious form of betrayal. Therefore, all the major actions and most of the minor are as close as I can make them to the real thing. I have pondered this matter hard and have come to the conclusion that it is acceptable as a working principle to keep to what actually happened, but for the sake of narrative flow, in some cases, vary the *time* when it happened. For instance, Admiral Howe's ships did not venture for France until some time after I say—I did not want to have Kydd start his sea adventures in a ship that first swings around its anchor for several months. My ships are actual vessels of the times; I have changed the names only. Engagements are based on real actions of the time with some variation in the time or place described.

As for Thomas Kydd—in the circumscribed world of eighteenth-century society, there were those fortunate enough to be well-born, and there were the lower orders who knew their place and in the main accepted it. Yet in the twenty-two years of warfare at the end of the century, a total of 120 men crossed from the fo'c'sle to the quarterdeck through their own exceptional merit, passing thereby from common seaman to gentleman. They include Lieutenant Pasco,

—who was signal officer at Trafalgar and who famously amended Nelson's immortal signal "England expects every man to do his duty"—and also Nelson's own first lieutenant of *Victory,* a pressed man like Kydd. And of these, twenty-two went on to become captain of their own ship, and three ended as admiral!

These men must have been titans—hard minded, iron willed and utterly resolute—but little is known of them, for none left an autobiography, with the single exception of Bligh, who for all his faults went on to fight like a tiger as captain of a ship-of-the-line at Camperdown and for Nelson at the bloody battle of Copenhagen.

Today it is hard to get a focus on such men. The distorting lens of Victorian sentimentality gradually changed public perceptions of the sailor to one of Jolly Jack Tar, an object of patronized quaintness. The eighteenth-century seamen were hard men who lived a hard life, and it is equally nonsense to think they were the dregs of humanity, as some more modern writers would have it. The mighty ship-of-the-line was as complex in its day as a moon rocket today. Most seamen were proud, self-sufficient and resourceful men sharing a remarkable culture, but they were not articulate. This book is my tribute to those who became masters of the sea in the greatest age of fighting sail.

ACKNOWLEDGMENTS

Writing one's first book is an adventure, but a perilous one—necessarily trusting untried skills and sailing into uncharted waters with no certainty that there will be a successful outcome to the voyage.

I count myself blessed by the help I have received from others in this odyssey, the chief of whom is certainly my wife, Kathy. She persuaded me to set forth, and her sureness of touch and unwavering vision have kept me from the doldrums of self-doubt and the rocks of ill-practice.

I readily acknowledge the debt I owe to the staff at the National Maritime Museum and the Public Records Office at Kew, the excellent services of the Society for Nautical Research and the Navy Records Society, and to that band of people on both sides of the Atlantic who have patiently distilled the overwhelming range of primary sources into a coherent, usable and fascinating account of this heroic period. I think particularly of Nicholas Rodger, Brian Lavery, John Harland, Peter Goodwin and Karl Heinz Marquardt, and others who are no longer with us—David Lyon, Christopher Lloyd, Michael Lewis—and William Falconer (lost at sea 1770), whose warmth and humanity transcended his century.

And, of course, the professionals: professor of eighteenth-century studies Jack Lynch; my literary agent, Carole Blake; marine artist Geoff Hunt; and finally my publisher, McBooks Press.

THE THOMAS KYDD SHIPMATES NETWORK

IF YOU ENJOY THE KYDD SEA ADVENTURES, why not join the Shipmates Network and keep in touch with Julian Stockwin and his hero, Thomas Kydd, on a regular basis?

Each month you'll receive the free email newsletter *Bosun's Chronicle*, packed with information about the Great Age of Sail, details on author events, advance notice of new publications, news about Shipmates around the world, and contests for signed editions of the Kydd books and other great prizes.

There's also an opportunity to have your own questions about the sea and ships answered in the "Ask Julian" column.

It's easy to join the network.

Just register via the website-www.julianstockwin.com

Naval Adventure
with a Wry Sense of Irony!

A Sailor of Austria

In which, without really intending to, Otto Prohaska
becomes Official War Hero No. 27
of the Habsburg Empire.

by John Biggins

**Lovers of great military history
rejoice! The beloved Prohaska
books are back.**

This ironic, hilarious, and poignant
story, the first in a four-book series,
will delight and entertain—and leave
you wanting more. Otto Prohaska is a
submarine captain serving the
almost-landlocked Austro-Hungarian
Empire. He faces a host of unlikely
circumstances, from petrol poisoning
to exploding lavatories to trigger-
happy Turks. All signs point to the
total collapse of the bloated empire
he serves, but Otto refuses to abandon the Habsburgs in their hour of
need.

A Sailor of Austria
by John Biggins
978-1-59013-107-7
376 pages • $16.95 trade pb.

"Stark realism and finely crafted
humor…use of narration, his thorough knowledge, and good technical
details make this novel compelling
reading."

—Library Journal

Night of Flames
by Douglas W. Jacobson

WHAT PRICE WOULD YOU PAY

TO KEEP YOUR SOUL?

In 1939 the Germans invade Poland, setting off a rising storm of violence and destruction. For Anna and Jan Kopernik the loss is unimaginable. She is an assistant professor at a university in Krakow; he, an officer in the Polish cavalry. Separated by the war, they must find their own way in a world where everything they ever knew is gone.

When Anna's father is deported to a death camp, she must flee to Belgium where she joins the Resistance. Meanwhile, Jan escapes with the battered remnants of the Polish army to Britain. He returns to Poland in an undercover mission to contact the Resistance and seizes the chance to search for his missing wife. Through the long night of Nazi occupation, ordinary people across Europe fight a covert war of resistance against the overwhelming might of the German war machine. The struggle seems hopeless, but they are determined to take back what is theirs.

ISBN 978-1-59013-136-7 • Hardcover • $23.95

"Suspenseful, rich in convincingly detailed incidents, and impeccably researched."   *—Library Journal*

"Well researched and skillfully executed . . . a highly readable work which is both informative and imaginative."
—The Historical Novels Review

"A taut and twisting thriller with memorable flesh and blood characters."   —James Conroyd Martin,
author of *Push Not the River*

Douglas Reeman Modern Naval Library

By the author of the Alexander Kent/Richard Bolitho Novels

Rarely does an author of nautical fiction so fully initiate his readers into the life, the heart and soul of a ship. Fans of the best-selling Bolitho Novels will find Reeman's modern naval fiction shares the same masterful storytelling and authoritative descriptions. These riveting World War II novels are the latest in Douglas Reeman's epic collection of 20th-century naval fiction, now available for the first time in trade paperback.

$15.95 each

Available at your favorite bookstore, or call toll-free: 1-888-BOOKS-11 (1-888-266-5711). To order on the web visit www.mcbooks.com

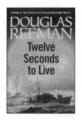

Twelve Seconds to Live
Lieutenant-Commander David Masters now uses all his skill and training to defuse "the beast" wherever he finds it.
ISBN 978-1-59013-044-5

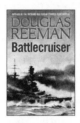

Battlecruiser
Captain Guy Sherbrooke still reels from the loss of his previous command; now he's out to even the score.
ISBN 978-1-59013-043-8

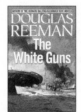

The White Guns
The crew of *MGB 801* face the challenge of revenge and sacrifice during the occupation of the German seaport of Kiel.
ISBN 978-1-59013-083-4

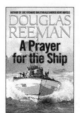

A Prayer for the Ship
Sub-Lieutenant Clive Royce must quickly learn to play the deadly cat-and-mouse game of attack and survival against the mighty German fleet.
ISBN 978-1-59013-097-1

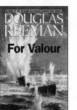

For Valour
The crew of the crack destroyer *Hakka* are weary but determined to face down the enemy one more time.
ISBN 978-1-59013-049-0

The Matty Graves Novels
by Broos Campbell

1. No Quarter

In 1799, the young U.S. Navy faces France in
an undeclared Quasi-War for the Caribbean.
Midshipman Matty Graves is caught up in escalat-
ing violence as he serves aboard the *Rattle-Snake*
under his drunken cousin, Billy. Matty already
knows how to handle the sails and fight a ship.
Now, with the sarcastic Lieutenant Peter Wickett
as his mentor and nemesis, he faces the ironies of a
war where telling friend from foe is no mean trick.

ISBN 978-1-59013-139-8 • Trade Paperback • $16.95

"[Campbell's] characters are sharp, genuine and fascinating, his
plotting fast-paced and authentic."　　　　　—James L. Nelson
author of *The Only Life That Mattered*

2. The War of Knives

Matty Graves, acting lieutenant in the newly
formed U.S. Navy, becomes a spy in the French
colony of Saint-Dómingue and plunges headlong
into a brutal world of betrayal. At first the bloody
civil war between former slaves and their mixed-
race overseers simply offers a way to test himself,
but soon Matty is drawn into the heart of the con-
flict when he meets the flamboyant Juge and the
mysterious Grandfather Chatterbox—and faces an
interrogation by the brutal colonel known as "The Whip."
ISBN 978-1-59013-104-6 • Hardcover • $23.95

"Entertaining . . . a colorful cast of shady characters . . . an elaborate
swashbuckling tale."　　　　　　　　　　　*—Publishers Weekly*

"Don't start this one at bedtime; you'll be up all night!"
—William H. White
author of the Oliver Baldwin Novels

The Sea Officer William Bentley Novels by Jan Needle

1 A Fine Boy for Killing

Under sealed orders for a long, arduous voyage, Captain Daniel Swift must forge an efficient crew from a ragged group of old men, criminals, and young boys under his command, including his nephew and favorite, William Bentley.

0-935526-86-2 • 320 pages, $17.95

2 The Wicked Trade

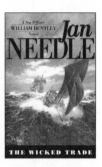

The "wicked trade" is smuggling—customs men and smugglers battling over piles of booty. Surrounded by corruption and greed, young Bentley confronts ever more ruthless companions and crew while the dark shadow of his brutal uncle, Captain Swift, looms over him once more.

0-935526-95-1 • 384 pages, $16.95

3 The Spithead Nymph

First Lieutenant William Bentley of the *Biter* begins a harrowing journey to Jamaica. The brutality of Will's shipboard companions further hardens him to navy life, but nothing can prepare him for the inhumanity that fuels the slave trade.

1-59013-077-4 • 288 pages, $14.95

green
press
INITIATIVE

McBooks Press is committed to preserving ancient forests and natural resources. We elected to print this title on 30% post consumer recycled paper, processed chlorine free. As a result, for this printing, we have saved:

9 Trees (40' tall and 6-8" diameter)
3,339 Gallons of Wastewater
6 million BTU's of Total Energy
429 Pounds of Solid Waste
804 Pounds of Greenhouse Gases

McBooks Press made this paper choice because our printer, Thomson-Shore, Inc., is a member of Green Press Initiative, a nonprofit program dedicated to supporting authors, publishers, and suppliers in their efforts to reduce their use of fiber obtained from endangered forests.

For more information, visit www.greenpressinitiative.org

Environmental impact estimates were made using the Environmental Defense Paper Calculator. For more information visit: www.papercalculator.org.